BACK STORY

Caught Dead in Wyoming
Book 6

Patricia McLinn

✧ ✧ ✧ ✧

Dear Readers: If you encounter typos or errors in this book, please send them to me
at Patricia@patriciamclinn.com. Even with many layers of editing, mistakes can slip
through, alas. But, together, we can eradicate the nasty nuisances. Thank you!
— Patricia McLinn

MONDAY

DECEMBER 26

Chapter One

"A TRAGEDY THAT no one in Cottonwood County has—or can—forget is being revisited upon us this very day. More on that tragic and unforgettable event when we return."

I looked up at the ceiling-hung TV screen in time to see that KWMT-TV anchor Thurston Fine's countenance matched his lugubrious tone. Then, blessedly, the five o'clock news broadcast in Sherman, Wyoming cut to a snowmobile dealer's commercial.

"Did I miss something while I was gone? Something worthy of doubling down on *unforgettable* and *tragic*?" I asked the newsroom at large.

Don't be misled by that phrase *at large*.

The KWMT-TV newsroom is the opposite of large. Also the opposite of cutting edge. In fact, the opposite of from-this-century.

I added, "Did Thurston's favorite golf course get invaded by prairie dogs again?"

"Yes, but he won't know about it until spring," said Leona D'Amato. Leona had been with the station since it started. She worked part-time, covering what she called "social dos" and was no fan of hard news. That was by preference, not from any lack of awareness of what made a good story. Which meant she didn't hold Thurston in high regard.

"And let me tell you," she continued, "it's a lot of work relocating the critters to that one golf course."

That drew a laugh from all of us. *All* was Leona, Audrey, and me. The KWMT-TV's staff runs lean-and-not-so-mean at the best of times. During this week between Christmas and New Year's it was leaner than usual. Of the few who had been here today, the rest had left early.

Glowering twilight seeped in from the few windows, leaving the décor more colorless than usual. And since usual was battleship gray desks, chairs, and floor, that was saying something.

The only reason I was here was to wait for Mike Paycik to finish his sportscast before we met more friends for dinner and— inevitably—a slice of chocolate pie at the Haber House Hotel restaurant.

I might have said I was here to complete my work day, since I'd come in late after a return flight to Cody from Illinois, where I'd spent a few days for Christmas with family.

But it wouldn't have been the truth. If it weren't for this dinner, I'd have worked a half-day with no qualms. And that wasn't only because the News Director, Les Haeburn, was off, though that didn't hurt.

I would have expected Thurston to be off, too.

True, he trusted few people to sub as anchor, a group that did not include yours truly. I almost said *despite* my having experience anchoring, but it's almost certainly *because* of that experience.

On the other hand, it was such a slow week it would have been the smart time for a paranoid anchor to take off.

Thurston Fine's strongest supporter would have a hard time saying he wasn't paranoid or—in Fine-esque phraseology—obsessively protective of his self-perceived prominent position.

Yet here he was, on the air, tossing out *no one can forget* and *unforgettable, tragic* and *tragedy* in two sentences.

"He's talking about the Yolanda Cruz case," Audrey told me. "A woman was murdered by the boyfriend of her employer's teenage daughter. The daughter committed suicide. The boyfriend was convicted and sent to prison for life."

"Thurston wasn't here when that happened," Leona said. "How does he know anything about it?"

"Apparently he got a tip about a new angle and did some digging. By which I mean he ordered the news aide on duty—that would be Dale—to get him the clip files from the library. And—" Audrey paused for dramatic effect. "—Thurston read them."

That deserved a moment of awed silence.

Fine's reporting usually consisted of receiving news releases and taking them as gospel.

"What's the new angle that's stirred him to such excesses?" I asked.

Audrey shrugged. "Thurston threatened Dale divine—or at least Fine—retribution—" A short break for her audience to groan. "—if he breathed a word. And with Jennifer not here, we couldn't get it out of him."

Jennifer Lawton was a sort of news aide heroine to Dale. I suspected he dreamed of a closer relationship. But since she stayed fully occupied with her duties at KWMT-TV, with computer magical arts beyond my comprehension, and now and then with plying those arts on behalf of a group of us who'd looked into crimes, I also suspected Dale's dreams were unknown to their object.

This week, Jennifer was among the staff on vacation. She had gone with her family to visit relatives in Idaho.

That's why it was Dale, not Jennifer who called across the mesa of empty desks to me, "You have a phone call from Deputy Shelton. Line Two."

"Oooo," Leona and Audrey chorused in the same tone and with the same expression they would have used if Dale had said Sasquatch was on Line Two for me.

Deputy Wayne Shelton, born and raised in Cottonwood County, was a dedicated, respected, and effective law enforcement officer. He was also a pain in the ass for anyone in the media. Particularly me.

Our paths were unlikely to cross for my official beat as the "Helping Out!" consumer affairs correspondent, but on some of the extracurricular inquiries I'd been involved in they'd crossed, clashed, and—for rare, fleeting moments—coincided.

Through all that one thing could be safely said: We did not call each other to say hi out of the blue.

"Elizabeth Margaret Danniher. KWMT-TV's consumer affairs reporter. Have a problem? Tell us all about it. KWMT-TV will consider it as a potential topic for 'Helping Out.'" I made the answer as long and chirpy as I could.

"I want to talk to you."

"I hate to jump to conclusions, but I was leaning toward that conclusion when you called me."

"Smart ass."

Was I deluding myself that he said that with a modicum of affection?

Yes.

"I hope you had a good Christmas, Deputy Shelton."

"Yeah. I'll pick you up—"

"I did, too. Thank you for asking. Got back from Illinois earlier today. And, yes, my family is well. Thank you for asking about that, too."

His growl deepened. "—in fifteen minutes."

"I'm not available tonight. I have plans."

He was silent for half a beat. "Morning might be better," he said, as if that were the only reason he accepted my response. "Seven. Meet you then."

"Seven? The sun's not even up then."

"That's what headlights are for. Be at the EZ Gas at seven—"

"Oh, no. Not that early and especially not when I'd have to get into town."

The EZ Gas wasn't actually in town. It was worse from my standpoint, because it was on the far side of town from the direction I'd be coming from—the cozy place I rented on the ranch belonging to my co-worker and favorite camera person, Diana Stendahl. Mind you, the opposite side of Sherman wasn't exactly like driving in traffic across D.C. or like driving across Manhattan any time. It would add five, maybe ten, minutes to my trip.

"Seven-thirty at Diana's," I countered.

"Out of the way. Seven-twenty at the EZ Gas."

"Seven-thirty at the station."

Thurston came on screen, but I wasn't worried about missing what he said. I could listen to two things at once, especially when one was Thurston.

"…summer visitors to our county…"

"Seven-twenty at the EZ Gas." Apparently, Deputy Shelton had maxed out his negotiating ability.

He had an advantage, and he knew it. He'd caught me by most sensitive attribute—curiosity. "All right, all right."

"Dress like you're not an idiot." He hung up.

"…the convicted murderer in the tragic death twenty-six years ago of Yolanda Cruz has been released from prison."

I looked up to see an old, grainy photo of a young man in hand-cuffs.

I turned to the others. "Did you know about this?"

Dual head-shakes.

"Not only is this murderer being released, but he is being released into our peaceful, idyllic Cottonwood County—"

"He clearly doesn't read the weekend police report from the Kick-ing Cowboy," Leona said of a Sherman bar that did a thriving trade in alcohol and fisticuffs, especially on Friday and Saturday nights.

The possibility flitted across my mind, like a delicate late-season butterfly, that Shelton's call might have something to do with this convicted murderer returning to town.

Then a fire hose of reality shredded those gossamer wings.

Shelton.

Inviting me into a case—uh, potential story.

Yeah, right.

"—after serving only twenty-five years of a life sentence for that brutal murder of beloved housekeeper Yolanda Cruz, the mother of five and much loved in the Cottonwood County community. Now, Dean Isaacs will be on parole—"

"At least they're going to keep track of him, not just releasing him," Audrey muttered.

"—living among us with no oversight, with impunity for whatever he might do—"

"Fine doesn't know the meaning of parole or impunity?" I asked rhetorically.

"—to follow up on his heinous act of twenty-five years ago—"

"He said twenty-six before," I said. "Which is it?"

Audrey said, "The murder was twenty-six years ago, the conviction twenty-five years ago."

"—Yolanda Cruz was shot in the head in her room at the home of renowned professor Nora Roy on that late June night twenty-five years ago—"

"Twenty-six," we chorused. It wasn't like Thurston didn't know the dates. He must have in order to get it right once.

"—then Dean Isaacs was convicted of the ruthless, execution-style murder—"

Groans followed that cliché. Mine might have been the loudest. "Execution style for a beating?" someone scoffed.

"—the following year and sentenced to life in prison. Instead, the parole board let him out—"

"They *have* to consider him for parole," Audrey said. "Since the Supreme Court ruling about juvenile murderers sentenced to life having to be eligible for parole."

I was impressed. Nodding, I said, "The *Miller v. Alabama* ruling said juveniles couldn't be sentenced to life with no possibility for parole, even for murder."

"And *Montgomery v. Louisiana* made it retroactive to those already sentenced," she added.

Very impressed.

"—and now we will have him walking our peaceful streets. KWMT—and I, Thurston Fine, personally pledge to keep you, our valued viewers and fellow citizens, fully updated as this story develops."

"Which will be when the next news release arrives," grumbled Leona.

"And now in other news…"

We all tuned out at Thurston's transition.

"It was a good story," I said into the momentary silence.

"He should have had the background of those Supreme Court rulings. Should have included that context instead of making it sound like the parole board did it on a whim," Audrey said. "So it could have been better."

"You could say that after any Thurston effort." Leona paused, then added, "*Every* Thurston effort. Probably mine, too."

The last was said cheerfully.

"Audrey, is there still family in the area?" I asked.

"Of Isaacs'? I don't know."

"That's what I meant when I asked the question, but it would also be interesting to know if Yolanda Cruz's family is around here. And the family of the girlfriend, too."

She shrugged.

"Laura Roy's family is still here," Leona said. "Her mother, Professor Roy, her father, her sister, and brother-in-law. They moved to a new place after the murder, but stayed in the county."

"Could be worth checking into them," I nudged as I looked up those Supreme Court rulings to refresh my memory.

That was me being diplomatic.

It absolutely was worth checking into. It should have been in the initial report.

Audrey knew that. Moreover, if she'd been the producer it *would* have been. Though Thurston might not have read it. He had a tendency to skip things when he read his copy. That way he had plenty of time to toss in his oh-so-wise perspective.

But it didn't hurt to remind Audrey, who'd been down since mid-December, when a job she'd applied for in Seattle went to someone else.

I'd talked to her about taking at least one intermediate step before she tried for a Top 20 market. Leaping from a Bottom 20 to a Top 20 market was darned near impossible. There was too much competition.

The rejection shouldn't have surprised her, even if it did disappoint. I hoped she shook it off soon.

"It's Thurston's story," she said gloomily.

Thurston claimed every good story. He also held on to them with a death grip, even as he screwed them up, underreported them, gave only one side of the story, or all the above and more.

Sometimes, he could be persuaded a story wasn't worthy of his great talent. I'd managed to sell that argument a few times. But even Thurston had recognized the zing of this story.

Darn it.

"Perhaps he'd be open to someone else exploring one of the smaller angles," I suggested gently to Audrey. Missing an impossible leap left bruises. "It's at least worth asking Dale if Thurston's already checked—"

But there would be no asking Dale at the moment because he was answering another call.

He turned and shouted, "Call for you, Elizabeth" without covering the mouthpiece.

If it was Shelton calling back to say he'd thought it over and decided I'd had logic and reason on my side, so we'd meet when and where I preferred, he'd surely been deafened by Dale's shout.

Chapter Two

I PICKED UP. "Hello?"

"Hello, Elizabeth, this is Mrs. Parens calling." As if I couldn't tell from the precise enunciation.

"Mrs. Parens, I hope you weren't deafened by our enthusiastic news aide. He's been told he mumbles too much and I fear he's overcompensating."

"I developed adaptive hearing during my years interacting with students." The official line was that Emmaline Parens had spent her adult life as a teacher and principal in the Cottonwood County school system. The more accurate description was that she'd run the system and still had her fingers on its pulse point, though officially retired. "I'm pleased to hear Dale speaking up. He will acquire moderation as he matures. I hope you had an enjoyable visit with your family and a happy Christmas celebration."

"I did, Mrs. Parens. Hope you had a Merry Christmas, too. I just got back today."

"Thank you. I did. I am aware that you returned from Illinois earlier today and went directly to work. I am also aware that you have an engagement this evening. I was unsure, however, of the time of that engagement." Mrs. Parens being unsure of anything was a news flash. "I called you at the station number to ensure I could speak with someone if you were not available. I prefer that to leaving a voice mail message."

"No need for a message now," I said cheerfully.

"Indeed." I'd just been chastised in two syllables for stating the obvious. "I am calling for the purpose of inviting you to a gathering tomorrow evening."

Inviting was a euphemism. Royal command covered it. I knew that more from her tone than the words.

Although, I probably would consider it a euphemism any time Mrs. P *invited* me anywhere.

Accepting the inevitable, I said, "I'd be happy to come to your house tomorrow evening." Since she didn't drive and public transportation is non-existent in Cottonwood County, that was a safe bet. "But you have my cell number and you're welcome to call me any time. I hope you know that."

"I will bear that in mind, Elizabeth. In this instance, calling you through the station was most efficacious. The gathering tomorrow night is not at my home."

Which is why I don't bet.

"A dinner will be held at the Sherman Western Frontier Life Museum for the museum committee, as well as a number of people important to the museum. Their numbers will include three tribal representatives I look forward to you meeting, John Bear Charley, Anna Price Fox, and O.D. Everett."

"How do I fit into that group?"

"That will become clear tomorrow evening. We should be there by seven o'clock."

She allowed even less negotiating than Deputy Shelton had.

"Would you like me to pick you up?"

I offered because she didn't drive.

"That would be most agreeable and relieve me of the necessity of making other arrangements. Thank you."

Her most frequent driver was her next-door neighbor, Gisella Decker, who was also Mike Paycik's Aunt Gee and the head dispatcher for the sheriff's department's substation at O'Hara Hill. She could have run the dispatch department if she'd wanted, and probably a lot more.

Mrs. P didn't come out and say it, but I had the impression she hadn't wanted to ask Gee for a ride. Presumably because the other woman wasn't invited to this museum dinner.

"My pleasure, but… Are you… Is something wrong, Mrs. Parens?"

"Nothing is wrong, Elizabeth. I look forward to seeing you tomorrow evening. I hope you have an enjoyable gathering with your friends this evening. Good-bye."

I responded in kind as the call ended. At least I was pretty sure I did. I was a bit distracted.

Had I misread Mrs. Parens? She wasn't exactly an emotive open book, but I'd swear something had been worrying her.

Or irritating her?

Or distracting her?

Or it was all in my head because I was off-kilter.

First, I hadn't had much sleep with the oh-so-early flight from Illinois, bookended by drives to O'Hare and from Cody on either side of it.

Second, I'd had the emotional whiplash of leaving my family, then returning to KWMT-TV. Nothing like an uninspired concrete block bunker to remind you of how far your career had dropped.

It was enough to make you think there was something seriously wrong with the universe.

Come to think of it, something *was* seriously wrong with the universe when Thurston Fine had the best story in sight, while my calendar consisted of a fun dinner tonight with friends, a highly unlikely-to-be-fun-or-rewarding outing with Deputy Shelton in the morning, then a slim-chance-of-being-fun-or-rewarding dinner at the command of a retired schoolteacher/principal.

I felt a little jolt in my head. Like a nerve in my neck had twanged.

Or like an invisible fairy had gonged my head with a paddle.

Seriously wrong? No. That had been a knee-jerk reaction.

Because I didn't truly care Thurston had this story. I was greatly looking forward to this dinner with my friends. I was curious about what Deputy Shelton had in mind. And obliging Mrs. Parens was fine with me.

"Ready?" Mike said from beside my desk, having already ditched his studio sports jacket and grabbed his outside gear. "Diana texted. She and Tom are already there."

Between my conversation with Mrs. Parens and my thoughts, I'd totally missed his sportscast.

"Ready."

Chapter Three

OUR SERVER'S NAME at the Haber House Hotel restaurant was Kelly.

She didn't tell us that. Her nametag did. Also, I'd encountered her before.

She wore black eye makeup in such quantities that I wondered what percentage of her income went to those supplies. As we'd discovered when we'd needed to ask her questions last summer, she smoked heavily and chewed masses of gum to try to mask the smell from the diners and her bosses.

Kelly was the opposite end of the spectrum from an overly attentive staffer hovering to add to your order or whisk away your plate. No worries about feeling pressured or rushed by her.

I know it's considered old-fashioned, but waitress (or, if you prefer the gender neutral, wait-person) suited her better than server. She didn't do much serving and you did a lot of waiting.

We didn't mind. The Haber House's dinners kept a body fueled, but didn't bother the taste buds with over-stimulation on the way down, so we were here more for the conversation than the meal.

Well, for conversation and the chocolate pie.

Plus, the red brocade and dark wood motif was beginning to grow on me.

With our orders given, I asked if the others had heard Thurston's big story tonight.

They hadn't.

Tom Burrell had been driving here from his ranch northwest of town.

Diana Stendahl had been on the phone with her kids, a pair of teenagers making the most of their Christmas break by spending as much of it as possible with kids they saw every day in school.

But not even Mike, who'd been in the station prepping his sportscast, had caught the news.

"You don't listen to the rest of the news?" Tom asked him with mild interest.

Sometimes I caught a bemused look in the eyes of Thomas David Burrell, and I suspected he was wondering how he'd become caught up with three media types. Especially in the instances when we ventured into investigating.

"Not usually." Mike generously buttered a roll from the basket. "I pick up the top stories during the day and since Thurston puts the kibosh on the happy talk most stations' anchors do with their colleagues on set, I don't need to listen to him drone on."

I caught a couple heads at nearby tables turning toward us, including a man and woman with salt and pepper hair at the table behind Tom. She had more salt than her companion, but then again, she also had more hair, especially across the crown of her head.

They'd possibly tuned in to the name "Thurston." Possibly recognized Mike, who'd been a local football hero long before he played in the NFL, retired, and returned to town for his first TV experience. Possibly been curious about Tom's conversation, since he'd been a basketball hero even before Mike was a football hero, as well as being involved in every civic and otherwise good for the county effort there was.

Or they were nosy.

In that case I empathized completely. Restaurant eavesdropping was one of my favorite sports. Though I preferred being the eavesdropper rather than the eavesdroppee.

"It's about the Yolanda Cruz case. Do you guys remember it?" Unanimous yesses. "Seems the guy convicted of her murder is getting out of prison and coming back here."

Mike frowned. "He was sentenced to life. I was a kid, but I remember that."

"He was a minor when he received that sentence and the Supreme Court found in *Miller v. Alabama* in 2012 that sentences of life without the possibility of parole were unconstitutional, even for those convicted of murder. Then in 2016, another case reached the Supreme Court—*Montgomery v. Louisiana*—and it ruled *Miller* wasn't just for cases going forward. The same standard had to be applied retroactively. So the states had to get busy. Some abolished life without possibility of parole for minors. A few responded with laws saying they had to serve up to forty years before being eligible for parole review."

"Wyoming didn't wait for *Montgomery*," Tom said. "It passed a law in 2013 that stopped sentences of life without parole for minors. It makes the prisoners eligible for parole after twenty-five years. As long as they don't commit serious crimes in prison."

I raised one eyebrow at him. He raised both back at me.

I'd known the gist of the Supreme Court rulings, but had looked up the details in the past hour.

He knew the information off the top of his head. As with Audrey, I was impressed. But with Burrell, I should have known he'd follow the Wyoming legislature the way some people follow baseball.

"They get out after twenty-five years now?" Mike asked.

"Not necessarily. It's the *possibility* of parole. Not the certainty. As Tom said, it depends on what they've done in prison, and then it's still up to the parole board."

"Also depends on how far away the parole board members live from where the murderer's going to live," Diana said dryly.

"Because they wouldn't want one let loose in their backyard, but it's okay farther away? Isn't that rather harsh?"

"I was thinking of the impact of the memories. It might have faded for people living in other areas, but I can't imagine anyone in Cottonwood County not remembering that vividly. It was the biggest event around here until—"

"You came to town, Elizabeth, and people started dropping like flies," Mike interrupted cheerfully.

The gray-haired man and woman at the next table whipped their heads around toward us. Neither face showed any sign of sharing his cheer.

Diana stepped up to my defense. "You can't blame Elizabeth. She's solving crimes, not committing them."

"I wasn't blaming—"

"Tell me about the Cruz case," I interrupted.

"Tom will do it best," Diana said.

Mike grinned. "Because he's oldest."

Tom didn't argue. "Teenager named Dean Isaacs was having a romance with the daughter of a college professor. Her parents didn't approve, tried to keep them apart. Their housekeeper had been enforcing the rules. Kid killed her, the girl committed suicide over it."

If that account had been a holiday turkey, he would have just served up a carcass, rather than a plump, juicy feast.

"Killed herself because the boy was caught or in horror at the housekeeper being killed?"

Tom made a slight who-knows gesture with his long, tough hands.

"What about Dean Isaacs' family?"

"None around here. Father left when he was a kid. The mother took a couple older sisters and him to Oregon. He came back less than a year before the murder, living with an aunt. The aunt died a few years after he went to prison."

"No relatives of the victim, no relatives of the murderer around here," I murmured. So Fine hadn't screwed that part up.

"Family of Yolanda Cruz was in Colorado the last I knew," Tom said. "Do you not count Laura—the girl—as a victim?"

"What do you mean? Fine called her family summer visitors."

"Originally. Professor Roy kept bringing them back here every year for a while. Around the time her book hit big, they moved here permanently. It was a big deal, a young, single mother professor suddenly the worldwide expert."

These people should have been contacted before Thurston's story. Did he know about them? If not, could I pitch a follow-up that sounded interesting enough to get on the air but not interesting enough to tempt him to try to poach it?

"What about the survivors of the housekeeper? I asked Audrey, but she didn't know."

"Boy, she's really been down the past few weeks," Mike said.

"She didn't get that job, remember?"

"Oh, right. But … she didn't really expect to, did she? She told me she didn't, with it being such a big jump."

"Her brain might have recognized that, but hope and desire rarely give way to reality when it comes to the darned near impossible."

"Nice," Mike said.

"Thanks. Anyway, the basic question Fine should have pursued is if families of the soon-to-be-ex-con murderer and his murder victim are within interviewing territory. What about the scene? Could we—?"

Diana interrupted. "Let's save the rest for later."

"But there's something I should—"

Mike stopped his protest as he encountered a slight head tip from Diana. He followed the direction of it to the table behind Tom, where the gray-haired couple looked frozen. He sat back in his chair with a disappointed exhalation, but nodded.

"So, Tom," Diana said, "what did Tamantha get for Christmas?"

As usual when the topic of his daughter came up, Tom Burrell's Lincolnesque bone structure softened slightly. Say from granite to sandstone.

"A drone."

"Like on Star Trek?" asked Kelly, leaning over my shoulder to refill my water. It was the most animated I had ever seen her. In fact, she was so interested, I nudged up the lip-side of the pitcher so she didn't flood the table.

"Don't know. Never saw it. Did they have little flying machines?"

Everyone gawked at Tom.

"You *never* saw *Star Trek*?" Mike demanded. "How is that possible?"

"Ranch work, school work, basketball," Tom said succinctly.

"Still… reruns on cable," I said.

"No cable."

"Miss?" called the gray-haired man from the neighboring table to Kelly.

She ignored him, insisting to Tom, "But... But, you *have* to have seen Star Trek."

"Sorry, Kelly, never have. Did it have drones?"

"Oh, yeah. The Borg. Assimilation. Resistance is futile."

"*Miss,*" the man at the other table said louder.

Tom looked as if he were waiting for a punchline.

Mike weighed in. "Star Trek drones are people—well, they don't have to be people exactly. They can be humanoids and, I suppose, other species. The Borg take them over by force—"

"Nanoprobes," Kelly said.

"Right. And the Borg put nanoprobes in them so they lose all individuality—"

"—and become part of The Collective," Kelly concluded. "Except Seven of Nine, who—"

"Kelly." It was the hostess. "You might not have heard Table Six asking for you."

The woman had a future in diplomacy.

Kelly's expression sank back into apathy, she muttered a "yeah," and shuffled toward the other table. The hostess returned to her station at the door.

"The drone you got Tamantha? That was the kind that flies?" Diana asked Tom.

"Right," he said with apparent relief.

"I'm guessing not a toy one."

His mouth quirked. "She got one of those in her stocking. Wasn't too pleased with it until she got the better one she'd wanted under the tree. Now she tells me she's using the small one to work on her skills before risking the other one outside. Waiting for the right weather, too."

"June?" I asked. Then I remembered some of the June nights I'd experienced in Cottonwood County, Wyoming. "July?"

The natives ignored me.

"What made Tamantha ask for a drone?" Diana asked.

"She's interested in aeronautics and computers. Wants to see about flying those drones to check on cattle. Though weather and the difficulty with range, especially in areas where the grazing's not real flat—" *Not real flat* was his way of describing the Rocky Mountains. "—make it a bit tougher."

I had a vision of Tamantha Burrell revolutionizing the cattle industry with computers and drones. Though that might be a come-down from my usual vision of her revolutionizing the world.

"First space cowgirl," Mike muttered, indicating his thoughts had followed a similar direction.

"What about your Christmas?" Diana asked me. She's the true diplomat in the group. When I practice it, it's usually to get a story rather than from altruism.

"Yeah," Mike said, "how was Christmas in Chicago? Did you go downtown to Macy's to see the windows or—"

"Bite your tongue."

"—go ice skating near Michigan Avenue? Why bite my tongue?"

"To my family it will always and forever be Marshall Field's. They hold a grudge against Macy's for changing the name. Arrogant barbarians with no regard for tradition is the general theme. They won't shop there, much less go downtown to the Walnut Room. As for skating, that's done locally. Among other Danniher traditions."

Tom's face stayed solemn, except for lines fanning out from the corners of his eyes. "Thought big-time media types went for glitzy Christmas vacations."

"Yup, they do."

When I was ascending the network ladder, working in D.C., then New York, colleagues would jet off for weeks in Bali or exclusive Caribbean resorts or private yacht cruises or the more mundane skiing in Europe or Aspen. I'd fly into O'Hare, then drive west to just past the tentacles of the Chicago metropolitan area, where I'd settle in for jigsaw puzzles, family meals designed for stevedores, and that favorite wintertime sport of shuffling cars so Dad had an open driveway on which to demonstrate his latest superior snowblowing technique that surpassed all previous superior snowblowing techniques. That car-shuffling exercise was inevitably followed by digging out and pushing out cars that got stuck in unplowed areas.

After I'd explained that Danniher family tradition, Mike asked, "If you have all that experience with digging and pushing cars out of snow, why are you so worried about the weather here?"

"*Because* I have all that experience with digging and pushing cars out of snow."

There were some more comments about my entirely logical desire to avoid heaping helpings of snow, but the chocolate pie had finally arrived and I concentrated on my heaping helping of that.

As we walked out to the parking lot later, Tom asked suddenly, "What was all that about humanoids being assimilated? Doesn't sound like a present for a third-grader."

"Like a flying drone is?" Mike asked.

"Remember, it's Tamantha we're talking about," I said. Then I chuckled.

They all looked a *What?* at me.

"Trying to imagine a present for Tamantha that had anything to do with losing individuality. Talk about a non-starter."

A LITTLE OVER an hour later, Shadow and I looked at each other across a swath of hardwood floor and area rug in the bunkhouse I rented from Diana.

The dog—I'm not against him being *my* dog, but he's so much his own dog that even thinking of him that way seems a bit presumptuous—had flicked his tail a few times when I followed Diana into her house to retrieve him from where he'd spent Christmas.

The tail flicks were his equivalent of rolling over on to his back in ecstasy.

Since I'd first spotted him—fleetingly, hence the name Shadow—in the backyard of the house I rented when I arrived in Sherman in April, the pace of his thawing would have delighted any iceberg-studying scientist. Plenty of time to get all the measurements before it disappeared. No rush, no rush.

For tonight's reunion, he'd come up to me in Diana's living room and let me pet him for a minute. Maybe even sixty-four, sixty-five seconds.

But when it was time to leave for the bunkhouse, which was really a studio apartment I rented, Shadow gave me a look.

I interpreted it as saying I was on a level with the Tom Hanks character leading innocent John Coffey to his death in *The Green Mile*.

Okay, that might be a little over-dramatic, but it felt a bit like that taking Shadow away from the activity and warmth of the main house—not to mention the attentions of teenagers Jessica and Gary Stendahl and the food tidbits I'd spotted Diana slipping Shadow.

Also not to mention that Diana's house was chock full of holiday cheer, including a robust real tree brightly decorated. The bunkhouse was clean and comfortable, but with no hint of Christmas.

It hadn't made any sense to decorate since I'd known I'd be in Illinois.

We're not even going to be here. We're always at your parents' in Illinois.
Wes, if you want to go to your family—
God, no.
We could stay here, have a little tree or—
What's the point? It makes no sense to disrupt everything.

Under the weight of ex-marital memories, I sat on the floor.

Shadow stood at some distance and looked at me. I parsed his look out as equal shares of surprise, caution, and confusion.

I dug in my pocket and pulled out treats Diana had dropped into it as we left the main house, saying, "Give them to him, Ms. Grinch."

Now, I extended my arm.

He didn't advance, but he did take the treats by stretching his neck and nose to full length.

When he'd finished, he retracted neck and nose, and sat directly in front of me, barely beyond arm's length away.

"Shadow, come," I said.

He didn't move for what seemed like a long time.

Slowly, he stood. Then, with his eyes on my face, he advanced three steps.

"Good dog, Shadow."

I brought my hand up in easy stages and showed him another treat on my palm. "We can pretend this one's just from me, okay? Merry Christmas."

He still looked at me, but the softness at the side of his muzzle puffed out, then in as he absorbed the scent of the treat.

I raised my hand.

He delicately took the treat.

I leaned forward. Despite his stiffening, I kept coming, until my face was in the fur on the side of his neck.

"I missed you," I said aloud.

I felt him pull back slightly.

But then he nuzzled at my hair at the back of my head.

A few tears might have dropped into his fur.

"Merry Christmas, Shadow."

TUESDAY

DECEMBER 27

Chapter Four

"I WANT YOU to do something for me."

Cottonwood County Sheriff's Deputy Wayne Shelton scowled at me, then returned his attention to the road ahead, scowl intact.

But I'm getting ahead of myself, because that didn't happen until well after we'd left the EZ Gas.

When I arrived, he was already there in a sheriff's department truck. If he hadn't told me he'd be on the north side of the building—known to civilians as the back—I wouldn't have spotted the vehicle between the windbreak and dumpsters.

He made the grand gesture of lowering his window and ordering, "Get in."

"I want to get some coffee to take with."

"Bad idea. No indoor toilet until we get back here."

"How long will that be?"

"Don't know."

I considered the situation, specifically the cold wind, the lowering sky, and the great outdoors that would be my only option.

I skipped the coffee.

"Quit wasting time. Get in."

"You're not by any chance trying to hurry me because you don't want us seen together, are you?"

No response.

"Because if I were paranoid, that might make me wonder if I were about to get disappeared."

He turned his head to look at me. "Think I wouldn't have done that already if I thought it would work?"

Odd. That made me feel better.

I went around the vehicle and got in.

Not that I *really* thought the deputy meant me harm.

He drove north out of Sherman on a road that went to gravel fast. I hadn't been on this road that I remembered, but I was guessing it paralleled the highway that passed a turnoff to Tom Burrell's ranch, the Circle B, then continued on to O'Hara Hill—Cottonwood County's second-largest town, which made it mostly a bump on the road—before eventually reaching the border and venturing into Montana.

I'd thought that highway was basic. This road made it look and feel like the Autobahn.

Actually, *feel* was the more active sense, because seeing was limited.

Snow slanted across my field of vision, which was what the wipers managed to clear from the windshield.

In movies and TV shows, snow drifts ever so gently from above thanks to programmable snow machines. Wyoming's snow machine was pumping out the white stuff fine, but the directional controls were on the fritz.

This snow mostly slanted from lower left to upper right, with a subset from upper left to lower right. A few lost snowflakes went straight across. I didn't see a single drifter.

I generally prefer to be the one behind the wheel, but was fine with Deputy Shelton driving this morning.

"Didn't know they were predicting snow," I said.

He grunted. "This isn't anything worth predicting."

Thus ended another of my attempts to strike up a conversation during the silent, somehow stealthy drive.

I'd previous asked if he'd had a good Christmas (grunt), how he saw the NFL playoffs shaping up (grunt), and how he liked this sheriff's department vehicle (grunt.) At least with my weather sally he'd added a few words to the grunt.

The Cottonwood County Sheriff's Department had a few sedans, but I'd never seen Deputy Shelton in one. Mostly he drove a four-wheel drive or a truck. I had no idea how it was determined which he'd be in when.

With the computer and other communication equipment taking up the console area I would have appreciated being in this larger vehicle at all times. With the snow, I also appreciated its heft.

At this particular moment, I further appreciated its size for the distance it put between me and his scowl.

Now, the fact that Shelton scowled at me might lead you to think *I* was the one who'd said *I want you to do something for me.*

You'd be wrong.

Asking me to do something for him clearly caused a state of agony that only a man as resolute as Deputy Shelton could push past.

That was the only reason I was willing to ask, "What's that, Deputy?"

A lot of journalists are allergic to asking wide open questions because the answers can get you in to trouble in an interview—especially on-air—that there's no getting out of. But I had no hesitation asking that particular wide-open question, because logic told me that if he'd been about to say that what he wanted me to do was to get lost, leave Cottonwood County forever, or go soak my head in a vat of acid, he wouldn't have looked pained.

"Look at a case."

"What? *What?* You want me to look at a case?"

I'd been stunned when he'd called and asked me to meet him, though *asked* is giving it a lot more graces than it deserved. But to look at a case? I was beyond stunned.

His expression of pain deepened. "That's what I said."

"I didn't even know you were working a case. There's been a murder? Or—Oh. Is this about Dean Isaacs getting out of prison and coming back here?"

"No."

But I hardly heard the denial. I turned to bring his profile into focus. "That's why you called the main line instead of calling me directly. You didn't want a record of a call to me."

Grunt.

"You also don't want Sheriff Conrad to know you're talking to me, so that explains the spy games at the EZ Gas."

Not even a grunt.

"But you're in an official vehicle, which you wouldn't do if this wasn't at least semi-official."

A flicker of his eyes, but that might have been in reaction to the snow's angle shifting as he turned right, into a worse road. This one didn't even pretend to be more than a single track, now with white lining the bottom of the twin ruts in the rusty brown earth.

He yanked the steering wheel to pull the tires out of the ruts and bumped us up to a spot that looked across lower ground to the south and east.

No, I couldn't tell the direction from the sky or even from the mountains being to our west. Because I couldn't see the sky or mountains amid the snow, haze, and clouds.

The vehicle boasted a compass indicator amid all its gadgets.

Either the snow had let up or this angle was protected somehow, because I could see that below us and a little distance to the southeast there was a ranch. A large house, a barn, three other outbuildings, several corrals. A wide creek ran close to the barn, then wiggled around, with a trail of bare tree trunks following it. More bare trees curved around the house, beyond them stood a more distant swath of evergreens. Evergreens also gathered in front of the house, which would block the view from a road that looked significantly better that the one we were on.

"Why didn't we take that road, if you want to—? Wait a minute." I'd stopped myself in time to prevent complete revelation. I opened the SUV door and climbed out to cover my near-miss and for a better view. "I know this place."

Sort of.

I'd observed it from satellite views online.

I'd also driven past the front road, which provided an entirely different angle than this did. For one thing, it didn't allow much of a view of the house, which I had never been inside.

He'd come out, too, remaining on the opposite side of the hood.

"Yeah, big surprise you know it, considering it's Mike Paycik's place. Got himself a tidy little spread."

Chapter Five

MIKE'S PLACE.

The place Mike had yet to invite me to see. So far I'd withstood the temptation—temptations—to wheedle an invitation out of him.

Mike had first come to my then-rental place in May and many times after. I had never been invited to his *tidy little spread.*

My friend-competitor-sometimes-colleague Wardell Yardley had spent several nights there in November. On a visit from D.C., he'd taken shelter with Mike when his original accommodations were otherwise occupied.

You might ask why I didn't ask Dell about the place if I was curious.

Asking questions is, after all, what I do for a living. And unlike lawyers, journalists do ask some questions they don't know the answers to.

The difference was that was for business. This wasn't.

Dell would never let me forget that I'd asked him for the answer to the mystery of why Mike didn't invite me to his house.

We would be in the old journalists' home decades—many decades—from now, with not a tooth in our mouths, no hearing to speak of, and as blind as those statues of justice, but he'd still manage to roll his wheelchair up next to mine and rumble, "Remember when you had to ask *me* about Mike Paycik's house in Sherman, Wyoming, because you didn't know what the big secret was that kept him from letting you see it? When I knew and you didn't have a clue? Remember that? Huh? Huh?"

And my only comeback would be the pitiable, "Not in Sherman. His house was in the county—Cottonwood County. Hah! You don't know everything."

Deputy Shelton clearly expected that I was familiar with the place. Familiar enough with it that he apparently thought I was yanking his chain.

"Used to be the Roys' place. Bought it when they first moved here permanently."

"The—?" I stopped.

Michael Paycik owned the ranch where Dean Isaacs had killed the housekeeper, Yolanda Cruz, and where his girlfriend, the daughter of Professor Roy, had killed herself.

And he hadn't said a word about it. Not last night, not ever.

Of course, I'd known he owned a ranch and that the ranch had a house, but not that the house had been—

"Wait a minute. His house isn't old enough to have been here then." Diana had told me that the previous owners had built the house Mike now had.

"They tore the other place down, pretty much. Course, some of it fell down on its own. Had been left empty for a long time after the Roys moved to another place, closer to town. They'd always rented out the land and they just kept doing that. But the house was left to fall down. Took years before some newcomers bought the whole place— acres and home ranch. They cleared it out to build this house. They probably didn't know the history."

"Mike did, though. He knew the history."

"Sure, he did. So what? Wasn't any of his doing. More places than not have had shi—stuff happen in them. And after his family…" He stared straight ahead. When he spoke again it was as if he'd mentally erased that foray toward Mike's family and was sure I'd do the same. "It's been good, him having a ranch and this place belonging to him. A Cottonwood County boy. Everybody thinks so."

I turned to face him over the hood. "Why'd you bring me here, Deputy?"

"Told you. I want you to do something."

"What?"

"Look into some phone calls."

"Phone calls?"

"Consider it like that bit you do on the news. You know, 'Helping Out!'"

"Yeah, I know that bit I do on the news. What I don't know is what it has to do with—"

"It's a scam."

"What is?"

"Phone calls people are getting."

I huffed out a cloud. The charms of being outside to get a better view had worn off. "It's like I tell people on 'Helping Out!' you need to tell me everything, openly and honestly, before I can possibly help you."

If I'd said he needed to strip naked and run around the car five times he would have looked happier than he did now.

"But first," I added, "I'm getting back in. I'm freezing."

Inside once more, he said, "Residents have reported getting phone calls that are scams."

I'd figured that out on my own, but restrained from saying that. If someone's keeping score, I get points for that. Maybe even a gold star.

"How does the scam work?" I asked with infinite patience.

It paid off, because that kicked him into professional mode.

"A male caller tells citizens that they have failed to appear for federal grand jury duty and if they don't pay a fine immediately, they will go to jail. They can only avoid jail by paying the fee promptly, using money cards. The scammers are smart enough to have the money directed to a reloadable card with no name to trace."

"Okay," I said slowly. I was more confused than ever. "What does Sheriff Conrad say?"

Silence.

Oh. "You haven't told him."

"No and don't you, either. Not him or anybody."

"You might have noticed that the whole idea of 'Helping Out!' is to tell people about scams. It's what I do."

"Never watch the thing. But this just started. Needs more looking into. Lots of calls but only a few days."

I shook my head to see if that would right the axis of the earth, which had gone off-kilter, as evidenced by Wayne Shelton coming to me instead of handling it himself or going to the sheriff. "If no one's lost any money…?"

"They have."

I looked at his profile. "What else are you not telling me?"

"The male caller identifies himself as a deputy—a Cottonwood County deputy."

"You."

"No. Deputy Alvaro."

"Oh."

Richard Alvaro was a young, smart, promising deputy. He'd provided valuable information on the first inquiry Mike, Diana, and I did last spring.

Since then, he'd been less forthcoming.

Oddly, his less-forthcoming period coincided with Shelton taking him under a wing.

"Sheriff Conrad's not stupid," I said. "He recognizes Richard's value."

Another silence.

"You think Conrad won't give him a fair hearing?"

He didn't answer directly. "It's a department that's had issues. He's the new broom meant to sweep it clean. He can't afford scandal. Might think he can't afford questions, either. A lot easier and cleaner to cut the one who might be tainted."

"Does Richard know?"

"Not yet." In other words, Shelton had waited to see what I said about looking into this before telling Richard his name was being used in vain.

"Okay, give me everything you know."

"First, you can't tell anybody."

I raised my eyebrows. "I have to talk to the people who received these calls."

"I mean your little band."

What he really meant was Diana, since she and new Sheriff Russ Conrad had formed a connection the first time they met at the start of November.

I'd seen it happen and still didn't believe it.

Outwardly they were taking it slow, undoubtedly because of Diana's children. But it clearly hadn't escaped Shelton's notice. Possibly it was the electricity that arced between Diana and the new sheriff when they were within a block of each other.

I came to my friend's defense. "Diana would never—"

"Don't tempt her. Besides, it's your show. That 'Helping' thing."

That was a point. "Okay. Talk."

I took notes as he talked. Deputy Shelton intermittently turned on the heater, though only when I mentioned that my fingers had become too stiff to function.

"Told you to dress right," he grumbled at one point.

"You didn't say anything about needing Eskimo mittens. Wouldn't be able to take notes with them on, anyway."

He resumed his recitation of facts.

When he finished, I had the material I needed to get started. And confirmation of one of my earlier questions.

His request truly didn't have anything to do with Dean Isaacs being released from prison or the events that had led to his being there in the first place.

I was still confused about one element, however.

So, I asked again, "Why did you bring me *here* for this, Deputy?"

His face eased slightly. "Best dead zone this close to town. Should be back before anyone wonders where I am, but even if they do, they won't have any idea where I've been, and that makes it a lot harder for anybody to say I was with you."

If I'd still been thinking along the lines of being disappeared by Deputy Shelton, that speech might have made me uncomfortable.

But I had other things on my mind.

One of those things was looking at the problem Wayne Shelton had asked me to take on.

Another was Michael Paycik and his tidy little spread.

Chapter Six

I HAD SO many episodes of "Helping Out!" banked that I would have ignored most other leads.

Not this one.

For Deputy Richard Alvaro's sake.

As soon as I got back to the station, I made one pass to see if Mike was in yet—he wasn't—then got started. It didn't take much research, once I was defrosting at my desk, to discover this scam was widespread.

I couldn't find any region where it *hadn't* been employed. Plus, it had swept across the country multiple times, as the scammers added refinements to their recycled classics.

Sometimes the scam callers pretended to be deputies in the same county as the victim, sometimes in nearby counties, and occasionally they impersonated U.S. Marshals.

Some scammers bolstered their stories by including badge numbers, the names of real federal judges, specific court hearing times, and accurate courthouse addresses.

They'd leave callback numbers that would be answered with the name of the jurisdiction the initial scam caller identified. Sometimes they'd get more elaborate with "court clerks" or other purported courthouse officials answering the callback numbers.

A few scammers tweaked it for any who denied receiving a summons. Never got a summons? Fine. All we need to clear this up is your birthdate and social security number.

Nothing like a threat that you'll be thrown into jail to short-circuit good sense.

And there goes your identity.

If the first call didn't work, they'd call again, ratcheting up the pressure, increasing the fine, lengthening the threatened jail time.

That hadn't happened in Cottonwood County, most likely because there hadn't been time yet. From what Shelton had given me, the calls had just started.

Considering their recent experiences with phone calls, the targets of the scam would likely be more amenable to in-person interviews.

That might have been vetoed by the weather, but the day had transitioned to brilliant sunshine and—more importantly—mild breezes. The mild breezes were vital because that meant the early morning's snow wasn't being shoved back on to the road surfaces.

At least not as much as usual.

I called the people who'd received the recent calls purportedly from Deputy Alvaro to set up the interviews, but left all questions other than where and when off the table. In an hour, I had two background interviews set up for tomorrow morning, another possibility awaiting confirmation, and one in half an hour on the other side of town.

That left time to skim the Internet for anything on Dean Isaacs.

No, I wasn't going to try to take over Thurston's big story. I was just curious.

There were several photos of Isaacs, all with floppy teen-boy hair over one eye and a lopsided grin.

The grin was there even when the hair had been trimmed and he was dressed for court. All the photos showed him as thin, but that one looked as if he had shrunk inside the clothes. Was it cynical to wonder if that had been a ploy by the defense to make him look young and helpless?

He did look young. He did not look helpless. Those eyes looked old and shrewd.

The most frequently run photo of Yolanda Cruz showed a gray-haired woman with gaunt cheeks smiling at a blurry girl doing a cartwheel. The caption said the blurry girl was Laura Roy the summer before they both died.

There were also photos of the stricken faces of Yolanda Cruz's husband and grown children. And of Professor Nora Roy, who stared straight ahead, while her husband turned his face away from the cameras.

There was a photo of the ranch, including the cottage where Yolanda Cruz had been killed. About the only things I recognized from this morning were the wide creek and the trees, younger then.

The online accounts were wire service clips, short on detail.

They presented the prosecution's theory that there'd been an argument when Yolanda found Dean Isaacs in the house and threw him out. Laura was upset with Yolanda and her family for coming between her and Isaacs. Isaacs, the prosecutor said, circled back to the property and, feeling Yolanda was the biggest obstacle to his being with Laura, found her alone and killed her. When Laura realized this—most likely, told by Isaacs, the prosecutor suggested—she felt such remorse that she committed suicide.

The defense said Isaacs left when he was told to and—despite a witness testifying to seeing him nearby hours after he was kicked out— was miles away when Yolanda Cruz was killed and Laura died, and knew nothing about either.

It struck me that none of the accounts were from the *Independence.* Cottonwood County's twice-a-week newspaper, which I would have expected to have good coverage and lots of it. There might be clips in the station's library, but that would involve more dust than I'd have time to remove before my cross-town appointment.

As I was leaving for the scheduled interview, Diana was coming in from an assignment. We stopped between the two sets of double doors at the main entry.

"Where are you off to?" she asked.

"Running some background interviews for a 'Helping Out!' segment."

She raised her brows. Not only does she know how many segments I already have in the can, but she's my favorite shooter, which means I generally let her know when I'm going to be wheeling and dealing in order to get her assigned to my stories.

"Way down the road," I said, not looking at her by pretending I needed to change settings on my phone right then instead of when I reached my destination. I usually turned my phone off or at least muted it during interviews as a courtesy to interviewees. This time I was also turning off my location. With Jennifer not around I wasn't sure if anyone at the station would, much less could, track where I was, but why take the chance? "Want to take advantage of the good weather."

"Uh-huh. In case we get blizzarded in for the next eight months and you run out of 'Helping Out!' segments. Admit it, you need to stay busy."

I laughed and waved as I pushed through to the great outdoors.

But I felt a little guilty.

Possibly also a little hypocritical, since I was ready to hit Mike with both barrels for not telling me about his "tidy little spread's" history, but here I was keeping something from Diana.

On the other hand, Mike had held out on telling me about his home's connection to a murder for nine months—not to mention never inviting me to his house—while I wasn't sharing a scam I'd learned about a few hours ago.

THE SCAMMER HAD picked the wrong person when he called Enid Harter.

She owned a printing business in town that she'd started on her own nearly thirty years ago. She was nobody's fool. She also had a point she wanted to get across immediately.

"I know the Alvaros and it was not Richard on the phone."

She waited until I nodded, acknowledging her certainty.

"I almost hung up on the guy, but then I figured it was better to get as much information as I could."

She handed over some papers. A quick look showed they included a copy of her handwritten notes, apparently taken during the conversation, then a printed transcript of the notes.

It would have been embarrassing if I'd fallen on her neck in gratitude, but if every source were this organized, I could spend a lot more of my life with my feet up, sipping margaritas.

"This is great. Thank you. I would also like to hear your account, as we talked about on the phone."

"Of course."

She recounted what the scammer had said during the phone call—only once did she say "Wait, I forgot. He also said I could call back—the number's in my notes" before proceeding.

Someone who gives a straightforward accounting of what happened is the unicorn of witnesses or sources.

Embarrassing or not, I might fall on this woman's neck.

At the end, I asked two questions.

"Did you call back?"

"No. I knew it was a scam. I didn't say that to him. But I wasn't going to spend more time investigating. That's for the professionals. That's why I called Wayne Shelton."

"What made you say so emphatically that it was not Richard Alvaro?"

Instead of rushing into a character defense of the young deputy, she stared, unfocused, over my shoulder a moment.

"The cadence was wrong." She shook her head. "That's not quite it, either. He said the right words and there were no obvious mistakes. Nothing mispronounced, for example. It was... Ah. It lacked Richard's sincerity. And integrity. There was something undercutting everything the caller said."

It made sense. And I think I understood what she meant. The problem was that wouldn't hold up—not in court, not in the court of public opinion, and probably not in the court of Richard Alvaro's new boss' judgment.

As I prepared to leave, I asked the standard, "May I call you if I have any further questions?"

"Yes." She walked with me to her office door. "I've heard about you from Linda Caswell. That gives me hope you'll get whoever's doing this before it costs someone a lot of money or hurts Richard

Alvaro's reputation. I understand this kind of scum often preys on the elderly. Good-bye."

I wouldn't pretend I wasn't pleased that Linda's report on me was positive.

Linda was an intelligent and interesting woman, who ran family businesses in Cottonwood County and was on nearly as many civic committees as Tom Burrell.

We hadn't met under the best of circumstances, yet I believed we respected each other. We'd had a very enjoyable lunch in early December—a lunch we'd been talking about having since the summer.

It didn't surprise me she knew Enid. Or that Enid took her opinion to heart.

Back in my car, I turned my phone back on and saw I'd received a message.

Mrs. Parens, asking me to call her. I did.

"I apologize, Elizabeth," she said, "but I must ask if you would be available to pick me up earlier than we had arranged."

"Sure, what time?"

"Now."

"Excuse me?"

"It would be beneficial if you can arrive here at your very earliest convenience. I recognize this is abrupt and intrusive. In addition, it might well make it necessary for us to then go directly to our dinner engagement." To go directly from where? There wasn't time to ask, because she was continuing. "If you require time to go to Diana's to change for the evening—"

"No, I brought my clothes to the station, so—"

"Excellent. Then I will look for you shortly."

MRS. P WASN'T talking on the drive from her neat little house in O'Hara Hill back to Sherman.

I couldn't tell if she was embarrassed at making the request that I pick her up immediately, angry, or worried. Or all three.

We were nearly back to Sherman when she finally said, "Our destination is Sally Tipton's house. I believe you will recall where she lives."

I did.

Now, I guessed there was a fourth ingredient in her mix: frustration.

She'd known Sally Tipton most of her life. I'd only met the woman last summer and could not conceive of dealing with her for decades.

The front door of her small house had a Christmas wreath on it. As far as I knew, that door was mostly for decoration, even if the current decoration was hanging askew, with a red ribbon faded by the sun, and its greenery browned around the edges from the cold.

We went to the back door, which opened to the kitchen.

Mrs. Parens knocked commandingly.

A sound came to us, and a shadow showed through the curtained window then retreated.

"Sally, we have seen you. Open the door."

The shadow didn't move for a second, then advanced. Sally Tipton opened the door a crack.

Sally's gaze skidded past Mrs. Parens and came to me. "Oh, my, Elizabeth Margaret Danniher. What a delightful surprise." She glanced back over her shoulder toward the front of the house. "Though this isn't the most convenient—"

"Back up," Mrs. Parens said. "We're coming in."

I gawked at Edward G. Robinson's delivery coming out of this down-to-her-toes lady.

Sally dithered. "Oh, dear, oh, dear, I'm afraid this isn't a good time. Perhaps another day—"

Mrs. Parens wasn't taking another day for an answer.

She delivered a block that would do the NFL proud. I followed her in.

Not waiting for an invitation, Mrs. Parens was already shedding her coat, displaying a formal black sweater set with pearls.

Sally delivered an anti-invitation. "I'm sorry, but you have to go. Really, this isn't the time. I wouldn't have called you if I'd known—"

"Tell her," Mrs. P ordered Sally.

"I don't know what you're..." Sally wisely let that die and turned to me as the easier target. Her white hair, usually fluffy, now had the full finger-in-a-socket look of Einstein on a really bad hair day. Her wide, pale eyes held more emptiness than usual. "It's really nothing. Emmaline is making a great fuss over nothing. It's... I, uh, I have someone staying with me. Temporarily."

Mrs. P made a disparaging sound.

I was completely lost.

"That doesn't sound like such a bad thing," I started tentatively. "For you to have some company, I mean. Someone to look after you a little—"

"Company. Look after her." Mrs. P repeating my phrases in a disgusted mutter left me braced for the earth's crust to split open and swallow us all whole. Surely it was a sign of the apocalypse.

"I don't need looking after." Sally said that with the surprising bit of snap she occasionally displayed. "I'm fine on my own."

"Well, that door to the bathroom sure needed looking after."

I turned at the male voice coming from the archway to the rest of the house.

Older, a lot less hair, but still recognizable.

Dean Isaacs had walked into Sally Tipton's kitchen with a long, heavy screwdriver in his hand.

Chapter Seven

I MIGHT NOT have even noticed the screwdriver in someone else's hand.

There was something about knowing the holder was a convicted murderer that concentrated my attention.

But since his hold was loose, my mind let a few other thoughts in.

Thurston had screwed up the story.

Dean Isaacs wasn't *going* to come to Sherman at some point in the future. He was already here.

Prison is supposed to be physique pump-up central, especially twenty-plus years' worth of prison.

Dean Isaacs was the exception.

He wasn't as skinny as in the old photos I'd seen this morning, but he also hadn't gained much muscle. What he'd lost was most of his hair. What remained was wispy over a front-to-back ridge along his crown. That emphasized the shape of his head, which strongly resembled an egg stretched into a caricature.

With the receding hairline at the top and a receding jaw below an almost delicately pointed chin, his face gave the impression of small, unremarkable features stranded in that elongated and lopsided egg.

"But it's all fixed now," he said.

Sally made a sound. Giving her the benefit of the doubt, it was the beginning of "what" rather than simply a "*waa*."

"The bathroom door," he said. "It'll close all the way now. Locks, too. I tightened up the hinges so it hangs straight. You have any oil— household oil, WD-40?"

"Oh, dear. I don't know. I might. But I might not. I don't—"

"That's okay. I'll look in the basement where I found the screwdriver. Otherwise we'll add it to the list."

"The list. Oh. Yes. Okay. Good. Yes, do that. Good, good."

He lowered his head, looking at Mrs. Parens and me from under his eyebrows as he passed us.

When a door, presumably to the basement, closed behind him, I turned to demand, "Dean Isaacs is staying *here?*"

I made the demand of Mrs. Parens, rather than Sally.

That might seem unreasonable, since it was Sally's house. But wanting a truthful answer fast, my choice of sources was clear.

"Apparently," she said with grim brevity.

"You knew?"

"I did not know for a certainty. I was aware that Sally had opened the door to the possibility, in a manner of speaking. I had hoped I had persuaded her that it was not a wise decision and to act swiftly in order to preclude it from occurring."

"I didn't have a choice," Sally whined. "I didn't want to… Though I do feel sorry for him, poor soul."

"Poor soul?" Mrs. P repeated with a snap. "Don't start that muddle-headed, soft-hearted, and soft-brained nonsense, Sally Tipton. Remember, I know you and have for the better part of our lives. Elizabeth sees right through you, too, now."

That last word was a jab. One I deserved. I had fallen for the vague elderly woman act, not only by Sally, and it could have turned out a whole lot worse—for her and other people, including me—than it had.

"But I mean it," Sally protested. "I *do* feel sorry for him. That awful skin condition he has. It must be so difficult to go through life like that. I know they talk about the heartbreak of psoriasis on TV, but this is so much worse. I can't imagine anyone wants to touch him. And you know what they say about babies in orphanages."

"What are you rambling about, Sally?" Mrs. P demanded in her best schoolteacher voice.

"Babies in orphanages who are never held and touched get a disorder. Surely you've heard about that, Emmaline."

I thought Mrs. Parens might be driven to the extreme of saying something ungrammatical, so I stepped in. "Not about the babies in orphanages. About your feeling sorry for Dean Isaacs."

"Oh, yes. That. His horrible skin condition. You must have seen it."

"Skin condi—?" I giggled. I tried to cover it with a cough, but it came out as a snort.

And now Mrs. P turned the full force of her schoolteacher trained glare on me.

"Elizabeth." It was both an exhortation to behave myself and a demand to know what was causing my disruptive behavior.

"Tattoos," I got out in a fairly normal voice. "I believe she's talking about his tattoos."

Mrs. P pivoted to look in the direction Isaacs had gone, apparently mentally reviewing his appearance.

"They can't be tattoos," Sally objected. "It's down at the bottom of his arms. On his wrists, and where his collar opens on his ... Where his collar opens."

Good heavens, the woman was shying away from saying "his chest."

"Have you remained unaware of popular culture these past decades? It is termed a full sleeve," Mrs. Parens said.

"What's a full sleeve?"

Swallowing my surprise that Mrs. Parens knew the term, I said to Sally, "That's what they call tattoos that cover the entire arm. Didn't you ever watch *Prison Break*?"

"Watch what?"

I waved that off. "Or any prison shows. Or pro basketball for that matter." I considered that. "Or baseball."

"Good heavens, all those poor people have it? Isn't there a lotion they can use?"

"This is all beside the point." Mrs. Parens' declaration ended that discussion. "The issue at hand is that you have a convicted murderer staying in your house."

"Yes," Sally said miserably.

At that moment we all turned toward the basement door, having heard footsteps on the stairs.

"Found a can of WD-40." He shook it, releasing a death-rattle sound. "But it's about gone. I'll see if it will help the hinges, but you need to add more to the list, Sally."

"Oh. Yes. The list. I'll add it. WD...."

"WD-40," he filled in, gesturing slightly with the can.

She jumped and hurried to where a piece of paper sat on the spotless countertop.

He followed her, leaning against the counter and watching her. She repeated the name as she wrote it on the list.

"That's it, Sally."

He sounded almost caressing. It creeped me out. It made Sally lose color in her already pale face.

Mrs. P, on the other hand, stepped forward.

"Good day, sir. I am Mrs. Parens."

"I know who you are. From Cottonwood County High School. Wasn't there long, but I remember a lot."

"Indeed. I wish to talk with you about your living situation now that you have returned to Cottonwood County."

"Thanks, but I'm sure I'll be real comfortable here with Sally."

"You cannot waltz in and demand to stay at someone's house."

"No, ma'am," he said with an excessive courtesy that edged toward mockery, "absolutely not. I came because I was invited."

We swung back around to Sally.

"Sally?" Mrs. Parens demanded in her most terrifying *calling on you in class when you just woke up from a catnap* voice.

"The prison wrote me a letter."

She seemed to stall there.

"What did the letter say?" I nudged.

"That he—" A hand flapped toward Isaacs. "—was getting out of prison and as a condition of his parole he needed a place to stay and they liked to place them with... With, uh, people, who are good citizens."

"And you volunteered to have him stay here?"

"I never," she gasped in horror at my question. "I never volunteered. They *asked* me if I would let him stay here and I said yes, but I never thought he'd actually *come*."

He smiled slightly. "But I did."

In that youthful photo, I'd ascribed the lopsidedness of his look to his grin. But now I saw it wasn't the grin. That side of his face was visibly shorter than the other side, the line of his eyes tipped down, his mouth slanted up.

It formed a permanent expression now. Still a youthfully cocky grin? Or should it be describe as having hardened into a smirk? And had the lopsided grin caused the lopsidedness in his face or vice versa?

"Why on earth did you say yes, Sally?" Mrs. Parens demanded.

"I have to. He's, uh … a relative."

We all looked at her.

"A sort of, uh, cousin," she said weakly.

I said, "You are under no obligation to let anyone live with you, much less *a sort of cousin*."

Isaacs stirred, pushing away from the counter. "You're not from around here, are you? Blood's still thicker than water in Wyoming. And Sally here and I are a lot thicker than cousins. I'm her grandson."

Chapter Eight

"YOU PROMI—" SHE fluttered toward him, then abruptly veered back toward us. "No, no, he's confused. Family tree, you know. Very complicated. So confusing. Why, I've never been married."

"Makes that family tree kind of twisted, now doesn't it?" He said it with a glint of real humor.

Sally's face went even paler. I didn't think there was any paleness left before she'd keel over.

"You're my cousin." She looked at the floor as she said that. Then she looked from me to Mrs. P and back. "He's a cousin."

"Sally," Mrs. Parens began.

"Cousins," Sally said desperately. "Twice removed. At least."

It hung in the balance for an instant, then Mrs. Parens relented. "Whatever the relationship, you are not obligated to take in anyone, Sally."

She was not going to dispute Sally's account. At least not now.

"I told them I would."

"Told them? Who did you tell?" I asked.

"Well, first there was a form. And then a man came. He said he was part of, uh, Dean's transition team."

"Plain folks call him a parole officer," Dean contributed, now at the end of the counter, a step or two away from leaving the kitchen.

"I signed the paper because I didn't know what else to do."

"What else to do was to decline to sign the paper," Mrs. Parens said tartly.

"But he's been writing me for months and months."

"In prison, I saw a story on local TV news about your friend getting killed in the case about some thieves here in Sherman," Dean said. "The Tipton name caught my attention. Checked the genealogy I'd pulled together. And there it was, clear as day. As you said, our family tree."

"Yes, well," she said hurriedly, not making eye contact, unless it was with the microwave's clock. "Never mind."

"That's when I wrote to you. Knew my chance at parole was coming up and they like you to have a place to stay before you get out. What could be better than my grandmo—" He broke that off and ducked his head, as if in apology. It was hard to tell if it seemed deliberate, even sly, because his lopsided face shaded everything he said in that direction or because it truly was deliberate and sly. "What could be better than staying with a relative, right here in Cottonwood County? Fine, upstanding citizen and all, too."

I looked at him for a moment, then turned back to Sally and our conversation. I said, "If you don't want him here, you tell him to leave. If he won't leave, the police will see to it. He cannot force you to let him stay here, no matter how many forms you signed. You're allowed to change your mind."

She looked at me with a glimmer of hope. "But if I don't let him stay, where would he go?"

"They have halfway houses."

"They do? Here in Cottonwood County?"

"He doesn't have to stay in the county. He probably doesn't even have to stay in the state. States usually have agreements with other states to keep track of parolees."

"He could go to another state?" Hope raised Sally's voice.

Then she looked at Dean.

He smiled. Lopsided and sly.

Her hope vanished.

"Leave Wyoming? No way," he said. "Cottonwood County's my home. I'm not leaving here. But if I didn't have a place to stay, I'd have to go public with my story and see if anybody'd be willing to take me in. That old newspaper's still around isn't it? I bet they'd want my story. Or I bet this pretty TV lady would want to hear how I found a real interest in genealogy and started researching my parents in prison. Only there was hardly anything about my dad's background because he was adopted. So it took a lot more research to find out who to talk to, then writing letter after letter, and filling out forms before I could discover his family history. Leastwise bits of it. Sure would like to know more. That's why I came here. Thing is, you've got lots of time in prison to write all those letters and fill out all those forms and search all those sites.

"But there's some information you can't get to inside. I'm real optimistic I can find it now that I'm here. If you can't tell me, I'll keep asking around until I find out more. That's something I learned in prison. Cast a wide net for information, talk to everybody you can, because you don't know where the one, little piece of information that breaks everything wide open is going to come from. Another thing I learned in prison? Being real persistent. Just asking and asking and asking."

Sally swallowed convulsively.

"So, what do you say, *Cousin* Sally? You going to have your friends kick me out?" There was no overt threat in his voice.

"No," she said in a small voice.

He smiled at me, then at Mrs. Parens.

BACK IN MY vehicle, I didn't start the engine right away.

"Try not to worry, too much, Mrs. Parens."

"I am less worried than I am exasperated with her. If she had stood up to his bullying from the start, she would never be in this position. Indeed, she had the option of simply not responding to his letters."

"But now that she is in this position, her meekness might stand her in good stead. He doesn't seem to want more from her than a place to stay. If she provides that, maybe…?"

She sent me a look.

I decided to start the engine and begin the trip to the museum.

Driving provided sufficient distraction that I could pretend I hadn't noticed the withering in that look.

"It is an entirely unsatisfactory state of affairs when an elderly woman must wager her comfort and well-being on the hope that a person who might not appear overtly psychotic is not, in fact, psychotic in a more subtle manner," she said.

Hard to argue with that.

Remembering his comment about the high school, I asked, "Did you know him when he was growing up here?"

"He did not grow up in Cottonwood County. He came here only for his last year of high school. I did not have him in class, nor was I the principal of the high school at that time."

Last year of high school, not senior year. With Mrs. P, that was not a slip. "Did he graduate?"

"He did not at that time. I have been told he did receive a GED while in prison."

"Were you aware of any problems with him? Before the murder, I mean."

She paused a moment. "After he left school and had obtained part-time employment with a truck repair establishment, he would appear at the high school at the end of the school day, mingling with some of our students, especially girls, with the offer of rides and snacks."

Snacks. Right.

"Was that how he met Laura?"

"I have no direct knowledge of that."

We'd nearly reached the museum, so if I was going to get in any questions before our dinner, I needed to do it now.

"Okay, he's blackmailing Sally—presumably about some family scandal—into giving him a place to live here in Sherman, but why?"

She looked straight ahead for a long moment, then clicked her tongue. It was a remarkably impatient sound coming from her.

"Because she still has not learned her lesson. I thought that after that business last summer... But clearly not."

"What does that have to do with this?"

Mrs. Parens emitted a soft sigh, crossed her glove-covered hands in her lap, and sat up even straighter, though I wouldn't have thought that was possible.

"Sally Tipton found a way to exist many, many years ago. Now she is afraid to try any other way of being. I might consider her extraordinarily foolish in allowing this fear to dictate her actions in this and other circumstances. However, it is not my place to make those decisions nor to share her secrets. I am sorry to be disobliging to you, but I shall be in this instance."

Chapter Nine

THE WESTERN FRONTIER Life Museum was transformed.

After a volunteer secured coats and hats at the door, we entered the lobby area that then opened to exhibits.

Straight ahead, I saw Leona listening with apparent interest to a tall, bulky woman with resolutely black hair. *Apparent,* because Leona wasn't taking notes and without looking away from the woman she winked at me.

Three rectangular tables were set with white tablecloths, white plates, water and wine glasses. Bright blue napkins, white flowers in small blue vases down the centers of the tables, and greens made for simple yet elegant arrangements.

Automatically counting the place settings, it looked like a dinner for thirty. Not bad for a small museum.

I suppose candles were out of the question with the historic artifacts around. They'd adapted with the lighting on the displays turned down to soft backgrounds, highlighted with flickering lights showing through false firelogs in the Native American and frontier displays. String lights provided more light near the tables.

I recognized a few volunteers passing out pre-dinner glasses of wine, including a woman named Vicky Upton who worked in the gift shop and who proved once again that she was not one of my biggest fans when she pointedly bypassed me with the tray.

I secured two glasses from another volunteer, passing one to Mrs. P.

"Ah, Mrs. Parens, how nice to see you. And Elizabeth."

Turning, I saw it was the curator of the museum, Clara Atwood.

Her perfectly trimmed hair reminded me that I'd meant to find out where she was getting it done.

Clara gestured to the woman beside her. "Mrs. Parens, you'll remember Professor Nora Roy."

I was surprised. I shouldn't have been. Of course, Mrs. P knew her.

The professor was the woman I'd seen Leona talking to. Her dark green dress was expensive. The matching jacquard jacket made her look squarer than she actually was. She had to be past her mid-seventies. Her blue eyes were sharp.

The two older women nodded at each other, not smiling.

I had a sudden image of two retired gunslingers, fully capable of a final showdown, but mutually deciding to delay it for another day.

Clara gestured to me.

"Professor Roy, I'd like you to meet Elizabeth Margaret Danniher, though you might know her as E.M. Danniher from all the important reporting she did before she came to our local station."

Hey, I'd done some important reporting since I'd come to Wyoming, too.

But I knew she was trying to be nice. At least I thought she was.

"It's very nice to meet you, Professor Roy."

I extended my hand. She gave me one of those overhand fingertips-only returns as if expecting to have her hand kissed. I stepped in, making her bend her arm and shake like a normal person.

"I'm afraid I have not observed any of your work." She spoke with a strong accent I couldn't place at first. "I watch only BBC news coverage. Unless you have appeared on the BBC?" She clearly didn't think that possible.

"Nope." I said cheerfully. Could the BBC-watching explain the accent? "Though I have worked with some great journalists who've left the BBC because they weren't allowed to do the investigative work they wanted to."

She raised her chin to try to look down her nose at me. "Indeed," she said with a stronger accent than before.

I smiled down from several inches above her.

I'd been *Indeed?-ed* by Mrs. Parens. Professor Roy needed to up her *Indeed?* game if she hoped to compete in that league.

Apparently thinking she'd been too subtle to this point, she said, "Having been born in England, I find the BBC the only worthwhile news outlet."

"Born in England? How interesting, then, that you chose to specialize not only in American history, but in the history of the frontier West."

I'd pegged the accent now.

Losing or acquiring an accent is all over the map. Or, as a dialect coach I knew said, variable and individual. Most people adapt some to new surroundings. A few fight tooth and nail to hold on to their birth accent, despite the odds.

Professor Nora Roy had the more-English-than-England accent of the latter group, with a side order of BBCism.

Having encountered variants of that accent in D.C. and New York, I should have identified it immediately.

"This is the professor's daughter and son-in-law," Clara Atwood said quickly, presumably to keep me from responding to the professor. "Kitty and Graham Young."

I turned. And was face to face with the gray-haired couple who'd been sitting at the next table at the Haber House restaurant last night.

The sister and brother-in-law of Dean Isaacs' girlfriend who'd committed suicide. Surely acquainted with Yolanda Cruz, her mother's housekeeper.

Who'd been sitting there listening to us talk shop about the cases.

Wait a minute, Tom must know them. Why hadn't he—?

Because he'd had has back to that table. He'd never seen them.

Something glinted in the woman's eyes. Satisfaction? Or did I suspect that because she'd caught me at such a disadvantage? A fair number of people would have been satisfied at catching me at a disadvantage. But I became less sure the glint was satisfaction when I realized she was looking at her mother, rather than me.

Before I could turn to see the professor's response, the man extended his hand and said with faint disapproval, "Ms. Danniher."

I shook, forcing my focus on him, rather than on his wife. "How do you do, Mr. Young."

"Professor," he corrected.

"He's a professor of history, too," Clara said.

"Come, Kitty, Graham," Professor Roy said, "we must circulate so no one important feels we have overlooked them."

With the pair trailing behind her and Clara running interference, the professor marched toward a group at the far side of the room that included Tom Burrell. Our eyes met, and he nodded a greeting. He didn't look surprised to see me. I suspected he'd known ahead of time that I'd be here.

I hadn't known he'd be here, but also wasn't surprised to see him. A civic event in Cottonwood County? Of course he was here.

I smiled, raised my eyebrows, and added a slight tip of my head toward the approaching flotilla.

His brows came down and he said something to Linda Caswell, standing next to him.

Linda looked around, saw what was heading her way, and adopted a smile. It was polite, but not the smile that changed her collection of features that most would call plain into what only a fool wouldn't see was charming and genuine and warm.

She slipped her hand in to the arm of the athletic man next to her. Grayson Zane had done quite well in the National Finals earlier in the month. He deserved to take some time off the rodeo circuit over the holidays. No big surprise he chose to spend the time with Linda.

The professor steamed up to the group that also included two men and a woman I didn't recognize.

"The tribal representatives I mentioned," Mrs. P murmured from beside me.

Linda made introductions.

Professor Roy said something—something long, leaving no space for anyone else to talk. The body language of everyone around her stiffened slightly.

"Spreading joy and light," muttered a familiar voice at my shoulder.

I didn't need to turn to identify the speaker as Needham Bender, the editor/publisher of *The Independence,* but I turned anyway—to smile hello at his wife, Thelma.

"Typical?" I asked.

"Her specialty," he confirmed.

I look around at him. "Including within her family circle?"

"Now, whatever would make you ask that?"

"Just a wild idea."

As I turned back, I caught Linda and Grayson Zane exchange a look, she gave a slight nod, then he raised a hand to someone across the room—possibly a mythical someone.

Linda made what looked to be the appropriate excuses, then the entire group moved away from the professor and her entourage.

No question who'd orchestrated that. Linda. Another sign of her good sense.

"C'mon, I'll introduce you," Needham said, nudging me to intersect Linda and the others.

"Mrs. Parens said she'd introduce—"

"Oh, in that case, I bow to the greater authority." He smiled and actually gave her a small bow.

"What matters is that Elizabeth makes the acquaintance of these intelligent and kind people," she said graciously.

But she *was* the one who introduced me to John Bear Charley, Anna Price Fox, and O.D. Everett. O.D. Everett even said he watched "Helping Out!" and mentioned segments about running yard sales and insurance scams. I would have like to talk to him more, since he showed such fine judgment in television viewing. But introductions were all we had time for before an interruption came.

"Ms. Danniher." It was Sandy, the pleasant volunteer who usually manned the museum's front desk. "You'll be sitting at the main table, if you'll come this way."

"That'll be fun for you," Needham said. I didn't ask what he meant by that, because I thought I knew. "We're sitting with Linda, Grayson, and Tom, along with their guests over at that table."

"Now you're just bragging."

He laughed.

Thelma tapped his arm sharply in reproof. "Stop teasing her, Needham. It's a sign of what high regard you're held in that you're at the main table, Elizabeth. Needham has forfeited that honor by being untactful once too often."

"That I have," he said happily. He presented his bent arm to his wife. "Shall we?" He winked at me over his shoulder. "See you later."

I looked longingly at the table where they were heading. It was clearly the cool kids' table.

Chapter Ten

OUR TABLE WAS more heated than cool, while still managing to be boring.

Not an appetizing combination, which was unfortunate, because the food was delicious.

Crabmeat stuffed mushrooms came as an appetizer, with a main course of glazed pork chops, grilled pineapple, green beans, and balsamic caramelized onions.

It was a bold choice.

Not for serving onions to a group that was breathing on each other in close quarters, but for skipping any form of beef.

Though considering the conversation, it had also been a good choice. There was enough verbal red meat served up around that table.

It started even as Mrs. Parens and I were being herded toward the table and ran up against the slower moving group that centered around the professor.

That group had been augmented by several more people, including a thin man with the front of his hair combed back, then long and loosely curled at the back. He was talking animatedly toward the professor.

"... and prove the Cottonwood County encounter changed the entire complexion of the balance of the Indian Wars in the north."

"Even with proof, a battle in Cottonwood County—" started Clara.

"Massacre," the professor said. "If it happened, it was a massacre."

"I must agree with Professor Roy," the thin man said. "As many as twenty soldiers were lost."

The curator opened her mouth to respond, but Mrs. Parens beat her to the punch.

Not only as a figure of speech, either.

A punch is precisely what her tone appeared to deliver when she said, "It is a carryover from a distant and less enlightened age to term encounters won by the Euro-ethnic forcers *battles*, while calling those won by the indigenous forces *massacres*."

Score two for Mrs. P, since both Professor Roy and the man pulled their heads back as if the blows had landed on their chins.

The man recovered first. "The Cottonwood County *encounter*," he said with a finicky smile, clearly intended to show he was humoring Mrs. Parens, "never received the attention it deserved, being overshadowed by the Fort Phil Kearney *encounter* before it and Little Bighorn after it."

"That is because it never took place." Professor Roy appeared to be speaking almost absentmindedly.

His face turned red, veins protruding up his neck and tracing on his forehead. "It did. I have the research that proves it."

"A fairy tale. Never been able to find the spot, never been able to find documentation—"

"That's the *point*."

"—or contemporaneous accounts. Because it never happened."

He sucked in a breath. "You said—you *promised* you'd look at my new material from this trip before you said anyth—"

"Fine, fine." She turned her back on him. Which didn't help his vein-popping any.

"Dinner is about to be served," Clara announced loudly.

As we moved to the table, I said under my breath to Mrs. P, "What was that about?"

I doubted she would have told me, especially right then and there, but as it was there was no chance.

First, the professor barreled between us.

That led to a slow-mo scrum at the head of the table, as she caught up with the curator at the same moment the professor's gray-haired son-in-law converged at the position of power.

Roy left the other two in the dust, sliding in to the chair, taking a drink from the water glass, and snapping the napkin open.

It was the social equivalent of a cat marking its territory.

I stopped myself from laughing only because Mrs. Parens directed a stern look at me.

The son-in-law clung to the chair below her. His wife took the chair next to him. She seemed grim, though it was impossible to tell if that was because he'd missed out on the prime spot or because she would have preferred being farther away from her mother.

Clara took the spot at the bottom of the table. The red-faced man gravitated to that end, along with a young woman who I gathered was a graduate student.

Mrs. P and I took seats across from each other in the middle of the table.

The other seats were filled in by a man with faded blue eyes, who sat beside me, and the only one in the room wearing only a long-sleeved shirt with no sports jacket, and Sandy, who took the last seat at the table—the other one next to Professor Roy.

The red-faced man turned out to be another professor, by the name of Belknap.

He had become somewhat subdued. I gathered that he taught at the same Colorado university where Roy chaired the department and Graham Young also taught. As his color faded back to a more familiar human skin tone, something struck me as slightly familiar about Belknap, though I was certain we'd never met before. Perhaps I was responding to his clearly cultivated *look*.

I made a stab at conversation with the unknown man I guessed to be his mid-to-late sixties, by introducing myself and asking if he, too, was a professor.

"Nope. Married to one." He never looked up from buttering a roll.

Since Graham Young was clearly married to Kitty and Professor Belknap was demonstrating his hetero bent by preening before the graduate student and Clara, I was pushed to the conclusion that he was married to Professor Nora Roy.

"Do you also have an interest in the Nineteenth Century history of this region, Mr. Roy?"

"It's Zblewski. And no." The appetizers arrived then and he devoted his attention completely to the food.

Vic Zblewski, Nora Roy's husband, as I knew from the clips.

Those clips had referred to him as Laura's father, not stepfather, yet had offered no clues to why she had used Roy, rather than Zblewski as her last name.

His only role in the investigation had been as the witness that had seen Dean Isaacs driving away from the vicinity of the house hours after Isaacs said he left.

I had a feeling I wasn't missing out on much by being deprived of Zblewski's conversation.

To my right, the graduate student, whose name was Jasmine Uffelman, was too entranced by Belknap's domination of that end of the table to talk to me. At the opposite end, Professor Roy spoke at length with only occasional murmurs from Sandy to confirm someone was listening.

As I picked up bits and pieces from either end, I realized each was riding a historical hobbyhorse that seemed to touch on the battle/massacre discussion that had earlier raised hackles. I began to wonder if the curator had truly arranged this as the head table or had segregated the troublemakers here.

If I bet on horses, I'd put money down that these two hobbyhorses would collide before the meal was done.

What proved me wrong was the earnest graduate student. In the temporary lull while both Roy and Belknap watered their overused vocal chords, her clear young voice came.

"As I was saying to the professor—" With three professors at the table, I had no doubt "the professor" referred to Roy. The next phrase confirmed that supposition. "—during her office hours before the break, it's a shame that in the name of so-called progress things have to change from when they were so much better, say for instance, for the indigenous peoples, if it could have just stayed the way it was, with their beautiful lives in balance with nature and the environment, with peace and—"

"Utter nonsense." Professor Roy's voice reached down the table, stopped the young woman in mid run-on sentence, and slapped red spots onto her cheeks. "As I told you then. Yet here you are spouting on about a mythical utopia on the Plains. Precisely when was this perfect bastion of enlightenment and nonviolence?"

She left only enough silence to make it clear the graduate student couldn't gather her wits to respond, before continuing. "Which moment in history would you choose? Before conflicts among the tribes pushed tribes into this area that had not previously been here? Before—"

"Bbb-ut that happened bbb-because—" Jasmine Uffelman got it out, but it was a rocky start to the interruption. "—the pressure of settlement on the coasts, especially the East Coast, pushed tribes—"

Roy talked over her. "—the Indians—or Natives or indigenous, or whatever you prefer—had horses? Before they had guns? When exactly? History does not freeze in place. It continues on whether you like it or not."

Roy had a point.

It hurt to acknowledge that.

Then she did me a favor by continuing, which quickly got me past that moment of agreeing with her. "All the hand-wringing. All the revisionist historians falling over themselves in making the forces of progress and the future unrelentingly evil."

"B-bbbecause we know better now. We've evolved—"

"Or because their efforts were effective and the revisionists choose not to see that."

"Effective?" Belknap struck in. "Taking lands? Outlawing language? Eliminating religion? What—?"

"It is the way of the conqueror. And a necessary component to complete the process—to snap the cultural ties that supported the military aspects."

Clara gaped. Mrs. Parens' ramrod back became even straighter. Graham Young was blank-faced. Kitty Roy Young, on the other hand, did not gape, look shocked, or withdraw. She appeared sharply concentrated.

Vic Zblewski kept eating.

As for me, my Grandmother Danniher took over my mouth. It's the only explanation for what happened next.

Perhaps there was also a faint echo from Needham and Thelma's discussion of how one got oneself permanently struck off the list for future assignments to the miserable main table, but, really, it was mostly Grandmother Danniher.

"Guess they learned that from how the English government handled the Irish, huh?" Grandmother Danniher said through me. "Kicking landowners off their land, outlawing Gaelic and Catholicism, denying them jobs—or food during the potato famine while declaring help was bad for their characters."

Peripheral vision told me some gapes were now turned on me.

I was more interested in Professor Roy. She'd caught the red face and popping veins from Belknap. It didn't look any better on her than it had on him.

"As I said, effective." From the snap of that, she slid to snide. "Since England conquered Ireland."

"Not so effective, since England had to keep reconquering over and over and over because Ireland wouldn't *stay* conquered. Its cultural ties never snapped, nor did those of the natives of North America."

Into the silence that followed, Kitty said clearly, "Perhaps we should move on to another topic for discussion. The local news of the day?"

"Local news—" Professor Roy started disparagingly.

"Yes, news. Ah, Mother, it wouldn't have made the BBC broadcasts, so you might not be aware that Dean Isaacs has returned to Cottonwood County on parole. It's not related to your preferred period, but it is part of history—our family history."

Chapter Eleven

CLARA HAD THROWN herself on that hand grenade, chattering madly about plans for the museum through the next year.

Nobody paid her any attention, but it kept them from talking, so that was a major benefit.

Professor Roy hadn't tried to answer Kitty, but from her blotchy complexion and aggressive use of utensils—those beans really didn't deserve to be stabbed that way—the shot had hit home.

Her daughter calmly ate her meal.

All the rest of us followed her suit as best we could under the white noise of Clara's chatter.

By the time it was over, I seconded Mrs. P's excuses to Clara about making it an early night and followed her out with barely a glance at the table where the cool kids were happily talking and smiling.

"What was that about?" I asked Mrs. P, but only after I'd pulled out of the parking lot and the heater had kicked in.

"I believe you heard the discussion. Indeed, you participated quite—" She delicately cleared her throat. "—effectively. For which I say, brava."

Grandmother Danniher took a bow. "Apply the question more broadly. What was that whole evening about and all those currents and cross-currents? Why did you want me there?"

"I believed you would find the characters interesting."

"Yeah, I definitely found them interesting. Not conducive to good digestion, but definitely interesting. I picked up on a lot of strain between Professor Roy and her daughter and son-in-law."

"In what way?"

"How about that little jab about Dean Isaacs being in town?"

"That turn of recent events was bound to heighten tensions among the members of that family as well as others."

"You can't pass it off as recent events that having a daughter with that much gray in her hair makes it impossible for Nora Roy to credibly pull off that dark hair look. Showing up her mother in that passive-aggressive way must have been going on for some time."

A delicate *tsk* was all Mrs. Parens allowed herself. I interpreted that as a full-blown condemnation of Professor Roy's choice of hair color. But all she said was, "Kitty Young began to go gray quite young. In fact, when her sister died."

I considered that a moment.

"That reinforces that the hair wars were not a recent or spur-of-the-moment difference. I still say Professor Roy doesn't seem popular with her family." I amended that. "Certainly not with her daughter. It was harder to get a reading on her son-in-law other than *Not A Happy Man.* As for her husband, Vic Zblewski, who knows? Though he clearly did like the food. So he's capable of enthusiasm. He just wasn't directing any of it toward his wife."

Mrs. P made a mild sound. Might have been a chuckle, but I was concentrating on the driving as we hit an open area that let the wind bully not only the snow, but also my SUV.

With that handled, I picked up, "As I was saying, Professor Roy doesn't seem very popular with her family."

"Blood will tell in the end," Mrs. Parens said.

Her calm statement jolted me.

Should it have? In many ways, Mrs. P was a throwback to an earlier age. Although I'd never have expected the ways to include the sentiment that blood ties counted more than anything else. It seemed contrary to her interactions with people and her dedication to education to raise people up.

Not a discussion I was going to open, however.

"Or very popular at all, for that matter," I resumed, "considering her interactions with Belknap, Clara, and that graduate student,

Jasmine Uffelman. Was I imagining it or was the professor purposely kept away from the representatives from the tribes as well as the major donors? Actually, make that professors, all of them."

"Clara has learned from history."

In other words, I hadn't imagined it.

"I could see that the news about Yolanda Cruz's murderer getting paroled and returning here could ratchet up tensions, especially among Professor Roy's family. But you asked me to that dinner before you knew about Dean Isaacs being at Sally Tipton's, so what...?"

She stared straight ahead.

Oh, brother was I slow or what?

"I see. You *did* know. You knew *before* you invited me to this benighted dinner. You knew all the back story about the professor's housekeeper being murdered as well as her daughter committing suicide. Of course you knew Dean Isaacs was responsible. And you knew he had arrived to stay at Sally's house."

"I did not know that then," she said precisely.

I shot a stern look at her. Then thought better of it.

First, the wind was back to blowing snow across the highway, so my attention was better aimed at the road.

Second, no look of mine, stern or not, affected Mrs. Parens.

"You didn't know he was at Sally's house," I repeated. "*Then.*"

Her silence confirmed my emphasis.

"You didn't know he was at Sally's house when you invited me—" Commanded me. "—to this dinner. But you had reason to believe he might be there at some point."

She sighed. "You are correct to chastise me, Elizabeth. I apologize to you for drawing you further into Sally's affairs. I am disappointed in myself that I did not correctly assess the situation. Further, I blame myself for subjecting you to a far less than pleasant evening."

"Chastise? I'm not chastising—" I took a breath and focused on the road. "Mrs. Parens, you don't need to apologize. Or blame yourself, for heaven's sake. But you could explain a lot more. I know you know a lot you're not telling me. You'd go a long way toward making up for that miserable dinner company if you'd spill it all."

"I do, both apologize and blame myself." That had the faintest whiff of dry humor to it. Perhaps because she was so blatantly side-stepping the explaining and spilling aspects. "At this point in my life, as well as my long acquaintance with Sally, I erred in not accounting for the danger posed by weakness. The weak can do as much ill as the evil, because the weak act from fear, they are always fearful, and there are far more of them than the truly evil."

If that wasn't a fitting epithet to that dinner party, I don't know what was.

"Specifically, I apologize for drawing you in to Sally's situation." In other words, she wasn't apologizing for not answering my questions about the dinner party guests. "I am certain you noticed that Dean Isaacs was aware of your identity without an introduction."

I had noticed. *Pretty TV lady.*

Yet I had not been on the air, not live, and not with a "Helping Out!" segment, since his release. He'd been in prison in another part of the state and it was highly unlikely that anyone, much less a state prison, took pains to add KWMT-TV to its offerings.

"It is, indeed, disobliging of me to ask for your involvement, then decline to answer your questions, Elizabeth. It is neither gracious nor grateful."

She knew and I knew that I was going to let her off this hook without insisting on answers. I almost certainly wouldn't have gotten them even if I did try to insist, so what was the point?

I smiled at her. "You are always gracious. And I am grateful to you for all you've done for me."

She patted my arm. "Nonsense. I have merely welcomed a wonderful addition to our community. Now, tell me about your Christmas with your family."

I did.

She asked numerous questions, drawing out far more detail than most people expressed an interest in knowing about the holiday traditions and inner workings of the Danniher clan.

But after dropping off Mrs. P, as I drove from O'Hara Hill to my place at Diana's ranch, I was thinking about the conversation.

Not dwelling on the one on the drive from the museum to take her home, with all the dodging and weaving and outright refusing she'd done when it came to giving me answers, but, instead, examining the one before we'd arrived at the museum for that memorable dinner.

It struck me that there was a second, very different track to follow from my initial *He's blackmailing her into giving him a place to live, but why?* question.

That was another one Mrs. P had given me no answer to, essentially saying it was Sally's business and she wouldn't share secrets the old woman apparently had been keeping for ages.

Yes, my curiosity chafed over what he was holding over her head. But I accepted that the woman was entitled to her privacy.

That still left the question of why Isaacs would *bother* to blackmail Sally Tipton?

That answer might seem fairly obvious: He'd wanted to come back to Sherman, to Cottonwood County.

Obvious was often right, but not always. So it would be smart to stay aware of other possibilities.

But, assuming for now that the obvious was true, that led directly to the next question:

Why had he wanted to come back here?

Surely, the memories weren't great.

And with him needing to blackmail Sally into giving him a place to stay, it didn't seem like he had friends or family—close family, unless Sally really was … Nope, not going to speculate—who would draw him here.

Though that might be something to look into.

When the heck did Jennifer get back from vacation?

WEDNESDAY

DECEMBER 28

Chapter Twelve

MY FIRST SCHEDULED background interview of the day was in the eastern part of the county, so I went directly there from the bunkhouse.

It wasn't precisely dawn, but with the sun lollygagging around about rising this time of year it was a lot closer than I liked to come.

Especially since I'd stayed up last night going over my notes and the recording from interviewing Enid Harter.

I'd also taken advantage of it being so far from business hours that it was highly unlikely anyone would answer to make some calls. First, I called the courthouse to hear the real message, then the scammer's callback number. The two were close. Very close. Except the scammer told the caller to leave a message, not wanting to let a prospect wriggle off the hook. The courthouse message was more along the lines of call again when we're here.

The interview followed the same general outline as yesterday's, but with less detail. Let me clarify that—with less *informative* detail.

The woman, whose name was Marcia Odom, gave me plenty of detail about what she'd been doing in the hours before she'd received the call, how her children had misbehaved during the call, despite her having been a high school teacher and knowing how to deal with kids, and how their new dog was untrained because of her kids.

The dog was definitely untrained, though rather sweet in a knock you over and lick you to death way. So were the kids—untrained, I mean. As teenagers, they definitely weren't sweet.

I had to bite my tongue from pointing out where the lack of training likely originated.

Marcia Odom did not know Richard Alvaro, certainly couldn't say if it had been his voice on the phone or not, though "of course I know the family." This *was* Cottonwood County.

The second interview was mostly south of Interview One, putting it in the least populated part of a not very populated county.

That made it good time to call back Mel Welch—friend, lawyer, and convoluted relative-in-law—who had left a voice mail before I woke up. Even hands-free calls can be distracting, but this area helped a lot by offering few natural distractions.

When Mel's assistant put me through, he answered, "About time you called back, Danny."

He and numerous other friends and family had picked up the nickname I'd first used with a source with the FBI lab. Hearing it now reminded me I hadn't talked to Dex in a while.

"I just saw you at Christmas." I'd known Mel since I was six when he became my mother's cousin's oldest daughter's high school boyfriend. It was instant crush on my part. He'd shown more tolerance than most teenage boys would have, leaving no scars. When, in due course and after law school, he married my mother's cousin's oldest daughter—Peg, by name—our relationship settled into a comfortable, trusting friendship. "Besides, you called too early. It wasn't even seven o'clock."

"It was almost eight here," he answered cheerily and irrefutably. Mel had this theory that time only existed where he was and everyone else should adjust. I wonder if *he* could be related to my mother somehow. "You know what they say about early birds."

"Yeah, but who wants worms?"

"Apparently you did at one time, because you married one."

A lot can be forgiven a friend who dislikes your ex without reservation.

When I divorced Wes, I had no idea he'd react the way he did. That saying about you never really know a man until you divorce him?

It's true.

And if it's not a saying it should be.

He worked through his pain—or bruised ego—by doing his best to end my career. We'd worked our way up, me in news, him on the executive side, in the same network and he used his pull to isolate me here in Sherman.

It wasn't his fault that the wide open spaces had started providing me unexpected benefits.

I acknowledged Mel's point. "True. What's new with the worm?"

"Squirming. I got a response to our most recent demand for your share of the proceeds from the sales of the house in D.C. and the cottage in Virginia. He and Slocum are scrambling around for more excuses to hold on to those monies. I have our people in New York on notice to get on the schedule with the judge if this goes on any longer. I don't know why they're dragging their feet on this last financial tie."

"I can guess why. Wes wants that money to show up as his for both calendar years because he wants to impress the co-op board for the place in New York. That's the one he really cares about."

I, on the other hand, had liked the house in D.C. and loved the cottage in Virginia. The apartment in Manhattan we'd rented and he was trying to buy? That had been Wes' baby.

"Sneaky," Mel said with a trace of admiration.

"He and that co-op board deserve each other. I want my share of the money, but what I really want are the contents in storage in Virginia."

"Which he knows. That's why he's holding off releasing his rights to the contents. Slocum raised selling those items again."

"No." They were a mix of things from the D.C. house and the cottage, none of which Wes had considered worthy of making the move—stepping up, according to him—from Washington to New York. Some of them were Danniher family pieces, all of them mattered to me.

"Just be aware they're a weapon he can use against you because you do care about them."

"Yeah." I sighed. "Thanks for the update, Mel. Keep tugging 'til that worm comes loose."

"If it weren't for that, I'd step on the worm and squash him flat."

"Pleasant thought."

We hung up, and I was certain he was smiling at the other end just as I was.

Chapter Thirteen

THE WOMAN WHO answered the door looked to be well under twenty-five and very pregnant. Photos over the mantel added up to her being the wife of a deployed soldier.

This scammer truly was scum.

But it turned out the scam hadn't been aimed at her. It was her mother who'd been targeted. Candice Wynn was a bookkeeper who worked from home and was training her daughter in the black arts of the trade.

She'd dismissed the scam caller quickly and efficiently, so she didn't have as much to share as the others.

She couldn't say if the caller had sounded like Richard Alvaro or not. She knew his oldest brother, having gone to school with him, but wasn't sure she'd ever met Richard to do more than nod to him in town.

My third call was going to be on the western edge of Sherman, with this scam target being a name I recognized from my earliest days in Wyoming, but not anyone I'd met.

Before I went to the Radey home, however, I had two stops to make.

First, was the station, to check in.

Also to see if Mike Paycik was there.

He was.

In fact, he was at my desk, writing on a pad.

"Hey, Paycik."

He jumped up. "Elizabeth, I was leaving you a note to come see me when you get in."

"I'm in. Thanks," I added when he held out the chair for me. But then I had to spin the chair three-quarters of the way around because it only turns to the right. "Why did you want me to come see you?"

He sat on the desk, close enough that with our voices low no one else in the newsroom would hear us. That would have been true at its most crowded, which was never very crowded. Today he probably could have sat at the next desk over and nobody would hear us.

"Elizabeth, I know you're interested in Dean Isaacs getting out of prison and all that because Thurston broke the story—"

"It's not because Thurston—"

"—and is screwing it up royally. There's something about that case I need to tell you."

"There's something I need to tell you, too, but you first."

"The murder he was convicted of committing and the suicide of that girl, those happened on my ranch." He stopped, watching me.

"I'm glad you told me."

"You already knew," he accused. "How? Who? Diana?"

"Shelton."

"*Shelton* told you that?" He considered that an instant. "Shelton told you *anything?*"

I distracted him from wondering about that by asking, "Mike, why didn't you tell me—us?"

He shrugged and also let loose a sigh. "Folks 'round here all knew. Didn't need to be said." He met my eyes. "With you it would've needed saying."

"But what's the big deal? Is this why—?"

"Why what?"

"Never mind." Almost as soon as the words came out, I changed my mind. "No, I'll say it. After giving you grief about not saying, I will say… Is that why you've never invited me to your place?"

He flushed.

That's not the word that came into my mind, but it seemed wrong to say a former NFL player blushed.

"It's not much to look at inside."

"Are you serious? You didn't want me to see the *décor*? After the times you spent at the Hovel?" I said of my former rental house.

He grinned crookedly. "The Hovel had a certain quirky charm. My place is... plain."

"Plainer than the Hovel?" I couldn't imagine that.

"Well, the living room's set up as a gym. And that's the most finished room, other than the kitchen. Only because the kitchen already came finished. They even left a table and chairs."

"Dell didn't complain when he stayed with you." Wardell Yardley, a long-time colleague and competitor in the Washington press corps, had spent a couple nights with Mike during the fall when Dell was in Cottonwood County for a story, then ran into an ... issue.

Since Dell was nearly as well known for his pickiness as his reporting, his not complaining was significant.

"Might not have complained to *you*. He sure did to *me*. You should have heard him going on about what my place looks like."

"I can imagine, but I'm confused now. Did you never let me see your place because of the décor or because it was the site of a murder?"

"Oh, I knew it being the site of a murder wouldn't bother you," he said breezily. "I started to tell you at the Haber House the other night, until Diana gave us the sign that those other diners weren't amused by our topic of conversation. Besides, hardly any of the murder stuff is still there. The house got knocked down before they put this one up."

"Shelton said that some of the original main house's structure was still there as part of the barn."

"That's what I was told, too, when I bought the place. They have to reveal stuff like that. And I kept pressing it."

"As a negotiating tactic?" I asked with a smile.

"Sure thing. Every dollar I didn't spend on the place was a dollar kept in my nest egg."

"Do you know you're ruining the image of pro athletes as empty-headed spendthrifts who blow wads of cash?"

He looked a lot more serious than the question warranted. "Athletes aren't the only ones. Did you know seventy percent of wealthy families lose their wealth by the second generation and ninety percent by the third? So, yeah, some athletes still blow their money, but it's getting better. A lot of guys never had much money until they signed their first contract and then it seems like it's more than anybody could ever spend. A lot of bankruptcies proved otherwise, and now the young guys are getting told about that. The league, the union, the teams have been educating the players on finances. Me, I was fortunate in that way. Never made a huge bundle, always thought it would go away any moment."

"That's fortunate?"

"Sure. Made me keep looking ahead, seeing how short football income was, how long life after football was likely to be." He paused. Looked down, then back up at me. "I also had the example of my dad losing the family ranch."

I'd heard references to that piece of his history, but he hadn't talked about it before. From his silence, it seemed like he might not want to now, either.

"Must have been tough," I offered quietly.

"Yeah. Used to think it was tough on me, not having that legacy. When I got a little older—"

"Mike! It's Eduardo Tarcosa on the phone for you."

I recognized the name as a baseball player. Apparently an important one, from Dale's excited bellow.

Mike popped up. "Gotta take this. We'll talk more later."

I was sure we would.

Though I noticed he still hadn't invited me to see his house.

My second stop before going to the Radey house, was Hamburger Heaven.

I picked up lunch for three with plenty of extras, including multiple choice sides.

The man who answered the little house's front door, clearly gave a great deal of thought to food and acted on those thoughts frequently.

"Mr. Radey? Ed Radey? I'm Elizabeth Margaret Danniher from

KWMT-TV's 'Helping Out!', here for our appointment. I brought some lunch."

I had a soft spot for Ed Radey, because he'd been among the very earliest callers to "Helping Out!"

Possibly a soft spot in the brain, since what he'd called for was demanding that I take him and his wife out to dinner ... or cook for them.

When I hefted the shopping bag, his eyes lit up. "Come in, come in."

"Who is it, Ed?" asked a plump woman coming along the hallway.

"She brought lunch," he said, homing in on the essentials. "Right this way. Back to the kitchen."

He led me through the kitchen to a small table set under a window looking out on their backyard. Snow outlined beds that promised to hold vegetables come summer.

I couldn't really tell that from how the beds looked now, but we'd passed shelves holding glass jars neatly labeled with the names of vegetables, so it seemed a reasonable guess.

"Sit here," Mrs. Radey instructed, holding a third chair. She added a third placemat and brought three plates and sets of utensils.

Mr. Radey was pulling items out of the bag, muttering at a salad, then crowing when he came upon the burgers and fries.

"What would you like to drink, dear?"

I opted for water. She brought steaming coffee mugs for each of them.

"Who are you again?" he asked.

I noted that he hadn't asked that until he had his hands on the food.

"That girl from the TV station," his wife said. I warmed to her instantly. Being called a girl at my age, by someone who clearly meant it, can do that. "The one you told to come today. About the phone calls."

"Oh, yeah. You're the one I called back in the spring to come make dinner." He frowned. "You never came."

"I'm here now, with lunch."

He humphed, but dug into his meal.

Mrs. Radey *tsked* as she gestured for me to sit and did so herself. "Doctor put him on a diet last spring and you'd think I was trying to kill the man instead of trying to keep him alive. Now, dear," she added to me, "don't look so alarmed. A little indulgence now and then won't kill this old coot. Though we will help you, Ed, by taking our share of the fries. You can have some salad."

That didn't go over well until his wife suggested piling most of the salad onto a burger. Clearly he found that more palatable than salad on its own.

"We're learning little ways to adjust. He's lost almost forty pounds. I'm very proud of him."

He didn't respond as he ate his way through a container of cole-slaw.

At the end of the meal, with nearly everything gone except some potato salad Mrs. Radey had whisked to the refrigerator, he patted his substantial belly and said, "Best lunch I've had for coming on a year."

Mrs. Radey stood, taking the plates to the sink. I started to join her. "No, no. You sit. I'll have this taken care of in a flash. You'd best get your questions asked before Ed takes his afternoon nap. After this meal, it could happen fast."

I took her advice.

He'd started by berating the would-be scammer for ever thinking Ed Radey would be taken in by such a scheme.

That motif returned frequently as he answered my questions.

He knew Richard Alvaro, but not well. "The boy" had been a student at the high school where Ed had been a maintenance supervisor. "Knew all the Alvaro kids. Not well, 'cause they were good kids and smart. Not the kind stupid enough to think I could be taken in. The ones I saw a lot of were the troublemakers. Always trying to get into places they weren't supposed to be."

"Why?"

"Mostly to get away from the teachers and such trying to pound something sensible into their thick heads, one or two thinking they'd find a way to do real damage, but all of them to make more work for me."

He wouldn't recognize Richard's voice. *Not* because he was going deaf, he added with a frowning look at his wife. Because he didn't know him that well. Never had any trouble with the police or any trouble that required the police, so how would he know a deputy? He was a law-abiding citizen who paid his bills, lived within his means, voted regularly, kept his house and yard the way they should be, and didn't wait until spring to shovel his sidewalk.

Ed *had* called the callback number.

Not, mind you, because he was in danger of falling for the scam. Because he wanted to see what lengths they'd go to.

Mrs. Radey gave me that number from where she'd written it down. "Just in case."

It was the same number I'd called last night.

They'd been quite sure they hadn't missed a grand jury summons—"Haven't been away since that doctor put me on that diet. When you're starving, doesn't much matter where you are," he said.

Using the speakerphone, he called back the callback number right then, receiving that same recording I'd heard the day before.

Something was tugging at me, but what?

I did another round of questions, coming at the same issues from different angles, hoping whatever was tugging would surface.

It didn't.

And Ed's eyes were drifting closed even when he wasn't looking longingly at the recliner in the front room.

I excused myself and left.

The challenge now was going to be looking wider than these Shelton-approved scam-call recipients. Finding one who'd fallen for the scam would be ideal. We might even be able to trace the transaction back to the perpetrator.

When did Jennifer come back from vacation?

Otherwise, Shelton either had to give me something more to work on or untie my hands about revealing the scam.

Or both.

Wait a minute. He'd said someone had lost money. But none of the people Shelton had sent me to had admitted losing money. He was holding out on me.

Time to track down Wayne Shelton and shake loose more information.

While my SUV's engine warmed up areas of the interior not reached by the bright sun beating through the windshield, I checked my phone.

All hell had broken loose.

Chapter Fourteen

I HAD NINE messages—Diana, Mike, Mrs. Parens, Mike again, Clara Atwood, Tom, Mike's aunt Gee, Diana again, and Audrey Adams from the station.

While I was absorbing that, a text came in and I saw I had twelve of those. Diana and Mike dominated these, but also Tom, Clara, and once again last, Audrey.

I started with that last text, but since it simply said, "Call!" it didn't tell me a lot. And I didn't want to call her until I knew what was happening.

If this was going to turn into an official KWMT-TV report for me, I was going to take two extra minutes to know what I was jumping in to.

And, yes, whether I wanted to remain a free agent longer.

I scrolled through the other texts, hoping one would say what was going on.

Nope. They all just said, "Call."

I tried calling Mike, Diana, and Tom in quick succession. All busy.

So I went back and started listening to the calls.

Diana and Mike each said "Call me. Right away" in hushed voices.

Mrs. Parens, in her usual voice, said she hoped I would have the opportunity soon to return her phone call.

"Where the heck are you?" Mike's second message demanded. "Call."

I tried him, Tom, and Diana again. All busy again.

And they weren't picking up when they saw it was me calling.

Clara Atwood won the most-irritating message contest by saying, "You've probably already heard. I hope—" A long pause then. "I hope we can talk soon." Click. She'd sounded like she'd been punched in the first part of the call. After the pause, she was back to herself.

Tom asked me to call him in his usual give-no-hints tone.

Mike's Aunt Gee asked if I'd talked to Mike yet and to have him call her "as soon as possible."

Audrey went with the succinct, "Call."

I was trying Mike again when a live call came in from Diana. I clicked over to that one.

"What's going on, Diana?"

"I'm driving to the scene right now. I got the assignment."

"What assignment? What scene?"

There was a momentary pause. Not silence, because I could hear road noises as she pushed the sonic barrier as she always did when she drove without her kids in the car.

"You haven't heard?" She immediately added, "It looks like Professor Roy has been found dead in her garage. The husband called it in."

"Dead of what? Heart attack? Or an accident? Or—Garage? Carbon monoxide?"

"Don't know yet. They haven't said much, not even officially saying she's dead. But the way they're saying the little that they are saying, doesn't sound like a heart attack to me. We picked it up on the scanner and I was the first one out the door. When I left, Leona was trying to persuade Thurston to cut his lunch short, skip his nap, and get out to the scene. *Leona,*" she repeated.

Leona D'Amato was one of the few people in the newsroom Thurston might listen to. Partly because she'd been around KWMT-TV since before he and most of the rest of us were born. But mostly because she didn't threaten his job because she was perfectly happy doing what she did.

"Cut his lunch short *and* skip his nap? Never going to happen. Might have a long shot at one of them. But both? No way. As for Leona, she's taking it seriously because of the museum connection."

While I'd been saying that, my brain was working on other matters. "The professor has a daughter and son-in-law. Any idea where they live?"

"With her."

Damn. That meant they'd be sealed off by law enforcement.

"What about Professor Belknap?"

"Never heard of him."

"Good. Don't mention the name to anybody. Where does Professor Roy—" I almost finished that with *live*? Didn't apply anymore. "—where's her house?"

"Ranch," she corrected.

She gave me directions to the southwest corner of Cottonwood County. Definite high side territory, as the locals designated the area of the county with more plentiful water and more fertile grazing, and therefore more profitable ranches.

"What's law enforcement calling it?" I asked.

"Interesting you should ask. Mike pointed out that they keep saying that it was *called in as a suspected accident.* But they're not calling it an accident directly. Always ascribing it to the husband calling it in that way. Including the people on the scene."

"It's way too soon for them to even guess. Plus, they don't like to say someone's dead until the medical types confirm it. Still, it's interesting. Who's at the scene for law enforcement?"

"Shelton's on his way to take lead."

That figured. It was good for the quality of the investigation that would follow. Not so good for working journalists getting up-to-date information, much less a scoop.

It also nudged the likelihood of this being natural down the scale.

"Is Sheriff Conrad going to the scene?"

She answered precisely. "There's been no traffic about him going to the scene."

In other words, she wouldn't tell me if he'd told her privately that he was going.

That was fair. If the two of them weren't seeing each other, we wouldn't have known unless and until he did show up, so we didn't lose anything by her not sharing. Nor did we gain anything.

I might have a fleeting longing for the potential gains, but, yeah, it was fair.

"It *could* be a natural death." But Diana didn't really think so. "Even so, she was well known and a sudden death like this... You coming now?"

"No. The sheriff's department will have that locked down. I'm going to try some other angles that might be more open, at least temporarily."

"What—? Gotta go. Or they'll wave me into the next county."

She was gone.

I considered calling Mike next, but he likely would tell me what Diana had just shared and timing was going to be crucial on these other potential angles.

Despite the pressure of time, however, I didn't start driving yet. I had to know where I was heading first.

I called Sally Tipton's number.

"Hello?" came her hesitant voice.

"Sally, it's Elizabeth Danniher. Is—"

"Oh, hello, dear. How are you? It's a lovely day, isn't it?" Not only did the hesitation clear away, but she'd immediately picked up her usual way of talking—drawing out each word while leaving little to no space from one sentence to the next. It made it very hard to dive in without bordering on rude. "The sun feels so strong and warm I could almost think it was spring, but of course that's because I'm inside where it's warm. If I were outside—"

Sometimes bordering on rude was the only reasonable choice. I dove in. "Sally, is Dean Isaacs there?"

"Dean? You *want* to talk to him? But yesterday you said he should leave and—"

"*Did* he? Did he leave?"

"This morning after breakfast, because he doesn't like corn flakes, not even with sugar and milk—"

"For good? Did he leave for good?"

"For good? You think he might have left for good? I know it's wrong to say so but that would make me so happy if—"

"Sally. Is he there now, yes or no?"

"No, but—"

"When did he leave?"

"As I said, after breakfast. Really, he was almost... I hesitate to say it, since he has fixed a few things and he did say he'd pick up the items on the list from the hardware store, though I am paying for it and whether I receive any change from that money I gave him, I do wonder, and, truly, wouldn't you consider it rude, saying he was going somewhere to get a real meal? Because I *did* serve—"

"Has he been back since he left—what time was it that he left?"

"—a real meal. And even when you don't particularly want some-one staying with you, to have your hospitality—"

"Sally. Has he been back since he left this morning?"

"Oh, yes, this morning ... About nine-thirty, I believe, though—"

That time was when he'd left. I thought. Unless she meant that's when he came back... "Has he been back since he left at nine-thirty?"

"No, unless he slipped in while I was washing a load of tablecloths. They do make a table look so much more pleasant, I always think, so even though food does fall on them—"

"Did he take any of his things?"

"Oh, I would never go in his *room*."

I dropped my head to the hand that wasn't holding the phone. "Does he have a car, a vehicle? And—" I added quickly, hoping asking two questions would cut the number of times I had to interrupt. "—if he does, is it at your house now?"

"The vehicle he's driving is not here at the moment." And then, miracles of miracles, she anticipated my next question. "It's dark blue. Some might think it is black, but it is definitely dark blue and when the sun's out like it is today—"

"Thank you, Sally. I have to go now. Good-bye."

I'd considered asking if she knew what he'd intended to do today beyond the hardware store, but even if he'd told her—and I could get her to tell me in a reasonable amount of time—he'd been gone long enough that his plans could certainly have changed.

Tracking Dean's movements could be done later, and might already be of interest to law enforcement.

Though if Professor Roy's death truly was an accident...

I had another angle that would still be of interest and would stay fresh for a very limited time.

I shifted gears—literally, putting the SUV in drive and starting forward as I hit the main number for the Haber House Hotel on my phone.

Chapter Fifteen

I ASKED FOR Professor Belknap's room.

He answered on the third ring with the breathless impatience of someone who'd been pulled away from something important to answer the phone.

I hung up on him.

I also picked up speed as I headed to the center of town.

He wasn't going to tell me what I wanted to know on the phone.

By the time I took one of the angled parking spots that is the surest sign of a highly evolved civilization, I had a plan.

I didn't even try at the front desk. They're not supposed to tell you guests' room numbers. Most live up to that, even in Sherman, and then you're on their radar. Even if you get one who messes up or doesn't know and tells you the room number, they remember you later.

I went straight to the restaurant. A few tables held diners who seemed like they might be looking for their waitress.

Hot damn.

Kelly was on duty.

I wasted no time looking for her here in the dining room or in the kitchen, but went directly to a side door that opened to a tiny brick-enclosed space that Kelly had turned into a chimney with her cigarette smoke.

"Hey, this is for employees on brea—Oh, it's you."

I didn't waste time being affronted by the lack of enthusiasm. "There's a man staying here. Medium height, thin. Hair combed back, then long around his neck."

"The mullet with curls," she mumbled.

Not only was that a good description, but it triggered a memory. A deep down memory. "Yes. Wha—"

"Terrible tipper," she grumbled. With her level of service I wondered if she ever encountered anyone who was generous enough to *not* qualify as a terrible tipper.

"What room is he staying in?"

"Why?"

Not "how the heck would I know?" Good, good, good.

"Because I'll pay you ten dollars if you tell me his room number."

"A hundred."

"You're nuts. Twenty."

"Fifty."

"Twenty-five."

"Okay." She held out a hand.

"Not until I've confirmed that it is his room number."

"You mean I have to trust you that you'll come back and pay me?"

"That's right. Tell me the room number, I confirm it, then I come back and pay you. Or don't tell me or tell me the wrong number and you get nothing. That's your choice."

"Two-forty-four."

"How do you know?"

"He ordered room service and they make me do that, too."

"I'll be back." I pivoted as I spoke.

"What about some up front? A down payment? Twenty now and—"

I closed the door on her smoking closet without answering.

ON MY WAY through the dining room, I ordered two slices of pie from a guy who'd interrupted his task of taking inventory behind the bar. I also wheedled a tray, napkins, and forks out of him.

His service far surpassed any Kelly had ever provided. I tipped him generously enough that he grinned at me.

Upstairs, I knocked on the door and when Professor Belknap's voice asked who it was, I called out, "Room service," in my best terminally-bored Kelly imitation.

Wearing a velvet jacket in deep navy, he opened the door. Rather than the looseness of a smoking jacket, it was cut like a military uniform. "If you're here for the tray—"

I sailed in past him before he reacted. "Hello, Professor Belknap. We met—"

"Hey, you're not room service. You were at the dinner at the museum."

"Yes, I'm Elizabeth Margaret Danniher from KWMT-TV. But I did bring you room service—a slice of the Haber House's famed chocolate pie. I highly recommend it."

I'd also brought myself a slice, which happened to be a little larger. I picked up that plate, a fork, and a napkin, and made myself comfortable on the rocking chair made of antlers.

"I was so fascinated by what you had to say at dinner last night, but you never finished and when I heard you were staying here, I completely gave in to impulse in hopes you'd tell me more." I lifted my plate and smiled, "With a small inducement."

He was cautious for a moment, but ego won out. Possibly helped by pie, since he picked up the other plate. He slid aside a cream hat to make room to sit on the side of the bed closer to the rocking chair. The hat was broad brimmed, but unlike a cowboy hat, the brim was flat. One side was hooked up to the crown.

I kept looking at that hat. Maybe because after last night's visitation from Grandmother Danniher at the dinner, her customary exhortations about never putting a hat on a bed were bobbing up into my consciousness.

"The TV station? I'm glad to know somebody was interested." He punctuated that petulant lament by closing his lips around a forkful of pie. After a moment, the chocolate appeared to work its magic, because he waved the now-empty fork and said with would-be ruefulness. "I knew how it would be, of course. No surprise. I just wish Clara had placed me at another table where the conversation wouldn't have been dominated by the eight-hundred-pound gorilla."

He clearly hadn't heard the news of the gorilla's death yet.

Even so, it didn't seem the wisest thing to be disparaging her to a member of the media.

Deliberately using present tense, I asked, "Does Professor Roy actually have that much influence?"

"She does with those with limited knowledge of my area of expertise." From that lofty tone he descended to, "Unfortunately, that includes the university administration, which thinks having a popular book is preferable to serious scholarship."

He said *popular book* as if the words tasted the way the corpse flower that botanical gardens make a big deal about smells. I once covered the opening of the rare blooms. It wasn't rare enough for me. Think garlic, onions, limburger cheese, sweaty socks, rotting fish, mothballs, all rolled together, and then top it off with a stomach-roiling whiff of a sickly sweet medicinal something.

Oddly, I thought I could catch the faintest hint of that stench now.

"How popular was it? A bestseller?" I already knew it was. I wanted to hear how he characterized her success.

"She's not David McCullough, if that's what you mean." He huffed, and though much of it clearly was for Professor Roy, some was for McCullough, too. Not the first reflexive disparagement of the popular by an academic that I'd heard. "She managed to reach a few of the lists with it, though for quite a short time—"

And now he was dissing her for not being popular enough.

"—but during that time she leveraged every last iota of attention she could get. She was on this show and that one and the other. They made a big deal of her being young then. And all of them lapping up that fake accent. Taken in by a *poseur*."

I made my eyes wide. "Taken in? You mean she wasn't born in England?"

"Born, perhaps, but raised in Toad Hop, Indiana."

"*No.*"

"Yes. She'll admit to Terre Haute, but I have it on good authority that her family home was, in fact, in Toad Hop. Further, her antecedents in Britain were decidedly plebian. Not at all in keeping with that accent."

"Good authority?"

He waved that off with his fork-holding hand. Good thing there wasn't any pie on it. "My lips are sealed. Yet she maintains that ersatz accent. Those with even a minimal level of observational skill who happened upon her appearances on the talk shows, saw host after host going glassy-eyed as he or she recognized the fatuity of her conversation."

Happened upon? If he didn't study recordings of them, I knew less about human nature than I did about the Abominable Snow Man.

"Then the attention died down?" I asked.

As I'd hoped, that kept him going.

"By that time it was firmly fixed in the small minds of the administration that she was a Great Person and she was enshrined as the head of the department forevermore. And refuses to be budged even though it's blindingly clear she's far past her prime. The administration could have moved her out, but instead, gave her an exemption on the retirement age. Now she'll *never* budge."

"But I don't understand."

"Who does?" he muttered, showing me far more of his last bite of chocolate pie than I cared to see—good thing I'd finished mine already or I might have lost my appetite, and that would have been a shame.

"She lives here full-time, doesn't she? How does she chair the department in Colorado?"

"Well might you ask. That *is* the question. Though in reality, she is given all the perks and none of the humdrum responsibilities of running the department. No, those go to Graham Young. Oh, I'm not saying he's not perfectly adequate for running the department."

"He lives in Colorado and is just visiting here?"

"One would expect that to be the way it was, wouldn't one? But, no. Although there is a home there—it, like the one here, owned by Professor Roy—the Youngs, in fact, spend the majority of their time here, in a wing of the house."

Now I really was confused. "He runs the department from here?"

From his earlier faint praise of Graham Young, he shifted to cattiness. "Better I'm sure than she would if she were actually doing the work—trying to do the work."

"But how is that possible?"

He shrugged. When his hand came down from that gesture it brushed the hat, which turned into a stroke.

"They claim they have to be here because of the cooperative agreement with the local junior college."

"What cooperative agreement?"

"They ship us students down there and we ship students and those two up here."

"Surely there's more to it than that." I made it mild.

He flipped a hand. "Our students do research up here. On site, so to speak. Graham Young says he has to be up here to administer that. He claims the university department mostly runs itself and he can handle the rest from here. I suppose he also teaches a few classes up here for our students as well as the locals."

I felt a twinge of annoyance. Surely, I wasn't feeling protective of Cottonwood County against the slights of Belknap.

He was continuing, "If he focused the free labor of those students on something useful…"

I allowed no annoyance to come through when I said, "Such as your research. I can see that."

"Exactly. A couple years of those classes examining the grounds and I'd have all the proof I need. If they weren't blocking me at every turn, I'd have it by now."

I caught a hint of that Corpse Flower stink again, though now it reeked of despair, fear, irrationality, and ego.

"The only thing holding up my publishing is a final piece of proof. Once I have that, *I* would be the star. *I* would be the eight-hundred pound gorilla in the department, *I* would run things. Everything—"

I grabbed at my phone as if it had been vibrating hard enough to shake me to my core, even though it was actually turned off.

"Sorry, sorry, I have to go. It's work. You know how it is with a boss. If only I could stay—"

"When do you want to do the on-camera interview?"

I'd said nothing about an interview. No sense, though, in slamming that door in case I wanted to use the possibility as my entrée for another chat.

"Let me check with my boss about scheduling."

I was up and to the door, swinging it open, before he got off the bed.

Looking out, I saw a door at the hallway's far end open abruptly and out came the graduate student, Jasmine Uffelman. She started toward me, but didn't appear to see me, probably because of the stack of clean laundry she was trying to keep balanced as she closed the room's door.

I suspected from her expression of shock and excitement that she'd heard the news about Professor Roy. And she was coming to tell Belknap, no doubt. To discuss with him how this might affect his standing? Like a devoted wife who saw none of his flaws and put his standing above all else...

Click.

I finally realized why Belknap had seemed familiar last night, why Kelly's "curly mullet" twanged a memory string, why the jacket had tickled at me, why the hat had bugged me.

On impulse I turned and looked back into the room. He'd picked up the hat.

"Professor Belknap, what's your opinion of Custer?"

"Custer?"

"George Armstrong Custer. The Boy General of the Civil War? Battle of Little Bighorn? Last stand? *Please, Mister Custer.*"

"Please, Mr. Custer?" he repeated blankly.

"It's a song." A soldier laments being ordered into battle by Custer at the Little Big Horn. My father would sing bits of it throughout my childhood, mostly as a protest of some social outing Mom had committed him to.

"Never heard of it."

"But you have heard of Custer."

"He's not my specialty."

"Still, he's quite an important figure at that time, isn't he?"

"Important?" he repeated dismissively. "Certainly well-known. Though known more for being controversial and flamboyant than any true ability. I suppose nowadays, he'd be famous on the Internet."

That sounded like the worst curse he could think of.

"I see. Thank you so much. Sorry I have to go now but I look forward to continuing our conversation."

I closed the door and moved quickly to the stairs, starting down them as Jasmine passed, and getting a suspicious glare to hurry me on my way.

Chapter Sixteen

CLARA ATWOOD LOOKED up from her desk at the museum, saw me, and groaned, "Oh, God."

"Hey, you called me. And I was going right past the museum." Because I'd driven here on purpose.

"I called in hopes of persuading you not to say anything about last night's dinner on air."

"I can't imagine I'll be saying anything on air about anything, but you know Leona will about the dinner, and if she and Thurston don't mention the facts of that and the timing with the museum dinner—"

She groaned louder.

"No use burying your head in the sand. I'm not saying causation—"

"Causation? It was a heart attack. It had to have been. She didn't have a strong heart."

"It might have been a heart attack."

She groaned again, correctly interpreting my tone as not believing it for a second.

"I'm not saying causation or consequence, but there *is* a sequence at work here. Dinner at the museum one evening with evidence of strains and stresses in numerous relationships, Professor Roy dies the next day. Nobody can deny that sequence. Law enforcement won't miss it, either. By the way, how did you know Professor Roy had died?"

"I had a phone call."

"From?"

"A friend of the museum."

"Must be nice to have friends in high places."

"The friend is for the museum. Not me. I'm merely a conduit. I am associated with the people in high places, but not one of them. Neither fish nor fowl."

There was a lot behind those words. But exactly what?

To push or not to push? I had to decide.

Not to push, I decided. On that topic. For now. "Tell me about Professor Roy."

"Why?" Suspicion stood out all over her.

"C'mon, Clara. No camera."

Even if I'd had one, I wouldn't have tried persuading her to give background video, comments from those who'd known the deceased. That sort of footage wasn't worth the risk of irritation.

For one thing, I likely would need her as an ongoing source. For another, she wasn't a suspect.

Suspect.

Oops. Where had that come from?

"Fine. Ask your questions," Clara conceded. "I'll decide on a case by case basis what I'll answer." Partially conceded.

"Fair enough. Tell me about Professor Roy," I repeated.

"Too broad."

Sometimes that question got people sharing what they wanted to get on the record about the other person, good or bad, which could be revealing.

And sometimes it didn't work at all.

"Start with the basics," I told Clara. "How long have you known her?"

"I inherited her when I became curator here. She'd already been a big deal for quite a while in the circles interested in her topic."

"Interested in her topic? So that makes it a narrow field?"

"Quite narrow."

"She did have that bestseller book."

She puffed out a breath. "It was the Beanie Babies of history books. A brief, inexplicable comet across the sky that captured every eye, then was gone in a flash."

"Yet her field coincides with a lot of the interests of the museum."

Her mouth quirked. "It's a niche. Time and place. Those of us who live and breathe it do so because we love it, but we—most of us, anyway—recognize it's not a major driver in popular culture. Not everyone shares our passion."

"That graduate student, Jasmine, and Professor Belknap were quite passionate."

A flicker gave her away.

She, too, thought they were involved with each other.

Was my belief a leap? Possibly. But I also couldn't think of a lot of other reasons for a grad student to be going to a professor's hotel room with a stack of clean laundry, including his undies. Not only involved, but she was doing his laundry.

I doubted Clara knew that detail. Yet she'd reached the same—if not conclusion, then working hypothesis. But she wasn't saying it and I wasn't asking.

The expression she was willing to show me consisted of raising one eyebrow. "You were fairly passionate yourself."

"I was."

"So I'm sure you understand that Professor Roy could stir passion in others," she said.

"I do. What else could she do?"

"Too broad." She was really being tough.

"Could she also derail the careers of others in the field?"

"Possibly."

"In the department she heads?"

"Stronger possibility."

"Has she?"

"Not to my immediate knowledge."

Nice side-step, Clara.

I could call her on it. But that might end this conversation and I had more I wanted to cover.

"What about her daughter and son-in-law? How well do you know them?"

Without any obvious movement, she seemed to withdraw. "I know them only from events like the dinner—in other words, slightly and socially."

"What about the cooperative program between the community college here and their university in Colorado?"

"The museum is not involved in that directly."

"How is it involved indirectly?"

"It's not a secret."

I eyed her. "If the museum's involvement is something I can read in back issues of the *Independence* you could save me the time and—"

"The museum has right of first refusal for any physical finds that stem from the cooperative program."

"Anything so far?"

"No."

I considered that. "You must be pulling for Professor Belknap's theory to turn out to be true. That would be quite the coup for the museum."

"I don't pull for theories. I recognize proof."

"Graham Young's specialty is in a related area, isn't it? You must have had more interaction with him."

"Perhaps a little. He has consulted with the museum as we're putting together our claim for the gold coins."

Ah, yes, the historic gold coins found in Sherman earlier in the year. A number of parties, including the museum, were claiming them, while the court system ground slowly, slowly, on.

"And you've clearly observed the tension between Professor Roy and the couple?"

"What makes you think that?"

"Because you're not blind, because their reactions to each other had the air of long-established habit so last night surely wasn't the first time that familial tension showed up, and most of all because of how you arranged the tables."

"If I'd known the woman was going to die I sure wouldn't have put you at her table."

I nodded my understanding. "I can see that. I was supposed to be cannon fodder."

"I wouldn't go that far."

"Okay. Make it grease to keep the friction between some of the people at that table from working up to a fire that would burn everyone there. Mrs. Parens was, too. And, to give you your due, you put yourself in there. Though you both went in knowing your role, while I did not."

"Hard to say you kept the friction down with your speech about Irish history."

"You know how firefighters sometimes control a forest fire by starting another fire…" I grinned. "Anyway, it didn't bother any of the other guests—the ones you really cared about—which was always your goal."

"I cared about everyone—"

"Sorry. Yes. Of course, you did. But the people at the other tables were people who could do things to benefit the museum—money, backing, interaction, interest. Professor Roy was isolated because she could mostly hurt the museum."

"You're not quoting me on any of this."

"Absolutely not."

"There have been previous incidents, which could have had a negative impact on the museum. Those made me feel it was wiser to limit certain combinations of people."

I was so tempted to ask about those incidents and about which combinations had been worse. But, again, there was more territory to cover. Plus, I had a number of other potential sources for that.

"I'm also not quoting you when you tell me how you have observed Professor Roy and her daughter getting along."

She sighed. "Never any better than last night, on one or two occasions significantly worse."

"Worse?" My phone vibrated in my pocket.

She raised one hand, palm up. "They don't—didn't seem to be aware of how rough they got. Not foul language. Almost wished they would. Might've been easier to listen to without wanting to squirm. Or get far, far away."

"How about Professor Roy and her son-in-law?"

"Last night was typical."

The phone vibrated again.

"You're saying the professor would cut him down, Mrs. Young would respond, but he would not?"

She nodded. "Pretty much."

Two more vibrations in quick succession. If this kept up my phone might really blow up.

I had more I wanted to ask her, but it could wait.

I stood.

Nothing like seeing relief cross someone's face when you indicated you were leaving.

I turned back. "Another question off something you said earlier. Did Professor Roy share that recognition that the pond she thought she ruled wasn't a major driver in popular culture?"

"I have no idea."

"WHERE ARE YOU?" Mike demanded when I responded to his urgent messages by calling.

"In town. Where are you? I assume you know—"

"Yeah, I know. That's where I am. With Diana and Leona."

"*Leona?*" Leona D'Amato on a hard news story?

"Yup. She tried to tell Thurston he needed to be here. He flat refused. She gave him a short, pithy speech about being outdone by an old lady and walked out. I was right behind her, though she declined my offer to drive her. Said we needed maximum flexibility in case different angles came up to pursue. And now she's giving Shelton hell about freedom of the press and the public's right to know. She's a trouper." I could hear the grin in his voice.

"Good for her."

"Yeah, but why aren't you out here? Diana said she gave you directions ages ago. Getting in early on a murder—"

"Have they said—?"

"No, no, but—"

"We should hold off thinking it is."

His snort scoffed at that. "By the time Shelton would let us in on it, the murderer would be tried, convicted, and off to prison." He paused a moment, telling me his thoughts had followed the same direction mine had. "And out on parole."

"I've got one more stop to make, then I'll be on my way there," I promised.

✧ ✧ ✧ ✧

I GRABBED WATER, bottled coffee, a spare pair of sunglasses, cookies for me, and snacks to keep the others away from my cookies, then got into Penny Czylinski's checkout line at the Sherman Supermarket.

To my astonishment, she did not start in about the death of Professor Roy.

Don't misunderstand, she knew about it. I heard a snippet of her conversation with the customer leaving as I came in and it was definitely about the professor's death.

Yet the best news gathering—and disseminating—source in Cottonwood County chose to start her monologue to me on a different topic.

And one that started with an indefinite pronoun that had me mentally scrambling to figure who, as well as what, she was talking about.

"Said she could hardly move for all the people connected to the murder of Yolanda Cruz coming into her library lately. None of 'em regulars, either, except Vic Zblewski. Now, him, she's been seeing forever. On a computer, reading magazines, leafing through books, and sometimes sleeping in one of the easy chairs. But lately, she said she's also had Kitty—that's the daughter—and Kitty's husband, and that professor who thinks he's going to find a battle that nobody knows about, all in the library. Why even Professor Roy was there yesterday, and Ivy Short couldn't ever recall seeing her there before, not since her book came out ages ago. Not that you'd think it was so long ago to hear her going on about it. Too important to ever go to the Cottonwood County Public Library, you'd think. Unless she went in while Ivy was out having gallbladder surgery—with one of those little robot things. Amazing how fast she bounced back. Not like when my mother had to have hers removed. Why that scar oozed—

"Professor Roy at the library?" I inserted desperately.

"—for a month or more. And that was a scar, let me tell you. Went diagonal all across one side. Not those little pinpricks people get nowadays, either. So would've had to be in those couple days and that isn't likely, now is it? So, it's nearly hundred percent Ivy would see who was there."

Back to the library. I breathed a little easier now that we'd left the topic of scars.

"So, I'm willing to say that Professor Roy's never been there before yesterday, which is odd, with her being a professor and all. You'd think she'd be there all the time. Though it's still not as weird as these past few days, Dean Isaacs been showing up there. First time he's ever been to a library, I'd bet. Ivy says he was this close to running into Professor Roy. Says he's on the computer all the time. Butter wouldn't melt in his mouth toward most everybody, except he nearly ran over Lorraine Flicker's mother, who was here for the holidays. All for a seat at one computer. Seems he and that Vic Zblewski favor the same computer—though why anybody'd get attached to one individual box over another I don't know. How folks can get lost in a computer I don't understand. Now, a good movie—"

"Why was Dean at the library?"

"—like *Singing in the Rain* or *Seven Brides for Seven Brothers*, those are something you can truly get lost in. And sing along. Humming those songs all day long I am after watching one. Well, they're supposed to look for jobs when they get out of prison, aren't they? And jobs are supposed to be all over the Internet. Like he should be free to get a job and keep living his life while that lovely woman's been in her grave all these years. Why—"

"You knew Yolanda Cruz?"

My shocked question actually broke her train of thought, an occurrence in the same stratum of rarity as total solar eclipses.

"Of course, I did. You don't think Professor Roy was in here buying groceries for her family, do you?"

I supposed not.

"Yolanda first came in when it was just the professor, little Kitty, and Yolanda, coming for a few weeks in the summers, while the professor was doing research for that book that eventually came out and everybody made such a fuss about. Yolanda and Kitty, always together, just like Yolanda and Laura, after she came along. Kept staying longer and longer each summer. That's when Arturo started bringing theirs. Guess he had to—"

"Arturo?"

"—or they'd never have seen each other for months at a time. Course everything changes with time, everybody getting older. And then poor Yolanda getting killed that way. Sure makes me sad. And mad. Shouldn't have happened to such a nice woman."

I was debating whether to try again to find out who Arturo was, when Penny announced my total, handed me a receipt, held her hand out for my payment, looked past me, and said, "Well, hi there."

There'd be no more from her now. She was on to fresh meat.

Not a very successful stop at the supermarket. Except for the cookies.

Chapter Seventeen

I CAME AROUND a bend in the graveled road and saw a snow-dusted compound laid out below.

A central part of the house, constructed of stone, wood, and glass, rose three stories high with two-story wings angled gently off either side. All that had a view of the river downslope from the house.

Farther along the river's meandering ribbon appeared a cluster of what appeared to be outbuildings.

Off the house, and clearly having no river views, a long, low building extended. Taking a wild guess—based on the driveway leading to it, then seeing tire tracks branching in to four and running right up to its side, this was the garage.

Right now, a sheriff's deputy car and a fire department vehicle were run up close to what was probably the bay second closest to the house. Several more official vehicles formed an untidy semicircle some distance back. Behind them came a cluster of other vehicles. I recognized the Newsmobile—the rough and ready KWMT-TV SUV Diana drove. Or in some instances flew really close to the ground.

A few ant-sized forms stood as close to the semicircle of official vehicles as possible, facing off with a solitary ant-sized form who appeared to be wearing a sheriff's deputy's uniform.

Only then did I realize I'd come to a stop to take in the scene.

Good thing there wasn't traffic on this road.

I started to ease my foot off the brake, then a second realization sank in, and I stopped again.

Tree stumps marked the edge of the road and as far down the side as I could see. Not neatly lined up stumps as if they'd been set there as an orderly arboreal guard rail, but more as if a random forest that had once grown right up to the road had been cut down.

The only reason for that I could imagine was to provide this view of the compound below.

It certainly wasn't for safety.

Without those buffering trees, a bump from behind could push a vehicle right over the edge here.

On that cheery thought, I drove on.

The road down to the river valley level was twisty, but more tedious than terrifying. Approaching an open gate set between stone piers, I had no view of the house or other buildings—hidden off to the right by trees—but a perfect view across a nearly flat section to mountains rising sharply.

My four-wheel drive clattered across a bridge over the river, then kept going before it connected with another gravel road, this one coming from across the plain then turning toward the compound. I followed it in that direction.

And there they were, all the vehicles I'd seen returned to normal size, all the ant-like figures turned into people.

People I knew, including Diana and Mike, along with Needham Bender from *The Independence* standing in the gap between a sheriff's department truck and SUV. Deputy Lloyd Sampson stood about fifteen feet back, facing them. Apparently prepared to stop them if they stormed that gap. Or, at least, to holler for help.

"About time you got here," Mike said by way of greeting. "You've missed everything."

After quick hellos that ignored that, I asked, "Where's Leona?"

Mike answered. "Went to the hospital when the ambulance left with Professor Roy. Actually a couple ambulances. They took everybody."

I turned from surveying the garage, which had regimented racks of supplies along the back wall. The only sign of disarray was a green towel wadded up near the step from the interior door to the garage. "Everybody?" I'd only heard about the professor. If everybody—

"Precaution," Diana said. "I caught a bit of one of the EMTs telling Shelton that. They'll be checked out at the hospital for exposure to carbon monoxide, probably kept overnight for observation and the fire department's checking out the whole house in case some leaked in there."

"Has it been officially confirmed?"

"Not by Shelton. But the EMT folks and the fire department said enough—not to us, but to each other. Before she left, Leona said she was going to try to get the hospital to say it officially, but she'd go with 'consistent with carbon monoxide poisoning' if she couldn't get anything firmer."

That was a good move. "How about the other occupants of the house?"

"The husband, the daughter and son-in-law, a housekeeper."

Shelton approached our journalistic huddle.

"Nothing here to see. Go on home, all of you."

Needham choked down a chuckle, which was why Mike got out the first question.

"Was it the generator that Vic Zblewski turned on in the garage last night that killed her?"

Generator? That was news to me.

"Go away." Shelton said generally, then directed his glower at me. "Don't you have other work you're supposed to be doing someplace else?"

It might have sounded like his usual get-lost non-greeting, but he and I knew it wasn't.

Mike chuckled. "She's got so many 'Helping Outs!' in the can she could go lie on a beach somewhere for months."

"Don't tempt me," I murmured.

"She has been working on something," Diana said slowly, looking from Shelton to me, then back. "Yesterday and this morning."

"Then she should get back to working on it," Shelton said. "Nothing for her—for any of you—to do here."

"Wayne," Needham said, "there's been a death—"

"Not confirmed."

"—and the public has a right to know—"

"Not about this. Family tragedy. An accident. They're all at the hospital getting checked out now."

"*Was* it an accident?" I asked. "For sure?"

Needham picked up on my point, pressing it. "You're officially declaring it an accident, Wayne? For attribution."

He growled. "No. Not official and not for attribution. We're investigating. That's all you get officially. Now, go away."

"Not even confirmation of the name of the victim? It's all over town already. You might as well confirm."

Another growl. Then, "Professor Nora Roy was taken by ambulance from here to the Cottonwood County Hospital this afternoon. The medical authorities there declared her dead."

"When?" Needham asked.

"Ask them. Go on, get out of here."

Shelton started to walk away.

Needham went after him.

"Whoa. Needham's going to try to pry more out of Shelton? Didn't think he went for impossible feats," Mike said.

"He needs enough to make this a real story for the Friday edition. It's a slow news week. Nothing happens between Christmas and New Year's."

"Slow news week? Speak for yourself," Mike objected. "There's lots going on in sports. Pro football, basketball, hockey, major college bowls, then holiday basketball tournaments for high school and college, winter sports. It's no slow news week in sports."

"Then why are you here?"

He half grinned. "Didn't want to miss out. But I do have to leave now to get my block ready for the Five. I'll be at Diana's right after I'm done."

"Oh?" I turned to her. "When was this planned?"

She shrugged. "Mike suggested it. It's okay with me. He's right about if we wait for official word about it being an accident or murder we'll be way behind."

I refrained from mentioning how Sheriff Conrad would view the situation. It certainly didn't include any concern about our group being *behind*.

"And you're right about it being a slow news week—for non-sports people—so we might as well. You want to call Tom or should I?"

GLAD YOU GOT the extra fries." Mike dug another container out of the shopping bag collapsing in on itself now that it was mostly empty. "Hamburger Heaven fries are a necessity when we look into murders."

"Nobody's said it's murder," Diana said, giving me a teasing look.

"You expect that to stop this group?" Tom asked at the same time Mike said, "It might be a murder."

They looked at each other, then chuckled.

Tom gave a single nod, conceding. But only partially, which became evident when he said, "Or might not be."

"You're welcome, Mike. Feast on those fries, because I'm sure not going to be able to offer much information for you to chew on." I'd ordered myself a salad. Two meals in one day from Hamburger Heaven was just daring my arteries to clog. Not that I could tell them that. As long as I was under Shelton's gag order, I couldn't tell them about any of my scam-related interviews today. "Besides, Diana's right, we're *not* looking into the professor's death. Thurston is already screaming about anybody else touching it. We need to pick our battles with him and this one might well be an accident, so it's not worth it."

"Right."

I turned from Mike's skepticism to face Tom's. "On the other hand, you wouldn't be here if you didn't think there was *something* to look in to."

"Fair enough. Even with no murder, it seems to me there's a chance something's going on. That dinner last night…"

"True. And Mrs. P must have had a similar feeling beforehand or she wouldn't have corralled me into going."

"Besides Elizabeth already has a lead, don't you?" Mike looked at me like a baby bird waiting for the worm straight from Momma's beak.

As much as a former NFL player with great hair, broad shoulders, and bone structure like that can look like a baby bird.

"Me? What are you talking about? I told you all I struck out."

"You said you had something to tell me about the Cruz murder."

"I said—? Oh. Yes, but it's not a lead."

"What is it then?"

"I was going to tell you that I knew where Dean Isaacs was staying in town."

"Oh? Where?"

I felt bad. Really.

Don't be fooled by the trouble I was having suppressing a grin. I truly did feel bad. Because it was about to get worse for the baby bird.

"Dean Isaacs is staying with Sally Tipton."

"Sally Tipton?" He groaned. The baby bird had gotten a mouthful of plastic worm. "No. Anywhere but there. That woman goes on and on and on without making any sense at all."

"There's usually a core of sense in what she says," I objected. "Somewhere way, way deep."

"And she keeps fluttering around and insisting on feeding us."

"There's this tactic called saying no thank you," I said.

"Then she looks at me like I'd pulled the plug in her kiddie pool."

Considering the weather, I had to squelch a shiver at that image as I described yesterday's visit with Mrs. Parens to Sally's house.

When I got to the part where Dean said he was her grandson, each of my listeners demonstrated surprise. Mike gave a low whistle. Diana murmured a "Holy moly." And Tom raised his eyebrows.

"You never heard that rumor?" I asked.

Diana and Mike shook their heads.

We all looked at Tom.

"Never remember hearing it. Though there was something about Dean having family in the area in addition to the aunt. He wasn't here that long before the murder and I never heard more about it."

"Interesting, though I don't know that it would add anything even if we knew for sure."

"But Sally Tipton," Mike grumbled.

Diana patted his shoulder. "There's still hope. If there's no murder, there'll be no reason to talk to Dean Isaacs, so you won't have to see Sally."

"I should be so lucky."

"Well, you are lucky, because Thurston's claimed the Dean Isaacs story, too. So, it's hands-off for us."

They all grinned at me. That wasn't what I'd been going for.

"Of course," Diana said to Mike as if I hadn't spoken, "that does mean you have to make a choice of which you want more. A murder to investigate or a free pass away from Sally."

"I wouldn't shirk my duty, even if it means dealing with Sally Tipton."

Chapter Eighteen

"YOU KNOW," I said, "Accident is far more likely. While I was waiting at Hamburger Heaven, I did a quick look-up on carbon monoxide statistics. I think I'll do a 'Helping Out!' on it—and try to get it on the air before spring. Of course, that leaves me months and months."

"Quit picking on Wyoming weather," Mike said.

"I will as soon as it stops picking on me."

"Don't you like all the sunshine?"

"I do. I just wish I wasn't looking at it from the bottom of a freezer."

Diana frowned. "Are you cold in the bunkhouse?"

"Not at all. So, as long as I stay inside it until June..."

"Hey, days are getting longer."

I glared at Mike in disbelief.

"What? They are. Ever since December twenty-first."

I knew they were in theory. But theory didn't do much for me when I was still getting up in the dark.

"In fact, a lot of people think the twenty-first is the shortest day of the year, but most of the time it's the twentieth. The days start getting longer on the twenty-first. So if the early Christians had been trying to co-opt the pagans by connecting Christmas to the solstice, they should have had the eve on the twentieth, then Christmas on the twenty-first to celebrate the turn toward spring."

"Are we going to talk about the professor's death or not?"

I clapped a hand to my throat. "Thomas David Burrell actually urging us to start one of our discussions?" It drew a bigger laugh from

Mike and Diana than it deserved.

"I've learned that you three can't be dissuaded from looking into these deaths. Sooner it gets started, the sooner it's over."

"All right, but keep in mind that it's really Thurston's story and this is all academic," I said, tossing my garbage into the shopping bag. "Let Diana start, since she was the first on the scene."

"A lot of good it did me. They kept moving me back and moving me back."

"So, you didn't see any more than I could when I got there?"

"Didn't say that."

I laughed. "Diana does smug."

"And does it well," she said.

"Don't antagonize her," Mike said. "She saw a lot more than I did, too. What did you see, oh, mighty Diana?"

"With that appropriate level of respect, I will tell you."

But before she did, she ate some fries and took a gulp of her soft drink.

"Okay, when I got there, one sheriff's deputy SUV was there—Lloyd Sampson—and a rescue vehicle. The garage doors were wide open."

I opened my mouth, but before I could ask, she said, "All four doors, the same way you saw it. One bay was empty. The one farthest from the house. Next in was a pickup, then a small luxury SUV, then a large SUV closest to the house. None of them were running.

"Just as I pulled in, some EMTs were taking someone—presumably Professor Roy—from the sort of walkway in front of the vehicles, in line with the door to the house." She had her eyes closed, recalling the scene. "I can't say for sure, but I had the impression she'd been about even with the gap between the first two vehicles. Like she might have walked out of the door from the house, started toward her SUV, but hadn't made it all the way there. They were working on her."

Her eyes opened.

"I didn't get it on camera because of the angle. I couldn't see real well in there, either, because of the narrow space between the vehicles, plus they were moving around her, so I can't be sure. It was more of an impression. Leona, then Mike arrived. As soon as the emergency services folks had her loaded in, they took off. So, that's when Leona left, too.

"At least two EMTs stayed. One was with Vic Zblewski, Professor Roy's husband. The EMT had Zblewski out of the garage, well away from it. Zblewski seemed woozy, unsteady. Then another rescue vehicle and another deputy—Shelton—arrived. Shelton parked right in front of me. Had to move around for a view. Almost immediately, Lloyd came out the front door with the daughter, son-in-law, and housekeeper. They all seemed fine, but the EMTs took them as a precaution. Mike, anything else? You were closer to them."

"They were asking what happened," he said. "The housekeeper seemed to be the most upset. She said she'd been sure she smelled exhaust Monday, but Professor Roy said she was imagining it. But today she hadn't smelled anything. The daughter and son-in-law ignored Shelton and went directly to Zblewski. I got close enough to hear him. He didn't make a lot of sense. He kept saying that he tried, he tried. And if only she hadn't insisted on his turning the generator on last night."

"What was that about?"

He shook his head. "Tried to ask Lloyd, with no luck. That's why I tried the question on Shelton. You know what he said." He looked at Tom. "Wouldn't give us anything. Some people around here do use generators in their garages to take the chill off in the winter. With what Zblewski said it wasn't much of a leap to the question. But how we'll pin it down for sure—"

Mike interrupted himself by pulling out his phone and checking it. Usually he would have then slipped it back in his pocket, having assured himself that it was something that could wait.

Not this time.

"Excuse me. Got to take this."

He retreated toward the kitchen, presumably so we could continue to talk among ourselves. He should have known better. We were all listening to his side of the call.

"Hello…. Yes…. Yes, ma'am." He glanced toward us then focused on the floor in front of his feet. "Yes, but that's going to be pretty late, especially the return—Uh-huh.... Uh-huh. ... I won't. ... Yes, ma'am."

He hung up.

"What does Mrs. P want?" I asked.

"How the heck did you know it was Mrs. Parens?"

"Because you only sound like you're taking orders from a general when you talk to her or your Aunt Gee," Diana said.

"And you don't call your aunt 'ma'am' every other word," Tom concluded.

"Smart asses," Mike muttered, but with a grin as he came back and sat down. "You're going to get yours, because Mrs. P is coming here later."

"Okay, you won that round," I said.

"Later when?" Diana demanded.

"I've got my marching orders—" He gave a dry smile. "—to pick her up after the Ten and bring her here. Apparently, she has something to say to all of us."

"But that'll be so late—"

Mike interrupted. "Exactly what I said. She said she wasn't letting a late night stand in her way. Not a late night for her or for me, by the time I get home after taking her back to O'Hara Hill at whatever hour."

"I'll take her home," Tom said. "I'm partway to O'Hara Hill any-way. And I might go on up to my sister's tonight instead of waiting until morning to drive there to pick up Tamantha."

"Thanks, Tom. That would be great. Save me a lot of driving. Let me get to bed at a decent hour. What?" he demanded of me.

"Let you get to bed at a decent hour? What you really mean is it will save you from spending that time with Mrs. P testing your knowledge of topics she views as vital."

He shook his head. "Nah, she'll already have done that on the way here. Yeah, go ahead and laugh all of you. She doesn't grill you the way she grills me. C'mon, c'mon, that's enough laughing. Let's get back to where we were. Where were we?"

"Something about a generator."

"Right. Couldn't get any confirmation out of Shelton, as you heard. A guy I know from high school's an EMT. Wasn't going to interrupt him when he was trying to revive the woman this afternoon, but I'll see what I can find out from him."

"Good."

Tom cleared his throat. "How about asking Leona?"

The rest of us looked at him.

"Good point," Diana said. "Who listened to her report on the Five?"

"Not me, I was doing finals on my own," Mike said.

"Not me, I was getting the food," I said.

"Not me, either. I left my video at the station, then came home and was busy getting dinner for the kids before they took off for the basketball tournament at the high school," Diana said.

We all looked at Tom again.

He nodded. "I caught it at the Kicking Cowboy."

"You were in the Kicking Cowboy on a week night—actually on a weekday afternoon?"

"Yup. Supper."

"At the Kicking Cowboy?" It was a honky-tonk kind of bar. Good for a beer on a Saturday night, maybe, with the right company. But a meal?

"Yup."

Sure, I wanted to ask more, but it would come at the cost of adding to the glint already in his eyes. No.

"Okay. What did Leona say?"

"She said Professor Roy was declared dead at Cottonwood County Hospital this afternoon. She said the death was consistent with carbon monoxide poisoning, although the official cause of death would be determined by an autopsy, with the body being sent to that forensic pathologist in Montana."

Mike nodded. "Richard Alvaro's sister's boss."

"She said the police had no official statement, although multiple sources indicated that Professor Roy likely died of carbon monoxide poisoning in an apparent accident in her garage. She said Nora Roy was known to have heart issues, which would have made her more vulnerable to carbon monoxide. Other members of the household were at the hospital being checked, but that all were expected to be okay. Then she talked some about the dinner last night—"

"Clara will be thrilled."

"—and Professor Roy's book and the cooperative program between Bison University and Cottonwood County Community College. And then she said..." He paused, drawing it out. "More at ten o'clock."

Chapter Nineteen

WE GROANED. HE grinned. He asked, "What were you doing this afternoon until you arrived at the ranch, Elizabeth?"

"First, I tried to find out where Dean Isaacs was right then and had been earlier in the day with absolutely no luck."

Mike sat up. "You think he might have—"

"I don't think anything yet," I interrupted. "Except that there was a connection between him and the professor, he had just returned to Sherman, and I was curious about where he was, where he'd been, and how he'd react. Unfortunately, I didn't find out any of that."

I condensed my conversation with Sally to the time of Isaacs' departure, his one stated destination of getting a meal, and that she had no idea where he'd gone.

Next, I recounted the visit to Professor Belknap, concluding, "He has no love for Nora Roy or Graham Young, that's for sure. I also stopped by the Sherman Supermarket—"

"Running low on cookies?" Diana asked.

"I did happen to pick up a couple bags of Pepperidge Farm Double Chocolate Milanos, but that was only so I would have something when I went to Penny's checkout lane."

"Uh-huh," they said in a chorus of amused skepticism.

"And," I continued with dignity, "I went by the museum to see Clara."

That knocked one of them out of amused skepticism. "Why Clara?" Tom asked.

He is protective of the Cottonwood County institutions he's interested in, and since that was all of them, it covered a lot of territory.

"Because she'd called me when she heard the news about the professor's death—which is interesting, don't you think?—and because she was obviously worried. I also hoped to get more background out of her."

"Did you?"

"Not much."

I repeated what little I'd gleaned from Clara.

For context, I went another day back to the tensions and exchanges at the museum dinner. Then I relayed what Belknap had said to me—focusing on the pertinent bits and skipping references to Kelly, pie, and Custer.

Mike whistled. "Now that's a motive. Sounds like she was ready to pull the plug on his pet project, sending his career down the drain."

"But he talked about her in present tense and pushed for her to retire," Diana objected.

"A ploy. All a ploy. What do you think, Elizabeth?"

"We don't know enough to think anything, yet. We've barely started gathering the seeds. Way too early to try harvesting."

On that homey note, I repeated Penny's not-quite-on-target contributions.

"Dean Isaacs went to the library?" Diana repeated.

"I don't find that any harder to believe than Vic Zblewski spending a lot of time there."

Mike ignored my point. "It's got to be Dean Isaacs. How can it not be? Look at the history. And the timing. He gets out, returns to Cottonwood County, and boom, Professor Roy ends up dead."

"It is interesting," Diana said. "In a lot of ways it would have seemed more logical for him to have killed Professor Roy twenty-six years ago instead of Yolanda Cruz—the mother keeping the young lovers apart, rather than the housekeeper."

"And he's finishing the job now? Why? Blaming her for Laura's death? That seems rather esoteric for Dean Isaacs. What's in it for him? Because I'd suspect that's always his first question."

"Revenge," Mike said.

"You're assuming Nora Roy's death is a murder," Tom said. "Could be an accident. You know carbon monoxide deaths happen every winter. People warm up their car in a closed-up garage or there's a leak from the garage to the house or somebody gets their electricity turned off so they use a backup generator, only they don't put it far enough away from their house, or—"

"Exhaust pipe gets clogged by snow when somebody's stuck," Mike picked up. "I know, I know."

"It does seem a haphazard way to try to kill somebody. And even if it *is* a murder, the sheriff's department will be all over this," Diana said.

Mike nodded, not happy. "Which leaves little to no room for poking around."

"On top of that, as Elizabeth said, Thurston's claimed the story," Diana added.

"That we could get around," Mike said. "I'm not so sure about the rest."

After a stretch of silence, Diana said, "Why are you so quiet, Elizabeth?"

"I'm thinking that all three of you are right."

Tom chuckled. "That's why you sound so down?"

I ignored that. "You're right that it might not be murder, Tom. Mike's right that the timing is awfully interesting. Diana's right that the sheriff's department is going to be all over it, so what is there for us to do?"

Sometimes, saying something out loud clicks a connection in my brain. I sure wished it would happen before I said things, but it's better than it not happening at all.

This was one of those times.

I sat up straight.

"They'll be all over Nora Roy's death and Thurston's glommed on to the Isaacs being released story, but that leaves us something else to look into."

I looked around at each of them with enthusiasm. They each looked back with mild confusion.

"The past. The back story. The B roll. What happened before."

Still mild confusion. "Look, whatever happened today, there *was* a murder, right? Yolanda Cruz."

"Yeah. One for which Dean Isaacs was tried and convicted. Think you're a little late for investigating that one. That story's done and gone," Mike said.

"But in addition to Yolanda Cruz's murder there was also the death of Laura Roy. There are still questions about that. But not only from the past. There are things going on now that could very well stem from what happened then. There's so much—there *was* so much tension between Professor Roy and her daughter, Kitty. Plus, that odd relationship between her and the son-in-law. Like she had a hold over them. What was that about? Does it stem from the younger daughter's suicide? And exactly why did Laura commit suicide? We have *that* slice of the story that nobody else is looking in to. We'll have to be careful not to bleed too much into Isaacs' release or Professor Roy's death, though."

"Yeah, we wouldn't want to do that," Diana said dryly.

Tom shifted his position and we all looked at him.

"After Laura Roy died, her mother claimed it wasn't suicide. She wanted Isaacs charged for Laura's death, too."

"Hey. Maybe Laura Roy didn't commit suicide," Mike said, warming to the idea. "After all, it was Sheriff Widcuff in charge back then." He paused after mentioning the sheriff ousted last spring. "Wasn't it? Or did that predate him?"

"Good question. We should find out who was in charge of that investigation. Whoever was might be a good source for us."

"Too bad Jennifer isn't here to—" Mike stood abruptly. "Oh, damn. I've gotta go and get ready for the Ten. I'll be back with Mrs. P as soon as possible."

Tom stood as the door closed behind Mike. "I'm going to call my sister, then catch some sleep in the truck. I started the day on rancher's hours and making that drive will be easier with a little shut-eye first."

"You will not do that in your truck," Diana declared. "You make your private call, but then come back in here where it's warm. As long as you can sleep through some cleaning."

"Sure. Thanks."

"No way are you going to sleep through one of Diana's cleaning frenzies." I shifted to her. "Why are you cleaning anyway? The place looks fine."

"Mrs. Parens is coming and I haven't cleaned since before the Christmas mayhem. Besides, it's my place—" She added a tune to the next words. "—and I'll clean if I want to, clean if I want to. You'd clean, too, if it happened to you."

"Okay, okay." I got that out around my laughter at her singing. "Tom, go over to the bunkhouse and get a nap there, take Shadow with you. He's not fond of the vacuum. We'll call when Mike gets back."

It took more convincing, including a demonstration of Shadow's impression of a noble soldier facing a firing squad but determined to retain his dignity when the vacuum was rolled out into the living area, before Tom took Shadow to the bunkhouse.

"Okay if I make a couple quick calls from the guest room, Diana? Then I'll come help you clean."

"Of course. But I have a question—what about that other story you're working."

I didn't meet her eyes. "Oh, I'll work that in. It's no big deal."

"Uh-huh. Go make your calls."

THE FIRST ONE wasn't a call, it was a text to Jennifer.

I wrote that I hoped she was having a great time on vacation, then asked whom she considered the next-best researcher among the news aides.

My phone rang before I could make a call.

"You've got a murder case," Jennifer said.

"No. And Merry Christmas to you, too. You're on vacation, re-member? If you'll tell me who's the best person to ask for some straightforward research—Dale?"

She groaned. "No. Nice guy and all, but no, no, no. I can do it from here. They only let me bring one laptop, but I should be able to tap into more power and—"

"Jennifer, no. It's the holidays. It's your vacation. With your family. Go, enjoy yourself."

"I would be enjoying myself if you gave me something to do," she said plaintively. "It was fine for a couple days, but now they're talking about staying through New Year's."

"That should be fun, Jennifer. You've been working a lot and with the extra research you've done—"

"Please let me do this, Elizabeth. *Please.* If I have to play that candy game with my little cousin one more time, I won't have a brain cell left. This kid's obsessive. She woke me up in the middle of the night to play with her. Just because I'm sharing the bunkbeds with her doesn't mean I'm her game slave."

Obsessive must run in the family.

I tried again to get her to recommend a news aide, but she was adamant. Okay, yes, I really didn't want anyone but her to do the searching.

In the end, I gave her as much information as I could about the murder of Yolanda Cruz, and asked her to find out the lead investigator, any other law enforcement on the case, who the sheriff was at the time, the prosecuting and defense attorneys, and as many detailed accounts of the trial as she could find.

I left a message with my friend and source, an FBI lab scientist named Dex. Sure, he was on East Coast time, but I didn't worry about waking him up.

He turned this phone off at night or when he was hard at work. His FBI phone was never off.

"Hi Dex, it's Danny," I said, using the nickname he'd developed from my last name when he first became a source for me it had added a layer between him and a journalist named Danniher. Now it was ingrained for both of us. "I'm hoping you can give me some background on carbon monoxide poisoning. Give me a call when you have a chance."

I considered another call to check if there'd been progress on a more personal matter, but it would likely wake up the recipient, who did not turn off his phone. And I would hear about waking him up. Especially if word got back to my mother.

Cleaning was preferable to that.

Chapter Twenty

MIKE, LOOKING ONLY slightly less beleaguered than I could imagine him being during the worst loss of his football career, escorted Mrs. Parens in, Diana took her coat, Tom led her to a chair, and I got tea for her. Plus a coffee for Mike.

"I beg your pardon, Diana, for descending on you this way," Mrs. Parens said.

"Not at all. You are always welcome here and we're all delighted to hear what you will tell us."

"In light of the death of Professor Roy, and after much thought, I have determined that there is information that I should share with you."

"Good, I have a lot of questions—"

She held up a single finger to stop me. Most people it takes a whole hand. One finger did it for Emmaline Parens.

"It will be more efficient for me to tell you what I came to tell you about the past."

In other words, she wasn't going to take questions.

"About the past," I repeated. "Why are we always having to dig through old files and dusty memories into the past?"

"Because," she said, "the sheriff's department and even the Sherman Police Department are admirably suited to responding to crimes of the moment, such as traffic infractions or robberies or domestic disputes. The matters you have been looking into have developed and grown over time. You must look at the immediate situation, but also peel back the layers of time to see how they lie, one upon the other, each dependent and deformed by what came before."

"Deformed?"

"Oh, yes. Because the past never lies smooth." She tipped her head. "Indeed, it can even be said to be fluid. Yes, Michael, fluid."

He jumped as if she'd called on him while he'd been sitting in the back of the room making paper airplanes. Which he might have been doing in his head.

I drew her fire. "Fluid? How?"

Paycik owed me.

"The past is not static. It changes, for good or ill, with our views, our priorities, our attention, or lack of it."

"I get the part about our views. That one period's views color the interpretation and re-interpretation of events. All the revisionists of history and then the revisionists of those revisions, and on and on. But does lack of attention change the past? Doesn't it simply remain there, like a fossil, waiting to be found?"

"The past is not a relic of a living being. The past that has no attention from current generations slides deeper and deeper down, getting no sunlight or oxygen, and stretching its connections to the present until they are gone completely."

I raised an eyebrow. "You mean primary sources die off."

She didn't answer immediately. "Or they bury the past in the interests of moving on, of living as best they can until something drastic occurs, which forces them to reacquaint themselves with the past." She put the already empty teacup and its saucer on the table beside her. "What do you know of Professor Roy's history?"

"We knew she wrote a book—"

Diana filled in the title. " 'Westward, No!' "

"—that became popular and that brought her a certain standing in academia as well as financial success. Penny also gave me a sense that the professor didn't exactly fit in here."

Saying that reminded me of Clara's comments about being connected to the top echelon in the area, but not truly part of it. Did Professor Roy fall into the same category?

She might also have been caught in another no-man's land—not a complete outsider, since she lived here and knew the history, yet not part of the native fauna, either.

I knew how that felt.

Most of the time I was fine with it, since it was part of a journalist's lot. I wondered if Nora Roy had felt the same.

After a moment, Mrs. P slowly nodded. "Penny has many admirable traits. I doubt, however, that giving a coherent and chronological account is among them." She barely paused for the assortment of stifled chuckles and grins that drew. "That is what I shall give you."

She resettled herself, sitting even more upright, with one hand cupping the other in her lap.

"Yolanda Cruz was a kind and lovely woman. She and her husband, Arturo, had five children close together, with the youngest a boy named Javier. He was not yet two years old when Arturo was laid off. To keep the family solvent, Yolanda became the housekeeper for Professor Roy and cared for Kitty Roy.

"At that time, Nora Roy was a young single mother, hoping to make her mark at the university in Colorado where she worked. She soon after began the research that led to her book. At first when she came to this area, she, Kitty, and Yolanda stayed in Cody, using resources there. The couple from whom she was renting a small apartment at the time discovered the approach of her research and ordered her to leave there."

"Good grief. What was her approach?"

"You must first have a clear idea of the viewpoints of historians before that. Michael?"

He started at being called on, but rallied impressively. "Early historians, uh, like Frederick Jackson Turner, saw the West as heroic. They set the image, the myths, the 'Go West, young man, Go West' image, with 'savages' marauding against civilizing whites. Then, in the last third or so of the Twentieth Century, things went the other way, with the history of the West being viewed as a paradise for the Native Americans that was torn apart by marauding whites."

Mrs. Parens gave him a slight nod. He visibly relaxed.

"So, what did Nora Roy do?" I asked. "Swing the pendulum back the other direction again?"

"Thomas?" Mrs. Parens called on her next student.

My ignorance on this topic exempted me. I didn't mind at all.

"Professor Roy essentially said the Native Americans *and* the whites were evil marauders who deserved each other."

"And," Diana added, not waiting for the next command from the former teacher, "she said the whites who came here were the dregs who couldn't make a go of it in 'civilization.' " She refilled Mrs. Parens' teacup.

"Including Buffalo Bill Cody?" I asked.

"Among many, many others," Diana confirmed. No wonder the professor had gotten kicked out of his town. "The academics, the big city reviewers, and the TV people ate it up with a spoon."

Mrs. Parens retook the lead. "The reaction in Cody to her research prompted Professor Roy to move her stays to here in Cottonwood County, though she continued to do considerable research in and around Cody."

"Was she accepted here?"

"Naturally, neither she nor members of her household were true residents, since they lived here only for short periods and they were not from—or of—Cottonwood County. However, Yolanda Cruz and Kitty were more familiar to many because they were out in the community, while the professor worked and her husband, when he eventually joined the household—" Her mouth pursed ever so slightly. "—did not. With the publication of Nora Roy's book, some of that changed. The publication of the book was itself an event. It drew considerable attention around the state."

"Not favorable, I take it?"

"In general, no, it could not be termed favorable. The sentiment in Cody could be characterized as both indignant over her portrayal of William Cody, among other figures, and triumphant that they, in their view, pushed her on to Cottonwood County."

"We didn't mind as much, because we don't have any major heroes for her to trash," Mike said.

He was taking a drink of coffee, so missed Mrs. Parens' disapproving glance.

She cleared her throat. "With the success of the book, she bought a small place to the east of Sherman. She, Kitty, and Yolanda began to spend all of the summers here, as well as other vacation times. That was when she met and married Victor Zblewski, though she maintained her last name since she had established it professionally."

Had she decided their daughter, Laura, would use that last name, rather than Zblewski? Or had Laura?

"Being here all summer must have been hard on Yolanda's family," Diana said.

Mrs. Parens nodded. "Her husband, Arturo, had returned to work and he would use his vacation to bring the children here to Cottonwood County to camp. They saw as much of Yolanda as they could. By extension, they also spent a great deal of time with Kitty. As time went on, the older Cruz children would bring the younger ones here when Arturo could not get away. Eventually, the youngest could drive himself. That era ended when Javier went to college. He then worked throughout the summer and during the year to pay the expenses his scholarship to Bison University did not cover."

So Yolanda's son had gone to the same school where Professor Roy taught. That made sense, since the Cruz home must have been nearby.

"Many changes happened in that period. Nora Roy had married Victor Zblewski. Yolanda had been very close to Kitty, but she went to a college preparatory school in what would have been her senior year in high school, then to college. It might have been expected that Yolanda would work less for the family. But then Laura was born. That was when Professor Roy sold the house where they had spent summers and bought the property that Michael now owns as her primary residence. Yolanda, who cared for Laura, came as well."

"They ranched?" I tried to imagine the woman I'd seen at the museum dinner in that role.

Mike shook his head. "It was only the home ranch at that time, about ten acres. The people I bought from were the ones who put most of the acreage back together to make it a viable ranch again."

I nodded. "Kind of rough on Yolanda wasn't it, to be up here year-round? Why didn't she quit?"

"It was, naturally, difficult for Yolanda to be away from her family, which remained based in Colorado. Yet she was devoted to Laura. In addition, the financial considerations remained. Her husband's health became such that he could not work. He lived with a daughter in Colorado. So Yolanda's income was essential."

"Still, she must have been torn."

"I saw no evidence that she ever considered not staying here with the professor's family."

I thought about the four members of the family I'd met at the museum dinner. Not a jolly group.

"What about that family? There certainly was tension among them last night." I could see Mrs. Parens' disapproval gathering, like storm clouds blotting out the sun. She did not approve of what she considered gossip and I considered background material. In hopes that old *background* material would be more palatable to her than any as fresh as last night, I added, "Were they always like that?"

"Like what?" Mike asked.

"Like four unrelated marbles without a connection contained in a sphere. They'd bump into each other now and then, the action ricocheting them away from each other fast. If I had to pick one word about their interaction, it would be antipathy."

"Yes." To my surprise that came from Diana. "I knew Laura a bit. She was friends with my oldest sister for a while when they were in middle school and I was in elementary school. In fairness, I can't say 'always.' But they were like that well before Laura died."

I teeter-tottered my pen between two fingers. "So her suicide might have exacerbated the divisions, but didn't cause them?"

"That would be my reading."

I nodded.

Tom stirred in his chair. "Sorry to break this up, but If I'm going to make Montana before I fall asleep, we'd best get going."

"But—" As I looked over to him I caught sight of Mrs. Parens. She didn't come anywhere close to a slouch, but her posture wasn't as erect as usual. Also, shadows showed under her eyes and the corners of her mouth turned down slightly.

"Of course." Diana stood. "We shouldn't have kept you so late. The coffee's all brewed for your thermos," she added, referring to an earlier conversation she and Tom had. "I'll fill it right now."

That pretty much ended the gathering.

Tom said to call if we had any chores for him, an offer that was probably the most forthcoming he'd been about any of our inquiries.

Which drove home Clara's point about Professor Roy not being truly part of Cottonwood County. Otherwise Tom Burrell would be telling us how impossible it was that anyone from here would be involved in a murder … despite evidence to the contrary. Not only in the months I'd been here, but also twenty-six years ago when Yolanda Cruz was murdered by Dean Isaacs.

Mike, Diana, and I didn't even sit down again after they left.

Though we did toss around ideas about what to look in to.

Mike repeated that he'd check with his EMT friend, plus see if Deputy Lloyd Sampson might let some things slip during a friendly conversation.

"I'll see if my sister or any of her former classmates and other friends remember more about Dean and Laura," Diana said.

"I think I'll go to the library. I have a couple other ideas, but have to wait for some information first."

"Did you call Jennifer?" Diana asked.

"No, I didn't." That was emphatic. What followed wasn't. "I did happen to text her, and she called me. I didn't ask for her help. I kept saying she was on vacation, but she volunteered. In fact, she insisted. She said Dale is a nice guy, but not the person for us to rely on."

"Uh-huh."

Unabashedly changing the subject, I said, "One thing that keeps tugging at me is how did the story of Dean Isaacs being released come to Thurston in the first place?"

"News release," Mike and Diana said simultaneously.

"Does the Wyoming Department of Corrections send news releases about prisoners being released? I find that hard to believe. They probably notify the families of victims, but that would be the Cruz family in Colorado. I doubt they'd notify the Roys."

"Why does it matter?" Diana asked—not challenging that it did, but curious.

Heck, I was curious why it was tugging at me, too.

And I wondered if it mattered or if it was a red herring that was leading me into a sidetrack.

"I have no idea. Maybe it's bothering me because it's a 't' that needs crossing, an 'i' that needs dotting. We'd usually turn it over to Jennifer to run down and it would all be settled."

"Let me see what I can find out tomorrow," Mike volunteered. "I'll be at the station and Dale is sports crazy, so I have some pull with him. He's no Jennifer, but he's the one who'd know."

I UNLOCKED THE door to the bunkhouse, then hesitated.

Shadow looked up at me.

"Good question," I told him. "I have no idea why I'm not getting out of this wind right away, either."

I swung the door wider.

Too far. The wind caught it and shoved. So I had to be firm with it, pushing it closed and locking it before I turned to the rest of the room.

The bed looked just the way it had when I'd left it this morning. Possibly better.

There was no Tom-sized mussing of the covers, no head indentation in the pillows, certainly no boot marks on the white bedspread. He'd straightened and fluffed the bed back into perfect order.

Had I really expected otherwise?

No.

So I certainly wasn't disappointed. Because that would make no sense at all.

THURSDAY

DECEMBER 29

Chapter Twenty-One

WHEN I GOT up, I discovered Jennifer had stayed up all night.

That wasn't a guess or a supposition. Unless she had rigged a program to send emails in her sleep, she had been up all night.

2:43 am—The name of a sheriff I didn't recognize, followed by a notation that he was deceased.

3:02 am—The name of a lead investigator I didn't recognize, also deceased.

3:31 am—Prosecuting attorney was Wayson Haus, the County Attorney at the time. Defense attorney was Henry Longbaugh. Both deceased. I suspected attorneys by those last names I'd encountered while in Cottonwood County were their offspring.

4:47 am—First pass of accounts of the crime/trial. The accompanying note read, "Haven't found *The Independence*'s stories yet. They're not in the usual place. I'll keep at it. These are mostly wire service stories, so mostly short and not a lot of detail. Best of the lot is probably the one from the Colorado newspaper from Yolanda Cruz's hometown."

5:38 am—Attached, a list of all law enforcement mentioned in accounts gathered so far.

I read them in the order they'd been sent.

The wire service stories were the ones I'd seen before. I skipped to the story from the Colorado paper. It was mostly quotes from Yolanda's friends and cousins who'd still lived in her small hometown.

It reinforced what Penny had said about the woman and reiterated a sketch of the family, which was less detailed than Mrs. Parens had shared, and didn't add anything.

While I was reading that, another email came in. "There is definitely something weird with *The Independence*. None of the issues we'd want to see are in the usual databases. Will keep looking after some sleep. And I promised that little pest another four games so she won't snitch that I was up all night."

A visit to Needham Bender at the offices of *The Independence* was added to the day's to-do list.

Then I read the list of all law enforcement who'd been on the case. Said a nasty word. And made a phone call.

One ring, then, "Shelton."

"Meet me where we talked yesterday morning. I'll be there in thirty-five minutes."

"I don't have time—"

"Make time, Deputy Shelton."

I hung up. I was pissed.

But before I left to chew his ass, I put in a call to Linda Caswell, in hopes of getting more museum background.

She might not be free today. If she did have a slot, she'd message me.

SHELTON SHOWED UP about two minutes after I did. Not even long enough for me to stew much about his being late.

Though it did give me time to notice a black SUV pulled over to the side of the road across from a back road to the barn and other ranch buildings of Mike's place. I couldn't see much inside the SUV from this angle, but a flutter of light-colored paper testified to someone trying to maneuver the folds of a map in an enclosed space. Probably no connection for GPS, going by what Shelton had said about the area.

I got into Shelton's vehicle without awaiting an invitation. "Who lost money on that scam? You said someone has, but none of the people you sent me to talk to have. I need the name or names."

"Not going to get it from me. You're supposed to be such a great investigator, go investigate."

If I'd needed confirmation for what I was thinking, his words provided it. I squinted at him. "You lied to me."

"Be careful what you say. I asked you to look into that scam and that was no lie, so—"

"Not only about the scam. About why you wanted to meet here. Solely because it's a no-service area my ass. You wanted to bring me here for a specific reason and that was to see the scene of a crime. What's left of it."

"Not much is. Like I said the other day, the main house was there, where the barn is now. Part of the structure's worked in to what's there now. The housekeeper's house, that was over to the west, beside those trees. Gone now."

As tempting as it was to crow over that tacit acknowledgment, not crowing would get me farther.

"That's a creek running through there?"

"Getting to be a regular nature scout, aren't you?"

"I've learned a thing or two," I said with false modesty.

"Right. Creek used to rise and flood her little house. One room, really, with a bathroom. It rained and rained that night. Creek came up, flooded the house, and wiped out a lot of evidence."

"Then how did Dean get convicted?"

"Didn't wipe out all the evidence. Left a broom with his finger-prints. A witness saw him leaving the area well after he should have and he had no explanation for that."

I eyed him. "Most law enforcement I've met have at least one case they're obsessed with. Yours is the murder of Yolanda Cruz, huh? The murder Dean Isaacs was convicted of. And now he's out on parole after twenty-five years." I paused, as if saying those words started up the calculator in my head. "Wait a minute, this couldn't have been your case."

He gave me a side-eye "No shit, Sherlock" look.

"Why the—" I swallowed *obsession* and substituted. "—interest now?"

"Always interested in justice."

I narrowed my eyes. Partly to focus deeper, but also because even in the vehicle it was cold enough that I wanted to cover as much of my eyeballs as possible while still seeing.

"You knew the victim. Yolanda Cruz," I said.

His blankness was a negative.

"Dean Isaacs and his girlfriend, Professor Roy's daughter."

Still blank.

"You were a brand new officer and it was your first call and you'll never forget the moment when—"

Disgust replaced blankness. "My father. My father was on the case."

I let him have that. I'd figured that out when I saw the name Wayne Shelton Sr. on the list Jennifer had sent, but sometimes you gained more by pretending to know less.

"Your father was a deputy?"

"Some kind of reporter you are." There was triumph in that.

There was a limit to what I'd let him have, however. "And yet you came to me for help on the scam using Richard's name and you happened to bring me here to do it, right after Dean's arrival back in town. So, what does *that* say?"

He almost grinned. I swear he did.

"It says I know all the official, real information. It says I'm happening to wonder if there's anything that flaky and off-the-wall thinking might produce."

"*Flaky* and *off-the-wall*? Go ahead, make yourself feel better about the answers we've come up with this year that the sheriff's department hasn't."

"Would've gotten it if you lot hadn't jumped the gun time after time. Cutting corners. Not thinking—"

"Keep telling yourself that." I raised my hand to stop his words. "Okay, so your father was on the case, but it was all settled, the murderer convicted. Even if you thought he should have served a longer sentence, what could you hope to…?"

I didn't finish because he wasn't going to answer me. Not to mention that I had a good guess anyway.

"You're not totally satisfied, because your father wasn't totally satisfied with the case. Good heavens, you and your father didn't think Dean was innocent…? No, not that." My squinted eyes were sure of that. "Still, whatever's bothering you, you could investigate yourself."

He didn't react, but he might as well have shouted *No, I can't.* That's how clearly I understood.

"Sheriff Conrad. He's blocking you."

"He's promoting me."

I laughed at his dour tone. He didn't.

"Got to be an example."

He meant it. As if he hadn't already been an example.

Not always a good example in my opinion, since I considered him largely responsible for turning Richard Alvaro into a taciturn law enforcement officer when it came to dealing with journalists, specifically with me.

"What is it you're hoping we'll do?"

"Not hoping anything in particular."

"What about Professor Nora Roy's death?"

"What about it?"

"You must be looking at whether it was really an accident or a setup to get the exhaust into the garage to kill her."

He snorted. "Her or whoever walked into that garage first."

"But you're investigating? Starting with the spouse, of course."

"Nah, we're not investigating at all. Wouldn't ever occur to us to check for recent life insurance policies or marital discord or one or the other fooling around or something else going on in the family. And if you're asking if there are fingerprints on the frozen tumbleweed, we haven't found any yet. The wind must have worn gloves."

What a sneaky, backhanded, smart-ass way of giving me information.

I admired the heck out of it.

We sat in silence a moment. Then I nodded, gripped the door handle, and said, "Good to know you're on top of it. As for us looking

into the Yolanda Cruz murder, don't think you can stop us if we start."
No need to tell him we already had started. "We're not operating under
your orders. Be clear on that."

As I exited, he said after me, "You're still looking into that scammer who's trying to drag down Alvaro." It was an order, not a
question.

"Yeah, I am."

DEX ANSWERED IMMEDIATELY.

As usual, I had to identify myself before I got a "Hi, Danny." He
has his doubts about caller ID.

"What do you know about carbon monoxide?"

Asking that was a mistake. Before I could rephrase, he started
telling me its chemical makeup and how it acted on the body and why
it produced the telltale cherry red signs on autopsy.

In danger of having my eyes roll back in my head—not good, since
I was driving back toward town at the moment—I interrupted with a
quick description of the set-up of Nora Roy's garage.

"Could that produce fatal levels of carbon monoxide?"

"With a gas generator that was not vented adequately and safely to
the outside running all night, carbon monoxide could certainly build to
a lethal level—"

"Even in a garage that big?"

"Yes."

"It seems more likely to have been an accident, though, rather than
murder, don't you think?"

"I have insufficient data to make such an assessment." A classic
Dex answer.

"I'm thinking it would be a rather haphazard way of committing
murder, so that makes accident more likely."

"It would not be difficult for a murderer to arrange for carbon
monoxide to reach lethal levels in that garage."

"But wouldn't the victim have smelled the exhaust and turned
back?"

"It requires 12,800 parts per million to cause unconsciousness in two to three breaths—" About as long as it would have taken Nora Roy to walk past the first SUV and collapse before she reached hers. "—and to cause death soon afterward. That puts it within acceptable limits to account for her not recognizing the odor in a period of time that allowed her to respond before being overcome, especially if, as you indicated, she had heart issues. A poorly functioning heart, as well as age, are factors that can accelerate carbon monoxide's lethality. Was the garage heated?"

"I doubt it, or why would they be using a generator?"

"A faulty assumption," he scolded. "However, if it was not heated, there would be little air flow and that would be an additional factor in building carbon monoxide to a lethal level."

"But no one in the house was sick or smelled anything. With a generator pumping exhaust into the attached garage all night and all morning, wouldn't some of it have leaked in to the house?"

"In many cases it would. However, you would have to have tested the air quality in the house at the time to determine that. Colloquial information could be gathered by asking the occupants if they noticed headaches or other symptoms. Otherwise, they were quite fortunate."

That *colloquial information* phrase was voiced with maximum distaste.

But it sounded like a plan to me. In fact, it sounded like a large part of my profession.

Chapter Twenty-Two

PULLING IN TO the KWMT lot, I felt my phone vibrate.

Just the way it always does when I forget to turn it back on after an interview. There wasn't anything different about this vibration. Nothing.

Yet I knew it was my mother.

Catherine Danniher has that sort of reach.

"Hi, Mom."

"Elizabeth, how *are* you?"

"Um. Fine. How are you? Dad? Everybody?"

"We're all fine. But we're concerned about you."

"No reason to be," I said lightly.

"I'm not," I heard Dad say in the background. "She's a very capable young lady, Cat."

Aw, Dad, still thinking of me as young. And a lady, for that matter.

My recent visit had sharpened my mental pictures of what actions went with the words spoken over the phone, so I could see Mom turning a shoulder to Dad, as if that would shut off his opinion. "We hadn't heard from you."

"Sure you did. I called you when I got back here, told you everything was fine."

"*Fine,*" Mom repeated, somewhere north of scoffing and south of despair.

"Yup." Unrelenting cheer was my best option.

"Do you have plans for New Year's Eve yet?"

I grimaced.

"Don't make that face, Elizabeth Margaret." Uh-oh. That mental picture thing went two ways, with my Christmas visit sharpening Mom's ability to envision my reactions, too. "Having plans for New Year's Eve is representative of being connected, of being part of a community, of a family."

That last one was her real point. She'd wanted me to stay in Illinois through New Year's, to celebrate with the family.

That would have meant all the grandchildren at my parents' house, along with those of the adults who didn't have other plans, which meant most of them would be there. There would be old movies, a jigsaw puzzle, and Scrabble death matches.

Most years I would have liked to have stayed. When Wes and I were married we seldom had. He'd had to get back to work, I'd had to get back to work, he'd wanted to leave, or all three. Wes' preferred celebration (when we weren't working) was attending a party with VIPs. More accurately, *working* a party with VIPs. I got so I preferred working that night.

I probably could have stayed in Illinois this year if I'd asked for the time off. I'm not exactly the go-to person in the newsroom for news director Les Haeburn. True, when I signed a new contract in the fall it included latitude for me to explore some stories on my own. But I hadn't had anything cooking—back to the slow news week idea—and this wasn't the time to start enterprise reporting if it required finding anyone who wasn't away for the holidays. My contacts list would be the cyber equivalent of a ghost town.

I hadn't asked for the time off.

This turnover from one year to the next was also the anniversary of my last newscast as the old E.M. Danniher—no, let's make that the original E.M. Danniher. The new—and I hoped improved—version had been pecking away at my past's shell for the past seven months, and that had been happening here in Cottonwood County.

It seemed appropriate to usher in the new year here.

If it was Shadow and me watching an old movie while munching on some popcorn, that was fine with me. It would be fine with him if he got a few kernels, too. The dog did like popcorn. How it came about that I knew was irrelevant.

"Do you have plans for New Year's?" Mom repeated.

"I do."

"With other people?"

"Cat, let the girl be." Dad to the rescue.

"I have to go now, Mom. Talk to you and Dad later. Love to all." Another dose of unrelenting cheer to finish off the call.

I climbed out of the cold SUV into the colder air. Nothing like frigid to make KWMT-TV's squatty block building look appealing.

"What are you doing?"

Diana's question brought me out of a montage of family memories—many from long-ago New Year's celebrations, some from a few days ago—and in to the realization that once I'd made it into the building, I'd stopped in the hallway, rather than continuing on to my desk.

Before I answered her, however, she piled on another question with sharper interest. "Get something good? You have that kind of look."

"Oh, no. It was my folks. They called as I was parking. Got me thinking about the holidays and family."

She tipped her head, frown lines appearing between her eyebrows. "You had a similar look day before yesterday after you flew in. When you left, I'd have said there was almost no chance you would go back to Chicago."

"Go back—?"

"But when I see this look…"

"Oh, that's the flying."

"The flying?"

I'd try to explain to other people about this, including my ex before he was my ex. None had gotten it.

The true essence of flying over the Midwest isn't simply a matter of it *not* being what ignoramuses call flyover country.

It's not the *absence* of ignorable. It's the *existence*—and recognition—of the pleasurable, even admirable.

There's a solidity to the land below, to the orderliness of the arrangements. Even in December and even from such a height, there's a sense of the fertility of the soil beneath the snow. Perhaps because the stretching, stalwart trees, outlining fields or gathering in conclaves around houses, speak of roots sunk deep and getting what they need to thrive.

Some people's hearts beat faster at the energy of New York, the gloss of L.A., the free spirit of New Orleans, the power of D.C. I've experienced all of those.

But what makes my heart beat slow and deep and true is the sweep of a Midwestern farm field, whether in full-fledged corn bonanza or the winter's stubbled state.

What can I say? I'm a Midwestern girl at heart.

Some say that's why I talk to people I don't know. If that's true, that open, fertile, solid territory across the middle of this country must have spawned a lot of journalists. As well as pleasant, pass-the-time-of-day folks.

"I'll tell you all about it one evening when we're sitting in front of a fire with some wine," I said.

She said, "Okay." But those vertical lines didn't disappear.

I'D CHECKED THROUGH my work email again and was weighing what to do next when a text came through from Jennifer.

If my math was right she hadn't gotten much sleep at all.

But I wasn't about to look a gift text in the mouth.

Especially not when she'd answered so promptly with interesting information.

I texted back my thanks, and went looking for a colleague.

"Mike? How's the reception at your tidy little spread?" I said from the doorway of the editing bay.

"Fine. Now." He saved his work. As he turned to me, he added, "Why?"

Avoiding answering, I asked, "What do you mean, now?"

"It's really bad all around that area. I paid a bundle to get it upgraded for the home ranch."

"How about, uh, the nearby roads or, you know, the fields and stuff?"

"That whole area? No way. It'd cost way too much. The house and barn. If they bring the cost down or start a subsidy or something for us rural folks, I might consider expanding it. Why?"

"That's the Internet. What about cell phone?"

"About the same. If you don't have access to my network, you're pretty much SOL. What's all this about?"

I might be going overboard with being suspicious.

Oh, not of Shelton. Him I was still suspicious of.

But turned out the guy in the black SUV really wouldn't have had connection when he'd lost his way and had to resort to a paper map, so he didn't deserve my suspicions.

"Just thinking about how lack of broadband makes it harder for rural areas economically." He quirked a brow at me, but before he could doubt my statement with words, I added, "Want to take a little drive with me? Ask some questions."

"Where? Who?" But he was already up.

"When we're outside."

As we passed through the bullpen, he grabbed his jacket from an empty desk—with more desks than staff it was easier to stow bulky outer clothing on the empties than try get all that cumulative puff compacted on a rack.

I waited until we were in his SUV to say, "We're going to pay Graham Young a visit at his office at Cottonwood County Community College."

"Why Graham Young?" Mike asked.

"Because, thanks to Jennifer, we know he didn't cancel his office hours this morning, which end in half an hour. So we can get there right before he'd leave. All of which means he's the one person from that crew that we can get to without Deputy Shelton interfering."

Chapter Twenty-Three

WE PASSED DOWN brightly painted concrete block hallways.

Not at all like the bunker atmosphere of KWMT-TV. This place made concrete block look perky.

A door with a poster taped to it saying "Special Vacation Week Symposium" stood open to a classroom with laptop-equipped students sitting around irregularly shaped tables. From the noise level, everyone in the room was talking at once with great enthusiasm.

I tried to envision Graham Young as the teacher in that energetically chaotic atmosphere and failed.

Past that it quieted again. A sign at a cross corridor directed us to the right, where we opened a glass door labeled *Social Sciences*. No one was behind the desk or sipping the cup of still-steaming tea. Five doors presented themselves to us. The two to our left were labeled with names neither of us recognized. Straight ahead, and bracketing the desk were two doors, both marked "Professor Nora Roy," though the one to the right also said "No entry." The one on our left was cracked open, showing a slice of a large window, a heavy wooden desk, tall black leather or leather-substitute chair, and an oriental rug. To our right was a single door: "Professor Graham Young."

Mike pointed to it. I nodded. Since he was closer, he knocked. A male voice instructed us to wait one moment. Listening closely, I heard a click and from the lift of Mike's eyebrows, he heard it as well.

The same voice told us to come in.

The sliver of Professor Roy's office we'd seen would have spilled out the sides of this minuscule office. Not only that, but there was no natural light and the place was ringed with bookshelves, which were packed. That left a square in the middle for a desk, desk chair, and two visitor's chairs, all small and undistinguished.

Graham Young was straightening from leaning over in his chair behind the desk, as if he'd been accessing something in the bottom right drawer.

"Professor Young, we met the other night at the museum. I'm Elizabeth Margaret Danniher and this is my colleague, Michael Paycik. We hoped you might be willing to talk to us for some background."

"I know nothing about Professor Roy's death other than what I have told the authorities and they have instructed us not to discuss it with others."

When one door closed in your face, you looked for a likely window.

"I understand, sir. We're not here to ask about Professor Roy's death. We'd liked to ask you about the cooperative program with Bison University." Selling him on talking about the program seemed the most likely.

"Have a seat."

It was less an invitation than a spatial challenge—especially for Mike. I knew those broad shoulders and that muscular physique had to have a downside.

As we maneuvered to fit both us and the chairs into the minute open square in front of the desk, Mike hiked one eyebrow and tipped his head toward the bookcase nearest him.

He ended up folding one chair, gesturing for me to sit in the other, then unfolding his in place and pivoting carefully to sit.

That maneuver gave me time to survey the bookcase he'd indicated. Top to bottom, side to side it held copies of Nora Roy's book and only copies of Nora Roy's book. Professor Young's office was a storage area for her back copies.

There was a real theme going here.

Graham Young was the professorial version of Cinderella. Only instead of sitting by the fireplace, he was at a desk that was such a tight fit that I couldn't imagine how he'd gotten around it to sit behind it.

"First, sir, let me say that while we're not here to discuss Professor Roy's death, we would like to offer our condolences on that tragic accident," I said.

"Thank you." Beyond those two flat syllables, nothing. Not a wince, not a flicker of discomfort, not a "that was no accident" declaration.

It never hurts to hope, as long as you keep going if and when hope is denied.

"We would like to learn more about the cooperative history program that Bison University and Cottonwood County Community College offer."

That did draw a reaction. First, a faint twitch of one eyebrow. Then, a stream of words. Most of them boring. It didn't surprise me when he said a government grant helped support the ongoing cooperative program. His detailed descriptions smacked of governmentese.

I made a show of taking notes, though I was mostly writing down questions to ask him.

Would the Fairy Godmother have ditched Cinderella if she'd droned on like this? The prince sure would have. The glass slipper would have been left on the step to be trampled and kicked by guests who didn't depart until well after the stroke of midnight.

I edged closer to our target by sliding in, "So, you all moved here full-time when the program started?"

"I was not yet involved with the program when Professor Roy established a residence in Cottonwood County. She did that before I—" The slightest of pauses came before he finished. "—joined the family."

"Oh? When did she establish a residence here?" I quickly added, "That must have been an important milestone for the program, a sign that she had faith that it would endure."

"She had faith in it from the start. However, she had not wanted to interrupt her daughter's schooling by moving."

"That would be her older daughter, Mrs. Young?"

"That is correct. My wife. It was when she left Colorado to finish high school at an academically challenging private school that Professor Roy bought her first house here."

"Oh, yes," I said, as if on impulse, "that's where that horrible murder occurred. You must have known that poor woman, Yolanda Cruz."

"Yes. It was a tragedy." No danger of this guy over-emoting.

"And that girl committed suicide over it at the same time. Laura. Professor Roy's younger daughter. And Mr. Zblewski's, of course. Oh. Your sister-in-law." I widened my eyes in sympathy. "How horrible for you."

"It doesn't have the level of emotional import for me that it has for my wife."

My sympathy appeared to have been wasted.

"Or the girl's mother and father," Mike said.

Graham Young inclined his head. "Of course."

"But you did know her?" Mike asked.

"Certainly. She was a child when we married. We were there as she grew up."

Very much *there* from what I'd heard from Professor Belknap about the in-laws' suite the Youngs occupied, rather than their own home.

"You've always lived with your mother-in-law? With your wife's family?" I amended quickly.

"Not at the beginning of our marriage, while I was completing my Ph.D. When I joined the department at Bison University and with the program here, it only made sense to combine households, rather than trying to maintain four between two states. What does this have to do with the cooperative program?"

Mike dove in. "As you said, the program is intertwined with family and where you lived."

"That was all a long time ago."

We'd heard that a time or two when someone didn't want to talk about the past. I didn't push that angle, however. "It was," I conceded. "However, with Dean Isaacs out of prison and in town, it's bound to be on everyone's mind. Including yours."

"What is on my mind is my wife."

He stopped there. Abrupt and a bit odd.

"Of course," I said. "She was very close to Yolanda Cruz, wasn't she?"

"Yolanda had been part of her life from a very young age."

Another abrupt response. Another oddity. I'd set that up with the expectation that the natural response would be a retort that his wife had just lost her mother. That would have been an opening I could have explored.

Possibly he'd chosen to respond the way he did to deny me that opening. If so, he was a lot more astute about interviews than I'd given him credit for.

But, even taking the angle he had, he could have said something about an emotional connection, something softening. His response still qualified as odd.

I decided to push.

"Were you notified about Dean Isaacs' release?"

"No."

"Neither you nor your wife?"

"No."

"Perhaps Professor Roy—?"

"No. What does this have to do with the cooperative program?"

"What's going to happen to the program in light of Professor Roy's death?"

Graham Young turned his head at Mike's question. Mike had been right to ask it, to break the string of *nos* and Young's growing stiffness.

"It will continue, of course."

"Will you be in charge of it?"

"Yes." Another single-word answer, though significantly less door-slamming than the *nos* he'd given me. "For now. I'm certain that in due course there will be discussion about whether the program requires a person at the helm who brings outside interest and attention."

"Perhaps Professor Belknap."

For the first time, his mouth moved from straight. The corners rose ever so slightly. "I doubt that."

"Oh? He has a ground-breaking theory, doesn't he? A lost battle in the Indian Wars? An encounter that shaped what followed, especially Custer's actions. I would think that would bring plenty of outside interest and attention."

"It would need to be proved first. Now, if you have no more questions about the program, I have a great deal of work to do, as I'm sure you can understand."

"Of course." I slid my arms into my coat. We did another close-quarters dance with each other and the chairs to get out of the office.

At the door, I turned back, "Thank you, Professor Young. I'm sure you won't mind that I call you if I have more questions about the program or to set up a time to interview you on camera about it."

I gave him no time to refuse before closing the door.

An auburn-haired woman in her fifties now occupied the desk in the outer office. She had intelligent eyes that examined us as we passed her.

I smiled at her. Never hurt to pave the way to returning for a later chat with her.

Her eyes went to Mike and I made a mental note to be sure to bring him along for the return trip.

"Okay, how did he get behind that desk?" Mike demanded as soon as we were in the corridor and out of the woman's hearing. "No way could a human being get between it and the bookcases. So what did he do? Levitate? Crawl over it?"

"Crawling under would be more in keeping with the rest of it, don't you think?"

"Oh, hell, yes. Forget having his name on it, that door should have been labeled Storage Closet. Did you get…"

"What?"

"It's going to sound weird."

"Say it anyway. You pick things up, Mike. Be confident in that. Follow it up with questions during an interview. Pursue it in your reporting."

"Thanks." He looked at me from the corner of his eye, then said more naturally, "Really, thanks. That's good advice. I'll put it to the test. Did you get a sense that he liked being like that?"

I stopped and looked at him. Partly to focus on what he was saying. Partly because we were about to go outside again and I didn't mind delaying a little longer.

"I didn't until you said it, but now that you have said it... Let's talk about that."

"**WHAT ARE YOU** doing?" Thurston Fine's resonating anchor voice demanded.

I looked around to see that he was glaring at me from where the hallway to the editing bays, studio, library, and other areas, including his private office, opened into the bullpen.

In addition to dropping off Mike, I'd stopped in to use the facilities and grab more spare notebooks and pens from my cache. Yes, I record and digital is great, but sometimes notes work better, as well as making a great prop.

"Getting ready to leave to work on a story." I pulled my coat back on.

"Don't think you can get away with it because you can't. It's my story. Mine. You should know that by now. I get the lead stories and I did the first report so there can be absolutely no question that the Dean Isaacs story is all mine."

"Sure thing. Good story, too. I heard Audrey had ideas about filling in some elements, exploring additional angles..."

And plugging gaping holes in the story.

Although I didn't say those words, everyone in the newsroom heard them.

The synchronized eye-shift from me to Thurston proved that.

Okay, not everyone in the newsroom heard the unspoken words.

Thurston was the exception, as proved by his pushing straight ahead with his agenda.

"You will not try to push in to this story. It's mine."

"Which story?"

"Either story," he said quickly. "That murderer's return to my county or the tragic accident that claimed Professor Roy's life. You will not interview any of the people involved in this."

I looked at him.

It was mostly absent-minded.

I'd talked to Dean Isaacs, true. But, really, as a private citizen.

An interview, though …

There'd been the interview with Graham Young. Interviewing Kitty Young could also be interesting. Javier Cruz if we could find him? Who else would be interesting, now that Thurston had raised the issue?

An interview can play to an ego.

An ego can make people say more than they intend.

But right now, a more immediate concern made itself felt.

"I gotta go, Thurston." With my coat, scarf, and gloves on, I was starting to bake. Which would make going outside all the worse. "We can talk more about this later."

"There is nothing to talk about."

"Oh. Good. I'm glad you feel that way, too. Bye."

"They're mine. Those stories. Both. Mine."

"Then you better get to work on them," Leona said from behind him. "I've been waiting in the editing bay. You're going to get this intro right. Let's go, Thurston."

She tapped him on the butt with the rolled papers in her hand, then pivoted and walked away.

Chapter Twenty-Four

AN OLDER MAN held the door for me as he exited and I entered the library.

Older.

I better watch that. It was hard to tell at a glance how much older he was than me. He was tall and straight. Fit. He had gray around the front of his dark hair, lines in his face, but not the weathered look of an outdoors worker.

I supposed as long as someone was actually older than me it was safe to consider him or her *older.*

But if I slipped up and thought of someone as *older* who turned out to be younger than me, then I was really in trouble.

Entering the library cut the wind, providing a temporary impression of luscious warmth. Judging by the bulky sweaters the two women behind the desk wore, that impression wore off as cold air rushed in around each arrival and departure.

Rather than approaching the desk immediately, I warmed up by looking up the things I could on my own. Sure, I could have walked up and asked for Ivy Short, but there were downsides to that. This way gave me an opportunity to suss out the staff members while also doing something useful.

Useful, but not initially rewarding.

The library's microfilm of the *Independence* had the same gap as the online resources, which left me unable to fill in details on the coverage of Yolanda Cruz's murder and Dean Isaacs' trial.

That added an item to my to-do list.

Next, I switched to a computer to access the Internet.

I would have preferred to do this on my laptop or phone or even at the office—especially since the teenage boy I'd seen sitting at the terminal when I arrived had left a drift of orange crumbs from cheese curls—but I was still trying to decide which of the two middle-aged women was Penny's source, Ivy Short.

Knowing which it was—brown sweater or blue sweater—would give me cues on how best to approach her.

As I sat down, my bag brushed the computer's mouse.

The screen came to life. And there was the last item the previous user had read: An article on fighting "bacne."

I couldn't resist. I looked. I had to read some to discover that "bacne" was back acne.

I hit the back button.

Another article on the topic. Two more back button hits, two additional articles. The fourth click back produced the previous user's search: "How to get rid of back acne."

Another tap on the back button. A piece on which tech stocks were likely to have the best return in the next year.

More backs, more tech investing information, until I hit the original search on that one, too.

And then came articles on decorating with shades of white. Going backward with the tap of a button through a *lot* of sites, used up all my patience. I couldn't imagine actually looking at them. Finally, I reached that original search, too.

This time, tapping back got nothing new.

The user before the shades-of-white decorator had cleared his or her search.

What had I learned from this? One out of four Internet users at Cottonwood County Public Library was a responsible public computer user.

Feeling a familiar vibration, I silently wished the "bacne" kid well, but most of my attention was on the just-arrived text.

Linda Caswell would meet me at four o'clock at her house.

Buckling down, I started a new session.

I was still wondering about the holes left by Thurston's reporting of Dean Isaacs getting out on parole, including whether the family was available for comment. Mike was going to ask Dale about the KWMT end. I intended to try from the other end.

By this point, I wasn't surprised to find no obituary for Yolanda Cruz from the *Independence.*

But pay dirt came with an obit from the Deer Forks, Colorado, *Tracks.*

As with many obituaries of murdered people, this did not focus on the crime that brought death, but on the life that preceded it, including her children. In the survived-by paragraph, it listed their names, along with spouses' names, married names for the daughters, and the towns where they lived.

I copied those down. I also took a photo of the screen with my camera.

Then I did a first skim through the Internet for Arturo. Nothing. No phone number, no address, nothing. But also no obituary.

Next, I tried the children's names, starting from the oldest. A few sites offered me basic information, but for a fee. I passed. Beyond that? Nothing. These folks were not newsworthy. No police reports was good news for the family, but not for me.

Then…

Bingo.

Not police reports, but the trail of a semi-public figure. Turns out, Javier, the youngest as Mrs. Parens had told us, was a lawyer in Denver. From the website for the firm where he was a partner and from articles referring to him, he was a big-shot lawyer who kept a fairly low profile—the biggest kind of big-shot lawyer.

If someone in the family had been up to date on being notified about Dean Isaac's status, Javier was most likely. I noted his firm's phone number.

Then I made a pass to see if I could find a likely home number for him. I wasn't surprised when that failed.

My sporadic surveillance of the women at the desk had informed me that blue sweater was the better bet. Not only was the color more cheerful, but she was more talkative. At the moment, she also was alone at the desk. Time to make my move.

"Ivy Short?"

She turned. "Yes. I—Oh. You're Elizabeth from TV."

Nodding, I put my hand out. "E.M. Danniher of KWMT-TV." A tinge of color came into her cheeks. I adjusted immediately, softening my approach. "Elizabeth. I, uh, know Penny from the supermarket."

Her smile came back. "Of course. Penny."

Something about the way she said it made me suspect I might have been the subject of a Penny monologue. Oh, goody.

"She thought you might be willing to talk to me a bit," I said. I figured Penny *might* have thought that if she'd ever slowed her talking enough that I had a chance to ask her.

"Oh. I can't leave the desk. Shara's on her break."

I squelched a triumphant smile because she sounded disappointed. "Perhaps in a little while?"

"Yes. If you're going to be here another ten, fifteen minutes?"

"I will be if you have the yearbooks from Cottonwood County High School."

I knew somewhere else I could find all the yearbooks, but that would involve a drive to O'Hara Hill, not to mention passing Mrs. Parens' stringent Need to Know requirements when a lot of my inquiries were Want to Know or even Who Knows If This Factoid Might Come In Handy Some Day.

"Of course. They're all in the local history room." She pointed.

"Thank you. I'll be there when you have a moment."

I headed the direction she'd pointed and found the compact room. It was a lot shorter trip than O'Hara Hill.

Yearbooks lined up in chronological order in a bookcase. The first couple yearbooks I pulled had nothing of interest beyond amusing hairstyles and heart-tuggingly young faces. Then, in the third one, I found Laura Roy in the Ninth Grade class.

She had dark brown hair, a triangular smile, and soft, huge brown eyes. Under her name was an assortment of activities. I figured out the drama club, volleyball, soccer, and track. I guessed at a couple more as student government and volunteer organizations, but a few were beyond me.

The next year I found her again in the same activities—part of a group in the football bleachers, building sets for a play, laughing with a young woman identified as Miss Reynolds, a teacher.

And then her class photo.

It didn't look like the same girl.

Her hair was striped with white-blonde. Uncombed hunks fell over her face, obscuring most of it. Her head tip, combined with a closed-mouth slant, reminded me of Dean's smirking younger photos. Her eyes looked straight into the camera.

Daring me.

Daring everybody.

But daring us to what?

I grabbed the next year's edition. She was not in it. Not anywhere. Looking at the date I realized why.

I knew she'd died at fifteen. Somehow it hit even harder that she'd died between her sophomore and junior years in high school. No opportunity to return to all those activities. No opportunity to return to who she'd been.

I propped up the yearbooks with her in them and took closeups of the pictures. Maybe a second look later would reveal what the dare was about.

Closing the yearbooks, the years on the cover caught my eye, and the calculator in my head went to work. I picked up the first one and flipped through it again, on a different hunt. Nothing.

If I was going to do this right, I needed a span of years to cover possibilities. In fact, I could get two spans…

I stacked the books to look at on the table, then returned to the shelf, my hand sliding along the tops of the upright volumes, spanning a decade, reaching with both hands—as the door opened on Ivy Short.

Pulling my hand back, I set to work making her comfortable in her own library. It wasn't hard. With the door closed, she settled in and repeated everything Penny had told me. Almost everything. She skipped over the surgical scar, thankfully.

"…and how strange was it that in the past week, for the very first time, Professor Roy's husband shows up and then Dean Isaacs right behind him and—"

"Right behind him, like Dean was following him?"

"Oh." She looked up at the ceiling. "I don't know. Vic Zblewski had come in a few times before, then the day after Christmas he came in and then this man I didn't recognize—not until Thurston Fine's report on TV about him jogged my memory—came in. One minute I looked over and Vic Zblewski was at the computer and then the next minute, it was Dean Isaacs."

"Like Dean kicked him out?"

She paused again. I liked that. She was thinking before she answered.

"I don't think so… I can't even say if they talked. Though I can say Dean Isaacs looked quite, uh, pleased."

Her hesitation made me think she'd really wanted to say he'd looked unbearably smug.

"I *can* say that the day before yesterday when Vic Zblewski came in, then Professor Roy came in a little later, they didn't talk. I'm not sure they even saw each other. She went to the fiction side, then to the movies, before she came right back to here, while he was over by the computers the whole time. I figured she was doing research, you know, like that other professor who comes here. Though he always wants all sorts of old diaries and journals brought to him in this room. In fact, he was here that day, too, and he was even—"

She stopped. Her cheeks went pink. She coughed a little. Then she continued, "He was here, in this room, when Professor Roy came in to the library. It seemed like… Well, he left and then she immediately came in here."

I heard her hesitation so I said it outright. "Right away? Like she'd been waiting for him to leave?"

"I can't know for sure, but she did appear to be whiling away time. She did not look at any of the books or at the movies. She entered this room directly when he left. I know some say she's difficult, but she wasn't that day. Didn't make a peep, God rest her soul. Even left the door open, while that other professor was quite, uh, particular that the door be closed. And insisting on us knocking like he owned the place and we were visiting."

"That other professor... Long hair, kind of curls at the back?"

"Yes, his name—Oh, perhaps I shouldn't say."

"Belknap. We've met." I smiled and saw she was relieved I already knew what she had worried about telling me. "Did Professor Roy stay in this room long?"

"Perhaps half an hour. She came out not long after Mr. Zblewski had left. She'd asked Shara about checking into rights of victims of a crime and revocation of parole."

She brought her gaze to my face. Apparently satisfied that I'd gotten the significance, she nodded twice. "Considering the complexities, she didn't spend a long time on it. Then she checked her watch and went out in a hurry like she had someplace to get to."

Like a dinner at the museum.

"I understand Kitty and Graham Young have been here, too?"

She frowned. "Their regular visit was beginning of last week. Haven't seen them since."

Could she have missed them with all the comings and goings? She hadn't missed the others.

When Ivy left, I looked around the room again.

Nora Roy shows up at the library where her husband is on a computer terminal and Professor Belknap is in the local history room with the door closed. She shows no sign of having seen Vic Zblewski. Her actions and timing might indicate she'd been waiting for Belknap to leave this room, because she came in immediately after he did.

There was an interior window that looked out on the nonfiction stacks, with a view of the computer terminals. I could see a sliver of an exterior window by twisting to the left, leaning forward, and peering at the sharpest angle possible.

I couldn't imagine Professor Roy doing that maneuver.

I paced the room, looking at the exterior windows on one wall—horizontal and close to the ceiling. Even if Nora Roy had stood on the table, her field of vision would have been mostly straight ahead. In other words over the top of the head of anyone on the sidewalk. Plus, there was that issue of imagining Nora Roy climbing up to stand on the library table.

Then I spotted a slice of window between bookshelves that otherwise blocked it.

The slice gave a direct view of the sidewalk out the front door. So she could have watched her husband leave. Belknap, too, for that matter. But why?

Chapter Twenty-Five

ON THE WAY to the *Independence*'s offices, I emailed Jennifer and asked her to try to find addresses and, better yet, phone numbers for the Cruz family.

I also asked her to try to find out who—if anyone—was registered to receive information about Dean Isaacs' parole status.

Next, I called Diana. She was out on assignment. I left a message saying if she could shake loose at any time this afternoon, I wouldn't mind company.

Company and a second pair of ears to filter and assess what was said. Plus, a second pair of eyes to add a different angle.

My second call was to Mike. I didn't reach him, getting the news from Dale that an interview for a weekend feature had Mike tied up until the five o'clock broadcast.

Then I called Tom.

When he answered with "Hello, Elizabeth" I heard highway noise, so I knew I was on speakerphone, which meant Tamantha was with him. "Need something?"

"Sort of. I just did the math."

"You have math homework over the holidays?" Tamantha asked.

"In a way. I have work to do, and it includes math. Adding up how old people are, who they might have been in school with, things like that."

"That's simple," she said.

"Speak for yourself." Before she could, I continued, "How was your visit with your aunt?"

"It was fun. Even though she wouldn't let me practice with my drone, not even the little one. Too much stuff she didn't want to get broken."

I *tsked* my shared disapproval of such short-sighted fussiness, since it was thwarting genius. "So you had a good Christmas?"

"Yes. Even though Daddy pretended he hadn't gotten me the real drone, when I got a toy one in my stocking."

"Your dad and Santa must have gotten their wires crossed about that, giving you two drones."

"I don't say anything to little kids, but Santa's not real."

"He is to me." It was a line that had let me skirt the issue with many a niece or nephew over the years.

"Elizabeth," she scolded. I envisioned Tamantha's intelligent eyes boring into the phone in lieu of boring into me. The phone was on its own.

"You called about math?" Tom asked mildly.

"Yes. About math, when you graduated from high school, who you knew from high school, and what you failed to mention last night."

"I knew a lot of people from high school." Before I could say more, he added, "Where will you be about supper time? We're going to check on things around the place, do laundry, then I'll be bringing Tamantha in to town. She has a sleepover tonight."

I swear that girl had more social engagements than the most active debutante. The upside was it meant he'd be free to be at tonight's gathering at Diana's.

"No idea where I'll be. Give me a call and we'll see where we both are then."

For now, I was on my own.

AT THE OFFICES of the *Independence*, which maintains its original late Nineteenth Century brick building in front with modern tech in an addition in back, I found Needham and Thelma Bender at his desk, eating lunch.

They saw me through the swath of glass that gave Needham a

window to the lobby, and waved me in.

After hellos, Needham asked, "What brings you here? Or—" His eyes glinted. "—does a who bring you here."

"Not the who you think and actually more of a what."

"Okay, you two, quit trying to out-puzzle each other," Thelma ordered.

Obediently, I said, "We've been trying to find out more about the trial of Dean Isaacs for the murder of Yolanda Cruz, so naturally we turned to the digitized editions of *The Independence*."

The compliment did not turn his head.

"We who? Sure isn't Thurston Fine, because I've never known him to delve into anything that wasn't bright and shiny and shallow. Come to think of it, I've never known him to delve into anything."

"No, not Thurston."

"In other words, your little group."

"That case was so sad," Thelma said. "Yolanda was a lovely person. Laura Roy had her problems those last months, but—"

"Don't all teenagers?" Needham said.

If I'd only been listening to them I wouldn't have picked up anything beyond their bland words. But I'd also caught a sharp look from Needham to his wife. A don't-say-more look.

So now I knew there was more.

"—she was a sweet girl."

Needham, tipping his head at me like a curious gray-haired bird, shifted the subject. "A murder trial from twenty-six years ago over a current death? Interesting."

"You know as well as I do that Isaacs' release makes that story practically brand new. But Jennifer and I can't find anything in the archives."

"Ah." He looked pleased with himself. "Certain of the *Independence*'s back issues didn't make it into being digitized."

"How many?"

"Oh, a handful now and then."

"That's a shame, since that means there's not a continuous record of the paper."

"Wouldn't say that. We have newsprint copies of every issue since the first one rolled off the old press."

"And you've been saving them just for me."

He grinned. "Yup." He pulled out a pair of gloves from a drawer and tossed them at me. "You'll need these."

"To protect the old paper?"

"And for the dust."

HE'D UNDERSOLD THE dust. It was monumental. I spent half my time in the basement room sneezing.

While the papers had much longer accounts of the murder, arrest, and trial, they did not contain any shocks.

The trial had lasted a week.

According to testimony, Isaacs had driven to the Roy-Zblewski ranch house. He had tried to slip in a back entrance at approximately ten-forty-five at night. Yolanda had intercepted him and told him to leave.

It was an "acrimonious" encounter, Professor Roy had testified. She had been drawn by the noise and had first joined Yolanda in demanding he leave. Then, feeling Yolanda had the situation in hand, she had gone to calm her daughter, who was at the top of the nearby staircase, crying. Professor Roy said she had accompanied Laura to her room, then went to bed herself.

Kitty and Graham Young said they'd heard loud voices. By the time they reached the entry, Yolanda, wielding a broom, had repelled Isaacs and locked him out.

They had retired to their rooms.

Graham Young testified to seeing Yolanda walking from the main house just before midnight to her cottage one-hundred yards away.

Zblewski testified seeing Isaacs in his car, driving away from the vicinity of the house. But that was not until nearly two a.m., when Zblewski was returning home from a "business meeting" in Cody.

When the household awoke the next morning, Kitty noted Yolanda's absence first and went to her cottage. Her screams brought her husband and, eventually, her stepfather.

Professor Roy did not respond to the furor at the cottage because she had gone to Laura Roy's room to see if she "was more composed after a good night's sleep" and had found her dead, an apparent suicide. There were pills in her system and a plastic bag over her head.

"This was the only point in her testimony that Nora Roy became emotional," the account noted.

Sure would be hard not to be emotional in those circumstances.

Yolanda had been beaten to death. The attack had started with a broom, though the fatal blow to her temple was delivered with an old-fashioned flat iron she used as a doorstop.

Isaacs' fingerprints were found on the broom handle, along with fibers and hairs. No usable fingerprints were found on the flat iron.

Isaacs did not testify. The defense vigorously attacked Zblewski's account, both on cross-examination and then by calling witnesses who said he'd been thoroughly drunk when he left a bar in Cody shortly after one a.m.

The defense also called an expert witness who said that, while Isaacs' fingerprints were on the broom handle, none of his fingerprints were in the blood on the handle, which he called unusual.

On cross-examination, the prosecutor pounded that it was possible the murderer had switched to the iron to avoid the blood, not realizing he had left fingerprints already.

The jury was out for three hours, including lunch.

To save note-taking, I took photos of a few paragraphs with more detail than I'd found elsewhere.

I also looked at editions from immediately after the murder to right up to the trial.

The only item of interest in those was Professor Roy's adamant insistence that her daughter had not committed suicide. But since there was no sign of forced entry, plus the pills—stolen from her father's medicine cabinet—she'd consumed in a soft drink and the plastic bag over her head showed no one else's fingerprints, the ruling was suicide.

When I came upstairs, I found Thelma in the hallway, across from the door to the basement … almost as if she'd been waiting for me.

Hoping that was true, I went straight to the main question. "Thelma, what kind of problems did Laura Roy have?"

"Oh, the usual, of course. Family, emotional drama." She glanced at me. "Boys."

"Someone other than Dean Isaacs?"

"I wouldn't know about that. He was plenty of trouble all by himself. And bad for her right from the get-go. Some girls are drawn to that sort. And then they get themselves into trouble, too."

"Thelma!" Needham called from his office. "Will you come in here, please?"

She rolled her eyes, grinned, and went.

I followed slowly, hoping he'd think we hadn't encountered each other. I wasn't optimistic about fooling him, but I hoped.

At his open door, I asked, "So, Needham, are there other events where the coverage wasn't digitized?"

"Yup. Here and there."

"You old fox."

"Wasn't me. Previous editor had a secretary who'd been here when he started as a copy boy and she had a file of copies she'd decided shouldn't be available to the public. She kept them out of the microfilm, so they weren't there to be digitized."

"A lot of stories?"

"I wouldn't say that. Ones she felt were sensitive."

Thelma snorted.

Needham and I turned to her.

"It was power with her. All power."

Needham started to chuckle. He stopped at a look from his wife. "I, uh, forgot you and she didn't see eye-to-eye."

Impulsively, I asked, "Any of those have anything to do with Sally Tipton? Something that would explain why she would take in a convicted murderer as a houseguest. I know there's a story behind that. I know it. What I don't know is what that story is. Mrs. Parens isn't talking."

"Sally's harmless," Thelma said.

"And I'm not talking," Needham added. "Not that I have anything to say."

This time it had been Thelma giving the say-no-more orders.

Still, that in itself was a piece of information.

Although, it was information on an issue we weren't exploring.

MIKE HAD CALLED and left a message, clearly regretful, repeating Dale's early account of the news release being addressed generically. "Nothing new there. And I'll still be tied up until after the Five."

This time when I called, I did reach Diana.

Not sounding the least regretful, she said she couldn't join me for the drive to Linda Caswell's ranch.

"It won't be that snowy out there," she added with no sympathy.

"I didn't call you because the back roads are likely to be snowy," I said with dignity.

"Uh-huh. Besides, you'll get more from Linda on your own. You two are practically *compadres*."

I wouldn't have gone that far.

But I was definitely feeling kindly toward Linda Caswell when I saw that the road into her ranch had recently been plowed. That didn't keep snow completely off. The wind saw to that. But it was a lot better than it would have been otherwise.

The house was white, a solid two stories with dormers indicating a third. It was settled into its surroundings with assurance and ease.

I liked it right away.

She offered me tea and cookies in a book-lined room capturing the early afternoon sun.

I said how much I liked the house.

She told me some of its history, which was also family history.

I asked more about the architecture, the workmen, the landscape.

She said, "Elizabeth, you didn't come to look at the house. Ask what you want to ask. I'll answer if I feel I can."

I huffed out a breath. "What a strange way of doing things."

She smiled, transforming herself. "You're adaptable. You'll manage."

I grinned back at her. "Tell me all the back story on the undercurrents at the museum dinner."

This time she laughed. "That story goes back to the first settlement on the East Coast. That was the first domino. No, it goes back before that, because there were a lot of dominoes that fell to set up Jamestown, Virginia in 1608." She grew solemn. "I believe you heard something about that from Professor Roy at the dinner."

"The moving target that is history. Yes, I heard that. How about something a little more current? Say from the time Professor Roy moved her family here."

"Not from when she began to do research here? Oh, wait. Of course, you've talked with Mrs. Parens."

"And Penny."

Another flicker of a smile. "I'm honored to be in that company. Though I'm sorry to disappoint you. My only contact with her or her family was through the museum. I did not know any of them well. Yes, we had numerous meetings over many years, but all of the sort you witnessed the other night."

"You mean when you orchestrated getting away from the professor and her entourage as quickly and smoothly as possible?"

She looked up with a startled frown, then chuckled. "You are observant. I hope no one else…"

"Not that I saw. It was very smooth. Both you and Grayson. A well-oiled machine."

She smiled, as she often did at the mention of the rodeo cowboy. Then the smile faded. "There is something…"

Hot dog. I'd take anything right now.

She said, "On the phone, you asked me to think back about any encounters with Professor Roy, her family, or associates. I did. And I have remembered something."

Often this was how it worked. You asked and asked and asked questions with few or no useful answers being returned. Then one of those seeds you'd cast widely takes root and poof, there's a seedling to explore.

Plus, there was the fact that she was telling me rather than Tom. It wasn't a competition—really—but I did appreciate that token of her trust in me.

"I don't... I'm not entirely comfortable with this, repeating something I overheard, but under the circumstances of Professor Roy's death..."

I didn't try to sell her or rush her. Neither would work with her.

I also didn't say we were more interested in the deaths of Yolanda Cruz and Laura Roy from twenty-six years ago.

She pulled in a breath. "I overheard Professor Belknap and Jasmine Uffelman talking after the museum dinner."

Her pause seemed to call for some response. "Oh?" was all I had. I would have sworn I didn't have an expectation of what she might tell me, but this was definitely not what I'd expected, so I must have expected something.

"I'm not as good at this as you are—I mean reporting. I didn't mean to imply that you—"

"Overhear things?" I laughed. "I do. Every chance I get. It's a skill that serves me well in my occupation. Like reading upside down, sometimes upside down and backward."

"Upside down and backw—? Okay. Never mind. Tell me another time. I only have a minute and I think you will want to hear this. I was standing just inside the cloak room. Grayson had gone to the back to get our coats. They must have been standing around the corner, by the doors to the restrooms."

She wasn't too shabby at this reporting thing. I knew precisely where she meant.

"He—Bruce Belknap was speaking. I recognized his voice immediately, then caught the end of it. Something about 'not difficult for heaven's sake.' He might not have used those words, but that's the gist.

"Then Jasmine Uffelman, the graduate student who works with him—" In response to a question mark in her voice, I nodded. "—said, 'If you'd just tell me where—'

"Belknap said, 'No. It must be natural. Organic.' I'm sure of that. Natural and organic.

"She said, 'But with what she said, it's urgent now.'

"He said, 'I'll take care of that. You do your part.' Then either they heard Grayson approaching from the back of the cloak room or they moved away, because I didn't hear anything else."

"Even though you didn't hear specific words, did you have an impression of what they were talking about—don't think, don't censor, say it. Whatever comes into your head."

"I'm not censoring, because there's nothing, Elizabeth. Truly, I have no idea."

I wasn't convinced, but I was sure *she* was convinced.

"Go back for a second, Linda. After Belknap said no, he wouldn't tell her 'where' and he used the words natural and organic, how sure are you of what Jasmine Uffelman said?"

She gave it a moment's thought. "I'm sure she said, 'it's urgent now.' As for the first part, the sense of it is correct. She might have used a different phrase. 'In light of what she said' or 'as a result of what she said,' maybe. Though neither of those really sounds like her."

"I agree. That's good, Linda. So you're sure of the two important beats of that—that Jasmine said it was urgent now and that the urgency stemmed from something 'she' said, whoever 'she' was."

"Yes. Certain."

"Okay. And the last part, what he said in response?

"That I'm sure of. He said he would take care of it—"

Take care of the urgency ... or the 'she' who caused it?

"—and she should do her part."

I didn't realize there'd been a pause until Linda spoke again.

"Do you have any idea what it might mean?" she asked almost tentatively.

Idea? No. But questions? Yes. Lots and lots of questions.

Chapter Twenty-Six

I HAD MY hand on my SUV's door handle when a familiar pickup came around the bend in the ranch road and pulled in next to me.

When the driver emerged, I said, "Hi, Tom."

"Elizabeth. What are you doing here?" He looked at the window of the sunny room as he spoke.

I turned and saw a curtain moving ... as if someone had just walked away from it.

"Had some questions I hoped Linda could answer."

"Did she?"

"No. But she had something else. I'll tell you all together tonight. What about you? What are you doing here?"

He glanced at the house again. "Stopping by to say hello."

That was a lie.

Holy moly. I'd recognized Tom Burrell was telling a lie. It was like figuring out Mount Rushmore was telling a lie.

"Really? You just happened to stop by now?"

He huffed out a breath, then grinned. "No. Linda called as I dropped Tamantha off at tonight's sleepover, asked me to come by. I swear, none of these kids are spending a single night at home during the Christmas break except for when they're the host."

Linda was matchmaking. But we weren't talking about that. "When is it your turn to be host?"

"I got it over with during the fall break. Every darned girl she invited came. I'd been counting on no-shows keeping the volume down. Thought I'd go deaf."

"Tamantha is an amazing kid. I'm just astonished her peers recognize it at that young an age."

His smile started slow and grew even slower. It wasn't until it was almost full width that he said, "Mostly, they don't recognize it. Not completely. But their parents do. And they're hoping it rubs off."

"Speaking of schoolmates, what do you remember about Laura Roy?"

"I knew of her, I'd recognize her, but I didn't know her. That's why I didn't mention it. Nothing to tell you. She was a year ahead and did different things."

So his photo would have been in those next yearbooks I hadn't had a chance to look at. "You weren't in the theater crowd?"

He smiled slightly. "I did sports, then I got home as fast as I could for ranch work."

"Your father insisted on that?"

"He mostly worked on the road construction company. The ranch needed more attention than he gave it."

I heard an echo of Mike's voice talking about his father and their family ranch.

Since I'd arrived in Sherman, I'd heard a fair amount about some members of the next generation not wanting to carry on family ranches but this was another aspect of it, with a younger generation working hard to hold on to them. That's if you counted Tom or Mike—or me—as the younger generation.

Although, the idea of Tamantha giving up the Circle B didn't fly.

"Is that why you're running it now? Because he wasn't that interested in it? Or because he reached retirement age?"

His smile flickered deeper, then disappeared. "There's no retirement age in ranching. That might be why my father preferred the road construction company. He hit sixty-five and he wanted golf, sun, and never up before sun-up. That's what they went after, that's what they have now."

It struck me as sad that they didn't have much contact with their granddaughter, however. Or their son.

Families. Complex creatures, aren't they?

"As for Laura Roy, I didn't know any more about her than you do now, even if I was in school with her."

"The last year she was in the yearbook, there were casual pictures of her where she looked like she had earlier—young, shy, pretty, sweet—but her individual picture was entirely different."

Slowly, he nodded, a frown gathering. "Yeah, I remember that. She started the school year like her usual self. It was some time in the early spring that she made that transformation."

"Early spring? But yearbook portraits are usually taken in the fall. It's backward. How did that happen?"

"Can't help you there. And by the time it came out, she was dead, Yolanda Cruz was dead, and Dean Isaacs was heading to trial."

"What did the kids at school think happened to her?"

"Everything from aliens killed her to she and Dean murdered Yolanda together then Dean killed her to cover it up, or then she regretted it and was going to tell on him, so he killed her to cover that up. With stops in between that would make even you say they were being paranoid."

"What do you mean even me?"

"Seeing murders everywhere."

"I've been right, haven't I? Besides, Mike and Diana see them, too." I considered that. "And sometimes it's so obvious even *you* see it's murder."

"Touché. But this time there was a trial and a conviction and a sentence served. Are you telling me you think Isaacs was innocent?"

"No." Hmm. No hesitation there. So, my gut was definitely saying he was not innocent. "But something's tugging at me."

"What?"

Elbows tucked, I snapped my open-fingered hands in the air between us. "You don't think I'd say if I knew? You always want the answers, Burrell, when I'm just figuring out that I have questions."

He held my eyes for an extra two beats.

Subtle, Burrell. Might as well shout that we were now double-tracking this discussion. Text and subtext.

"You always have questions. At some point you have to come up with answers." Slowly, he added, "Or won't you?"

I felt a hitch. In my breathing or maybe in my heartbeat. Worse, I felt a rush of heated moisture in my eyes.

He gripped my shoulder and that made it worse.

I knew what he wanted. I knew what Mike wanted.

I wanted it, too. Even if it was contradictory, because both of them, each of them… Oh, hell. It wasn't possible.

I knew some people, including some who cared about me, thought I was behind schedule with moving on. Sorry, folks. If I could snap my fingers and be back to who I was eighteen months ago…

I wouldn't.

Which was surprising and exhilarating.

And perhaps why, if I could snap my fingers and be who I would become in the next eighteen months I wouldn't do that either.

I was taking this journey as it came along.

Most of the time I wanted things to stay as they were. Sometimes, I wanted more. Sometimes, none of it, wanting to be on my own.

Except *not* on my own. Because I had friends—friends I was learning to turn to instead of closing off.

Diana, Shadow, Jennifer.

Mike and Tom.

"You can give up on me." My voice came out low. I was looking up, trying to keep tears from falling.

He was silent. A long, long time. Finally, with my back to the house, I dashed at the moisture at the corners of my eyes and looked at him.

"How are you going to figure out what's tugging at you?" he asked.

Still double-tracking. I nodded acknowledgement of that. "Keep moving ahead. It's gotten me this far."

Moving ahead. Not moving on.

He looked down, leaving nothing visible of his face. "Okay." I didn't know if that word was acceptance or something else. Especially when he continued, "I'm not any help with Laura. But when I leave here, I'm supposed to meet up with a few folks who might remember better for a drink."

"Then you better go, huh?"

"Yeah. See you at Diana's tonight."

"See you tonight."

DIANA HAD CALLED while I was with Linda. When I called her back, she said she'd be free unexpectedly early, because her last assignment had fallen through and KWMT-TV owed her enough vacation time for her to stroll around the globe a time or two.

I said I'd meet her at Sally Tipton's and to bring her camera—her camera, not the station's.

As I pulled up to Sally's house, another call came through. I parked, then answered, "Hi, Jennifer."

"I've got the names of Yolanda's kids."

"Yolanda and Arturo's children? Mrs. P told us. An obituary listed them, too."

"You mean you've already got all their names?" She sounded disappointed.

"Yes. But that's still good work, Jennifer. And when you come back from the holidays, we'll compare methods."

"Okay. I don't suppose you want to know the grandkids' names?" Definitely disappointed.

"Hold on to the grandkids' names. Just in case. But for now tell me what else you've got."

"Not much. I found Arturo. Yolanda's husband."

"You did?" When she got back we were also going to talk about burying the lead. "I had no success with him at all. That's great."

"Yeah, he's in Colorado." She'd perked up. "Looks like he lives with a married daughter's family, which made it harder to find because of the different last names. I found a number for Maria Guadalupe in Deer Forks. Along with what looks like her husband and kids, the listing included Arturo Cruz, age 85, at the same address."

"Good for you, but—"

"I didn't hack anything," she said before I could voice that concern. I must be getting predictable. "I keep telling you there's lots out there. Each of the sites only gives you a little piece, hoping you'll pay them for a complete report. But why should I pay? I add pieces from this one to pieces from that one to pieces from a third and then go back with those pieces and pick up a few more. So, I have a list of family members. His kids and it looks like a sister, which made her Yolanda Cruz's sister-in-law. There's something weird about the sister-in-law's family. It was on genealogy sites—"

I felt as if my eyes were rolling back in my head. It's not that I didn't appreciate history and ancestors. I just associated them too closely with Grandmother Danniher's pop quizzes on great-greats and cousins once removed. Or was it twice removed?

"Wait a minute," I got in quickly. "Let's get the rundown on Yolanda and Arturo's family before we go into a sister-in-law's weirdness."

"Okay. Yolanda and Arturo have five kids. Arturo Junior, Teresa, Maria Guadalupe, Sylvia, and Javier. Maria Guadalupe is the one he lives with. She's married to Ralph, who—"

"Do we need to know that?"

She considered. "Maybe not. I needed the husband's name to get the address and phone number, though."

"Phone numbers are great. Send those to me, will you? You hold on to how you tracked it down and if we need to recreate that later, you'll have it. But for now, if we can keep on the narrow path? Diana's going to get here any minute."

"Sure. As I said, Arturo Senior lives with Maria Guadalupe. Arturo Junior's working for a construction company, Teresa and Sylvia are nurses, Javier's a lawyer with a big firm. They're all around Denver. I'll email you everything I've got."

The email arrived as we hung up.

With Diana not in sight yet, I called the number Jennifer had for Maria Guadalupe.

"Hello?" said a cautious voice.

"Hello, does Arturo Cruz live there?"

"What is this about?"

Four words made it clear that if I hit this woman straight-on, she might hang up. If I came in at too wide an angle, however, she'd definitely hang up.

"My name is Elizabeth Margaret Danniher. I'm KWMT-TV's 'Helping Out' correspondent in Sherman, Wyoming."

"Sherman?"

At that apparently involuntary repetition, I heard a voice in the background. An elderly, male voice raised in questioning.

She didn't respond to him. Ignoring him? Or gesturing him to silence.

"Yes. I'm calling for comment from the family of Yolanda Cruz."

"Comment about what?"

"Were you not notified of the release of Dean Isaacs from prison? If you registered as a family member you should have received notification."

"Registered? Why should we register? The scum got life and no possibility of parole. That's what the judge said. I heard him. How could he be released? How—?"

I didn't interrupt her. She simply stopped.

But the man in the background was still speaking.

"We have no comment," she said.

She hung up.

That certainly could have gone better, but I didn't come away completely dry.

Like a lot of other people, I studied Spanish in school, but don't really speak it. My best sentence is *No me gusta albondigas,* which means *I don't like meatballs.* That's not real useful, especially since I do like meatballs.

I have retained some understanding. I'm better at reading it than listening to it, but even listening I can catch some. Especially nouns, for some reason. Arturo had said *hijo,* not *hija*—that's son, rather than daughter.

And another word he'd said had been *nieta.* Granddaughter.

✧   ✧   ✧   ✧

THE BAD NEWS was I hadn't gotten much from Maria Guadalupe.

The good news was she'd left me time to make another call before the close of business at a Denver law firm.

I identified myself to the smooth, confident voice, and shared my desire to talk to Javier Cruz. It had taken me two steps to get to this administrative assistant.

"I'm afraid that will not be——"

"——from KWMT-TV of Sherman, Wyoming."

"One moment." She put me on hold without asking my permission the way the lesser mortals on the firm's phone tree had.

But she was forgiven, because when she came back on, she said, "Hold one moment for Mr. Cruz."

Again, she didn't wait for a response, but who was I to gripe when she was giving me what I wanted.

"Ms. Danniher? My assistant said you're a consumer affairs reporter? There must be some mistake. I don't practice in that area."

And yet he took my call.

Must have been the magic of the name Sherman, Wyoming.

"I am a consumer affairs reporter for KWMT-TV in Sherman, Wyoming, Mr. Cruz. However, I am calling about the release of Dean Isaacs."

"The man who killed my mother."

That came in a very different voice.

"The man who was convicted of killing your mother."

He didn't respond to that prod. I suspected he was too focused to be detoured. "He was never supposed to be released. Ever."

"The Supreme Court thought otherwise."

"Yes." There was a brief silence. "That is the end of it as far as I am concerned."

Really? His tone said otherwise.

"Actually, I wasn't calling for a comment on that." *Keep him talking, Danniher. Keep him talking.* "I was hoping you could give me background on the events surrounding your mother's murder. You knew Professor Roy's family, didn't you?"

"They employed my mother. What makes you think I'd know them?"

I hadn't, not really. At least not consciously. But that tinge of wariness had me thinking otherwise.

"Well, Professor Roy got you that college scholarship that started you on the life you have now."

"Yes, she did that."

"Mr. Cruz—"

"No. I am not part of your story, Ms. Danniher. Good day."

I knew that click.

One of a reporter's least favorite sounds.

On the other hand, Diana had arrived in the Newsmobile.

Chapter Twenty-Seven

DEAN ISAACS ANSWERED our knock at Sally's back door.

That ended the hope of pumping her about his movements.

Also the hope of confirming what my eyes had told me as we walked up the driveway and past the deep, deep blue car that looked almost black.

The car Sally had described when I asked what Isaacs was driving was her own. On the front passenger seat of the otherwise pristine interior, there was an empty cigarette carton and fast-food wrappers.

Making the best of the situation, I smiled and said we'd hoped to talk to both of them.

"Of course, of course," Sally fluttered from the background. "Although I don't know what I could possibly tell—"

Isaacs cut across her. "I'm busy." But he didn't leave us, and a speculative gleam came into his eyes when he spotted the camera Diana carried.

"What are you doing?" I looked at the buffet of tools set out on an opened newspaper on the counter.

"Helping Sally."

"I heard you planned to go to the hardware store for supplies yesterday."

He shrugged slightly. "Decided against that until I know exactly what I'm dealing with. I like making one trip to get everything I need. And I like making one fix that takes care of lots and lots of problems. Efficient they call that."

"What fix are you making now?"

"Putting in a door stopper for that bathroom door. Doesn't sound like much, but it has to be an especially long one because the heater's behind the door. Right now when the door's open, it blocks the heat from the room. You could freeze your ass before you're done taking a—" His lopsided, smirky grin came. "Before you're done. Only starts warming up in there when you're getting ready to leave after taking a shower. With this long door stopper, there'll be room between the door and the heater, so some heat will circulate. And it'll keep the door from hitting that heater, knocking off its cover every time, so that means towels can be stacked on it—warmed towels, how do you like that?—making room on the shelves for me to keep my things."

"Oh, that's nice. Isn't it? Don't you think that's nice, Elizabeth?" Sally fluttered. "Warmed towels will be so … uh, nice."

"Very nice," I said, deadpan. I hadn't missed the inference that having a shelf for his things made him more and more settled in Sally's house.

His smirk widened. "Sort of an investment in my future. Keeping this place in good order. For Sally, of course. And, maybe, one day for me, since she doesn't have any other kin and us being family and all."

Sally shrank farther back into the corner created by the counter-topped cabinets. Her clasped hands pressed against her chest. She muttered, "We're not, we're not."

"Family?" My head tip reinforced the skepticism in my voice, all aimed at Isaacs.

"Yup. Like I told you the other day, I researched it. Got it right and tight. Paperwork and all. Course, I wouldn't want to air dirty linen in public—not unless I'm forced to. It's that family feeling, you know."

Yeah, I knew.

I knew it was blackmail. I also knew Sally not only wouldn't take the risk of calling his bluff, she'd walk on eggshells around him.

Never a respecter of eggshells, I said, "Speaking of family, I under-stand Laura Roy's family was not happy about your association with her."

Something like genuine emotion flickered, but before I could iden-tify it, his smirk resumed prominence. "They forced us apart, just like

Romeo and Juliet. There was a girl in that story who killed herself, too, because her family got all high and mighty and kept them apart."

"His family did, too. Romeo's, I mean. The two heartbroken families came together in the end."

"Yeah, well, my family didn't give a shit. I looked out for myself from the beginning. But Laura loved me. Loved me so much she couldn't live with the fact that her family was going to send her away from me. Off to some school in another state to make sure she never saw me again. She couldn't take that they were trying to keep us apart, so she killed herself. Because I was her one true love. Served her friggin' family right." Though he didn't say "frigging."

"Casting you in the role of Romeo?"

"That's right."

"Dean, do you know what happens to Romeo in the play? He kills himself. He finds Juliet, thinks she's dead and he kills himself from heartbreak."

"What a jackass," he muttered.

Spurred by anger, I smiled professionally at him and tromped on a few more eggshells. "As long as we're here, and since you seem to be taking a break from your labors, we'd like your comments on the recent news."

Not waiting for his response, I nodded to Diana, and she raised the camera.

Without checking that she was rolling—I knew she would be—I asked, "Dean Isaacs, what's your reaction to the death of Professor Roy?"

He stopped, but remained half facing away. "Why should I?"

I decided to take that as why should he have a reaction, rather than why should he talk to us.

"You were involved with Professor Roy's daughter, Laura, in the months before her death twenty-six years ago. That level of connection would be enough for most people to react to an individual's unexpected death." Nothing changed in his face or posture. Repeating the facts so they'd be available for sound bites, I added, "In addition, you were convicted of murdering Professor Roy's housekeeper, Yolanda

Cruz, and spent twenty-five years in prison for the crime before your recent release."

He turned back toward me, but he was looking past me, fully into the camera. "What have I got to say about Professor Roy that everybody made such a big deal of? That everybody ran scared of? I'll tell you. Instead of boo-hooing about her being dead, what they should look at is where she was when that woman was beaten to death. I know where I was and it wasn't bashing in the head of that cleaner woman. Had no reason to. Laura was running away with me. That very night, she was running away with me. I waited and waited, but she didn't come. Because she killed herself when that bitch of a mother of hers said she'd do whatever she had to do to keep us apart. And she did, didn't she?"

"What did Professor Roy do?"

"I told you. Whatever she had to do to keep Laura and me from running off together."

"Are you—? Are you saying Professor Roy killed Yolanda Cruz? And did so to keep you and Laura Roy apart? But how could she have known—?"

"Look at what happened. That's what you've gotta do, look at what happened. Cleaner woman gets killed and I get sent away. Just what that big-shot professor wanted."

"But her daughter—" I cut off the involuntary objection that her daughter's suicide certainly couldn't have been what Nora Roy wanted. *Let him talk. Keep him talking.*

"I didn't do that crime, but I sure as hell did that time. How's that for a joke? Ha-ha. But it gave me plenty of time to figure it all out. To figure out exactly what happened. And I did. I surely did. And now I've got the proof."

"What proof?"

For the first time, he shifted his lopsided smirk from the camera to me. "You think I'm going to tell you? No way."

He turned away from the camera. On the way past the counter, he picked up a drill in one hand and a hammer in the other, humming the tune about whistling while you work.

Chapter Twenty-Eight

DIANA, PARTIALLY HAMPERED by the camera, and I, with no such impediment, dragged Sally outside.

"But it's cold—"

My usual sympathy for such a complaint, especially with the sun gone and only cold twilight left, waned under more urgent issues. "Sally, did you hear what he said about *someday* possibly getting your house?"

"Of course I heard, but it made no sense. It's my house."

Perhaps because she heard my teeth grinding, Diana stepped in. "Listen to us. No matter what he says or does or asks, do *not* change your will to benefit Dean Isaacs."

"I'd be an idiot to do that." Surprise temporarily blew away fluff, making Sally's voice crisp and certain. It wasn't the first time I'd witnessed that, still it knocked me sideways. It was like someone suddenly turning off Niagara Falls, revealing all the rock behind the veils of mist and water. But the flow turned back on almost immediately. She blinked at us. "I mean, whyever would I do that? My will's all set and James Longbaugh has it nice and neat."

"Isaacs is going to start bugging you," I said. "He won't let up. Do you understand that? To change your will or put his name on the deed to your house or put the title of your car into his—What? The car?"

The fluff was back in full force. "Well, it's true I don't drive very much and he did take the car to the hardware store, though he says he needs to go again to really start repairs around here. I didn't know the hardware store stays open that late, but he is fixing things. In the bathroom, for instance. The door and making it so it will be warmer in there, but also door handles that were loose, and a drawer in the kitchen that wasn't closing right. It wouldn't be right not to be grateful for all that. It wouldn't be natural. I am grateful to him. And there's the practical, too—with him running errands for me—"

"You didn't. Tell me you didn't already change it."

"No." That came out wobbly. "I told him I'd think about it. But, he does bring it up a lot and I don't know what to say to him."

"Tell him to get lost," I suggested. I knew it was useless even before Diana frowned at me. She was right. As Mrs. P had said, Sally Tipton endured by giving way. Standing up to Dean Isaacs was not in her repertoire.

Diana said, "What if you told James Longbaugh that you need some help and ask him to make sure you keep your car and your will as they are now? Then you say to Isaacs or anyone else that your lawyer's in charge of all that and they need to talk to him."

Sally brightened at that. "You think James would do that?"

"I'm sure he would if Mrs. Parens and Gisella Decker went with you to ask him," Diana said.

I was impressed. I hadn't given Diana credit for that much deviousness.

James Longbaugh wasn't going to know what hit him.

AFTER A QUICK consultation, we decided Diana would return to the station with her tape alone. My presence could only lessen its chances of it being run.

Without News Director Les Haeburn on hand—and sometimes when he was—Thurston ran roughshod over the producers who were supposed to make such decisions.

With Thurston making the decision, I was a liability.

In the meantime, I would hit the grocery store for tonight's goodies and another shot at Penny's storehouse of knowledge.

Bad, bad timing.

Apparently, I'd dropped in to the Sherman Supermarket at the height of the mid-holidays groceries buying binge. There were people, mostly women, everywhere. Including being backed up at Penny's line.

So much for worming more out of her.

With a heavy heart I did the only thing I could do. I grabbed a cart and started shopping.

At least I could replenish Diana's stock of snacks from the ravages of our gatherings.

Ten minutes later, I heard, "Hi, Elizabeth. How are you?"

I'm usually focused on what I'm buying, but since I happened to be in the salad dressing and pickle aisle, rather than the cookie aisle— I'd gone there first—it wasn't a major surprise that I'd recognized Marcia Odom from our meeting two days ago even before she said hello.

What was a surprise was that I now recognized her from some-where else, too—the Cottonwood County High School Yearbook.

"Why, hello, Marcia. I just was looking at your photo in the year-book."

"*My* yearbook picture? Oh, you mean when I was teaching. Good heavens, how did you come to see that?" I didn't bother answering because she wasn't really interested. "That was a million years ago."

"You knew Laura Roy then, didn't you?"

"Oh, my goodness. Imagine you bringing that up. I hadn't thought about it for ages, but of course with her mother dying in that horrible accident—carbon monoxide, I hear. I keep telling the kids how important it is that they pay attention. My Don had them out at the beginning of the season giving them lessons on not letting the engine run without being absolutely sure there's plenty of space for the exhaust. Can't have it pushing back in to the car. No running the car with the garage doors closed—I can't believe the professor did that."

I didn't interrupt her flow to say it was actually a generator at fault.

"The silent killer, they call it," she said with wide eyes. "They say you get sleepier and sleepier and even if you realize what's happening, you can't do anything to save yourself. That poor family. First Laura— their housekeeper, too, of course—and now the professor. How much can they bear?"

"Funny you should bring up Laura, Marcia," I started, hoping that if I made it sound like it had been her topic that she'd stick with it. "I saw her yearbook photos at the same time I saw yours. Looked like you two had a real connection."

"We did. Which made it all the more tragic. I could hardly—"

"She changed a lot in a short time, didn't she? I mean, it looked like that from the photos. Of course, you were there and knew her and had a connection, so you'd know much better. Did she go through a transition during her sophomore year?"

"Oh, yes. Day and night, it was. Practically overnight. Spring of that year. Over the break. She left one girl and came back as another. And then, by the start of school the next fall she was gone. So tragic. Such a loss. When I came back in the fall—I'd been working at Yellowstone over the summer—and I heard that she'd died over the summer, I couldn't stop crying. Crying and crying and crying. I told the other teachers—"

"Here's what I don't understand about her photos in the year-book—" It was a small thing, but sometimes small things nag. You have to clear them out so there's room for big things. Plus, it would keep the conversation on Laura's life and death, not Marcia's feelings. "—The candid photos and the activity photos show her the way she looked the previous year. It's her portrait that shows a major change. But portraits are done early in the school year, right? So if she changed over spring break, how did her new look get into the yearbook?"

She looked at me without expression. I was about to try another way to explain, when the light switched on.

"Oh, I remember. My goodness, I'd totally forgotten all that. There was *such* an uproar, too. If you'd told me then that I'd ever forget I'd say you were crazy, because it turned the school upside down. All the individual photos were wiped out of the computer system—all of them, senior portraits, underclassmen, everybody. Not only the system at the school, either, but backups at the photography company. The company said it had never happened before, not in decades and decades of doing high school yearbooks. But it happened to Cotton-wood County High." She laughed. "They had to retake all the photographs. Every single one. The yearbook didn't actually come out until the following fall."

She was clearly satisfied with herself for clearing up that mystery for me. A vague feeling of deflation made me push for something more. "Did they figure out what happened?"

"Oh, yes. Everyone was quite certain who had done it. Dean Isaacs."

Nobody was more surprised than me when a minor question bugging me leads to a connection. But it happened far too often to ever ignore a minor question bugging me.

"Really? He could do that sort of thing? I knew he was good with cars—uh, vehicles—but..." Of course. Vehicles had become more and more computer dependent over the years. "He was good with other computers? Regular computers?"

"Oh, yes. All electronics, really. They tried to get him to help with the plays—you know, lighting and sound, but he lasted about a day. I think that's how he and Laura met. Computer class was the only thing he wasn't failing. Not that he got a good grade in that class, either. But I was dating the teacher who had him in a computer class at that time and Dean was a whiz with tech."

Dean Isaacs had tech skills.

I wasn't sure what that meant in the scheme of things, but it was worth remembering.

"Suspicion centered on him pretty quickly. He said Laura was his alibi, that they were together when the intrusion occurred. By then he'd been in a lot of trouble. Even without proof it was the straw that broke the camel's back. He was finally expelled."

"What kind of trouble had he been in?"

"Fighting. That's how it ended, anyhow. How it started was he slapped Laura across the face. Hard."

She seemed prepared to stop there.

That wasn't going to happen.

"She turned him in?"

"Oh, no. She never would have turned him in. At the beginning, she was ... besotted. That was around spring break. It broke my heart to see her disintegrate right before my eyes. One minute she's this normal, bubbly girl. The next she's withdrawn and silent and so very, very angry."

"Angry? But if she was besotted… Was it all from her connection to Dean Isaacs?"

"It must have been. It was the only thing that changed. She started seeing him and *boom*, she changed. I did try to get her to talk to me that spring, but she wouldn't. After I said something about Dean—just the mildest question about whether he was really a good person for her to be around, she wouldn't talk to me at all. I tried when he was expelled. I thought with him not around as much there might be a chance, but she shut me out. Except…"

"Except what?"

She delicately chewed on the side of her thumbnail. "The last day of school. I couldn't tell you exactly what she said, except something about now everything was going to be different. But I thought maybe she was bouncing back. I had hope—I was really optimistic that come fall she'd be back to herself. I left for Yellowstone the next day and that whole summer was crazy with the guy I was dating and—"

"The fight," I slid in before I was treated to a rundown of her romantic history. "If Laura didn't turn him in for slapping her, how did Dean get in trouble for it?"

"Oh, a couple of the older boys went to her aid and Dean went after them."

"Who were they?"

She lifted her shoulders. "They were upperclassmen. I didn't know them. That first year I mostly knew the kids in my classes. I only knew about it because it involved Laura Roy. They stopped him from hitting her. There was a scuffle, then…" She put a palm to her jaw. "There was something. I don't remember exactly what. He pulled a knife? Or hit one of them with a rock? Something like that." She took out her ringing phone. "Something that made it more serious or—Oh, I have to get this."

"One final question. Who were her friends, before the transition and after?"

"None after. Before? There was a group that hung out together. Um… a Mary, I think. And a Sue. Yes, I'm sure about the Sue. Oh, and a CeeCee. Though last names… Sorry." She grimaced at the screen. "Kids."

I nodded my understanding and mouthed, "See you later."

She gave a wave with her free hand, while she told the screen, "Stop shouting. I can't understand what you're saying your brother did that's not fair."

A *Mary*, possibly, and a *Sue* without last names.

Great.

Though, if CeeCee wasn't a nickname, maybe that would be a lead.

Could the yearbooks be cross-referenced for photos with Laura in them and note any other names with hopes of finding CeeCee, Mary, Sue, and possibly more? That would be a fun search.

Was it mean to wish Jennifer's vacation was over?

I WAS WHISKED through Penny's line with distressing speed. The only meat sandwiched between her greeting and dismissal was:

"Saw you chatting with Marcia Odom. Wanted to be one of the kids herself that one. That's why they liked her, not best for them, though. Same with parents wanting to be friends with their kids. What they need is parents. Grown up parents. Poor girl, poor girl. A lot to take in all at once for a young girl. Threw her for such a loop. Clear as day. All that nonsense. And with him. Not at all like before. Not the real thing, just swinging wild and the first thing she lit on. Still and all, might have come out of it with time, but never had a chance. None of them did. Maybe never will."

And with that I was out the end of the line with my order.

Chapter Twenty-Nine

AT DIANA'S, AFTER the five o'clock news, Diana and Mike filled the rest of us in about the newsroom drama when Thurston hadn't wanted to run the clip.

He'd argued that it was sensationalism.

"It's sensational all right," Mike said. "Because it's news. That's what I told him. 'You can't *not* run it, Thurston.' And everybody agreed. Still it was hard. Without Haeburn there—what is it with his disappearing all the time?—Thurston tried to pull the I'm-in-charge crap. Finally, he saw reason. Though not until the end of the C block. The idiot."

Despite being buried deep into the newscast, it was sure to be what people buzzed about tomorrow.

It would reach beyond Cottonwood County, because Audrey—bless her growing news chops—had let other Wyoming stations, as well as those in Colorado and Montana, know about it.

"What I don't get is why Isaacs said that on camera in the first place," Tom said.

"I know," Mike agreed. "Other than being crazy, why would he do that?"

"It wasn't crazy," I said slowly. "I don't know what the reason was, but there was nothing impulsive about it. He did it deliberately."

"The family was devastated and this punk goes on about how the girl couldn't live without him," Diana grumbled. She and I had filled them in on Isaacs' take on Romeo and Juliet.

Tom said slowly, "He has a lot of ego invested in her killing herself over him."

"That's sick. And then to try to put Yolanda's murder on to Professor Roy?" Mike shook his head.

"Yeah, he was definitely trying to blame her, now that she's dead," I said. "But if he didn't kill Yolanda, why didn't he present a better defense at the trial or any time since then? Or find a way to refute Vic Zblewski's testimony that he saw Isaacs leaving the area hours after he was told to get out."

"Secret meeting with Laura?" speculated the mother of two teenagers.

"Then why didn't he say so?"

"The good sense to know how it would look using the dead girl as his alibi? Or his lawyer's good sense to know that? Or guilt that he was with Laura right before she killed herself?"

I looked up at that last suggestion of Mike's.

"Like he should have known and stopped her?" Diana asked.

I shook my head and sighed. "Sorry. None of those are very satisfying. We'll come back to that later. Tom, were you ever involved in a fight in high school that got the other boy in trouble?"

His eyebrows went up. "Where'd that come from?"

"I heard about a fight that got Dean Isaacs in a lot of trouble that spring. He was harassing Laura and two upperclassmen came to her rescue and had a fight with him."

He shook his head. "I was a freshman the only year he was there. Didn't have anything to do with him."

I'd known he wasn't an upperclassman then. So, why had I thought...?

Because rescuing a damsel in danger—whether she wanted to be rescued or not, whether she knew she was in danger or not—was such a Thomas David Burrell thing to do.

He was continuing, "I remember it being talked about, though."

"Do you? Who were the guys? They might be able to tell us more about it. Maybe it would shed some light on what was going on in Laura's life, help explain why she committed suicide."

He was back to the head-shaking. "I don't remember who was

involved. Just the rough outline of what happened. Too bad the Lawtons aren't in town," he said of Jennifer's family. Her father and Tom had been friends since childhood. "One of them might remember."

"I can text her to ask them." I pulled out my phone.

"Better not. They'll figure out what she's been up to and won't be happy."

I put the phone away.

"I'll add that to the things I'm asking around about," he said. "I didn't get much today. With her list of assignments, Diana asked me to talk to her sister, but her friendship with Laura had faded well before high school. She recommended a couple people to try and I talked to a few more I could think of, but I didn't find anyone who knew Laura or Isaacs well. She was quiet and most kids stayed away from him. He—"

My phone rang. I glanced at the screen.

"I didn't arrange this, I swear. Jennifer," I announced to the room, then repeated it as a greeting when I answered the video call.

"You're meeting, aren't you? You're all at Diana's and talking over the murder of Professor Roy, aren't you? I know you are."

"We are at Diana's and we are talking, but no one knows if Professor Roy was murdered. Besides, we're asking questions about what happened twenty-six years ago."

"Now you sound like Shelton. What have you all said so far? Put me on."

I faced my phone toward the rest of them. After hellos and belated Merry Christmases, she demanded a recap.

"We were just getting to that. I was asking Tom—" Just in time I veered away from the fight questions, which she might ask her parents about, which would make them not happy with how she was spending her holidays. "—about Laura's friends from high school, but he doesn't remember. I'm hoping you might be able to get something."

I gave her the few clues Marcia Odom had shared, plus the information about the yearbooks.

"A lot of yearbooks are online. I'll see what I can get. What else have you done?" she asked.

"Mike and I went to see Professor Young. That's Professor Roy's son-in-law, Graham Young. Mike, you want to fill everyone in?"

He obliged, including answering a couple questions from Diana.

At the end, I said, "You know what's interesting? Clara—Clara Atwood, the curator at the history museum—introduced them at Tuesday night's dinner as Professor Roy's daughter and son-in-law, Kitty and Graham Young. Then she added that he was a professor of history, too."

"Why's that interesting? He is. They are," Mike said.

"What's interesting is she viewed them within the context of their relationship to the professor, not in their own right. She gave the relationships first—"

"I get it," Jennifer said. "She—that's Clara—said the daughter first because she was closer to the professor, then the son-in-law and then their names, and only last what the guy does."

"Exactly. Even though the son-in-law is in the same business."

"Where does that get us?" Diana asked.

I sighed. "Nowhere."

"Here's something else that gets us nowhere," Mike said. "I went back to the campus this afternoon."

"I thought you were tied up with an interview."

"I squeezed out some time."

"And got Dale to lie for you?"

He shrugged. "I talked to Mrs. Eldercott—you saw her, Elizabeth—she was Professor Roy's assistant, which left only a little time to do things for the rest of the professors in that section. She wouldn't say anything bad about Roy, but clearly didn't like her. She was happy to say Belknap is a jerk, a lousy teacher, and if he gets his just desserts, she won't cry. She has a soft spot for Young, possibly out of pity. She insisted the students love him, pointing out his heroism in offering office hours at all over the holiday week for kids participating in that special symposium, and second keeping them despite the death in the family."

"She said all that to you?" Diana asked.

"Reading between the lines. Someone told me to be more confident in what I pick up," he said airily. "The first takeaway was that Roy bullied him and he took it with dignified reserve, if you go by her view. The other possibilities to explain his lack of response being seething silence and defeated pessimism. The second takeaway is that Mrs. Eldercott is relieved at Professor Roy's demise, because Mrs. E feared Roy was threatening Young's tenure as chairman of the cooperative program and at that university in Colorado. What's it called?"

"Bison University," Jennifer said, accompanied by the sound of typing. "Found it. Bison University in Deer Forks, Colorado."

"What's their mascot? An elk?" Mike asked.

Jennifer said, "An elk? Why would it be an elk?"

"Figured they were covering all the animals."

More typing. "Mascot's a buffalo."

"Bison," Mike and Diana corrected.

"Better not let Mrs. P hear you call it a buffalo," Mike added to Jennifer. "A bison for Bison University. That's boring."

"You were hoping for a banana slug or okra?" I asked.

"UC-Santa Cruz and Delta State," he said immediately. "Horned Frogs?"

"You're going to have to do better than that—Texas Christian—or the Richmond Spiders. How about the Geoducks?"

"I know this… I know this." He raised a fist to his forehead, making me wonder if Rodin's The Thinker had been trying to remember which school used the world's largest burrowing clam as its mascot.

"What are you two doing?" Jennifer demanded. She'd quit typing.

"Playing mascot trivia. Which is a very poor use of our time, when we should be—"

"Got it! Evergreen State." Mike could have now modeled Triumph for Auguste Rodin.

"Good one, Paycik. Coming through in the clutch."

"Will you two, please, pay attention," Jennifer scolded.

We looked at each other, then grimaced at the phone.

"Of course," I said, sounding saintly.

I recounted my trip to the library, skipping the part about being interrupted before I could look through yearbooks that might apply to

Tom and Mike.

"What do you think?" Mike asked. "If Professor Roy was following her husband wouldn't she have left there sooner? Do you think she saw Dean? Would she have recognized him?"

I'd shrugged to each of the previous questions, but for the last one I had words. "I recognized him. Right away at Sally's house and I had a heck of a lot less reason to recognize him than she had."

"Good point."

My largely unfruitful diggings in the *Independence* archives didn't take long.

"They're holding back copies?" Jennifer demanded indignantly. "Those should be on the Internet."

Next, Mike shared what he'd learned from his EMT friend.

"For starters, they got official statements from each member of the household, but my friend also heard Shelton's going to do a group interview with the family again, and he wants to talk to all the EMTs together again."

Everything the EMTs had observed was consistent with Nora Roy being overcome by high levels of carbon monoxide.

His friend's estimates of how quickly she would have passed out and died matched Dex's almost exactly.

"The generator had been used with no problem for several years. It was in good working order. But a big clump of tumbleweed had gotten back in the little area where the exhaust comes out. With the snow and thaws and refreezes, it was solid as a block of ice. It *was* a block of ice. Probably had been since we had that ice storm two days before Christmas." Ah, a piece of Wyoming weather I'd missed. Of course, we'd had snow and sleet in Illinois, but still... "Zblewski told them he'd checked everything before they used the generator this season but hadn't since then. That frozen block of sage brush was waiting for the next time it was used. The professor wanted the garage warm before she drove to town Wednesday and *bam*."

"That kind of wipes out looking at alibis, doesn't it," Diana said. "Even if someone placed it right there to block the exhaust, they could have done that any time since the ice storm. Unless Zblewski checks the exhaust periodically?"

"Nope."

That started a discussion of venting generators properly and whether Zblewski had been negligent.

My mind went a different direction.

"Elizabeth?"

I looked up to find them all—all except Jennifer, who could only see where the screen pointed—staring at me.

Diana asked, "What are you thinking about, Elizabeth?"

"Hmm? Oh, Custer."

"Custer?" she repeated.

"Uh-huh. As in George Armstrong. The Boy General of the Civil War. Battle of Little Bighorn. Last stand. *Please, Mister Custer.*"

None of them—at least the ones I could see, because the angle left me with no idea of Jennifer's reaction—blinked over *Please, Mister Custer.* I really liked these people.

"I know who Custer is. But why?" Mike asked.

"I was thinking about how psychologists looking at him now talk about deep insecurity often being behind that kind of dramatics and misjudgment."

"Oh-kay," Mike said slowly. "You want to connect that to what we're talking about here?"

"Even some of his contemporaries saw that," I went on as if he hadn't spoken. "Yet others were devoted to him. Could see no wrong in him. Were certain anyone who mentioned flaws as simply jealous of his abilities."

"Like his wife," Diana said with a small smile. "Libby—short for Elizabeth, right?"

"Uh-huh. Exactly like that. A woman entirely devoted to him. Then to his legacy after he died."

"But nobody in this case has a devoted wife."

I turned toward Mike. "You don't think so?"

He thought it over. "You think Kitty is devoted to Graham Young?"

"Mmm." I turned away, letting my gaze go back to Diana's rock fireplace.

"I don't get it," Mike said.

"Someone," Diana said softly, "reminds Elizabeth of Custer. Who?"

"That's the question, isn't it?" I murmured.

"Professor Belknap," Tom said.

Chapter Thirty

"BELKNAP?" MIKE REPEATED. "Why?"

"There's definitely the hair." Diana started clicking away on her keyboard. "The light eyes and the narrow face."

"He has this jacket…" I wasn't sure I could explain. "And a hat."

"I've seen that jacket. And the hat," Tom said. "Heard he wore them to the museum dinner last year. It did not go unnoticed. Linda was ready to kick him out herself."

"Linda? I don't see her making a scene."

"In her quiet way." His mouth quirked. "She told Clara she refused to sit at the same table with him and she would not ask the tribal representatives to do so. That's why Clara kept him away from some guests this year."

"But you said he was really critical of Custer," Jennifer protested to me.

"Of course, he is. Custer gets the attention Belknap wants for the so-called Battle of Cottonwood County. If it happened."

"But his wife isn't here," Mike said.

"No, she isn't. But Jasmine Uffelman is."

"The grad student, right?" he asked.

"Right."

"Look at this." Diana turned the laptop around so we could see the screen. She'd pulled up a photo of Belknap in the coat and jacket on one side, Custer on the other.

Tom whistled softly. "Didn't realize it was *that* close a resemblance."

"Let me see."

Diana picked up my phone, angling it to give Jennifer a view of the laptop screen.

"Creepy," Jennifer said.

"Okay," Mike conceded. "I accept that Belknap looks vaguely like Custer and apparently he cultivates it with that get-up. But I come back to why? And what does it have to do with this? And how does Jasmine Uffelman figure in?"

"Men are so naïve," Jennifer said. "Just because she has a pretty face doesn't mean she's not capable of deviousness and murder."

"What are you?" Mike shot back, "the wise old crone?"

"Hey—"

"Actually, that's a powerful archetype—"

"And way off topic," Tom said. "What about this graduate student, Elizabeth?"

I told them what I'd observed at the museum dinner, along with the laundry delivery at the hotel. Then added in what Linda had heard.

"Belknap and Jasmine conspiring?" Diana asked. "Over what? Research at the library?"

"Over dealing with Professor Roy," Mike said. "Has to be. Remember what Elizabeth told us about before the museum dinner, when Professor Roy said the battle never happened and Belknap got upset at that and said she'd promised not to say anything for a while. That's what made it urgent. It all fits."

"That's logical, but not conclusive. We need to keep open to other possibilities."

"What about the library?" Diana asked. "I don't mean as another possibility. I mean how it might fit in. Zblewski's at the library, then Dean starts coming in to the library. Belknap's at the library pretty regularly, then Jasmine starts going there every day this week. And Professor Roy shows up there the day before she dies—along with her husband, Dean, and Belknap. All that coming and going? There's got to be some import to that."

"I'll give you Dean and Vic Zblewski, but two professors and a grad student at a library doesn't seem surprising," Tom said.

"With the timing and the fact that Professor Roy was rarely, if ever, seen there before?"

He lifted one shoulder. "Maybe. But as Elizabeth said, not conclusive."

Into the silence that followed, Jennifer asked, "Did you get anything from those phone numbers I got for the Cruz family?"

It didn't take long for me to recount that Maria Guadalupe, Arturo, and Javier had not wanted to talk, ending with "...and then Diana showed up and we went into Sally's. Isaacs was there, in all his charming glory."

I repeated what Isaacs had said before Diana began filming.

That led to showing Jennifer tape of what had run on the Five.

"You know what's bothering me?" I asked.

"Besides Custer?" Mike asked.

I ignored the chuckles. "How did Thurston find out about Dean Isaacs getting out on parole?"

"Department of Corrections says they did not send a news release. Meant to tell you that earlier," Jennifer said through the phone.

Diana lifted one eyebrow. "You asked her to check on that?"

"I was curious. How *did* Thurston find out?"

"Dale says it was a news release that came in an envelope addressed to 'Anchor, KWMT-TV.' No return address," Jennifer added.

I gave Jennifer an approving nod for taking the question the next step, though it might have been a brief nod, crowded out by more questions burbling up. Not to mention, she couldn't see it. So I stuck a thumbs-up in front of the screen.

"That's more than I got out of him," Mike complained. "I even promised him UW basketball tickets next month."

Ignoring Mike's complaint, I said, "That means it was sent by someone not aiming at a specific person, but rather at a position. And—"

"Can I tell Thurston that? Please let me be the one," Jennifer said.

"—someone who didn't know who held that position, yet knew the name of the TV station in Sherman."

"Like maybe someone who used to live around here but had been away for a while? With *being away* as a euphemism for being in prison?"

"That's a reasonable possibility, Mike," I agreed.

"Why do we care?" Jennifer asked.

"Because it's an interesting question. Was it a concerned citizen who wanted the populace of Cottonwood County to be aware of a convicted murderer about to settle among them? That's one scenario. Or was it someone who didn't want Isaacs to have a chance to settle in quietly? Or, as Mike pointed out, was it someone who had been away for a while."

"Why would Isaacs want people to know he was coming back to Cottonwood County?" Diana asked.

"And *that* is the most interesting question of all."

"A message to his sweetheart that he was coming home at last."

"His sweetheart died the same night he committed murder."

"His secret sweetheart. Or one he acquired recently—one of those prison gate Hannahs." We all looked at Mike. He said, "You know, the prison equivalent of rodeo's Buckle Bunnies or law enforcement's Badge Bunnies."

"Got it," Diana said for all of us. "Just never heard them called Prison Gate Hannahs."

"Should be Prison Patsys," I muttered.

Now they all turned toward me. "That's not bad," Mike said. "Wonder if we can trademark it."

"We?"

"If you're going to be technical, *you*."

I nodded at his acceptance of my proprietary rights to the phrase. "Rather than searching for a trademark lawyer any time soon, how about if we—including me—get back on track. Putting aside the sweetheart angle, because, why wouldn't he write to her directly—?"

"Because she's married," Mike said immediately.

Diana tipped her head. "Did you watch soap operas over the holiday?"

"She could be," he insisted.

"We don't even know there is a she," Jennifer pointed out.

I jumped on that opening to return to the main point. "Right. So what other reasons—?"

"A threat." Tom's slow voice stopped me mid-question.

"A threat?" Diana repeated thoughtfully. "Telling the county, look out, the horrible murderer's back."

Tom nodded. "Or letting somebody know he was returning to Cottonwood County."

"Why not call and say 'Hey, I'm back'?"

"More dramatic to have it announced on TV."

I nodded at Tom's answer, then added, "It also avoids direct contact."

"Why would he want to do that?" Jennifer asked. "Oh. They were conspirators before and he doesn't want to give away the other person?"

"Possible. That seems more altruistic than I'd expect of him, but possible."

"I was thinking he's come back to blackmail his conspirator and doesn't want to get caught doing that, so he's keeping some distance."

I nodded, then did another thumbs-up to the screen. "That's good thinking, Jennifer."

"What conspirator?" Mike demanded.

"We don't know. But now we have ideas to help us keep our eyes and ears open for possibilities, including the sweetheart, the conspirator, and anything else. We should also keep our eyes and ears open for anything that seems off."

"I have something," Jennifer said.

"What's that?"

"First, the Cruz family *was* registered for notices about Dean Isaacs. But it was Arturo's name, but the address was for that lawyer who's his son."

"Javier Cruz. Yes." So his calmness when I "broke" the news told us nothing, since he probably already knew.

"The other thing is he's in Sherman. Javier, I mean."

"What? *What?*" I leaned over to stare at the phone screen.

"He's staying at the B&B."

No need for her to be more specific, since there was only one in

Sherman—The Wild Horses Bed and Breakfast.

"How do you know?"

"Don't ask her," Mike warned. "Just take the information and say thank you."

"But—"

"I didn't hack. Not really. But there is a way to back-door and get the information. And the back door was kind of, uh, open. Then I called and confirmed it with the B&B."

"The B&B gave you information about a guest?" Diana asked.

"They're real grateful to Elizabeth and the rest of us for figuring out what happened there in November. I kind of told them it was for Elizabeth."

"Jennifer," Tom said sternly.

"I know, but it *is* for Elizabeth," she protested.

"Now that she's done it, we might as well know, right?" Mike said. "Telling us doesn't make it any worse. In fact, it makes it better, since, as she said, it is for Elizabeth."

Diana asked, "How much does it help us to know he's here? With his family's ties with the Roys and with the history, once news about Professor Roy's death hit—and I'm sure it was reported in Colorado with her ties there along with still being remembered for her book— it's not that surprising he'd come here."

"He was already at the B&B."

"What? *What?*" I had to stop doing that in response to Jennifer's statements.

"Uh-huh. He arrived Tuesday night. Been there since."

So, his assistant and he had both let me think he was in his office in Denver when we spoke on the phone, rather than being a few miles away.

"Why would he do that?" I said aloud.

"He's up to something," Jennifer said with satisfaction. "B&B people said he's been out a lot and then he stays up really late on his computer."

"In fairness, isn't it understandable that he's interested in what's going on, what with Dean Isaacs being released on parole?" Diana asked.

"He certainly didn't express that interest to me on the phone. And he denied knowing Isaacs was out—Damn. No, he didn't. I asked if the Department of Corrections had contacted him. He said no. He didn't say he didn't know Isaacs had been released. That was a bad question. Bad, bad question. Jennifer, will you see what else you can find out about him and the rest of the family?"

AS I HELPED Diana with the last of the cleanup after the others had left, she said, "You do know it's scary, don't you?"

"What's scary?"

I'd been thinking it was a sad state affairs that I was going to be dependent on someone else finding out something tomorrow to have a new thread to follow. Best bets I could see right now were a return trip to the library and another chat with Belknap and Jasmine. Oh, goodie.

If there was nothing more to pursue on the small mysteries surrounding the death of Yolanda Cruz decades ago and the recent release of her murderer, I'd pursue inquiries about the jury duty scammer invoking Richard Alvaro's name.

"The way you beam with pride at Jennifer when she comes up with some dark, devious idea or digs up, well, hidden information."

"She's come a long way in a short time. Of course I'm proud."

"It's like Morticia Adams complimenting her daughter on mastering a poison recipe."

"Ha. Ha. That's funny."

"Who's being funny?"

FRIDAY

DECEMBER 30

Chapter Thirty-One

I'D GONE PAST the Wild Horses B&B on the way to KWMT-TV. Had a great frosted Danish fresh from Krista Seger's oven, but no success finding Javier Cruz, who'd already left for the morning.

One of those people who got up with first light—before first light at this time of year. All the more reason not to trust him.

I'd also already read the new edition of the *Independence*, which comes out on Tuesdays and Fridays.

The big splash was on Professor Roy's death, but Needham had also laid out a solid secondary lead on the release on parole of Dean Isaacs, complete with a sidebar on the Supreme Court rulings and new Wyoming laws that led to it.

But nothing new to chew over.

That had left only one thing to do. Go to the station.

Jerry, the studio cameraman, had brought in post-Christmas cookies and left them in the break room. More specifically, he had brought in cookies his wife had made, packaged, and told him to bring to the station.

She showed impressive initiative. The newsroom had been awash in cookies and other sweets before the holiday, despite the nearly vacuum-like consumption. Dale had been particularly impressive. His metabolism deserved its own arm of scientific study.

But since Christmas there'd been nothing.

Many thanks to Jerry's wife for ending the drought.

The "break room" wasn't a room and, with only one small round table and two chairs, it was clear management didn't have a lot of breaks in mind. There was a small refrigerator, which was the source of many mysteries—what stuff was and where it disappeared to. A microwave, a trio of cabinets, a scrap of countertop, and a mammoth garbage can completed the decor.

I'd returned to my desk with enough cookies to last me the day— and for a mouthful for Dale—when Leona joined me, carrying a few cookies herself.

But my phone rang at the same time. Seeing it was Diana, I held up a give-me-a-minute finger to Leona.

"Elizabeth, meet me at Hamburger Heaven," Diana said.

"Thanks, but I'm full. Besides, I thought you were out on assignment."

"Don't ask questions. Come now."

"Why? What's going on?"

"Not saying until you get here. You'll be sorry if you don't."

Who can resist an invitation like that?

Not me. "It'll be a minute. Leona's here."

"Make it fast. I'm not kidding."

Leona might have heard Diana, because before the phone left my ear, she said, "What have you found out?"

I raised my brows. "Found out?"

"I know you and the others are talking to people." Her intelligent eyes zoomed in on me over a cookie adorned with a chocolate star. "Me, too."

"Who have you been talking to?" I asked.

"Clara Atwood, Linda Caswell, Ivy Short, oh, and Emmaline Parens."

"Then you know at least as much as I do and probably more." Especially if she'd gotten Mrs. Parens to spill.

"I know the sheriff's department is still investigating Nora Roy's death." I raised my eyebrows. She nodded and added, "Actively. They've talked to the family and housekeeper, and are going to again. They've got forensics going over everything. The whole deal."

"You definitely know more than we do. We've been looking into the past. The murder of Yolanda Cruz and what surrounded that, the professor's family history."

"Uh-huh." She said knowingly. "That family history's pretty interesting, isn't it? Happens it includes a suicide in the family and a murder practically in the family. Did you know Nora had heart issues, speaking of history. That made her more vulnerable to carbon monoxide, according to what that sweet young doctor at the hospital told me."

"Another person could have survived the amount of carbon monoxide she was exposed to?"

She grinned. "That's what I asked. The answer is probably not if they'd been exposed just as long to it. But they might not have passed out as fast as she did. Another person might have saved herself. Or himself. The way her husband did."

"Speaking of the husband and the rest of the family, how are they viewed by the movers and shakers in Cottonwood County?"

"You should know that as well as I do. Oh, wait. Is Emmaline being discreet again?"

"Unforgivably discreet. I did talk to Clara Atwood and some to Linda Caswell."

She nodded in approval. "I probably don't have much more or different to tell you than they would. They were treated with courtesy, of course. And they were accepted as part of the museum and community college group. But they've always held themselves apart. And that was fine with the folks here. Even when the girl—who was liked—was alive. That was kind of surprising because having kids in school usually pulls the whole family into the mix."

"I suppose Professor Roy wasn't exactly the room mother sort."

She chuckled. "I'd feel sorry for kids who got her as a room mother. Though Yolanda Cruz…"

"You knew her?"

"A little. Got talking one day at the library when she'd brought Laura in as a little girl. We hit it off. Would get together for coffee pretty regularly."

How could you not like this woman? She covered "society" while befriending a housekeeper.

"How'd she feel about not being with her family?"

"She always said her children were grown. They still had her love, but they didn't need her support. Not the way Laura Roy needed love and support."

"Because of her mother?"

"Better to say because of the entire family set-up."

I nodded acceptance of that while my brain took a detour.

"Leona, what do the museum people think of Professor Belknap and his theory?"

"They don't believe it. But they're hedging their bets in case the small chance that he's right comes through."

"What are you doing?" Les Haeburn's voice came from over my shoulder.

Darn. He was back from vacation. I'd been hoping he'd stay away until the New Year even though one of the women in accounting said he had to come back to work at least one more day or forfeit some management bonus retirement funds.

He already sounded irked.

Oh, wait. He always sounded irked.

"Leona and I were comparing notes."

"On what?" Thurston asked snidely from behind Haeburn. "The social scene?"

"Yes." Leona stared directly at him. His snideness melted under her challenge.

But his whine, like cockroaches, could survive Armageddon. "You're talking about that professor dying. I know you are. That's my story. Mine. And so is that guy getting out of prison."

"Professor Nora Roy," Leona said. "If you were so interested in the story, why didn't you get out to the scene like I did? Why weren't you the one at the hospital asking questions and getting the official statement?"

"I'm the anchor. I don't do leg work."

"*Leg work?* You think I'm your leg man? Only part of my legs I'd give you are my varicose veins. I like hard news as much as I like them, but when a story happens under your nose you've got to get off your butt and cover it. And anything I cover, I do on air. It's like my daddy said when he taught me how to shoot, 'The one who shoots it, eats first.' "

She gave him a hard stare, then spread it to Haeburn. Apparently satisfied, she stood, said "I'll talk to you more later, Elizabeth," and walked off.

That left Haeburn and Fine stranded in the middle of the newsroom with only me to take out their wrath on.

I might have exacerbated it by muttering, "Attagirl, Leona."

Haeburn struck a pose—I suspected he'd been watching leadership videos. "I still want to know what you're doing," he said forcefully.

"Leona told you."

"Not right now. Overall, since you've come back from your Christmas vacation."

"When I returned from my Christmas break Monday—and I hope yours was wonderful, too, Les—" He flushed, which was interesting. I hadn't expected my gibe at his longer break would get to him. Maybe his holiday hadn't been wonderful. "—I began investigating a scam I heard about that's affecting Cottonwood County citizens. It's a phone scam. Mostly going for money, with a side order of identity theft. It's a variation of a scam that's been hitting all over the country. To do the story right, I really should go to Washington and Los Angeles. Denver, too, but that's practically local, so—"

"No. No trips. Absolutely not."

"But it will be the New Year, a new budget—"

"No. You said there are local people."

"Yes. I've done preliminary interviews over the past few days." No need to worry him with the detail that they'd been intermixed with other interviews. "I'll need Diana for the next round. It's really quite—"

"Diana? She's always taking Diana," Fine whined.

"What would you use her for, Thurston? Planning to get out of the studio for a live report any time soon?"

"You're trying to poach my story on that murderer who got out of prison," he accused with no logic, but coming closer to accuracy than usual.

"What story? Dean Isaacs—that is his name by the way—is out on parole. You reported that. What else could there possibly be?"

Every other anchor I have ever known—those I've liked and admired, those I wasn't as fond of—would have been sure there were other angles and jumped on them. Then again, they all wouldn't have left the holes in the initial story and would have reported the heck out of the follow ups. Fine's follow ups were non-existent.

"You hear what she's doing, Les? Do you hear that? She's not denying she's going after that story. She's not denying it at all. What are you going to do about it?"

"I'll tell you what I'm going to do about it. You—" He pointed at me. "—go do that story for another damn 'Helping Out!' we don't need. And you—" Thurston this time. "—be quiet. I have bigger things to worry about than you two."

Haeburn turned and marched away, slamming the door to his office after him.

Fine stared at the closed door, open-mouthed.

✧ ✧ ✧ ✧

NOBODY CAN SAY I don't do what Les Haeburn tells me to do. At least when his orders coincide with what I want to do.

When I pulled in to the familiar Hamburger Heaven parking lot, Diana immediately got out of the Newsmobile—a four-wheel drive that was the cream of the KWMT-TV fleet. Consider that cream curdled.

She got in beside me. "Let's go."

"Where?"

"Start toward the Roys'."

I gave her a look but headed out.

On the highway, she refused to be drawn into conversation. Then she took care of any temptation to talk to me by pulling out her phone and having a nice chat with her mother, who'd recently returned to her retirement home in Texas after spending Christmas here with Diana and her kids.

She interrupted the conversation to point and say, "Take that right-hand Y."

That wasn't the way I'd driven here before. This road dropped down abruptly and I guessed we were going to come in from the road in the valley.

When she finally hung up, she checked her messages, returned one with rapid-fire tapping, then looked around. "We're never going to get there at this rate."

"The road could be slick."

"What are you talking about? The roads are fine. As you well know. Because I happen to know that Jennifer sends you the daily highway reports, the latest of which says all roads are in seasonally good condition."

"Reasonably good condition?"

"Not reasonably. *Seasonally* good condition. You know, in keeping with the season."

"In other words, crappy."

"Not as bad as it could be," she said cheerfully. "Turn left at that road up there."

"What road?"

"The gap in that sort of berm."

"Good heavens." We were turning short of the entry road I'd seen before. Once we cleared a group of trees, I could see we were coming in at the back of the Roy house.

Diana sighed. "You do know you don't have to come to a complete stop before making a turn?"

"I do before making *this* turn with *my* vehicle. You can abuse the Newsmobile as much as you want."

Once we'd turned she huffed in disgust. "If you don't hurry up, we're going to miss everything."

"Everything what? What's going on, Diana?"

"I'm giving you a belated Christmas present. Okay, now up there, follow alongside the corral fence. Around this curve. Uh-huh. Now pull into that gap and park."

It was beside a porch, with a back door directly in front of us.

"No excess noise," she warned me.

"Are you going to tell me what's going on?"

She grinned. "Nope. I want to spring it on you. You can thank me later. Me and my mom."

She went to the back door and a shadowy figure opened it.

By the time I was inside, the shadowy figure was slipping around a corner toward a lighted area, but I thought I recognized a maid's uniform.

Chapter Thirty-Two

DIANA GESTURED ME into a dark interior hallway.

As we moved forward slowly, we could hear voices. When I recognized one of them I almost fell on my face.

Deputy Wayne Shelton.

Diana had sneaked us in to a police interview.

It *was* Christmas.

Even if Shelton caught us, we'd been invited in.

But the voice that was speaking didn't belong to the deputy.

The near monotone belonged to Vic Zblewski, Professor Roy's husband.

"—and she was lying face down."

"She wasn't when the EMTs arrived," Shelton said.

"No. I rolled her over when I found her. I hoped that would give her some air. I couldn't lift her. I tried to drag her, but I got so dizzy. And it was like I couldn't get air in my lungs—"

No kidding. He *hadn't* been able to get air in his lungs because the carbon monoxide was taking up that space.

"—and part of me still knew I needed to get her out and get out myself, but all I wanted to do was lie down and sleep."

"It's a good thing you didn't, sir." Shelton's flat delivery robbed that of any shred of touchy-feely.

"I made myself get up and I sort of stumbled across the garage—you'll probably find my fingerprints all over the SUVs, because I used them to prop myself up—and finally got to near the door to the house and pressed the button to open a garage door. Once I got one, I hit a second one. Then a third. That must have been enough to get air in. I could start to think. I opened the door into the house and shouted and shouted and shouted. I could hear someone coming. Someone running toward me. Toward *us* and I thought they'd take care of Nora. Help her. Save her. I guess I collapsed then. I don't remember anything after that until the medical people were there."

"That was you, ma'am, running to him?" Shelton asked.

A voice said, "No. That was Lorraine. She heard Vic shouting." I'd only heard a few words from her at the museum dinner, but I was sure that was Kitty Roy Young.

"Lorraine?" Shelton repeated. I didn't believe for a second that he didn't know who she was.

"Lorraine Flicker. Mother's—our housekeeper."

"Okay, so Mr. Zblewski is on the floor in the garage near the door to the house. Ms. Flicker is going to his aid, having heard him call out. Where were you and Mr. Graham Young."

"As I told you immediately after this terrible accident, Professor Young and I were in our rooms at the other end of the house. When we heard a commotion, which turned out to be the arrival of the first rescue and law enforcement vehicles, we came out of our rooms together. When we arrived downstairs, Vic was on the ground near the step from the garage to the house, with a towel under his head. The EMTs said he had collapsed there, and was fortunate to have reached that spot. They insisted we get out of the house."

I realized I'd been staring at a photo on the wall since we'd stopped here. But I hadn't noticed it until now. It was a family grouping of sorts. I recognized Professor Roy, looking considerably younger. To her left stood Vic Zblewski. To her right, but with a little gap was a short, round woman, a handsome, tall, dark-eyed boy on the cusp of becoming a young man. Definitely not Dean Isaacs. The woman had a hand on the forearm of the boy/man. And both of them looking at the girl, who had to be Laura.

Laura's smile was relaxed, happy. Despite her light eyes looking straight into the camera, she practically shimmered with awareness of the boy/man. Aware, attracted, attached. There was something strong there. I was sure of it.

And from the way he looked at her it was mutual.

Who was he?

"Let's go back over what happened, starting Tuesday night."

"Again?" Zblewski moaned.

"Again."

"We got home from that dinner at the museum and I pulled into the garage—"

"What time would that have been, sir?"

"No idea. Wasn't watching the clock."

"Ten forty-five," Graham Young said.

"If he says so." Zblewski didn't sound impressed by Young's memory.

"Ma'am?" Shelton asked.

"I'm certain my husband is correct. I was not paying close attention to the time, either. However, I did notice that it was just before midnight when we turned out the light to retire and our usual bedtime routine takes approximately an hour."

"Nobody lingered downstairs, had a nightcap, chatted about the evening?"

There might have been head-shakes, but, even on its own, the silence that followed presumably confirmed that none of the household had lingered.

"Okay," Shelton said. "You pulled into the garage. What happened next?"

"Nora said it was freezing in the garage and asked me to turn on the generator."

"If you want a precise account, Deputy, before that discussion, she had expressed dissatisfaction with the parking arrangements," Graham said.

I tipped my proverbial hat to Shelton. He'd already taken their individual accounts, sanctified as official statements. By having them tell their stories in front of each other, he had picked up a discrepancy. Small, for sure. But every bit of information helped, especially in building a picture of the people and relationships involved. This little discrepancy said plenty about the relationship between Nora Roy's husband and son-in-law.

"Yeah," Zblewski said. "She liked her vehicle closest to the door, but we'd both been out earlier and I took that spot. I pointed out that put her right by the back door right then. That's when she talked about how cold the garage was and how in the morning she'd freeze before she could get to her car and I needed to run the generator."

That was a little different from his earlier "asked me to turn on." Didn't change the facts any but did mesh more with what I'd seen of Professor Roy and her relationship with her husband.

"So, I set up the generator the way I always do. You want details on that?"

"We'll get that when we go out in the garage," Shelton said. "Let's continue with the main outline of what happened."

"The generator started just fine. Then I came in, had a drink, and went to bed."

"The next morning?"

"Started like any other day. I heard Nora moving around her room—" So the married couple didn't share a room. "—then she went downstairs. Lorraine can tell you what happened then. Most likely Nora went to her office. I rolled over and went back to sleep. When I got up—"

"What time was that, sir?"

"No idea. Took a shower, got dressed, checked a few business things, then went downstairs for something to eat. Lorraine made me an omelet and some apple fritters. Nora came through while I was telling Lorraine what I wanted in the omelet. Said she was going to town."

"Where specifically?"

"Didn't say."

"Did you ask, sir?"

"No. Had no reason to check up on her. We didn't check up on each other."

I glanced at Diana. She didn't buy that last sentence, either.

"What time was it when you went into the garage to check on your wife?"

Had Shelton purposely used the phrase "check on" to push back on what Zblewski had said? Or was it unconscious mirroring?

"You keep asking about times like I checked every two seconds and wrote them down in a notebook. It wasn't like that. It was an ordinary day. I know I was eating an apple fritter when I realized I hadn't heard the garage door go up. Now, you don't always hear it, so I thought maybe I'd missed it. But I hadn't seen her SUV go past the window and that you usually do see. I decided to go see. That's when—"

"Wait a minute, sir." Shelton using a time reference in stopping Zblewski had to be deliberate. "Let's go back. Maybe we can figure out some time. Was it your first apple fritter you were eating?"

"No. But before you ask I don't know exactly how many. I don't keep track of those, either. I'd had a few, I guess. Lorraine might know."

"Yes. Trouble is, she was out of the kitchen, tending to the laundry, so she doesn't know when you went out to the garage, either."

"Well, there you go," Zblewski said, as if that had proved a point somehow. "Nobody knows exactly what time things happen—not in a normal day and not before a tragedy occurs, either."

"Somebody knows what time things happen," Shelton said in his usual gruff tone. "Your call came in to dispatch at two-forty-three."

"Then why are you asking me?" Zblewski complained. "I went out to the garage, saw her SUV still there, tried to get her out, realized I was going to pass out, got over to the garage door opener, so figure out how much time that took and you'll know exactly when I went out to the garage."

I could imagine how happy that answer made Shelton.

But he didn't get sharp or sarcastic, unlike the way he treated journalists. He said in much the same tone he'd been using throughout, "Mrs. Young, can you fill in any of the time factors?"

"Yes, Deputy. My husband and I rose at our usual time of seven. We were showered and dressed when we joined my mother at the breakfast table at eight. We were done at approximately eight-thirty or a few minutes later. My mother went to her office on the ground floor. My husband went to his office in our suite of rooms. I returned to the bedroom, where I made the bed, tidied the room, wrote a thank you note to Clare Atwood for the dinner the previous night on behalf of the family. I then began to respond to emails. That was shortly after nine-fifteen. To my knowledge each of us remained where we were until noon, when Lorraine served us lunch."

"It was twelve-ten," Graham said. "Nora was on a phone call until then."

"Twelve-ten," Kitty said, with nothing in her voice indicating she minded the correction. "We finished an hour later and—"

"You observed the time?"

"I did not. Lunch is always an hour." After a slight pause, she continued with no change in her voice, "Lorraine cleared. Mother returned to her office. Graham returned to his office. I returned to my correspondence."

"Did you know your mother planned to leave that afternoon?"

"No."

"Did you usually know each other's schedules?"

"My husband and I know each other's schedules."

Diana and I looked at each other again. Uh-huh.

"Did anyone go to the garage between your return from the museum dinner and when Professor Roy was found?"

Silence provided a negative.

"What about Lorraine? Did she go there?"

"No," Zblewski said.

"Not to our knowledge," Graham corrected.

"What about when she reported for work in the morning? Since she doesn't live in—"

"Professor Roy does not—" Kitty broke off, then resumed just as calmly. "She did not allow the staff to park in the garage."

A silence fell, then a slight sound of movement as if they'd all recognized a passage of time.

"What do you think happened, ma'am?" Shelton asked.

"Clearly an accident," Kitty said.

"Sir?"

Graham said, "I concur."

"Sir?" Shelton repeated.

"Must be an accident. If it's not, it must be suicide."

Shelton immediately said, "Suicide? What would make you think that? There was no note."

"Just like with Laura," Zblewski said. "Her daughter's death weighed heavily on Nora. With that scum back in town..."

A murmur too quiet for me to pick up sparked a "*What?*" from Shelton.

A throat was cleared, then Graham Young said, "There was a note. I saw it."

"You saw a note that Professor Roy left and didn't—"

"Not the professor. Laura."

"But Graham, Mother always said there was no note." Kitty's voice had picked up a load and a half of stress since the last time she spoke.

"Yes, she did. But I saw Laura first—"

"*You* saw her first?" Shelton sounded as if he were holding the top of his head on by pure force of will. "The reports said Professor Roy found her."

"It was a very unusual morning, with the upset from the previous evening and the absence of breakfast because, as we now know, Yolanda had been murdered. But I still had to go to work. I had a call scheduled that morning and was going to my office. However, Laura had driven the vehicle I favored the day before—only on the property, since she did not yet have a license—and had not returned the keys to their rightful place. I went to get them from her. The door was not completely closed. When there was no response to my knock, I pushed it open. She was there—and there was a note. I did not touch it, nor anything else in the room, and the note was there when I went to get the professor."

"Then what the hell happened to it?" Shelton demanded.

"I would imagine that's obvious, Deputy. I can only surmise that Professor Roy destroyed it."

Chapter Thirty-Three

"YOU'RE JUST NOW bringing this up?"

"I was never asked."

"You were asked during the original investigation when you last saw Laura."

"I believe if you check the transcript of my interview, you will find that I was asked when I last *spoke* with Laura. I answered truthfully that it had been the night before."

"And you never volunteered anything more." I don't know that I've ever heard Shelton sound nastier.

"No, I didn't." Graham Young was unperturbed.

"What did Professor Roy say when you told her you'd seen a note."

"I did not tell her."

"Why not?"

"There was no need. She must have known I'd seen the note. It was impossible to miss upon entering the room, as she did when I fetched her there."

"What did she say to you about the note?"

"Nothing."

"C'mon, she must have said something. You said she must have known you'd seen the note."

"She never said a word about it to me."

"What did you say to her? Don't shake your head. What did you say to her?"

"Nothing. If Professor Roy had wanted to discuss the contents of the note, she would have raised the topic. Absent that, I said nothing."

"Contents? You read the note?"

"I did. It was open on the bed where…" He hesitated. I listened closely for something that might indicate more reaction than his voice betrayed. I heard nothing. "Laura was."

"Do you remember these contents?"

"I do."

"What were they?"

Young cleared his throat again, then continued in a monotone:

> "This is too hard. All of it. This is not the way it should be. I know that now. So I'm ending it.
>
> That might be hard, too. But it's better. It will be better.
>
> Don't blame Dean. It's not his fault. He has been wonderful and has shown me so much.—

Young paused. "The next line was somewhat blurred because the letter had been folded and refolded, perhaps as she considered and reconsidered the step she was about to take. However, based on the context and what I could make out on the paper, the next line was 'I'm grateful to him.' Should you like further explanation for why I came to that conclusion?"

"No. Go ahead. Finish."

"Very well. After the sentence saying Dean Isaacs had shown her so much, it said:

> "I'm grateful to him. I hope you'll show your gratitude, too.
>
> You go around giving all your orders, but you can't make me do anything this time. Everything is in my hands.
>
> Good-bye,
> Laura"

"Was the handwriting—"

"It was not handwritten. It had been typed, presumably on her computer, then printed out."

"Did she have a printer there in her room?"

"Yes."

"Any sign that it could or could not have been printed from her printer?"

"Such as?"

"No ink. No paper. It was broken. Wrong color paper."

"No."

Shelton said, "I want to see that note—"

"As I said, I doubt it exists."

After a pause in which I imagined Shelton grinding his teeth, Graham Young added, "Have you any further questions for us concerning Professor Roy's accident?"

Shelton ignored that hint. "You remember that note awfully well all these years later."

"The emotional import of the words would likely have been sufficient to imprint them in my memory, Deputy. However, my recall has been bolstered recently."

"How's that?" I could imagine Shelton's gaze boring into Young.

When he answered, his voice carried no indication that he was discomfited. "I made a contemporaneous record of the circumstances of my finding the note and of its contents. I had occasion to review it recently. It is kept in a safe in my office."

I heard a sucked-in breath. I suspected it was Kitty Young.

I felt the same way—I'd bet that's what Graham had been doing that day at his office. Straightening up from putting the note back into his safe in the bottom right-hand drawer.

Perhaps Graham Young was not the dismissible character we'd been seeing him as.

"And you never mentioned this note to law enforcement, not even back when Professor Roy was all over saying it couldn't be anything but murder because there wasn't a suicide note?"

"It is obvious I had not, not until this conversation."

"Why?"

"I would think that, too, would be obvious." I thought so, too, and I suspected Shelton asked it mostly to make Graham Young say the unflattering truth. Though it didn't seem to bother the professor, judging by his tone. "As I previously stated, it was apparent to me that my mother-in-law had destroyed the suicide note Laura wrote. Therefore, it was obvious she did not want its existence revealed. Professor Roy had the capacity to make my life and that of my wife anywhere from deeply uncomfortable to desperate. She would undoubtedly have employed that capacity if I had contradicted her on the matter.

"By the end of that first day, Dean Isaacs was in custody. Shortly after, it was clear he was going to be tried for and likely convicted of murdering Yolanda Cruz. If he had been charged in Laura's death, I would—I believe I would have come forward. It was Professor Roy and only Professor Roy who intimated that he murdered Laura, not satisfied that in addition to his conviction for murdering Yolanda, he was being held morally responsible for Laura's death by most people. Perhaps she needed that to overcome her feelings about her daughter's death."

"Graham." That was Kitty. "Why didn't you ever tell me?"

From the change in his tone he turned to her. "This was one burden I could carry for you."

"All very nice about overcoming feelings and carrying burdens—" It was as close to a rage as I'd ever heard Shelton. "—but you withheld evidence and misled investigators and we'll be looking into all of that."

"After all this time—" started Kitty.

"Yes," the deputy snapped. "I want that contemporaneous account, along with you writing down every single thing you noticed about that note as well as your handling of it and what you know of Professor Roy's handling of it."

That clearly was addressed to Graham Young.

Young answered, "Of course, Deputy. As soon as you present a subpoena, I will produce the document immediately."

"I'd expect you to want to help the authorities look into this any way you can."

"The matter you are looking in to, however, is Professor Roy's unfortunate and accidental death a few days ago. Not the suicide of Laura Roy some twenty-six years ago."

Shelton jumped on that. "Did you see a note anywhere that could be associated in any way with Professor Nora Roy's death?"

"No."

"Do you have any information beyond what you have said today pertaining to the deaths of Professor Roy, Laura Roy, or Yolanda Cruz—*any* information, whether you have been asked about it or not?"

"No."

Chapter Thirty-Four

THAT DIDN'T SATISFY Deputy Shelton, of course. He kept at the questions from a number of angles, always with the same target.

He never came close to a bull's-eye.

Sensing he was winding up the interview for their shift to the garage, I nodded to Diana and we retreated back down the hall and out the door with no sign of our shadowy hostess.

Both of us were quiet as I drove back along the corral fence and the road connected to it, but when it came time to turn right to retrace our path, I impulsively turned left.

"You know we should have turned the other way?" Diana asked mildly.

"Yes. See that black SUV down there? I want to check it out."

It was closer to the main entrance road to the Roy compound than to the back entry we'd come out of, headed the same way we were, parked just off the side of the road with a scattering of trees and then a big outbuilding between it and the house.

"See if you can see anyone inside as we go by," I instructed Diana.

I also took a quick look. The man in the driver's seat was pulling out a paper map.

Again.

I was sure of it—it was the same vehicle, the same ploy as in front of Mike's place.

This time I had an impression of a tanned man with gray at the temples of otherwise dark hair, regular features coming together to make a handsome whole.

That was all I had time for.

"Well?" I asked Diana after we'd passed.

"Male. Probably late forties to early fifties, fit, dark hair with gray around the front. Blue plaid shirt under a dark gray sweater with a button placket. Top quality vest—probably Filson. And a Carhartt's jacket on the seat beside him."

"Good heavens. How many fillings does he have?" I was still checking out the vehicle in the rearview mirror.

"What you missed in all that were two important words. Filson and Carhartt."

"Sounds like a country duo, like Brooks and Dunn."

"They're clothing makers for outdoors. Filson says he has money. Carhartt says he knows work."

I made the left turn onto the road that would take us across the river and meet up with the highway route I'd taken here before, which would eventually complete the big rectangle we'd driven and bring us back to the main highway. As I did, I looked over at her.

"You got all this from one look."

"Yup. Speaking of which, you need to get shopping. You need better clothes."

"Hey, with all my stuff burned up not that long ago, I'm still picking up pieces here and there. And if you want to talk shopping, I did buy this thing." I patted the steering wheel of the SUV fondly.

"You also need boots."

"I have cowboy boots. You helped me buy them."

"Warm boots. Winter boots. Insulated and waterproof. Being a city girl, you probably don't know what's like—"

I groaned loudly enough to stop her. "Being a reporter I probably *do* know what it's like. I have an assortment of boots to get me through outside assignments—floods, winter fires, blizzards. You name it. But they're in storage along with a lot of other stuff in Virginia. My ex wanted the spare look for the apartment in New York."

"Okay, then we don't need to do remedial boot-buying instruction, but the ones in storage in Virginia are doing you no good here."

"You're right. Now, can we get back to—"

"What was that you said?"

"You're right. *You're* right. You're *right*. Was that enough?"

"It's a start. As for getting back to the guy in the SUV, did you notice it was a rental?"

"I barely had time to see the Wyoming plates. Darned driving. Took up all my attention. Rental, huh? That's interesting. Between that and the repeat fake map-looking exercise, under other circumstances, I'd say out of town reporter."

"Repeat?"

I flipped an airy hand, saying I'd seen what I thought was the same SUV elsewhere in the county and the guy did the same map trick. Then hurried on past the curiosity in her eyes. "But why would an out of town reporter be interested in Professor Roy's house? She's not that big a deal beyond this area anymore, is she?"

"I wouldn't have said she was that big a deal here, either. What do you mean re—"

"How did you get us in there, by the way?"

"Turns out my mother did Lorraine Flicker's mother a favor years ago. Apparently quite a big favor. I don't know the details, but Mom said she'd see what she could do when I called to tell her the big news in Cottonwood County."

"Well, tell her thank you for me next time you talk, will you? That was amazing. Now, do me a favor, will you? Call Jennifer. Use my phone and ask her to see what coverage the professor's death has gotten beyond here. Tell her to look specifically at Colorado, around Deer Falls, where Bison University is."

Jennifer checked while Diana was on the phone, telling us there had been a piece in Deer Falls about Roy's death, with only one story since. Other coverage had been spotty around the region.

The best news was that kept Diana adequately occupied so she didn't quiz me about the first time I'd seen that mystery SUV.

I'd come *this* close to saying I'd seen it at Mike's place. Then I would have had to either tell her about meeting Shelton there and break a promise or not explain, which would leave her to think all sorts of things that weren't true. A lose-lose choice.

✧ ✧ ✧ ✧

AFTER DROPPING DIANA at the Newsmobile in the Hamburger Heaven parking lot to pick up her day's assignments, I drove to the library again.

I was hoping a nudge would get Ivy Short talking more.

But first I called Dex again.

"More on carbon monoxide?"

"No. At least not right now. I remember you telling me about research into suicide notes. A group that's assessing elements that indicate if a note is genuine or not. Do you have any connections with that group?"

"Yes."

"I'll email you what I have. Unfortunately it's not the original. Just someone's memory of what the note said. And I need to know as soon as possible. This doesn't need to be perfect, Dex. Having an expert's reaction would really help at this stage. If it becomes important later, it could go through the usual scientifically rigorous examination. But for now, if there was someone who might give this a look... Is that possible?"

"I know somebody." This was Dex's version of "I know a guy." Though in Dex's case, it was "I know the top experts in this field in the world and I'll contact the one who best suits this particular question and redeem a favor."

I could have kissed him.

"Dex, there's also a case from twenty-six years ago—the trial was twenty-five years ago—where they say there were fingerprints on a broom handle that was used to beat a woman, though the fatal blow was from another implement, which had no fingerprints. News reports said there was something irregular about the fingerprints on the broom handle."

"News reports."

"Hey, watch it. That's my tribe."

"I know," he said solemnly.

"If I give you information about the case, is there any chance you can check into that?"

"I will see."

I THOUGHT YESTERDAY had set a good foundation between Ivy Short and me, but it wasn't going as well today.

She had to stay at the desk, she said. That meant she was distracted.

"Professor Belknap was telling me about his research," I said after the hellos, hoping she'd pick up that ball and run with it.

Nothing.

"About his theory that there was an encounter between the army and the tribes in this area that set the scene for the Battle of Little Bighorn."

Still no gush of information from her as she scanned the occupants of the computer terminals.

"I should go check on them," she murmured. "Never know what they're looking at. And it's not just kids. Dean Isaacs was looking up carbon monoxide the day before poor Professor Roy died."

"He was?"

She nodded absently. "Uh-huh."

"How do you know? What was he looking up? Was there specific information?" I stopped asking questions because I clearly didn't have all her attention.

"Saw it when I went to clear the screen after he left. Just that the headline was something about carbon monoxide. Don't recall any details. At first, when I heard about her accident... But as Shara said, he wasn't anywhere near their place, so... *Now*, what—?"

She bustled over to the line of computer terminals, administering a low-voiced admonition to a lanky teenager who reminded me of Dale, the news aide. He tried to plead his innocence, but she was having none of it. She marched back to the main desk leaving him vanquished.

"Games," she muttered. "They know they're not supposed to play them on those computers, but they'll try to do it anyway."

I *tsked* sympathetically, then tried to pull the conversation back on track. "Professor Belknap must be grateful for all you do for him, bringing him material, especially now that's he's going back over the same material to check citations. You must have been such a help to him researching his theory."

That elicited a *humph*, but at appropriate librarian volume.

At this rate we might be up to a syllable of true response in a week or so. Time to go for the direct questions.

"Does Professor Belknap ever talk with you about his research?"

"No."

"But you probably had some inkling of what he's doing from the materials he asks to see."

"That and what that young woman says."

Young wo—"Jasmine Uffelman? Light brown hair, blue eyes, studious glasses?"

"Yes. She did introduce herself." The slight emphasis on the pronoun made it clear Bruce Belknap had never bothered with that nicety. "And she has asked for recommendations on materials to look at. She was particularly interested in journals by original settlers. As I pointed out to her, however, there were no settlers in the locale Professor Belknap believes is relevant. On the other hand we have a number of memoirs that might be of interest. She looked through two Tuesday, but left earlier than usual."

The day of the museum dinner.

"Came back the next day and was looking at more when she rushed out of here in the afternoon—such a rush that she did not even return the materials to us, left them on the table in the Local History Room." Disapproval came through strong. But her niceness resurfaced with the next sentence. "I suppose that's understandable in retrospect. She must have just received word about Professor Roy, God bless her soul, so of course Jasmine Uffelman was upset."

Since I'd seen Jasmine at the hotel not long after, I suspected the rush had involved Belknap's laundry, not Roy's death.

"Has she been back since?"

"No, she hasn't. I suppose if she doesn't come today or tomorrow, I won't see her again, because she did say they'd be leaving New Year's

Day to get back to the college in Colorado. And that's a shame. Because I had thought of one more memoir she should take a look at. It was by the daughter of a man who'd been a fur trader as a very young man, then a scout for expeditions, and occasionally a scout for the army. He had very good relations with several of the tribes who passed through here at various time. If anyone knew about this battle it would be Ashtabula Prescott."

"Uh. I bet."

She grinned. "Clearly, you're not aware of who's descended from Ashtabula Prescott—Emmaline Parens."

Chapter Thirty-Five

CHECKING MY PHONE as I left the library, I saw there was a call from Mel.

When I was sure there'd be no additional tidbits from Ivy Short, I'd told her she needed to contact Sheriff's Deputy Wayne Shelton immediately and tell him what she'd told me about Dean Isaacs looking up carbon monoxide poisoning.

So I did my civic duty, just not until I'd wrung her dry.

Fiddling with my phone nearly made me miss that the woman whose path would cross mine as she headed to the main door was Kitty Roy Young.

She looked better now in the icy sunshine than she had that evening in the flattering low light of the museum. Her skin tone healthier. More alive and alert.

"Mrs. Young."

She wanted to walk past. Good manners stopped her. I'm not above taking advantage of someone's good manners.

I identified myself with a hand to my chest. "Elizabeth Margaret Danniher. We met at the museum dinner the other night."

"Yes."

Not a lot to work with there. "Please let me offer my condolences on the death of your mother. She seemed to be a remarkable woman."

"My mother had remarkable accomplishments." That was an interesting spin on what I'd said. No pride there. No affection, either. She said it the way someone else might say, "My mail carrier has brown hair." A fact, no more. "She needed not only to work tirelessly, but also to fight strenuously to reach her position. After my father deserted us when I was a baby, she worked to support us, while putting herself through college. Not only an undergraduate degree, but a masters, then a Ph.D. The second Ph.D. was somewhat easier since she had more financial resources by then."

That sounded rote. A history she'd repeated many times.

"As well as the support of your stepfather?"

She looked at me briefly. "You could say that. He took over the running of the household and supervised me to the extent that I required it, since I was in high school when they married. I suppose I did see more of him than my mother during those years." She didn't sound thrilled about that, though I was beginning to suspect she wouldn't have been thrilled if she had spent a lot of time with her mother, either.

"As you say, your mother worked very hard."

Her eyelids half lowered. "Yet she found ways to amuse herself. Do you know whose namesake I am? Have you heard of Kitty Leroy?"

I'd shaken her out of her script. No telling where this might go.

"I haven't."

"She was a well-known figure in what is referred to as the Wild West. She was a dancer, a gambler, a trick shooter, a saloon owner, and widely reputed to be a prostitute. Yes, my mother named me after a reputed prostitute. One who was murdered in a Deadwood saloon by her fifth husband when she was twenty-seven."

Whoa. Talk about Mom heaping a load of baggage on her kid. In other circumstances I might have whistled. Instead, I maintained a professional silence.

"I once asked her why she had selected that name. She said it had gone with Leroy, so she knew it would go with Roy. I don't have illusions, Ms. Danniher. My mother was not a nice woman."

With that statement, I figured it was open season on questions.

"What about your stepfather? Vic Zblewski," I added because she looked blank for a moment.

"Vic? Nice?" She gave a quick, single head-shake. "Vic is weak. She was strong."

"Did your stepfather have anything to fear from his wife?"

She laughed.

Not what I'd expected. Outrage, possibly. Confusion, maybe. Laughter, no.

"Not at all. Because she controlled him completely. There was no ambiguity there. When everyone knows and plays his or her role, all is calm, all is peaceful. Nor—because I can see this is going to be your next question—did she have anything to fear from him. What is there to fear from a doormat?"

"What is your role?"

She lifted one dismissive shoulder. "Non-entity."

"And your husband?"

"He doesn't enter into this." It was protective and a warning to steer clear.

I came at it sideways. "He *is* part of the family."

She stared away from me. "I did that, made him part of all this. It's none of his fault. I married Graham to irk her. She was grooming him as her protégé. Having him as a son-in-law—as *my* husband—was not part of her plan." Not the action of a non-entity. Did she recognize that contradiction? "I wonder if I also married him with a thought to saving him. How ironic that it's been the ruin of him. Though now... Yes, now, I think he might survive after all."

That was chilling, since the *now* clearly referred to her mother's death. Her mother's death had secured Graham's survival? That sounded like he and Belknap had more in common than they knew. Though I had a feeling Kitty's reference to survival was about more than career.

"Your family's faced tragedy—" I almost said *before*. But that only worked if she believed her mother's death was a tragedy. "—and survived."

A long-worn habit of wariness settled on her. "Yes."

I tried to break through it. "I know you're aware Dean Isaacs is out on parole. Did you share your mother's belief that he killed your sister?"

A flicker, but quickly tucked behind the wariness. "He was convicted of killing Yolanda Cruz" was her non-answer.

"Have you stayed in touch with the Cruz family?"

"No." Clipped and unemotional.

"Did you know Javier Cruz is in Cottonwood County? Has he contacted your family?"

"Jav—" After that one syllable I lost her. She shrank back deep, deeper even than the automaton she'd been at the museum dinner.

"I have told you truths about my family, Ms. Danniher. I will not talk about anyone else's. Good day."

I made no effort to stop her. I didn't have anything to reach as deep as she'd retreated. Besides, I was stunned she'd said anything at all to me.

TOM'S TRUCK PULLED up to a prime parking spot by the Haber House as I finished my frozen trek from the more distant parking lot.

Could feet go numb this fast?

Diana was right. I needed real boots.

He met up with me on the sidewalk. "You heading in to try to track somebody down?"

"That and to thaw out."

The lift of his eyebrows asked the question.

"Belknap. Or Jasmine Uffelman. Or both. Nothing dramatic, alas. Just want to fill in some things. What about you?"

I'd started to turn toward the door, but his hand on my arm stopped me.

"Got a bit of news," he said. "Rather share it out here than in there with all the ears."

"Whoever said no news was good news was wrong. Spill it, Burrell." Suddenly I wasn't as cold as I'd been.

"I found out who fought with Dean Isaacs when he got expelled. Gil Alvaro—"

I groaned. "Of course, it was an Alvaro. That family's everywhere."

"—and Rusty Harter. He's living somewhere on the East Coast now, but I gave Gil a call. He's Richard's oldest brother. He remembered it vaguely. Said he probably wouldn't remember at all if Laura hadn't died a couple months later."

Before I could open my mouth, he was continuing.

"I asked if he remembered anything that was said. He didn't. Also asked if he had any idea what it had been about—Dean Isaacs hitting Laura. He said not a clue. They'd seen a guy beating on a girl and they'd gone in to stop it. Did say Rusty did most of the heavy hitting."

"You're starting to get the hang of this question-asking, Burrell." The fan of lines at the corners of his eyes deepened. "Anybody else remember any specifics of the situation?"

"Nope. Gil and Rusty were the only ones nearby except Dean and Laura. Only thing other folks remembered was that it had happened and Dean Isaacs got expelled over it."

I tried to not sigh. "Okay. Thanks for covering the bases. Let's go in before I turn into a Popsicle."

My phone rang. "Mike," I told Tom, but didn't answer until we were inside.

Mike barely waited for my hello. "Jennifer called. She thinks she's got some stuff. Wants to talk to us all at the same time. I told her we'd call her from a late lunch at Hamburger Heaven. I got the back room for us. Diana's on board. If you can call Tom—"

"He's right here. I'll tell him, but why are you speed talking?"

"If I'm going to make this lunch I've got a shi—boatload of work to do first. Slow news week my ass."

He hung up on my laugh.

Chapter Thirty-Six

I'D FINISHED RELAYING Mike's message to Tom when I spotted Jasmine Uffelman steaming out of the restaurant and straight across the lobby toward us, with Belknap visible through the archway to the restaurant, standing beside a table, apparently caught up by paying the bill.

"Trouble in paradise. Hang on," I said under my breath.

Tom shot me a look, but I didn't have time to divine it. I was moving in.

"Oh, hello, Jasmine. How are you? It's so wonderful to see you again."

She sidestepped, as if she might plow right past us. Extending my hand might not be enough. I grabbed hers, shaking with my right, and holding her arm with my left.

"Elizabeth Margaret Danniher from KWMT-TV. We met at the museum dinner the other night," I said, as if her issue might have been with forgetting my name. "Tom, you met, Jasmine, too, didn't you? I know you were at another table, but I'm sure you had the opportunity to be introduced."

"How do you do, ma'am." He nodded to her.

"Oh. Yes. Hello."

Barely looking at him, she tried to pull her arm away. I held on.

"We had the most fascinating discussion at our table at dinner," I enthused to him. "Jasmine made some excellent points on history and how it needs to move with the times. But in all that I never heard what, exactly, is your area of study?"

She looked at me as if I were an idiot. "The Battle of Cottonwood County, of course."

"Oh, yes, of course. But Professor Belknap—"

"Is the lead, but I will get author credit, too."

"Author credit?"

"On the book." Her tone matched her earlier look.

But I hadn't been questioning what it was. I was questioning if she really thought Belknap would share any bit of whatever glory there might be.

"What happens if there is no book?"

Before she decided on arrogance, fear flickered across her face. "You know nothing about it. There will be a book. Proving the battle happened will be a sensation. Totally change the thinking on the Great Sioux Wars of 1876 and reshape the narrative of the actions of Custer and the other officers leading into Little Bighorn."

"But Professor Roy didn't seem to think…"

Her cheeks reddened. "She had no first-hand knowledge of the research. None."

"Oh?" Might as well take advantage of her low opinion of me. "Is that what you're researching at the library here in town?"

"Among other research," she said stiffly. "I'm accessing first-hand accounts that have not been explored by other historians because they were considered too unimportant because they're not by famous people and they focus on this area."

"You're looking in them for proof the battle took place?"

"Their facts will lead me to conclusions," she said stiffly.

Sure, sure that was the company line. But was it the truth?

"And Professor Belknap is looking at the same accounts?"

"No. He's been revisiting sources he'd previously examined. The ones that brought him to the realization that a battle was absent from the other accounts."

"Why revisit them?"

"In case he missed something." She seemed to realize that sounded weak. "He is meticulous in his research and wants to be certain he has crossed every t, dotted every i."

As if that reminded her of Belknap's presence behind her, she yanked her arm. I let go.

"I've got to... Uh, good-bye."

"So fascinating to talk to you, Jasmine," I said, adding distinctly. "Thank you for the useful information. That helps a lot."

Add another you're-an-idiot look to my ledger.

Ah, but she couldn't see Bruce Belknap closing in on us and that he'd heard what I'd said.

She scooted off.

As Belknap neared, he was clearly torn between going after her and trying to shake me loose of whatever "useful" information Jasmine had just imparted.

Tom shifted his weight, brushing his arm against mine.

To reassure me? To give Belknap a united front? Or because one of his feet was tired of carrying the load?

Belknap stopped in front of us. "Elizabeth, how nice to see you again. And Tim. Nice to see you, too."

Tom said nothing. I said, "Hello, Professor Belknap."

"What are you doing here?"

"Oh, you know what they say. All roads in Cottonwood County lead to the Haber House Hotel."

Tom's cough sounded suspiciously like "for chocolate pie."

"Saw you talking with my grad student."

"*Your* grad student? Oh, Jasmine Uffelman. Of course. You work with her. I've been hearing such wonderful things about her research..."

"Under my direction," he snapped. Hard to tell which had riled him more, my saying he worked *with* her or that she was doing *her* research.

"As you worked under Professor Roy's."

His head drew in. "Not at all. She was the department chair, and as such had some influence on the courses I taught, but she did *not* direct my research."

"Didn't she? She could influence if you received any more funding—or *not*." I paused, holding his gaze. "It certainly sounded Tuesday night as if she had decided on the not."

"That?" He tried a laugh. "That was nothing. She was always trying to push down everyone around her to make herself feel better."

I didn't disbelieve that about Nora Roy, though it didn't make me believe the rest of what he said.

"Besides," he continued, "nothing was going to be discussed until we were all back in Colorado."

I looked him down, then up. "And now there will be no discussion and you can sail on with your research without interference."

I didn't say, *now that Professor Roy is dead and, gee, that gives you a golden motive.* I didn't need to.

His cheeks went pale, then ruddy in a snap.

He tried for cool uninterest, but that's hard with your complexion flashing white to red.

"My research shall continue. Good day."

I looked at Tom. "You think it was something I said?"

"It was everything you said."

I smiled happily. "Oh, good. You know, if MacArthur had delivered his 'We shall return' line as poorly as Belknap's declaration, it would've been forgotten immediately. Let's go in and see if anyone heard what they were arguing about."

"And to get a slice of chocolate pie?"

"Of course."

"You haven't had lunch yet, have you?"

"Some days you start with dessert and work backward."

He didn't dispute that. Instead, asking, "How do you know they were arguing?"

I rolled my eyes at him. "Same way you know. We have eyes."

He chuckled. "Interesting to see you at work, E.M. Danniher. From over-friendly babbler to ice queen in a second. Real interesting."

"You, too."

"Me? I didn't say a word."

"Exactly. Unnerved him even more, Tim."

He chuckled as we continued on to the restaurant.

THIS TIME FINDING out that Kelly was on duty was not good news.

I'd been hoping the guy from behind the counter the other day might have been their server. Long shot, but I could hope. Second-choice hope was the hostess. After that was anybody but Kelly.

Kelly had waited on them.

She confirmed that when we tracked her to the smoking annex.

"Oh, yeah, that guy who tried to skip out without paying. Jerk."

I wondered how long Belknap had waited for the bill while Kelly had been in her annex.

"Yes, with a young woman."

"Uh-huh," she said through a haze of smoke I felt sinking into my lungs, my eyes, my hair, and every stitch of clothing I had on.

"What were they arguing about?"

"Dunno."

"What were they talking about?"

"Dunno."

"Kelly, come on. You must have heard something. You remembered about him getting room service and that was real helpful."

"You paid me."

"I tipped you," I corrected. "Are you saying you do remember what they talked about and you are not going to tell me unless I pay you?"

She held it for a couple beats, then dropped. "Nah. Only thing I remember them saying was their order. They were boring."

"Give me a piece of chocolate pie—to go," I finished with emphasis, threatening no tip as retribution for her lousy memory.

TOM LEFT, HAVING tipped Kelly despite my ferocious glower.

He said he was going to check on some things to see if he could track down Javier Cruz. You'd think in a town this size that wouldn't be hard. But in a county this size it could be.

He also said he'd meet the rest of us at Hamburger Heaven at the appointed time.

With the SUV's heater blasting, I drove directly there, figuring I'd reply to emails from sources on the jury duty scam from the back room.

But first, I had a phone call to make that I preferred to make from the privacy of the SUV.

Mel didn't have good news.

"...definitely going into the new year and making it clear they're going to keep trying to postpone handing over your share. Their latest tack is to say that your proceeds should be held in escrow since your position in Wyoming is—and I quote—'tenuous.' "

"It's none of his damn business what my position is. It's my money, and if I want to spend it on... on Grey Poupon mustard—" I pulled that from a memory of a woman who'd included that among her modest extravagances. "—it's none of his damned business."

"So I informed them, though in much more lawyerly terms. I also petitioned to have them pay interest on your money from the time of the closing until you receive the check. Fifteen percent. I have suggested we schedule a hearing on that in front of the judge. That should stir them into acting. Rest assured, I'll go for the jugular."

"Thanks, Mel."

"You're welcome. Don't let it get you down. You know his games. He's still trying to keep you under his thumb, even now. But I can make it unpleasant enough that he gives up that little game. By the way, Elizabeth, I'm not prying you know—" He was, we both knew it, and we both knew it was out of concern for me. "—but is there someone there who would, say, give you a glowing endorsement?"

He could have come out and asked if I'd made any friends, had any allies. I would have told him. But that wasn't Mel's way. Too much experience with the legal system, I guess.

"A camerawoman, a sportscaster, a retired teacher and, on a strictly professional level, maybe a couple of the technical types. But I wouldn't ask for any letters of recommendation from the news director, the anchor or—on some days—from a nine-year-old girl named Tamantha."

"I followed you up to that last one."

"It's a long story—" Having to do with her father. "—and it must be lunchtime there by now. Don't you always have business lunches?"

"Oh God, I do. I have to run."

Chapter Thirty-Seven

I WAS THE first in the back room, sending an email when Mike walked in, talking on his phone.

Actually, mostly listening.

He wrapped the call up with, "Love you guys."

After shedding his coat he sat across from me and said, "My parents."

"How are they?"

"Good." He shook his head. "Disappointed I'm not getting down there over the holidays." He paused again. "I've been thinking about them since the other day when we talked. I didn't want to leave you thinking I blamed them—him."

"I don't."

"When I went away, went to college and the NFL, I saw things from a broader perspective, and I gradually realized it was tough on him, too. He moved into town, got a job in real estate and he did okay. Supported us, saved real hard for retirement, so he and Mom are in New Mexico now. But those first years in town... He shrank. Literally. Lost several inches of height, not gradually like old people do, but almost all at once, and a heck of a lot younger than most people do."

"How does he feel about you having a place now?"

"Hates it. Won't say it, but thinks it's a slap at him."

"Do you wish you could have gotten the family ranch back?"

He glanced at me, then away. "No. There was a possibility I could have bought back a good part of it at the time I was looking at the place I have now. This was the better deal. Left me with a better cushion for moving ahead."

Silence settled between us, though I was certain there was no silence in his head.

When he abruptly spoke, he proved me right. He also proved right my suspicion that his thoughts had not been about the ranch—the family one or the one he owned now.

"He won't take a thing from me. Not a thing. Not even a Christmas present. That's why I don't go see them. They don't come here." He straightened his slumped back, stretched tall. "Used to come to Chicago now and then when I was playing. Never would stay with me. Always in a hotel. And he wouldn't let me pay for a single meal. Not one."

I thought of my father as I left for the airport Monday, pressing cash into my hand, in case I needed some. "Some fathers can't ever stop being the one to take care of everybody."

"Or feeling like they are."

"Maybe the two are closely related."

Another silence. His frown indicated his thinking wasn't pleasant. I deliberately interrupted it with, "But you know what's a really interesting question?"

He looked over at me cautiously. "Why I'm not ranching?"

I waved that off. "No, that's obvious. You want the ranch here for eventually and because it's important to you to own a piece of Wyoming, but you don't want to be tied down to being a rancher, certainly not yet. You've got places to go, things to do. Though why on earth you bought a huge house—Anyway, what's a really interesting question is why doesn't Vic Zblewski seem to figure in to things much? It's all about the females in the household—the girl, the mother who's the professor, the housekeeper, even the older half-sister. But what about the girl's father? Kitty's husband, too, for that matter. How do they figure in to all of this?"

"Sounds like a good topic to discuss tonight when we get together, since Jennifer seems to be planning the agenda for now."

"Tonight? At Diana's? Have you checked with her?" I asked.

"I thought, uh, we'd go somewhere else tonight. Uh, my place. I suppose you want to see it." With that tone he should have been digging the toe of his shoe into the dirt. He might, have, too, if any dirt had been available.

"Not if you don't want to, Mike. I'll admit I've been curious why you hadn't invited us—me. But it's your house, it's your prerogative."

"It's my house and I'm inviting you. All of you."

"Are you sure, Mike?"

"Yeah." He didn't sound or look sure. "Tonight."

MIKE'S ANNOUNCEMENT OF tonight's venue was greeted without a blink by the others, including Jennifer, who was on the screen of Mike's phone by then, and clearly impatient to get started.

"If Mike will hold down all that paper crinkling while he unwraps his burgers—plural—I have something to say," she announced.

"Hey. This is our lunch. Our *late* lunch. I'm starved."

"Forget your stomach, I got them."

I swallowed fast so her triumph didn't fall flat. "That's great, but got who?"

"Sue Martin for starters. I found a bunch of Sue Martins. Too many. If you want me to try to sort through them—"

"Not yet. Not if you found anything else on Laura's high school friends."

"I did." Triumph made a comeback. "Mary was actually Marilyn Backstrom. I did track her down. She's in Pittsburgh now. She was very suspicious at first, but said she'd talk to you if you wanted. Though she also said she barely remembers anyone from those first two years of high school. Her family moved after her sophomore year and she's never been back."

Great.

But Jennifer remained almost giddy, so maybe… "Anyone else?"

"Yup. I think so, anyway. I think CeeCee was Candace Carmichael. She and Laura were in a couple photos together. Involved with the theater stuff."

"You found Candace Carmichael?"

"Not exactly. But I did track her and I found her wedding announcement in the *Independence*. Her married name's Candace Carmichael Wynn and she still lives in Cottonwood County."

She sure did. Because I'd talked to her two days ago about receiving jury duty scam phone calls.

Fortunately, the others congratulating Jennifer and a french fry in my mouth stopped me from spilling that secret.

When I tuned back in, Diana was saying, "…at the high school because connections made at Cottonwood County High School are the real behind-the-scenes power networks… Elizabeth? I have the feeling we've lost you."

"High school." I said.

Diana raised her eyebrows. "Uh-huh. That's what I said. The high school. What are you doing?"

"Checking my notes."

"You're flipping back far enough to get to the beginning of time."

"Ah. Here's one." I ran a finger down the page. "Yup, exactly."

"More flipping?"

"Yes, that's what I thought. One more, one more. Now, where is it? Ahhh."

"You found it. But now what are you doing? Who are you calling?"

"Shh," I ordered. "Deputy Alvaro? Elizabeth Danniher. I have an important question for you."

"I'm not answering any questions. Besides—"

"Did one of your older siblings go to high school with Dean Isaacs?"

"How did you know—?"

"I'll tell you later. Gotta go."

"Elizabeth, how did you get this number?"

My very favorite question to be asked. Also my favorite question to not answer.

"Talk to you later, Richard. Thanks."

I hung up.

"Elizabeth?" Diana demanded.

"The high school. That's it."

"That's what?"

"The connection. Not random targets. People from high school."

"What are you talking about? We know the connections. And random targets? There haven't been any random targets."

I sucked in a breath to explain that I wasn't talking about the Roys, held it, then let it stream out slowly. "I can't tell you."

"You have to tell us," Jennifer protested.

"I really can't. At least not yet. Let me... I'll see if I can. But not now."

Mike said, "If it has something to do with—"

"I don't think—I don't *know* that it does. But either way, I promised."

"In that case, let's move on," Diana said briskly. "Elizabeth and I had an interesting morning."

She started to explain, but long before she got to what we heard, she was interrupted.

"Diana Stendahl, you are a *rock star*," Mike said in admiration.

"That is so cool," Jennifer said. "Like spies."

"Wayne Shelton won't like that if he finds out," Tom said.

"Then he better not find out, right?" I said.

When the reactions settled down, Diana told them what we'd heard of Shelton's interview of the Roy household.

At the end, I brought up the photo and my curiosity about the boy/man.

"Diana? With your great visual memory..."

She was shaking her head. "I only caught a glimpse of that one as we left. Otherwise your head was in the way."

"Too bad we didn't swap spots."

"Not sure I would've noticed even if I'd been standing right in front of it. I was focusing on what was being said."

"Jennifer," I asked, "would there be a way to get the identity of the guy I saw in a photo on the wall there? Without the photo?"

"Get back in the house and take a picture of it. Though a scan would be a lot better."

I turned to Diana. "Do you think Lorraine—"

"No. And I wouldn't ask her. That favor's been paid."

"I was just going to ask if you could ask Lorraine if she or any of the other members of the household had headaches or any other carbon monoxide symptoms Wednesday before Professor Roy was found?" I fibbed. "It might indicate if it was leaking into the house."

"That I will ask her."

That detour dealt with, I returned to the previous issue.

"So, Jennifer, there's no app or technology or something that you could—?"

"Suck the visual memory out of your head? Give it a few more years."

Foiled at every turn on that issue, I barely even protested as Tom gave his account of the encounters with Jasmine Uffelman, Belknap, Kelly, and a piece of pie.

Part of my thoughts rattled around that photograph, recognizing and not recognizing people, and wild ways to try to identify the boy/man. After all, I'd recognized Isaacs from photos that were twenty-six years old, so why couldn't—

I sat up straight.

"What is it, Elizabeth?" Tom asked.

"I recognized Isaacs from old photos."

"Yeah?" Mike asked.

"Why didn't other people."

"Oh," Diana said. "Good one, Elizabeth. You recognized him at Sally's right away. So certainly Professor Roy would have recognized him. But not just her. Kitty Roy Young, Graham Young, and Vic Zblewski, too. They all would have recognized him. So how could Zblewski and the professor have missed him in the library?"

"The same way Zblewski didn't spot his wife," Mike said. "She kept out of his direct line of sight and he's not a noticing sort of guy. Because from everything Ivy Short said to Elizabeth, he didn't see her, right? Elizabeth? Right? Elizabeth?"

I'd heard him before the repeat of my name. I'd have been fine expressing my agreement, too. But that mental train of thought had been shunted to a side track while an express came barreling through.

In the turbulent slipstream of that express, I said, "I should have recognized him."

"You did recognize Isaacs. As soon as you saw him at Sally Tipton's."

"Not him. *Him*."

"Him, who?"

But I had my device open and was typing away.

Why hadn't I looked at that photo? Or had I looked and I hadn't *seen*. Either way, I should have—"Got it."

Now I looked. And saw. And remembered.

Damn.

We'd wasted a whole day.

I turned the screen around so they all could see.

"*Him*."

"Never seen him before," Mike said.

"Me, either, but there's something familiar…" That was Diana.

"Who is he?" Tom said.

"That's Javier Cruz," Jennifer said. "That's from his law firm's site."

"Exactly. Yolanda and Arturo's youngest, as Mrs. Parens told us. The guy who'd get DOC notices about Isaacs' status, yet when I called him—supposedly in Denver—wiggled out of saying he knew Isaacs was out with a technicality. Thanks to Jennifer, we know he's *not* in Denver. He's here. Staying at the B&B and going places like the library where he held the door open for me when I was entering as he was leaving yesterday."

"You saw him?"

"I sure did. Several times. The most recent time, Diana did, too. She even knows where he buys his clothes. If I'd looked at his picture on the law firm website like any half intelligent person would have done, I'd've known who he was yesterday at the library. Dean Isaacs murdered Javier's mother twenty-six years ago and was sentenced to life. But now he's out of prison and back in Sherman. And so is Javier."

Chapter Thirty-Eight

WE ALL AGREED it was interesting.

We all agreed it wasn't coincidence, especially with him parked near the Roys' ranch house.

We all agreed we should find Javier Cruz.

But we didn't get much farther than that.

"We might not know what it means yet, but it's got to mean something," Mike concluded.

Frustrated with the accuracy and futility of that, I told them about my encounter with Kitty Roy Young outside the library. But that didn't get us any farther, either.

"Ivy Short wasn't any help about how much damage Professor Roy could have done to Belknap, but with what Mike got from Mrs. Eldercott, we have that covered." Nods all around. "But Ivy did say something interesting. She said Dean Isaacs was looking up carbon monoxide the day before Nora Roy died."

"He was?" Mike sat up straight, then slumped. "But he wasn't seen out at the Roy place."

"That we know of," Diana said.

"He was at the Kicking Cowboy from before they would have left for the museum dinner until well after they got back," Tom said. We all looked at him. "What? I can't figure out to check an alibi?"

"If he went out there in the middle of the night and rigged it up...?" Diana let her speculation die as Mike shook his head.

"From how my friend described it, he'd have had to be real lucky to find that frozen tumbleweed. Would he have gone out there just hoping something would pop up? We keep hitting dead ends," he complained.

Jennifer said, "What about that weird thing I told you about? You ready to hear about that now?"

"What weird—? Oh, right. About Yolanda's sister—"

"Arturo's sister. Yolanda's sister-in-law. She popped up on a genealogy site and that's how I connected her to him, because it would have been tough to find her married name. But there she was. And her three kids, including one daughter, Rosanna, who's married to Nando Alvaro."

"Alvaro?" at least three of us chorused in response. Wasn't sure about Tom, though he leaned forward in a display of interest.

"Richard's cousin," Jennifer said.

"You're kidding. Not a sibling? Now, that's a shock."

TO APPROACH RICHARD or not to approach Richard.

Ordinarily, I would have said not.

But we had two factors going in our favor.

Wayne Shelton had come as close as he ever would to asking me to look into this case.

And he had asked me to look into the scam calls citing Deputy Alvaro.

That didn't mean I walked in the front door of the sheriff's office asking for Richard.

Tom did that.

He wasn't particularly happy about it, but he did it.

I was in the passenger seat of his truck in the parking lot when Deputies Shelton and Alvaro climbed in the back.

I would have preferred that the short half of that combo hadn't come, but I hadn't held out much hope.

I twisted around in the seat and went right to the point. "Richard, you didn't tell me your cousin's wife has a connection to the Cruz murder and Dean Isaacs."

He looked taken aback, then puzzled, then faintly amused. "Oh, right. Isidora's aunt by marriage was the victim."

Shelton flickered him a look at that, but said nothing.

"That gives you a connection to the case, too, Richard."

"Oh, come on. This all happened when I was about a year old. Isidora was a kid herself and it was way before she even met my cousin, which happened when *I* was a kid. Not to mention the guy was caught and convicted."

"And is now out of prison and here in Sherman."

Without looking at Shelton, I was aware of his increased focus.

"Oh, c'mon," Alvaro said. He looked at Shelton, then back to me. "I probably heard about it once in my life before Dean Isaacs was released from prison."

"But you've heard about it since? From your cousin's wife?"

He hesitated for the first time. "Some."

"**AUNT YOLANDA STARTED** working for the professor when it was just her and the daughter—the first daughter. It was a regular job to start, though she did care a lot for that girl. What's her name? The older daughter?"

"Kitty Roy. Now Kitty Young."

One question had started the flow with Isadora Alvaro. Even with Shelton sitting behind her, which most people would feel as a black cloud hovering, she talked easily with Richard and me. Tom had left to pick up Tamantha, who had a free afternoon in her packed social schedule.

I'd seen Richard shoot a puzzled look at Shelton.

He had to be wondering why Shelton wasn't trying to shut me down, much less going along with this questioning.

Let him dare to ask Deputy Shelton.

"Right. Kitty," she said. "Aunt Yolanda liked her. Felt sorry for her, too."

Why? didn't come out fast enough to stop her from going on.

"After Laura, the younger one was born, that's when Aunt Yolanda would travel with them everywhere. They needed a lot more help, of course, with a baby. The professor had so much work and…" She glanced toward Richard as it trailed off.

"Go ahead, Isadora. Say what you were going to say."

"It's just what I heard. Mostly from my mother, remembering. So I don't know how true it is."

"But?" he encouraged her.

"But the professor was never very maternal. That's what Aunt Yolanda told my mother. Not with the older girl, which might have been because she was growing up, but not with the baby, either. Not even when she was a baby. The husband was useless. The older girl helped, but she didn't know how to take care of a baby and then she left home soon after." She shrugged. "So, Yolanda felt she was needed, really needed. And with her kids mostly grown … Plus, there was Javier."

"Javier?" Richard asked.

"My cousin. Aunt Yolanda and Uncle Arturo's youngest. Mamma always said the professor took advantage of Yolanda's gratitude."

"Gratitude?"

"The professor helped get Javier a scholarship to college. The whole family's always viewed Javier as the smartest one. The one with the best future. All Aunt Yolanda and Uncle Arturo's hopes for the next generation were on Javier. Which my mom always said was so unfair, since Arturo Junior and Teresa and Sylvia helped support the family and Marie Guadalupe kept the house going and did all the cooking with Yolanda away so much.

"Anyway, it turned out just the way they all hoped. Javier became a lawyer. He's making a boatload of money and he's helped his nieces and nephews—and his cousin's kids, including a niece of mine who's in college now."

"Why did your aunt feel sorry for Kitty Roy?"

She gave a half shrug, trying to play it down. "The mother didn't pay her much attention. Pushed her aside. Got impatient when the girl required any real attention. I remember there was something about her having the flu when she was in high school, and the mother couldn't be bothered. But well before that, Aunt Yolanda would say something now and then that made you know she didn't approve of how the professor treated her daughter. She never came right out and said it that I remember. She'd have thought that wasn't proper." She gave a little laugh. "She had a harder time sticking to her rules when it came to the professor's husband. I overheard her telling Mom how he was a good-for-nothing. A leach, that's what she called him. I remember asking Mom later what that meant."

"Would your mother be willing to talk to me…"

"She passed away a year ago."

"I'm so sorry."

"Thank you. But even if you could talk to her, it wouldn't give you much, not about the professor's husband. She always maintained that Aunt Yolanda was jealous. It had been the three of them—Aunt Yolanda, Kitty, and the professor. Most of the day Aunt Yolanda ran things because the professor wasn't home. Then that man came in."

"Were there specific issues?"

Isadora shook her head. "Nothing major. Not that I know of. Knowing Aunt Yolanda, it's not surprising she didn't like him. He could have been a saint and she wouldn't have liked him when he came in to *her* house."

✧ ✧ ✧ ✧

I CALLED SHELTON as soon as their vehicle was out of sight after they'd dropped me off at my SUV at Hamburger Heaven.

"Now what?"

"We have to meet. Same place."

"Why?"

"If I were going to tell you on the phone I would have already said. Same place. Tonight. Seven."

He grunted before clicking off.

That was a yes. I was almost sure it was.

Chapter Thirty-Nine

AT THE WYNN house, the young woman again opened the door. She looked at me a bit blankly for a moment—clearly not an ardent fan of 'Helping Out!'—then smiled her recognition that I'd been there before and invited me in.

Candace Wynn came from the kitchen, carrying a tray and smiling. "Coffee? Brownies?"

If only everyone responded to being interviewed this way. Especially since I'd called to ask if she'd talk to me again practically from her driveway.

As we sat on the couches at right angles to each other in front of the picture window, the daughter remained standing. "Mom, I'm going to go take a nap."

"Okay, dear. Have a good rest. I'll save you a brownie."

The younger woman gave a wry smile. "Better save me two."

"What can I help you with today? More about those awful phone calls? My mother always said, 'CeeCee, you do get yourselves into situations.' I haven't received any more calls, if that's what you wanted to know."

I skipped answering that. "Your mother called you CeeCee?"

"Oh, yes, that's what everyone called me. My name was Carmichael—Candace Carmichael—but I had terrible trouble saying Carmichael as a little girl. Candace, too, for that matter. I told everyone my name was CeeCee. That's what everyone called me from then on and all through school. Well, really, until I married, and then with the last name Wynn it didn't make as much sense. Though family and old school friends still call me CeeCee."

"Old school friends? Did that include Laura Roy?"

Her eyes went wide. "How on earth did you know that?"

"I was looking at old yearbooks from Cottonwood County High School. You and Laura and Sue Martin and Mary Backstrom were in a lot of pictures together your freshman and sophomore years."

She smiled. "We were. We connected our first day of high school and vowed to stick together." Her smile faded. "Poor Laura. Poor, poor Laura. Mary moved away with her family and Sue never came back after college, but Laura's gone forever. I think about her. So often." Her gaze went to the hallway her daughter had gone down.

"What was Laura like when you met her?"

"Why do you want to know this?"

"I'm not entirely sure," I admitted. "I had no idea you had a connection to Laura Roy when I first came here to ask you about the phone calls and now that I know you do… It seems like it's meant to be."

She looked straight ahead without blinking for two breaths, three breaths. Then, "Laura was fun. A little shy. But when you got to know her, she was such a good friend. Loyal and she'd stick up for you. We worked on sets for the plays and such. Some of the kids goofed off most of the time, flirting with each other and such. But Laura was always serious about getting the work done. She did more than her share, that's for sure."

"Did you see each other outside of school?"

"Oh, yes. Mostly at my house—my parents' house—or we'd meet at the movies or at the high school for some event, a game, a play, something like that."

"Her house?"

"Only once." She looked down at her folded hands. "I never wanted to go back. Nobody did anything overt, but…" Under her sweater, her shoulders gave a flicker of a shudder. "Even then, as a teenager, it made me appreciate my family. I really felt sorry for Laura. She knew it, too, and she didn't like it. But after a couple awkward days we got back to normal."

"I understand that didn't endure? She changed in her sophomore year?"

She nodded. "Everybody thought it was Dean Isaacs that changed her, but it was something else. Something… He was a symptom, not the reason. I'm sure of it."

"What was the reason?"

"I don't know."

"But you have a guess." Judging from the way her "something" had trailed off to a faraway stare.

She didn't accept that challenge. "It was a long time ago. She's at peace now."

Something in the back of my mind clicked and I could hear Thelma's voice saying *Some girls are drawn to that sort. And then they get themselves into trouble, too.*

Get themselves into trouble.

Had Laura Roy been "in trouble?"

My memory flashed to that photo in the hallway. Laura and the boy/man, who looked at her as if…

And just now, CeeCee talking of poor Laura as she looked to the hallway her very pregnant daughter had gone down.

"Was she pregnant?" The question came out before the thought had fully formed.

CeeCee Wynn's eyes widened. "How could you possibly—?"

"So, she was."

She shook her head. "I don't know. Not for certain. She said some things and I thought… We were awfully young and I was probably more naïve than most. But she and I talked, even after she changed so much. I think I was the only one she still talked to. Dean Isaacs used to tell her to stay away from all of us. Said we didn't like him, which was true. Said we didn't like *her*, which was *not*. Now you hear how cutting someone off from their friends is all part of a pattern of an abuser. I'm not saying he hit her. I don't know about that. But I do know he bossed her around terribly. Said she had to do everything he said or they were through. I kept telling her she didn't have to put up with that.

"Then, in the week before she died, she came over to my house—first time in months. She said she was sorry she'd been weird, sorry she'd let a guy interfere in our friendship. She said that wasn't going to happen anymore. And then she talked about needing to grow up and take care not only of herself, but others."

She looked out the window. The bright light from the blue sky reflecting off the shallow snow showed her age in well-earned laugh lines.

"After Laura...died, I was obsessed about it. I was sure there was a crime and I was going to solve it. That's when I thought back to what she'd said, and I was sure she'd been telling me she was going to break off with Dean. She had some pills—she'd stolen them from her father's medicine cabinet because Isaacs kept after her to do it. She said she'd give them to him then that was it. He'd be on his own.

"I tried to tell the sheriff and a teacher at school and my parents. They asked if she'd come out and said she'd broken up with Dean. I had to say no. They all said I shouldn't worry myself about it. It was a tragedy that I'd understand someday.

"I'd never known someone who'd died, much less a suicide and the murder of Yolanda who was always so nice to me... But in the end, I suppose I have to accept what everyone said happened was what really happened."

That might be what her head was telling her, but something deeper wasn't buying it. CeeCee still didn't believe her friend committed suicide. She couldn't even say the word.

"Only later did I realize she'd been trying to tell me she was pregnant. I was too inexperienced to recognize it."

"She never said it outright to you?"

She shook her head.

"Was she involved with someone before Dean Isaacs? A tall boy, attractive, dark hair."

She frowned, then slowly shook her head. "No. Dean was her first boyfriend. I'm sure of that."

"Maybe on vacation? A summer romance?"

She shook her head. "She would have told me, I'm sure."

She was sure, but I wasn't. Girls liked secrets. I certainly had at that age.

And he could be the perfect explanation for Laura's abrupt change over that spring break of her sophomore year in high school. A summer romance that spoiled from the separation of fall and winter. The final blow coming with spring.

She'd have been vulnerable for Isaacs' dubious charms.

"Did you know that Dean Isaacs likens their romance to Romeo and Juliet?"

"Give me a break." Her intonation and disgust reverted her to a much younger age, closely resembling the girl I'd seen in the yearbook photos.

"He said that just like Romeo and Juliet, they were being kept apart by family—her family."

A new alertness came into her eyes. "Her family? You mean her mother. But Yolanda was the one who had real influence over Laura. Yolanda was the one she turned to. They had a really close relationship."

"Laura and her parents weren't close?"

"She and her mother fought. A lot. She and her father had nothing to say to each other. He didn't have much to do with her."

"How about her sister?"

CeeCee lifted one shoulder. "Not close. Laura couldn't ever figure her out. Like why didn't she leave? She clearly disliked their mother as much as Laura did. Even if they couldn't get completely away because of her husband's job, Kitty and he didn't need to be right there all the time. They could have had their own life. Laura used to say she couldn't respect them because they chose to be Nora Roy's captives."

I asked more questions, but got no more information, though she promised to call if she remembered anything else.

I could see why Laura had liked and trusted her.

At the door, she said, "I'll never forget all those people who were adults saying that someday I'd understand it... I've long been an adult myself, about to be a grandmother, but I still don't understand it."

Chapter Forty

I WASTED NO time in following up on the Dean Isaacs angle with the remaining two, since I already knew Marcia Odom's connection with Isaacs.

Mrs. Radey welcomed me in, rousing Ed from an afternoon nap because, "that nice young lady's here."

"Bring any food?" he asked immediately.

"Not this time. I'll owe you another lunch. When I was here before you mentioned troublemaking students."

"Oh, dear, don't start him on that," Mrs. Radey said.

"Whaddya mean?" he demanded of her.

"Blood pressure," his wife said.

"Baloney. I don't get upset talking about those snotty little—"

"Blood pressure," she said in an entirely different tone.

Quickly, I narrowed to one snotty whatever, in hopes of whittling down his blood-pressure-hiking irritation. "Dean Isaacs."

He seemed to deflate from anger to sadness. "Oh, him." He looked from his wife to me. "The one who murdered Laura Roy. Poor girl."

"You knew her?" I hadn't expected that.

"Yeah. Nice kid."

"She'd bring Ed an apple every day."

"That's what I told you. Truth is, she brought me cookies until Isaacs got a hold of her," he grumbled.

"How did that start?"

"Had the door propped open because it was hot at the start of the school year. She came in and looked around, sat down, and started talking to me." He cleared his throat, but the next word still came out gruff. "Don't remember another kid who ever did that. Sweet kid. A shame. A real, real shame."

I'd meant how Isaacs had connected with Laura. "When she changed after starting to date Dean—?"

"Didn't."

I blinked at his irritation.

"Laura didn't change. Don't care what people said. Don't care what she looked like. Don't care what that jerk Isaacs did or said. She was the same girl. Brought me cookies that last day of school, same as she did the first day."

He blew his nose on a handkerchief as if it had insulted him.

After a beat to let him recover, I asked, "What about Isaacs? What were your encounters with him like?"

"Little pissant."

Not just a pissant, but a little pissant. Ed Radey definitely didn't like Isaacs.

"Encounters? You want to know about encounters? First one I found him pressing a girl up against a locker. This tiny little girl. I yanked him away, and he thought he was going to come after me until he saw I wasn't some tiny little girl. Didn't want any of that."

That fit with my impression of Isaacs. He wouldn't take on someone stronger than him—physically or otherwise. He'd take on Sally Tipton, but not Mrs. P. He'd intimidate a small, young girl, but not a burly man.

"Not long after, I found him in my storage room. Kicked him out and the principal gave him a slap on the hand. Same thing when the science teacher found him rummaging around the chem lab. Another slap on the wrist. Wasn't until he messed up that yearbook stuff that he got kicked out of school. Kept hanging around, though. Partly for Laura."

"Picking her up after school?"

He humphed. "And spying on her. Popping up like a bad penny all times of the day. I kept running him off. Made him mad as fire. Found him in my rooms again. Had an old cat who lived down there and he had it wrapped up in a plastic bag. I shoved him away. Ripped the bag from him, cat scooted away, and I dragged that little pissant out by the scruff of his neck. Tried to get the principal to get the deputies involved, but she still wouldn't do it. Sheriff's department sure as heck was involved when he killed that nice Yolanda lady and Laura killed herself."

His wife gave him a sympathetic yet scolding look. She turned to me. "He thinks he blames the principal. He really blames himself. You foolish old man. It wasn't your fault. The girl had parents and a family. They should have looked out for that girl, poor thing, and for that lady he killed."

I thought about that as I drove away. In most situations, the family was expected to look after its members, especially those younger or otherwise vulnerable.

But according to CeeCee, it had been something in the family that had spurred the changes in Laura, with Dean Isaacs as a symptom.

❖   ❖   ❖   ❖

"YOU NEED MORE information?" Enid Harter didn't look up from her office computer screen to ask the question.

"I do. Do you remember the circumstances of your son getting into temporary trouble for a fight with Dean Isaacs?"

That got her attention. "How on earth did you know about that?"

Before I could answer, she added, "And what does it have to do with the scam you're looking into for Deputy Shelton?"

"Possibly nothing. On the other hand, your answering my questions might provide the answer."

After a pause, she nodded. She even took her hands off the keyboard. "Shoot."

"What do you remember about your son getting into a fight with Dean Isaacs?"

"You're not going to tell me how you know that, are you? No. I can see you won't. Okay, what do I remember? Everything. Well, once I found out about it, everything. Didn't find out right away of course.

Teenagers. Especially teenage boys who think they're protecting their mother by keeping her in the dark. So it wasn't until the next morning that I found out he was in trouble with the principal."

The kid was in a fight after school and she considered it a long delay that she knew by the next morning. That hardly counted as keeping her in the dark. Not to me, anyway. But maybe that was from looking at it from the child's point of view, rather than the parent's.

"I grabbed him and we went to the principal before school. That woman thinking she'd punish him for protecting that girl. Wasn't going to happen."

"Did you have any contact with Dean Isaacs?"

"Yes. After that initial meeting with the principal, there were two more. The second meeting was the Alvaros, us, the principal, and the Isaacs boy and his aunt—that's who he was living with at the time— and a counselor. Started out with the Isaacs boy's account coming across like it was the complete and official story. I said wait a minute, and the Alvaros backed me right up. We asked our boys a couple questions and their answers had Isaacs whining and the principal and that counselor guy starting to look at things a little different. When we suggested they call in the girl and ask which story was true, that turned things around for good. Don't know if they ever did. But the last meeting sure was different. They'd held off on the threat to suspend the boys, but at that third meeting, they were commending them for helping that girl—about time."

"Isaacs wasn't there for the last meeting?"

"No. Still in school, though. Few weeks later he messed with the yearbook and that finally got that principal to act. If Emmaline Parens had been principal, never would have happened."

I WENT TO the back door of the Wild Horses B&B. Krista Seger opened it before I had to knock.

"Thanks for the message," I said as she returned to behind the large island. She was making something in a large baking dish with apples.

"He came in twenty minutes ago. He's taken a shower and I think he's getting ready to go out. He's in the room your friend was in. I'd rather he didn't know—"

"He won't." I figured that meant she'd rather her guest didn't know she'd informed me he was here or that the room he was staying in had not so long ago had a dead body in it. Nope, wasn't going to spill either of those. I put a hand on her arm as I went by. "Stay here."

I went up the back stairs and waited in the hallway, not in the direct line of sight as he came out. When the door did open, I waited until he took a couple more steps—so he couldn't easily retreat into the room—before advancing.

"Javier Cruz." He turned. "I'm Elizabeth Margaret Danniher."

Chapter Forty-One

HE WASN'T AS tall as Mike or Tom or Sheriff Conrad. But he was erect and straight. With that perfect amount of silver in his dark hair. And his dark eyes were direct and intelligent.

They now went from the back stairs to the front stairs, assessing my arrival and what it meant. "Are you a guest here?"

"No. Perhaps you don't remember that about Sherman from when you used to come here, but people rarely lock their doors during the day. As I'm sure you do remember, I'm with KWMT-TV. We talked Thursday when you misled me about your location."

"You had no reasonable expectation that I would share my location with you."

Lawyer-speak for *it was none of your business.*

I could see his point. Though it didn't make the fact of the concealment any less interesting.

"Your presence here in Cottonwood County leads me to believe you did know about Dean Isaac's release on parole."

He said nothing. The silence that neither confirmed nor denied.

"What have you been doing while you've been here?" In addition to driving out to both the scene of his mother's murder and to the Roys' new home.

"Pursuing matters of interest to my family, which I represent."

"I understand you've been working on your computer to all hours."

He smiled a tight *I'm a shark lawyer* smile. "I am keeping up with my work while I'm here, Ms. Danniher. It's my responsibility. And now I have an appointment."

"After your appointment—"

"No. Good day."

He strode away.

Running after and peppering him with questions was beneath my dignity. Particularly since I was certain it wouldn't work with him.

"DEPUTY SHELTON, THIS is getting to be our spot."

Having just seated himself in my SUV, he didn't respond.

I didn't waste any more time. "I've found a connection linking the people called by that jury duty scammer."

He scowled. "But not the scammer?"

"I have an idea about that, too, but let me explain the targets first. Ed Radey was a custodian at the high school for decades."

"Yeah. So?"

"Patience, Deputy Shelton." It sure was nice to order someone else to be patient. "Marcia Odom taught there seven years. Four years as Miss Rogers, then three more after she got married and before she left when she was very pregnant with their first child. That child will be nineteen on his next birthday."

He glared but didn't interrupt.

"Laura Roy was a sophomore at CCHS the year Marcia started teaching there. She was in the drama club. Candace Wynn was known as CeeCee Carmichael in high school. She was Laura's best friend."

"Is this—?"

"Enid Harter, is the mother of a son who went to Cottonwood County High School. Only trouble that son was ever in was when he and a friend got into a fight with a third student twenty-six years ago." His glare sharpened at the time period. "Turns out he and his friend were protecting a girl who was being hit by that other male student. Her son and his friend were exonerated. The other boy was kicked out of school a few weeks later. The girl ended up dead not long after. Laura Roy."

He started to say something, but I help up my hand.

"One more, Deputy. The friend who also came to the girl's defense, who also was exonerated? Gil Alvaro, Richard's older brother."

He chewed on that for half a second. He'd been putting the pieces together as I went along. "Proof?"

"Of those facts? Plenty. That Dean Isaacs is pulling off the scam? No. Though there is the timing—they started when he got out of prison, even before he arrived here. Did you know one of the bigger instances of these scams was a gang running them out of a Georgia prison? Reports say it's well-known in prison circles and they get a kick out of impersonating law enforcement."

His growl didn't count as a real interruption so I kept going.

"He has tech skills, by the way. Worked with computers as a kid. Still seems pretty handy with repairs and such. There might be ways to catch him in the act. But that's way above my technical expertise. I'd have to consult someone who knows all about electronics and computers and cell phones and—"

"No. We can't prosecute him with the way she finds things out."

"I understand. But she could still give us leads. Yes, I said *us*. I need to be able to tell the rest of them—Diana, Mike, Tom, and Jennifer—about this. With all of us putting our heads together... Though it might not be right away, what with the holidays and all, everybody's pretty busy."

"Yeah, right. You mean with all of you sticking your noses in the Roy death?"

"We weren't. We were heading another direction completely. But somehow things keep pulling us that way. So, I'll tell them—"

"Not yet." He relented only slightly in adding, "I'll talk to Alvaro."

"And the sheriff?"

"We'll see what you come up with first."

SEEING THE HOUSE from above had conveyed the footprint, but only coming around the trees that masked it from the road, did the mass of Mike's house become real.

Like Professor Roy's house, it was of stone and glass, angles and planes.

Yet those similarities created different impressions. In having Mike's house to compare it too, the Roy house's combination of these elements came off as not only less appealing, but gloomier.

Diana had pulled in ahead of me and waited on the stone-flagged front steps for me.

Mike answered the door with a dish towel over his shoulder and a sheepish expression.

"C'mon in. I, uh, gotta get back to the kitchen fast. Do you mind hanging up your stuff yourselves?"

"No problem."

He hurried toward the back of the house.

Diana and I looked at each other.

"More time to poke around," she said, voicing both of our thoughts.

As we took off our coats, we tipped our heads toward features, pointing them out to each other. The generous entrance, which swept up in a wide stairway with a gentle curve to a hallway along three sides of the two story-foyer. An empty room to the left, which, judging by the massive chandelier in the center, was designed as the dining room.

"Tara in Cottonwood County," Diana murmured as we hung our coats in the closet tucked under the stairway and behind wide wood doors.

"Scarlett O'Hare never had anything like that." I jerked my head to the room behind us.

In most households it would have been the formal living room. But instead of couches and easy chairs clustered around the large fireplace on the opposite wall, the open arch to this room showed weights in racks, a sizable rubber mat, a treadmill, a bicycle-type contraption, and three more machines entirely alien to me. Three mirrors rested against walls. The walls held nothing else. A rollable set of shelves held stacks of towels.

When he'd said he had a room set up as a gym, I'd expected the treadmill, but nothing like this.

Poking our heads into the substantial room, Diana and I raised our eyebrows at each other.

"Scarlett would have had the muscle to go with that willfulness if she'd had all this," she said.

We headed down a short, unadorned hallway to where it opened to the back of the house.

This was truly Mike's home.

To our right was a family room with a mammoth leather sectional, with one side facing a rock fireplace that dwarfed every other rock fireplace I'd seen, short of the one at Old Faithful Inn at Yellowstone Park. A comparable TV stretched above the mantel. The other angle of the sectional faced a run of wide windows and glass doors to a deck where a dozen cars could have parked.

In front of us an oval wooden table was surrounded by enough chairs to accommodate a large family. A nook designed for a break-front held a three-foot tall pre-decorated Christmas tree set on a red, upside down bucket. That and some cards on the mantel was it for holiday decoration.

The kitchen was to our left, with Mike in the middle of it, pulling out a tray from the oven designed for a serious cook.

"Taco dip," he said. "Got the recipe from a cornerback."

Four other trays rested on the granite countertops.

Mike glanced at them. "My failures."

Diana put the shopping bag she'd carried in on the counter, then went around the island to him.

"This one looks good. Stop now while you're ahead."

"Want to sit at the table or on the couch?"

Diana said, "Table to eat, then the couch to really talk. Now, what do you need us to do?"

Chapter Forty-Two

THE LAYERED TACO dip was delicious and a nice break from Hamburger Heaven fare.

I'd had my fill when my phone indicated a message. It was from Shelton. It said. "Those 3 only. No exceptions."

"Okay, guys, I have something to tell you."

With Mike and Tom still working on the taco dip, I had time to tell it my way. I'd pinned down the outline of the Cottonwood County High connections in my head, so that came out smoothly.

Of course there were questions. However, the only tension came when I emphasized Shelton's condition that no one else be informed. Including Sheriff Russ Conrad.

"He should know," Diana objected.

I didn't totally disagree. In fact, I wondered if Shelton's decision was swayed, in addition to his concern for Richard, by his desire for more information on the Yolanda Cruz murder. If Conrad knew I'd found the Isaacs and Cottonwood County High School connections to the scam calls, it cracked open the door to his discovering the digging we'd been doing on the Yolanda Cruz murder.

Most sheriffs lack enthusiasm for revisiting cases that ended in convictions.

"It's Shelton's call," I said.

"Russ wouldn't blame Richard. He's a reasonable man."

"He's also a hard ass," Mike said.

He looked at Diana quickly, as if realizing he said it aloud only when he heard the words.

"Yes, he is," Diana said with relish. "Thank you very much."

The laughter erased tension.

"I won't tell him—or anybody, but I reserve my right to urge Shelton to change his mind," she said.

"Fair enough."

More questions came when I said I'd seen Javier Cruz in a black SUV the first time when Shelton had brought me out here.

Diana jumped in. "*That's* what made you suspicious of the map guy in the rental SUV at Professor Roy's place."

"Yeah. I *thought* it was the same SUV, same guy, same map. But I didn't see it well the first time. It wasn't until we saw that picture of Javier on the law firm's website—"

"Wait a minute. Shelton brought you here to Bennett Rise?" Mike interrupted. "Why?"

First, I said I didn't know what the area was called. Then I gave them Shelton's explanation for preferring to talk where there wasn't good connection. Finally, I told them my guess about Shelton's interest in the twenty-six-year-old case and his reaction.

"That means we're on the right track," Mike exulted. "It's all tied in together for sure."

"Not for sure," I objected. "Isaacs' ties to the grand jury scam look promising. But how—or if—that ties to Laura's death? No, there's nothing. Plus, there's no link from either of those to Nora Roy's death."

"There's the timing," Tom said.

"Okay, yes, there's the timing."

WE'D MOVED TO the couch when Jennifer joined us.

First, she insisted Mike give her a live tour. He only did the back area of the first floor, promising more later.

Since Jennifer was not on Shelton's approved list, I slid past why, exactly, I'd been talking to them, but shared the information I'd gathered from CeeCee Wynn, Ed Radey, and Enid Harter.

Jennifer played it cool, but was clearly thrilled that CeeCee had turned out to be a gold mine.

Grumpily, Mike said, "All I did this afternoon was work."

Not grumpily, Tom said, "I ranched."

"In between assignments I did call Lorraine Flicker. She corroborated most of what the Youngs and Zblewski told Shelton, though with somewhat different emphasis in places." Diana gave a wry smile. "Zblewski's account of marital bliss was not backed up. Oh, and she said Nora Roy's reason for going into town Wednesday was she had planned to go to the library and then meet with Professor Belknap shortly before dinner."

"Belknap," Mike muttered.

"One other thing."

I looked up, hopeful.

"Lorraine is pleased to report that Kitty Roy Young has instructed her to park in the garage when she arrives for work."

Putting aside my disappointment that there wasn't anything juicy, I was happy for her.

"She might want to smell the air before she goes in there," Jennifer said.

I could feel the energy in the room dropping. Mine might have been leading the decline.

I forced myself to sit upright on the couch that encouraged burrowing. "We've been gathering information as fast as we can. Now we need to sort through it."

The others remained slumped, but Tom said, "I keep thinking about Dean making those statements to you on camera."

We all turned to him.

He nodded slowly, as if confirming something for himself. "It's like him sending that news release to Fine. He's sending a message. We didn't know what the message was or who he was sending it to, but look at where we do know who and what—Sally Tipton. He's been sending her a message all along that if she doesn't let him stay at her house and more that he'll tell something she fears being told. Whether it's true or not is beside the point. It's her fear he's working on. As you said from the start, Elizabeth, he's blackmailing her."

"You think his sending the news release was a threat?"

"Maybe not direct. But it was a way to put fear into people. Or into one or two people. A way to declare he's back in town. And then that clip. If it follows the same pattern, he was trying to put fear into someone then, too."

"And blackmail them?" I asked slowly.

"That's good, Tom," Diana said. "That's really good."

"We don't know who, not yet. But we have an idea of what," he said.

The rest of us nodded. Mike voiced it. "Something about Yolanda Cruz's murder. It has to be. But the who... He was implicating Professor Roy and she was already dead when he said it, so he couldn't blackmail her." He frowned. "But are we making it harder on ourselves looking so far in the past? We don't know Nora Roy was murdered, but with Isaacs hinting at it, if we look at it from that angle—"

"Yes," Jennifer said. "Get out of all that stuff that happened before I was born and look at the murder that just happened."

"We don't know it's mur—"

"Javier Cruz," she said. "He hears the story and hightails it up here from Denver, doing surveillance on the Roys' and Mike's place."

"Which used to be the Roys' when he spent summers here," Diana said. "But wait, he was doing surveillance *after* the professor's death. Even if he had a motive for killing her—and what would that be? That he'd nursed a grudge that the professor didn't adequately protect his mother from being killed?—why now and not any time in all these years?"

"And why not Isaacs? That's the murder that makes sense for him," Mike added.

"Okay, so not him," Jennifer said. "Then the husband. Spouse is the first one to look at. Plus, being the first one on the scene. Gives him a chance to remove evidence or stage whatever might need staging."

I nodded. "And he turned on the generator, even if it was at his wife's order. On the flip side, he didn't do anything to try to hide the generator or that he'd set it up. Didn't try to fake a note."

"If he were the guy, wouldn't law enforcement already be all over him?" Mike asked. "My money's on Kitty and Graham."

"Why?"

"I thought you'd never ask, Diana." He grinned. "Some of it's what you reported from overhearing that interview with Shelton. And then what she said to Elizabeth outside the library—*whew*. That Kitty is one cool, calm customer. Cool, or ice cold. Anybody going to disagree that there's evidence of a lot of resentment toward her mother simmering not too far under that icy exterior?"

Unanimous head-shakes.

"And then there's the son-in-law. He's been Professor Roy's professional flunky for decades. She gets the power and accolades. He does all the work. She treated him like crap. And then rumors about him being squeezed out—the last straw."

He spread his hands. "Could Kitty Young have killed her own mother to protect or rescue her husband? I say yes. Similar motive goes for him—escape for himself, protection of her. These double motives sure save time."

Diana turned to ask, "Tom, you've been around them for years, what do you think?"

"Don't really know them."

"At the very least," I protested, "you've been at that museum dinner every year with them. And if there have been other events…?"

"Yeah, there have. Okay." He half closed his eyes, possibly reviewing encounters. With his lids still partially lowered, he said, "Kitty's the more dangerous of the two. If there was homicide done, she planned it. Graham would follow her, but he wouldn't lead."

Whoa. That was the most committed he'd been to entertaining the idea of anyone's possible guilt.

"I'll buy that," Mike said. "Doesn't weaken my position at all. Because whatever applies for Graham could also add to Kitty's motive." He gave me the wait-a-minute gesture as I leaned forward. "They're definitely a team. And united against Professor Roy."

"I don't disagree about that, Mike. What will happen now, without being against the professor to unite them? Will they continue to stand together?"

"Could be a way to get them to talk. Stay tuned for your local news," Mike added dryly.

"Darn. I've got to—I'll be right back." Jennifer muted the connection.

"To recap, Jennifer thinks Javier or the husband. Mike thinks Kitty and Graham, or Kitty alone. Tom—"

"Isn't competing this go-round," he said.

I looked at Diana. "Who's your top pick?"

"Dean Isaacs."

"Because he's the trigger? Everything started when he got out of prison. That makes sense," Mike said.

"I bet it's something else," I murmured. "The Romeo complex."

"Exactly." Diana looked at Mike and Tom. "It's what Elizabeth told us about that conversation with Dean. He says Laura killed herself for love of him—more specifically, out of despair that her mother was going to send her away. So, to him, who was responsible for her death? Professor Roy. He gets out of prison and she dies. Interesting timing, isn't it?"

"Avenging the death of his lost love?" Mike said skeptically. "Wouldn't Javier Cruz killing Isaacs to avenge Yolanda make more sense than Isaacs killing Professor Roy, if revenge was the motive?"

"But what if it wasn't direct revenge? I was thinking of the chip on his shoulder and how much he hates being thwarted."

"I can see that," I said. "Plus his ego. That was the theme in his comments. Less about the tragic death of Juliet. More about how dare anyone get in Romeo's way."

"I don't know." Mike's doubt was clear. "I concede he's probably capable of it, but that motive seems weak to put him at the lead of the pack. Who's your top contender?" he asked me.

"Professor Belknap."

Six eyebrows went up.

"Possibly with an assist by his ever-faithful grad student, Jasmine Uffelman."

All six eyebrows went higher.

"Hey, if you buy it for Kitty and Graham, you need to buy it for Belknap and Jasmine," I said to Mike. "You thought the *rumor* of his career being in jeopardy was strong enough motive for Kitty and/or Graham. We know for sure that Professor Roy was threatening Belknap's career because Mrs. Parens and I heard her do it. He's hung his entire career on discovering this supposedly lost battle and she as good as said she was going to refute it. He was practically in tears at the museum dinner when he said she'd promised not to say anything until their official meeting next week. And lo and behold, she didn't have the opportunity to say anything more."

Mike waggled his hand side to side. He still hadn't bought it completely. "How would you stretch to the grad student?"

"Same motive. He's hooked his star to the tale of this lost battle. She's hooked her star to him. The battle's not found, he goes down. He goes down, she goes down. Think about what Linda heard. Although, if Nora Roy *was* murdered and if Belknap had something to do with it, he put on a very clever performance for me at the hotel Wednesday. He was quite open in his hostility to Professor Roy as well as his disregard for Professor Young."

"There she goes, arguing against herself again," Mike said.

"It also argues against Belknap being a suspect," Diana said.

"I wouldn't go that far. He might actually be that clever."

"That would mean he could be really hard to catch."

"A cheery thought."

I turned to Tom. "Which reminds me, will you talk to your friends among the tribal leaders to find out the view on this lost battle theory?"

"I can if you want me to, but I already know the answer."

"Share," Diana ordered.

"Their view is that it's bunk. There's no oral tradition of it at all. No physical evidence. Heck, they're so skeptical they point out there's no written record by the Army. They're not big fans of the Army from those days, but they say it kept darned good records about every encounter between its troops and hostile tribes. Skirmishes, and even sightings. Why would they suddenly miss a battle?"

I picked up that challenge. "Belknap would say because Custer lost and it was considered bad for morale so they covered it up. Didn't want Custer's reputation to be tarnished because they needed him as a heroic symbol."

"Then why the heck didn't they cover up the Battle of Little Big Horn?" Mike asked. "That couldn't have been good for morale. Sure tarnished Custer."

"I bet Belknap would say the opposite," I argued. "That it roused sentiment against the tribes. And any tarnish was wiped out by Custer's sudden death. We're looking at it from the point of view of now, when Custer is not considered a dashing, romantic hero, but more often seen as somewhere on the continuum from a bad decision-maker to deeply flawed to an idiot daredevil. But to much of the public of that time, he was still the Boy General from the Civil War, from a dozen years earlier."

"Even if you accept the motive that Professor Roy was threatening to pull the plug on his research—"

"And Jasmine goes down the same drain if that plug was pulled, just like Kitty and Graham," I reminded Mike.

"—what about opportunity? Do you see him—or her—out there in the dead of night tampering with a generator?"

"Plus," Tom said, "if you're looking at when Yolanda Cruz was murdered and Laura died, then he and Jasmine are out of it. They weren't here then."

"That we know of. Yet."

Three skeptical expressions faced me at that.

"Okay, okay. That's a stretch. But we still have a lot to figure out. For one, who was the boy/man in that photo? I'm telling you there was something between him and Laura."

Diana groaned. "Back to that?"

"Belknap would be around the right age." I didn't believe it, even as I said it. But maybe I didn't want to believe Laura would have been involved with Belknap. Even a younger, more appealing version of him.

"Would it help if you figure out who the woman was?" Tom suggested.

"I wonder if *you'd* recognize her."

"Good try, Elizabeth. But I'm not sneaking in to that house, or making up an excuse to go there—" I closed my mouth on that suggestion. "—to try to find out. What about Emmaline Parens? If you described the woman to her…"

"Might be worth a try."

With none of us willing to sneak into the Roy house—again—for stealth scanning, we had only my memory. I called up a mental snapshot of that photo in the hallway.

Vic Zblewski and Nora Roy. A space. Then the trio. The short, round woman, the boy/man, and Laura…

I closed my eyes to see it more clearly.

Wait.

Something was off. Something…

The clothes.

Chapter Forty-Three

THE CLOTHES WEREN'T right for what I'd seen in the yearbooks with Laura and her friends.

I tried to zoom in on the girl.

Using Nora and Vic as gauges, she was shorter than in the yearbook photos. This was summer. Even if she'd had a growth spurt before starting high school... No, at this height this photo had to have been taken when she was significantly younger than high school.

Yet there was that definite connection between her and the boy. Not platonic, no definitely not platonic... Could she possibly have been as young as her height indicated she was?

There was something else. Something more that didn't fit. It had been dim in that darkened hallway, but light had crossed her face...

Her eyes.

The eyes were different. They were light. Not the depthless brown of Laura's.

The girl wasn't Laura.

The clothes, the height, the eyes...

Kitty.

The girl in the photo was Kitty.

As for the age...

She couldn't have been much older in that photo than Laura had been when she died. Fifteen, maybe sixteen.

"Wait a minute, wait a minute." I had my hands up, my head down, eyes closed, trying to reassemble the pieces this new view had scattered, to bring them into order. "I think... It could explain everything." I straightened. "Well, not everything, but a lot. A whole, whole lot. Her eyes. The move. School. The timing. Yolanda's role. What Arturo said on the phone. In fact, he said it plain as day."

Mike shook his head. "I have no idea what you're saying."

I was hearing Mrs. Parens' calm, understated voice talking about the Cruz kids spending their summers in Cottonwood County to have time with their mother.

By extension, they also spent a great deal of time with Kitty.

Especially, no doubt, the one closest to her age. And there was something else...

Eventually, the youngest could drive himself.

The youngest. Javier Cruz.

A tall, attractive mature man, who once would have been a tall, good-looking young man with endless brown eyes.

Eyes that had lingered on Kitty.

And then another flash.

Laura Roy's huge dark eyes.

Like her father's?

"Javier Cruz was Laura's father. Just the way Arturo said."

"How do you get that from trying to remember what that woman looked like in order to describe to Mrs. P.?" demanded Mike.

"It was all the rest and—Oh. That was Yolanda. Must have been. Oh, my, she lost a lot of weight and... I wonder if she'd been ill when she was murdered."

"Okay, the woman was Yolanda, but how does that get you to Javier Cruz being Laura's father and what does Arturo have to do with it?"

"*Nieta,*" Tom said. "And *hijo.*"

"Exactly. Laura was his granddaughter. Javier is his son."

"Professor Roy and *him?*" That was Diana. "I can't imagine her ever being a cougar and at the time Laura was born, he would have been—"

Mike and Tom, apparently doing their own math, arrived at the same destination right behind her.

"Javier couldn't have been more than a teenager when Laura was born," Mike protested. "Professor Roy was no Mrs. Robinson, even back then. Are you saying—?"

"No, no, no, not Nora Roy. Didn't I say—?" It was so clear in my mind, but I might have skipped saying it out loud. "Kitty. *Kitty* was Laura's mother.

Mike whistled, then flopped back against the couch cushion.

After a moment, Diana said, "You're right, Elizabeth. That does take care of a lot of issues. She goes off to 'school' for her senior year in high school. Then the move from Colorado to Wyoming covers up Nora suddenly showing up with a baby. It fits."

I bobbed my head up and down as I drank from my cooling cup of tea. "It sure does. Including why Kitty never broke away."

A phrase Mel had used in discussing Wes' view of my pieces in storage in Virginia floated into my consciousness.

Just be aware they're a weapon he can use against you because you do care about them.

How much more powerful a weapon had Laura been against Kitty? And possibly, by extension, against Graham Young.

"Though why didn't they leave after Laura's death?" Diana asked.

"Graham Young's career was all tied up with Professor Roy by then and Kitty's very protective of that. We've seen it, but I also got that from Mrs. Eldercott," Mike said. He got nods all around. "Kitty and Javier being the parents can also explain why Zblewski comes across as less than a grieving father."

"What was that thing he said to Shelton?" Diana asked. "Something about her daughter's death weighing on Nora Roy. Sounded weird his not saying *our daughter's death*. Now that makes sense."

"Yup. And why Laura had brown eyes, while Zblewski's and Professor Roy's are blue—not conclusive, but indicative."

"What are you guys saying?" Jennifer demanded suddenly. "I missed some of it from my kid cousin screaming. Because she's a lousy winner," she added to someone beyond the camera. "Now get lost, like you promised."

"Laura was Kitty's daughter. Hers and Javier Cruz's," Mike said.

"Holy moly," Jennifer said. "Kitty was her mom, not her sister? That would freak out anybody."

Penny's words about Marcia Odom not being the one who could

have helped Laura came back to me.

Only one who could was the one who caused the trouble in the first place. Poor girl, poor girl. A lot to take in all at once for a young girl. Threw her for a loop. Sure did. Might have come out of it, but never had a chance. None of them did.

I'd thought she meant Laura's relationship with Dean, and a possible pregnancy.

But had she meant *this?* Had she meant Laura had figured out that the woman she knew as her mother was really her grandmother? That the woman who passed as her sister was really her mother?

Could finding out the deepest family secret have been the blow that sent her reeling over that spring break? That pushed her right into Dean Isaacs' arms?

"We're speculating," I cautioned. "We would need confirmation—"

"I'll get on it. See what I can find."

"Carefully, Jennifer, because—"

"Sheesh, Elizabeth, I know, I know. No hacking."

"Right. Also, be discreet. We don't want this to get around. Both because it's a private matter—"

"Unless it had something to do with the murder," Mike said. "If Yolanda got in their way... No, that's not right."

I nodded at his change of direction. "What could Yolanda have done to get in their way? But Nora Roy? She could have. She had the power. And to pull off the fiction that Laura was her daughter? It *had* to be her pulling the strings. It had to be."

Diana muttered something, then said more clearly. "It's surprising she wasn't murdered instead of Yolanda."

Mike straightened again. "You've got that right, Diana. Surprising Kitty and Javier didn't kill her when Laura was born. Surprising Isaacs didn't kill her twenty-six years ago, instead of Yolanda."

"Turn this over to Russ Conrad and Wayne Shelton, Elizabeth."

I met Tom's look.

"There's nothing firm enough, strong enough for them to move on. But we can make it firmer and stronger. We can. I know—" I held up a hand to stop his words. "Not yet. We need confirmation. We can't act until then."

SATURDAY

DECEMBER 31

Chapter Forty-Four

GLARING AT THE clock and rubbing my neck, which I'd twisted in the dive for the phone in the pre-dawn dark, I tried to make my "Hello" neutral.

And failed.

"What's wrong, Danny?" Dex asked.

Impulsively, I said, "I think someone might have gotten away with murder."

"Prove it and he or she won't have."

So simple in his world.

"Proving it is the catch, Dex." And I had the beginning of a wild idea that there might be another catch. A major one.

"Perhaps my information will help."

I sat up. "What information? The suicide note?"

"I am told that the likelihood that it was a fake is statistically significantly higher than the likelihood that it was a genuine suicide note, including accounting for the margin of error."

"Really? *Really?*"

"Yes. I would not tell you this if it weren't true." I could imagine the frown tucked between his eyebrows at my irrational response.

"Of course you wouldn't, Dex. Thank you. And thank your guy who looked at it so quickly."

"It was a woman. Do you want to know the basis for her opinion?"

"Sure. Absolutely."

"I can't tell you all of the markers, because that is proprietary. However, she did say I could share that it is quite rare in genuine suicide notes that the writer includes passages such as those about Dean Isaacs. Statistically, that is most likely to have been written by Isaacs himself."

"*Oh*" was all I got out. I was mentally stripping the note of those sentences … leaving what could so easily have been the draft of a break-up note.

> *This is too hard. All of it. This is not the way it should be.*
> *I know that now. So I'm ending it.*
> *That might be hard, too. But it's better. It will be better.*
> *You go around giving all your orders, but you can't make me do anything this time. Everything is in my hands.*
> *Good-bye,*
> *Laura*

Dex's calm voice snapped me back to the present. "There are interesting hints concerning the fingerprints and blood from the broomstick."

"What hints?" I asked eagerly.

"The information borders on speculation, because the examination was of photographs of the evidence rather than the original. In addition, the examiner is skilled, but not among the world's top experts."

"Was it you, Dex?"

"Yes."

"I trust anything you tell me."

"It would not hold up in a court," he warned. "The resolution of the reproduction alone—"

"I'm not a court. Please, tell me what you saw." As soon as I said it, I realized my mistake. Because he would. In detail. None of which would sound like English to me. "Tell me what conclusions you drew. Tell me what to think of the blood and fingerprints on the broomstick."

"The evidence would lead me to hypothesize that the fingerprints preceded the blood."

I was absorbing the implications. "Someone left fingerprints on the broomstick, but someone else used it to beat Yolanda?"

"That is an entirely unwarranted leap, Danny. I should not have hypothesized if you—"

"Sorry, Dex. I know better. Okay. Someone touched the broomstick before it was used to beat Yolanda?"

"Yes."

"Then the broomstick was used to beat her and that is most likely when her blood got on it."

"Her DNA does match the blood on the broomstick," he conceded.

"But there are no fingerprints in the blood?"

"None that were discernible in the photographs I received. There were smudges—"

"Like someone was wearing gloves?"

"That is one possible explanation. The photographs were represented as being complete, but unless I could see the original evidence, I would not commit—"

"Of course, of course, Dex," I soothed.

I was still soothing as we ended the call.

But as I got out of bed, I did a little jig that actually earned a tail thump from Shadow.

Then I sobered.

There was only one person I thought might tell us what we needed to know: What happened that night Yolanda Cruz was murdered?

Because what happened three days ago was set in motion twenty-six years ago and that was set in motion sixteen years before that, when Kitty's daughter became her sister.

I GOT THEM all on with me for a group call through the computer and told them what Dex had said, without, of course, revealing my source, other than to say I believed the source implicitly.

"Why are you happy?" Mike asked. "Doesn't this mean that Isaacs is innocent?"

"Nope. It *could* mean that, but it doesn't *have* to mean that. He could have touched the broom earlier with his bare hands, then gone back and used it as a weapon wearing gloves. That also would explain why the iron, which delivered the fatal blow, didn't have fingerprints on it."

"Seems to me we're going backward," Mike complained.

"Never going backward when we have new information, be-cause—Wait. Oh. I have an email from Jennifer." I skimmed it and gave a restrained, "*Yes.* Now we're getting somewhere. With this, we might get Kitty Roy Young to talk a lot more than she has. Diana, are you free to—?"

"What about Tom or me?" Mike asked.

"I have a quick assignment, then I'm free," Diana said. "Give me two hours and I'll meet you at the station."

"Will do. Sorry, guys. I think this will need a woman's touch. But I have a couple other ideas for you, if you're willing."

Two hours turned out to be too long. Because by then, Diana had another assignment.

I recognized the signs when I walked into the station to pick her up.

From the entry to KWMT-TV, I saw Diana standing in the hallway beside the slice of space designated as a break room.

"Elizabeth." Diana enunciated each syllable. That didn't sound like an ordinary hello. It put me on alert. She shifted her eyes toward Les Haeburn's open door and I knew it wasn't an ordinary hello.

"What's up?" I said as casually as I could.

"Leona and I are about to leave for the library. Breaking story."

"At the library? What's the story?"

"A potentially important document has been found in the local history room. It indicates—"

"What are you doing here?" Les interrupted, emerging from his office at a greater speed than usual. In fact, his usual was to stay in his office, door closed. "You have nothing to do with this story. Nothing."

Since he was looking at me, I said, "What story?"

"It's Thurston's story."

"Oh?" I looked around. "Is he going out on it?"

"That's my concern, not yours. And speaking of my concern, you haven't answered what you're doing here."

"Stopped in to touch base with Audrey about scheduling camera time for that scam I told you about. Then I have an interview to do." I looked at my watch to bolster my story. "Soon. But we should set aside time to talk about this scam story more, Les. I'm telling you, this is growing and growing. It's way more than a 'Helping Out!' It's worth an A block series. A week, maybe. Or two. Because what I'm finding out—"

"Yeah, yeah. Keep on it. When it's finished, we'll see."

"Really, Les, You're going to want to make time for this in the A block. Five and ten. It's—"

"There's Audrey. Talk to her." He bolted.

I'd scared him back in to his hole, but he left his office door open. The better to eavesdrop.

"Ready," Leona announced as she hurried from the back. She nodded at me. "Let's go, Diana."

"I'm going to check in with Audrey, then head out to my interview. See you later," I said.

Diana adjusted her camera bag on her shoulder and gave me the ghost of a wink. My message had been received. "See you later."

OTHER THAN THE Newsmobile and a pickup I thought I recognized as Needham Bender's, the library showed no signs of unusual excitement. On the outside.

Inside, I heard Professor Bruce Belknap proclaiming loudly, "This will be the making of Sherman and Cottonwood County. It will make this area the center of studies of the Army in the Old West. It totally rewrites the history of the West and it's right here. Right here—"

"What's right here?" Needham Bender demanded with enough asperity to inform me Belknap had been proclaiming for a while.

"The proof I've been saying all along existed. The absolute confirmation that the battle—the battle I shall formally name the Battle of Cottonwood County, since it has had no official name for nearly a century and a half—occurred. Found by a student working under my direction. This will be—"

"What's the proof?" Needham asked.

He, Diana, and Leona were at the front of a small group of library patrons and staff. Though some patrons had opted to remain at computers, in the stacks, or sleeping in an easy chair.

"A letter describing the battle as well as the determination to prevent it being known," the professor said triumphantly.

Jasmine Uffelman stood behind and off to one side of Belknap. She had her hands behind her back and her eyes down.

The gloss appeared to have worn off that relationship.

"How did it come to be found today?" Needham asked.

Belknap started to respond, then turned to Ivy Short.

"The staff of Cottonwood County Library will be able to answer that, since the letter was found here in their local history collection."

Diana turned the camera on Ivy.

She did the deer-in-the-headlights gape as she looked into the lens, but recovered herself after a moment with a little hiccup of an "Oh." With a deep breath, she gained more calm. "First thing this morning, we had brought a number of volumes as well as original journals to Miss Uffelman, as we do frequently. Among them was one from the daughter of an early rancher, along with his collected letters. Forty or fifty minutes after Miss Uffelman received the materials she burst out—ordinarily I would say emerged, but truly she burst out—of the local history room positively shouting, 'I have it! I have it.' At first we didn't recognize what she was saying, but when we did—oh, my. It was a joyful moment."

The joyful shouter did not look up from the floor.

"How did you happen to find it, Miss Uffelman?" Leona asked.

"I was going through the materials the way I always do. Checking each for any reference to the battle—"

"The Battle of Cottonwood County," Belknap interjected.

She glanced up. Not at him, but at the audience. "To the Battle of Cottonwood County." Was it reading too much in to her tone to think she repeated it dutifully? "I had gone through half of what they had brought me today when I found the letter. It was folded over several times and stuck tightly in between the pages of a book by the daughter of an early rancher that was reproduced by his family in the 1950s. It—"

"Which rancher?"

She looked up again, this time at Leona, who'd asked the question.

"Her name was Ashtabula Prescott."

"Hah."

Jasmine looked confused by Leona's reaction. I wasn't. That was the name of Mrs. P's ancestor.

"Yes, yes. The letter was folded and stuck tightly between the pages of the bound journal." Belknap took half a step toward Jasmine. How odd … it also put him in the path of Diana's camera.

"It was really stuck in there," Jasmine said abruptly. "As if it didn't want to be found. I had to be very careful in extracting it. It could have easily torn right in two."

"But it didn't and we now have the proof—"

Needham interrupted Belknap, still addressing Jasmine. "Had you found anything else today?"

"Nothing."

"How about before today?"

"Nothing."

Belknap talked over her. "We have found a number of references that made it ever more likely that we would find this source, which also underscores the authenticity of all the other pieces we've found."

"Speaking of authenticity," I said, "what will be the process for authenticating this and the other references you've found, Professor Belknap?

His left eyelid twitched.

"That will be seen to when the time is right. Finding the proper person with understanding of the context and circumstances will be a delicate matter. In the meantime—"

"But—" Leona started.

Belknap raised his voice. "—there will be free champagne tonight at the Haber House Hotel to celebrate this rare and vital find confirming the existence of the Battle of Cottonwood County!"

That drew excited voices from the staff and patrons, who gathered around him. Leona and Needham kept peppering him with questions, which he ignored.

Jasmine was gone.

I wasn't sure when she'd left, but looking all around, I saw no sign of her.

An enthusiastic patron in pursuit of information about free champagne, unbalanced me. To keep from stumbling, I sat in the nearest chair, which happened to be at one of the computer terminals.

The terminal, I realized, favored by Vic Zblewski and Dean Isaacs, according to Ivy Short.

Dean Isaacs looked quite, uh, pleased.

She'd said that the first time we talked. It wasn't until the second time that she'd said he'd been looking at information on carbon monoxide poisoning.

Had the two things happened at the same time?

As I had sat in the local history room trying to imagine what Nora Roy had seen, I sat where Dean Isaacs had sat, looking around. Was there something he'd seen that had inspired that amping up of his self-satisfaction?

If there was, I sure wasn't seeing it.

I looked at the darkened screen before me and saw my own frown-darkened face looking back.

Then something outside caught my eye.

Deputy Wayne Shelton, strolling toward a sheriff's department SUV.

Chapter Forty-Five

I SHOUTED HIS name as he opened the SUV's door.

He looked back over his shoulder as I kept hurrying toward him.

I figured he was going to get in and drive away. I was wrong. He closed the door, crossed his arms over his chest, leaned back against the door, and waited.

That let me slow my pace so I didn't pant when I reached him and said, "What are you doing here?"

"What do you think? That librarian Ivy Short insisted I come. Said *you* told her to."

"I thought you'd want to hear that Dean Isaacs had been looking up carbon monoxide."

"Yeah, delighted."

"Okay, Deputy. Next time someone tells me something like that I won't encourage them to share with you."

As if I hadn't spoken, he said, "Then all the shouting started. And bringing in the media. And phone calls to who knows who all. And speeches. And promises of champagne."

I tipped my head to adjust my angle on him. "You didn't have to stay."

He snorted. "You didn't have to come here."

Meeting his look, I said, "I came because Professor Bruce Belknap and his graduate student, Jasmine Uffelman, benefited greatly from Professor Roy's death."

It was an invitation to get everything out on the table.

He declined with a neutral "That so?"

So I said, "When you get a subpoena to check Graham Young's office at Cottonwood County Community College for his account of reading that supposed suicide note, check the bottom right-hand drawer of his desk."

He glared.

I braced for the how-the-hell-do-you-know-about-that. Instead, he asked, "Why?"

I explained, while my mind raced.

"You knew?" I asked him.

"Knew what?"

It was a dare to bring out in the open that I knew that he knew that Diana and I had been listening in to that interview.

Did he know before or find out after? Did it matter?

I kept quiet. Mostly for Lorraine Flicker's sake.

He grunted, reaching for the door handle. "What makes you think we'll get a subpoena for notes about Laura Roy's supposed suicide note?"

"Because you asked me why to look in that drawer *before* you tried to make me think you aren't going to pursue an investigation into Laura's death. When you *do* get the note, I recommend you have an expert in distinguishing genuine from fake suicide notes study it."

"You recommend that, do you?"

"Deputy Shelton, I'm beginning to feel downright used by you. If not abused."

"Works for me." He swung the SUV's door wider.

"Just remember we don't work for you," I said.

He raised a hand without looking back at me—the Wyoming sheriff's deputy version of "Whatever."

WHILE I WAITED for Diana in the KWMT-TV lot, I called Kitty Roy Young. It took two tries to reach her.

When I did, she was inclined to dismiss me. Until I said it was vital to Javier Cruz's future.

"You don't—You can't suspect…"

BACK STORY 293

"He has a lot of motive, Kitty. A lot of motive."

She agreed to meet at the spot in the highway that overlooked the Roys' ranch.

I closed my eyes and tried to arrange my thoughts.

Diana slid into my SUV just as I was thinking I might need to call Kitty to push back the time. Diana put a camera kit on the back seat floor, as I pulled out.

"Mine," she said, "not the station's. And I'm off the clock. Finally."

"Good."

"Boy, Audrey's still not operating on all cylinders. I should have been out of there in half the time. She's really been down since she didn't get that job."

"I know. But it would have been a huge leap. She should have expected it."

"That's logic talking. When you start dreaming about a big move, logic doesn't cut it."

Something in her tone had me studying her. "Are *you* thinking about going somewhere else?"

"I wouldn't, not until the kids are out of school. After that... Well, I had thought maybe to try. It would be nice to know if I could make it somewhere else, you know?"

"You could."

She looked at me. Startled at first, then pleased, then she chuckled. "That's it? A flat pronouncement?"

"That's it. You could be hired at any shop I've ever worked in. Might be a learning curve with up-to-date tech, but you'd have it in a snap. Don't believe me? Then ask Dell, he'd tell you the same. And few are pickier than Wardell Yardley."

Her amusement was gone. "You two have talked about...?"

"About you leaving KWMT? No. But he's seen your work and based on what he's said, he'd agree. Don't get me wrong, Diana. I don't want you to leave. Not as long as I'm here anyway." She gave a quick grin at that. "But you shouldn't stay here because you're not sure if you could make it other places. You absolutely could."

She released a breath. "I'm not going. The kids, the roots—"

"The sheriff."

"That, too, now. But it sure is nice to know I could." She grinned, then it faded. "I suppose Mike might feel the same."

I nodded. "And he doesn't have the kids or sheriff holding him here."

"He might stay if you... No, I won't say it. That's not fair to put on you. What about you? Just because you chose in the fall to stay here instead of going back to a bigger station, doesn't mean you can't change your mind."

"I could."

I supposed if I'd been an outsider looking at the Elizabeth Margaret Danniher story, climbing back up to bigger stations would be the obvious redemption after what could be seen as a life of success tumbling into failure.

But it wasn't the whole story, maybe not even the real story.

My true failure had been buried under the trappings of success.

That failure—allowing myself to move away from what was important to me—was now out in the open. Exposed, not masked, not buried.

Not the easiest thing to have happen to you, granted.

But once something's out in the open, it's a lot easier to work on.

"But I'm not changing my mind today," I said.

Chapter Forty-Six

KITTY STOOD NEAR one of the stumps, looking down at the house below.

For a second, as we got out of the SUV I'd parked next to her large Jeep, I had the thought that she was considering letting herself just fall forward.

But she turned as we approached.

"Thank you for meeting us, Kitty. This is Diana Stendahl, my colleague at KWMT-TV. We have a few questions—"

"Don't you think if I were going to murder my mother I would have done it a long time ago? A long, long time ago."

Okay, we were going for the rip-the-Band-Aid off style of interview. Because she saw it as a way to steer this conversation away from Javier Cruz being in Sherman when her mother died.

"I think there's a lot you can tell us that might well help clear up three deaths."

"*Three?*" But before the word was done I saw that she got it.

"Your mother's, Yolanda's, and Laura's ... your daughter's."

She didn't react at all. Yet she didn't retreat the way she had at the library, either. She was still with me, listening.

"We have a copy of the birth certificate." Jennifer had found it. But it wasn't ironclad. There could have been another Katherine Roy who gave birth to a girl at the right time and near the school where Kitty graduated high school. "DNA would prove it, of course. With your mother now dead, as well as Laura, it would be an unpleasant process..."

I let it hang, as if machinery were already warming up for an ex-humation. Yeah. I can just hear me trying to persuade Shelton, much less Sheriff Conrad.

"You don't need DNA." I wasn't sure I'd heard that right until she looked up. "You can go old school. Hospital records would do it."

It took me embarrassingly long to get it. "Blood type."

She didn't confirm or deny. She explained. Matter-of-fact. "Laura's blood type was AB. Mother was OO. The most basic geneticist will tell you it was not possible for Laura to be Mother's daughter. My blood type is AO. I was the bridge."

It was a strange way to say she was the mother of Laura Roy.

Blood will tell.

Mrs. Parens' words.

This was what she'd meant? Somehow she'd known and had tried to tell me?

Had I listened? No. Instead, I had mentally maligned Mrs. P.

Even though she had no idea, I regretted that deeply.

I also regretted that my conclusion-jumping about her meaning had stopped me from hearing what she was saying, which had kept me from getting to this point sooner.

I had the strange thought that Kitty might have preferred to get to this point sooner, too. She seemed somehow freer, more relaxed now.

"What about Javier?" I asked.

She looked up sharply.

After a long pause, she said only, "B."

"Ah." From what I remembered from high school biology, that fit.

A silence followed, which I deliberately let ride.

"How did you know?" she asked at last.

"I didn't. We didn't. We considered other possibilities—"

Kitty laughed. She had a pleasant laugh, though I was not tempted to join her.

"Oh, dear, not poor Vic as the father of my baby? No, no, no. That was the one flaw with Mother's grand plan—that anyone would believe Vic fathered a child."

"Yes. Well." I wasn't mentioning the Javier-Nora theory. No way.

"In the end, it was many grains of sand coming together to form the picture."

"Sand," she repeated slowly, with no hint of laughter. "I had one of those sand pictures back then. If I moved it slightly, it would shift and slide, assuming an entirely new formation. I can't tell you how many hours I spent looking at that, making it change, then staring at it again, imagining—trying to imagine—how Javier and I could ever be together.

"One image and we were there—the three of us, Javier, me, and the baby to come—in a perfect little house. Then a change and there was nothing. No baby. No Javier. No me."

That chilled me.

"You didn't consider...?"

"I don't know any more. I think... I've blocked memories of that period. I couldn't take the stomach-lurching ascents to the heights and drops to the depths. Over and over. Moments with Javier. The thought, the hope that I carried his baby. The fear. The joy. Then my mother's rage."

"When you told her?"

"I never told her. Never. She realized it. Eventually. I refused to deny it. I do remember the veins in her forehead. I thought she might have a stroke right then. She demanded and demanded. I said no. Until..."

"Until she threatened Javier?"

"Javier. And Yolanda. To ruin them. The whole family. Because they couldn't survive without Yolanda's earnings." She took a shuddering breath. "Or without the hope for the future that Javier was to them. To all of them. I couldn't do that to them. To him. Never to him.

"After I agreed to what Mother demanded, Yolanda held me..." She swallowed. "She held me together. Or she tried to. Mother wanted Yolanda out. She wouldn't leave. She made that clear. She would not leave. Not me and not the baby. Mother shipped me off and Yolanda came with me then, for those final months before Laura was born. And when I went to college, Yolanda stayed with Laura. She was

Laura's mother in the important ways. Certainly not Mother. Not me. In those first years Mother rarely let me be near Laura. I… We never bonded. Not in any real way."

"After you married, why didn't you and your husband—" *Get away.* I could practically hear Diana swallow the words. "—go out on your own? It must have been painful—"

"Mother wanted us nearby."

It was clipped and cold, signaling the topic was off-limits. She'd talked about being a pregnant teenager, about being kept away from the boy she loved, about her child being raised as her sister. Yet, she wouldn't talk about this.

"So Nora Roy arranged that she would raise your daughter as hers. Which worked until spring break of Laura's sophomore year in high school. That's when she found out?"

"Figured it out." There was an element of pride in that statement, definitely pride. "A project for biology class on blood types. She saw the fiction of being Mother and Vic's child immediately. When she realized I… It was difficult for her. She lashed out. Mother wouldn't budge. Kept insisting she was wrong. But after that first month, Yolanda persuaded Laura… We talked some. I thought—I hoped over time…"

"But she was pregnant," I said quietly.

She bowed her head.

"She was so young. Awash in all those hormones and rebellion and confusion. Mother—" She squeezed her eyes closed. "Was awful. It was history repeating itself. Except this time it wasn't happening with Javier, a good and decent man who—yes, man, even at that age. Instead, for Laura, it was with this worthless, conniving…"

"What really happened that night?"

"It was what we said at the trial. Except for what started the argument."

"Laura's pregnancy?"

She nodded. "It was already started when Yolanda found Isaacs trying to sneak up the back stairway to Laura's room, and used the broom to force him out. The rest of it was exactly as we testified."

I let out a long breath.

Now it got really touchy.

"We need to talk to all of you—you, your husband, Vic Zblewski, Lorraine, too. A few other people. This afternoon at the house. Say three."

"That's impossible."

"It's the way to clear this up. Without drawing the sheriff's department in until it's known what's happened. You've had only a taste of what an investigation can be like. If they suspect murder—"

"*Murder*? You truly think someone really murdered my mother? But when I said—I didn't mean it. Unless a murderer was ready to kill us all—"

"Revenge might drive someone to do that. Revenge for a mother's death, for the loss of a daughter. And the loss of love."

She didn't breathe for a half-dozen beats, then it rushed out of her all at once, "No. He didn't. He wouldn't."

"You haven't known him for forty-two years."

"No."

"Then this is the opportunity to prove it. Because if we don't clear it up, if law enforcement takes it over, you can be sure Javier Cruz will be the prime suspect."

That's how we got her to agree.

Now the trick was going to be getting the others there.

Chapter Forty-Seven

"WE'RE JUST IN time," Diana said as the Wild Horses Bed and Breakfast came in view. "Good thing we didn't go to Hamburger Heaven first."

Javier Cruz was loading up his pickup in the driveway.

I parked across the bottom of the drive, blocking him. He barely glanced up as we approached.

"You're leaving?" Dumb question of the day.

"I am. I have family and work to return to."

"So you accomplished what you wanted to accomplish here?"

That jab didn't even make him blink. Either he didn't realize I was intimating that he might have killed Nora Roy or innocence gave him immunity.

"Ms. Danniher, I have told you—"

"Now I have something to tell you. We know the whole story." Most of it anyway. We were still guessing at some. But that was the part beyond him and Kitty. "We know you and Kitty loved each other. That she became pregnant. That—"

"Bah." He half turned away.

"Kitty told us." He stilled at that. "How Professor Roy forced you apart. How she insisted that Laura be passed off as her own daughter to avoid scandal. How your mother stayed with the family to bring up Laura. Her granddaughter. Your daughter."

Still in profile, he was stone-faced until the last word.

"My daughter. To never say that. To never claim her. To never mourn her as my daughter."

"I can't imagine," Diana said softly.

Perhaps he heard the empathy, the understanding in her voice because he turned back toward us.

"Kitty told you this?"

"Yes."

He drew in air through his nose, then let it out through his mouth in a sigh that must have been building for decades.

"Kitty's mother threatened ruin for you and your family, didn't she?"

"Professor Roy was never subtle. She made very clear all that would happen, starting with my mother being fired. I would never get into any college. Her wrath would follow me to job interviews. Do you know why I accepted the scholarship? Because Kitty told me to. She said something had to be salvaged. That I could help my family. I have tried to live up to her faith in me."

"You can do one thing for her today—this afternoon. Be at the Roy house at three o'clock. I know you know where it is. We saw you parked nearby yesterday."

He looked at me. Then Diana. Then back to me. But no words came.

"Will you come?"

Now, he looked down, to a passing observer he could have been examining the condition of the front left tire of his pickup.

"I love my wife. I would die for her, for our children, for our life." The silence that followed echoed with an unspoken *but*. He looked up, past us. "Kitty... It was love. True love. We could have been a family. Happy together. Very happy."

IN THE BACK room at Hamburger Heaven we made our final plans.

Some of it we'd have to wing, but we had an outline, starting with Tom getting Belknap and Jasmine there, while Mike would round up Isaacs—physically if necessary. They'd already scouted where those three were and would get them right after we finished here.

For what came after that, we went over my theory of who had

done what.

Mike had answered one of my questions with a phone call to Lorraine Flicker, who'd agreed to be sure she was on hand this afternoon.

At the end, Mike sat back and said, "There are a lot of moving parts. I'm not so sure about that bluff, either."

"Which bluff?" Tom said, not happy. "There's more than one."

"It's the only shot we have. Javier was ready to leave. Belknap and Uffelman have no real reason to stay. The others could disperse at any minute. And this isn't the sort of investigation that will get better with age. Age is part of the problem."

"She can do it," Diana said. "I know she can."

Somehow her confidence made me more unsure than Mike and Tom's concerns.

"Are you okay, Elizabeth?" Mike asked.

"I was thinking about something Mrs. P said earlier this week. 'The weak can do as much ill as the evil, because the weak act from fear, they are always fearful, and there are far more of them than the truly evil.'"

Chapter Forty-Eight

I'D SENT THE vital message, hoping I hadn't sent it too soon.

They were all in the living room. All standing, because no one had accepted the invitation to sit. Lorraine was as close to the archway to the kitchen as she could be while still technically in the room.

There'd been a few tough moments.

One when Javier arrived.

Graham turned to his wife. "Kitty, what is this?"

Without looking at him, she said. "What does it matter now? Laura's dead. Mother's dead."

Another when Mike guided Dean Isaacs in, and Vic Zblewski had made as if to leave.

He'd ignored my cogent arguments, but acceded to Kitty's quiet, "Please stay, Vic."

He did. But it was clear Graham and Kitty Young, Vic Zblewski, and Javier Cruz were all edgy, braced for the secrets and emotions of decades to come out.

Dean Isaacs watched them with his usual lopsided slyness.

That's why I went first to Bruce Belknap and Jasmine Uffelman and hit them hard.

"You both had strong motive to kill Professor Nora Roy, as well as opportunity."

"What? No!" Jasmine gasped. "I-I-I never."

"You could have come out here and opportunely blocked the generator's exhaust so it filled the garage at any time during the night after the museum dinner."

"N-n-no. I didn't."

I turned to Belknap. "You were heard that night saying you'd take care of it. That you'd take care of what *she* had done that made your situation *urgent*. That's how you took care of it, wasn't it? Got rid of Nora Roy and that gave you an open field for the sudden 'find' this morning that so conveniently 'proves' your theory. It doesn't pass the smell test, Professor. Much less the authentication tests it's going to be subjected to."

"She's the one who found it." He pointed at Jasmine.

I wouldn't let myself look at Mike. He'd called this. *Glass jaw*, he'd said of Belknap. *Hit him head-on and he'll fold.*

"You're the one who hid it," she shot back.

"Shut up. Shut up." He took a step toward Jasmine. Tom blocked him.

"No, I won't shut up," she said, the slight stutter gone. "Not any more. He orchestrated the whole thing. He made me do that whole show today. He was sure Professor Roy was going to stop his research, end his career. He hid that fake letter Monday, then he told me to go find it. Wouldn't even tell me where to look. Wanted the discovery to look *genuine*." Who knew Jasmine Uffelman could snarl? "I wanted to forget it after the professor died. But he wouldn't. He insisted I keep looking and find it. He was happy—*gleeful* that she died, because he was sure he could pass it off as real more easily."

"Shut up. Shut up." Belknap broke out of that refrain with, "She's making it up. She did it all herself. Her career would go up in smoke, too. It's all her."

"But Professor, as you said, she always worked under your direction." Not giving anyone a chance to brace for the shift, I continued, "The other day Dean Isaacs brought up the idea that he hadn't killed Yolanda. And there might be forensic evidence to back it up."

"There is?" Isaacs forgot to look sly for a second.

"His fingerprints are on the broomstick—of course there might be a reason for that. Kitty?"

"Kitty, is this wise?"

She ignored her husband.

"He did grab at it when Yolanda was using it to shoo him out of the house."

"So that explains that," I said. "And then there are smudges in the blood, like someone wore gloves when using it to hit Yolanda."

Isaacs exulted. "Somebody else! I always said it. It was her—Professor Roy. She beat that other old woman, not me."

"But would she have had the opportunity?" I asked. "After Isaacs was driven out of the house, Laura ran up to her room, is that right, Kitty?"

"Yes."

"Graham?"

"Yes."

"Vic?"

"I wasn't there."

"That's right. You came home late, when you testified to seeing Isaacs lurking around the property."

"I didn't—"

I talked over Isaacs' protest. "So what happened next, Kitty?"

"Mother said Laura would be sent away and forced to give up the baby. Yolanda kept saying it would not happen again. It would not. Too many sacrifices had been made, and she would stop it this time. Mother went into her dictator stance and said they would discuss it later. Yolanda said they would talk right then so Mother would know that it would be as she—Yolanda—said this time."

"*Did* they talk then?"

"I don't know. Mother told us to go to our rooms."

Good heavens. They might not have had gray hair then, but they'd certainly been adults. Far too old to be sent to their rooms.

"And you did?"

"We did," she confirmed in her usual tone.

"See? See?" Isaacs said. "I told you that old Roy woman killed the other one. I told you."

"I know," I said soothingly. "And you came back to the house just to see Laura."

"She was all upset. I—" He broke it off, realizing what he'd said.

I continued as if he hadn't spoken. "You slipped in to the house again the way you had the first time. You wanted to soothe her, no doubt. To let her know how much you loved her. Romeo and his Juliet, after all."

"No. I left. Just like I said."

"I saw—" Zblewski started.

Mike punched him in the upper arm, quick and sharp.

"What I don't understand," I said as if there'd been no interruption and with as much perplexity as I could, "is why you killed Nora Roy?"

"Me? *Me?*"

"We know you were looking up carbon monoxide at the library."

"Not me. Him. *He* did it. I saw it when he left that computer and I sat down there."

I hadn't been sure. Not until then. But I'd wondered.

I sent a silent thanks to the boy with "bacne" for making me wonder.

Swinging his arm wildly, Isaacs pointed to Graham Young.

He turned, saw where his finger was directed and shifted it to Vic Zblewski.

"He did it, he did it. He murdered his wife."

That caught me by surprise. I'd expected him to deny with his usual smugness, never to react so strongly.

I'd been ready for him to make another accusation of murder, but not this one. I had to adjust. Fast. And figure out a way to get him to the *other* accusation of murder, because I needed him back in that night twenty-six years ago.

"How do you know?"

"I saw him. I saw him fiddling with the exhaust of the generator. Back there behind the garage. I saw him."

"When?"

His gaze shifted. "Early that morning. I was here and I saw him."

"Why were you here?"

He licked his lips. Looked around as if searching an escape route.

When his gaze came back to me, he tried his slanted smile that spoke of self-satisfaction and I'm smarter than you. It had deteriorated badly.

"All right, I'll tell you. I hoped to get some money from the old bi—From Professor Roy."

"Why on earth would she give you money?"

"Because I'm the one person who knew she'd murdered that Yolanda woman."

Javier made a sound but didn't move.

"So, you've said before. But what proof do you have?"

"I was there, all right? I was there and I saw her going in to that little house and I heard yelling. And I knew I hadn't done it."

"But you *were* at the main house—after Yolanda threw you out."

A muscle jerked in his cheek. "I got back in to see Laura. The kid was taking it hard, them trying to keep us apart."

"Was she?"

Red showed on his throat and cheeks. "Yeah. She was. I didn't know how hard until she committed suicide."

"What made you think she committed suicide?"

"Because there—"

Damn. He stopped himself short of saying *because there was a note*. Which he would have known if he wrote it himself.

"Because that's what the sheriff said. That's what they all said."

"What did Laura say to you?"

"She was crying. Taking it hard, like I said. Told her nothing would keep us apart. She seemed better then. So I left."

"Why didn't you tell all this at trial?"

"I was a kid, wasn't I?"

"Did you tell your lawyer?"

More slyness came into his eyes. He knew his lawyer was dead and couldn't contradict him. "Yeah. He advised against saying it at trial. And I was a kid, like I said."

"Why not say it later, when you weren't a kid?"

"Nobody listens to cons. I learned that fast. But then I got out and I thought…"

"That you could blackmail Nora Roy."

"Why shouldn't she help me out when I did her time? But when I got here I saw him." He gestured toward Zblewski, who was three or four feet to his left. "That morning. I saw him. I'll swear to it."

"What time?"

"Six, six-thirty." He knew he'd screwed up, but he wasn't sure exactly how. "I saw him," he insisted immediately.

"You couldn't have," Mike said. "Not enough light then. Days are too short. That spot's not lit by any outside lights."

As far as I knew, Mike had no idea if the outside lights reached that spot. But he sold it. He definitely sold it.

"It might've been later then. I don't know exactly what time. It could have been a little later. Seven."

"Then Mr. and Mrs. Young were awake." I turned to them. "Was Vic moving about inside the house or going outside at that time?"

"No," they said together.

"Lorraine arrives not long after seven," Kitty added. "And she comes in the road at the back of the house."

I turned to the woman. "Would you have seen someone if they'd been near the exhaust, Lorraine?"

"Yes, I would have. Nobody was there. Nobody was anywhere around the house. That's just what I told the deputy, too, because it's the truth."

Facing Dean Isaacs again, I said, "An excellent witness and another source to prove your story is false." I stepped back dismissively from him.

"I'm telling you, he did it." Isaacs shouted toward me as he extended his left arm to point at Zblewski again. "He killed her."

"Why would he do that?"

"To stop her paying me to keep quiet about her killing that cleaner woman. I recorded her and he wants—"

If anybody saw warning signs of what came next they didn't react to them. Because we were all caught flatfooted when Vic Zblewski wound up and slugged Isaacs under the chin.

Chapter Forty-Nine

ISAACS FELL BACKWARD, apparently unconscious, stretched out on the carpet.

Javier started toward Isaacs, but Tom barred him with one arm.

Without even looking at the man on the floor, Kitty asked, "But if Dean didn't kill Yolanda and he was with Laura, why didn't he use that alibi?"

"Because Dean Isaacs murdered her. That's what you're saying, isn't it?" Javier demanded of me. "That he murdered Laura?"

As understanding settled on Kitty, she shuddered. Graham took her arm, supporting her.

"It fits," I said simply. "There are strong indications that the note Graham saw and memorized was fake."

"What note?" Javier asked.

I shook my head. There was no time to fill in details now. But Laura's mother deserved an answer to her question.

"You asked why he didn't use the alibi of being with Laura. He didn't because it was more dangerous than saying nothing. Because if he used that as an alibi, they would have looked closer at Laura's death and he knew he *was* guilty of that."

"But why? Why?"

"Because she was breaking up with him. She'd already outgrown him, and he couldn't tolerate that."

She made a low, keening sound. Graham put his arm around her, even as she bent forward, as if from a blow.

"Guess that settles everything," Zblewski said.

"Not quite." I felt Mike on one side and Tom on the other move closer. "When we started looking into this, we thought carbon monoxide wouldn't have been a good method of murder. But that's only if the murderer was in a hurry. A patient murderer could set up the situation, then wait for the variables to fall into place—a way to block the exhaust that didn't look deliberate, enough time to build up the levels, the right person to walk into the trap, a time when there'd be no interference. And when all the variables aligned right, then it could pass off as an accident."

Everyone except Kitty and Isaacs, stirring slightly, looked at Zblewski.

"It *was* an accident," he said. "Everybody knows that."

"But Isaacs says he found your search for carbon monoxide information on the library computer." A treasure found from an accidental brush of the mouse as I'd experienced at that library? Or something more deliberate. "That was careless of you."

He huffed out a dismissive "Wasn't careful, because I didn't do it. That's his lying story. Like I said, an accident. Tragic accident."

"Then why were there fibers found on the bottom of the door from the garage to the kitchen? That's what you learned from the first try, isn't it? That the smell would come into the kitchen too soon if there wasn't something stuffed under the door. So Tuesday night when you started the generator, you took care of that. And you were careful to go out to the garage when Lorraine wasn't nearby, so she couldn't see you remove that plug. But you didn't count on the fibers."

This was the bluff.

The big, big bluff.

As far as we knew, no fibers had been looked for, much less found.

But Dex had said early on that the family was very fortunate the carbon monoxide had not leaked into the house. That and the mention of an earlier incident when Lorraine said she'd smelled exhaust got me thinking. And then the towel...

And came out as this bluff.

"What are you talking about fibers?"

"Fibers from the towel you shoved under the door. Green fibers.

Lorraine, what color was the towel Vic was holding when you first reached the garage?"

"Green."

I nodded. "The same green towel that's in all the video and photos, because people put it under your head. Lots and lots of documentation of that green towel and how it will match the fibers found under the door, where they never could have gotten by accident."

"Fibers." He shook his head. "Damned fibers. She was going to let that runt ruin everything. Always thought she was so smart. Smarter than me. Smarter than anybody. Thought she could outsmart Isaacs and keep him from putting his dirty paw out all the time. Taking my money."

"Your money," I muttered, almost dizzy with relief that the bluff had worked.

"Yeah, my money. I put up with her for all those years. About time I got something for it. And I still will."

He yanked at his coat pocket.

For an instant, what he pulled at caught on the fabric. Mike started to lunge forward.

But then the fabric tore and Zblewski was pulling out a gun. I grabbed onto Mike's arm. Tom hip-checked him. Not hard enough to knock him over, but enough to keep him from closing the gap to Zblewski.

Zblewski arced the gun from one side of the semicircle to the other like someone watering a garden bed.

"Nobody move. Get back. Or I'll shoot."

Clichés *and* a contradiction. How could we get back without moving?

I drew in a breath. Diana growled, "Don't say it" at me.

Zblewski backed up toward the door, fumbling for the doorknob with his hand behind him. "Nobody comes after me and nobody gets hurt. But I see anybody and…"

He didn't bother to finish the threat.

He opened the door just enough to get out and pulled it shut behind him.

I ran forward.

"*Elizabeth*—" Diana started.

But by then, Mike, Tom, and I were all at the door. Mike leaning against it, Tom and I both scrambling for the locks. He got the deadbolt, I got the knob lock.

"Yes," Graham Young said. "Kitty, get the porch door. I'll lock the doors from the garage and basement."

Not only did he sound more decisive than I'd ever heard him before, but also more chivalrous, because he'd taken the more dangerous option, since it was closer and Vic could get into the garage with his truck's door opener.

"Is there another door?" Javier asked.

"Yes. Come with me and get the door from the basement."

They left. Bruce Belknap stood with his mouth open and Jasmine beside him.

Diana took Jasmine by the arm and shook, then half pushed her toward Isaacs, who was moaning now. "See if he's okay. But don't let him up. Sit on him if you have to."

Jasmine froze halfway to Isaacs. Lorraine went to stand beside him, clearly prepared to do any necessary sitting.

"Somebody else is here." Tom looked out the edge of the narrow window beside the front door. "It's them. Three vehicles. Sheriff's department."

I hadn't sent the messages to Shelton, Russ Conrad, Richard Alvaro, and the 9-1-1 center too soon. I sure hoped I hadn't sent it too late, either.

Diana, Mike and I started toward the picture window.

"He can still shoot in the window," Tom said.

We all stopped. We could hear vehicles pulling up.

Graham—carrying a shot gun—and Javier returned from one direction, Kitty from another, stopping just inside the room. We were all frozen, as if being still would sharpen our interpretation of the sounds outside.

A shout came from the north end of the porch.

I recognized the voice as Richard Alvaro's before the sound resolved into the word, *"Gun!"*

Then a cacophony of shouts to *Drop the gun. Drop it now. Now, Zblewski! Drop the gun.*

"Let me go. Let me drive away and nobody'll get hurt."

Zblewski's voice sounded as if it were just the other side of the front door. Almost in unison, Tom, Mike, Diana, and I backed away from it, joining the others at the back of the room.

Were we far enough? Would the other end of the house be far enough if there were a barrage of shots? Maybe we should—

The shouting to drop the gun picked up pace and volume.

Then a single shot.

An instant of silence, then an expletive from Shelton, followed by an order. "Don't throw up until you've secured his weapon, Sampson."

Chapter Fifty

"SOME WAY TO spend New Year's Eve," I grumbled.

"I called Aunt Gee on the way here and said we'd probably be stuck for hours," Mike said quietly. "She says to bring everybody back to my place and we'll celebrate the New Year whenever we get there."

"Sounds like a plan."

Zblewski was presumably at the morgue. Isaacs was at the hospital under guard. The rest of us were in the waiting room of the sheriff's department's office in Sherman, watched by Deputy Lloyd Sampson while we awaited our turn to rotate in to one of the interview rooms for multiple go-rounds with grimly unhappy Sheriff Conrad and unreadable Deputy Shelton.

Speak of that devil, Shelton emerged from Interview One with Javier Cruz and came down the short length of hallway to the waiting room.

"When Sheriff Conrad finishes with—" He looked around, noted the missing person. "—Miss Uffelman, we'll assess how much longer we're going to keep you here tonight."

Javier had stopped, his dark, intense eyes focused only on Kitty.

She pulled in a breath, looking at him, then turned to her husband. She placed one hand over where both of his were clasped in front of him. I thought I caught a murmur of her speaking to him, but no words came through. And if he replied I didn't hear even the murmur.

She left that hand on her husband's as she stood and faced Javier again. It trailed behind her, until contact broke.

She went directly to Javier, stopped in front of him, and said clearly, "I am so sorry, Javier. So deeply, deeply sorry."

Tears sheened his eyes in a heartbeat.

I saw only her profile now, but that also revealed a trace of tears.

Graham Young stepped forward. I pulled in a breath, holding it.

"Deputy," he said. "Is there not a private space where they could have a word?"

My breath streamed out—admiration, surprise, relief—as Shelton opened the door to Interview One and gestured for them to enter.

"A few minutes," he said.

When they were inside, with the door closed, Shelton stood beside it, as if to ward off all comers. Graham Young pivoted and went out the front door.

Lloyd Sampson, frozen for an instant, was reactivated by Shelton's head jerk and "Stick with him."

The second obligatory blast of cold contradictorily unfroze the rest of us.

"That," Diana said to me, "might be the most romantic thing I've ever seen."

GRAHAM, WITH LLOYD behind him, returned in a few minutes.

It was longer before the door to Interview One opened. Both Javier and Kitty had been crying.

Graham stood.

Kitty stretched out her hand to him. When he joined them, she introduced the two men. They shook hands.

Graham and Kitty returned to their seats and Javier went to his.

Kitty slipped her hand into Graham's. United.

The glow of observing that ended abruptly when Sheriff Russ Conrad emerged from Interview Two, letting Jasmine listlessly return to her seat.

"Belknap, Ms. Uffelman, you'll stay. The rest of you can go. For now."

"What about Isaacs?" I asked.

"Since you all have signed statements saying you heard Vic Zblewski acknowledging he killed his wife, we will release Dean Isaacs from custody. When he gets out of the hospital is up to them."

"I'm convinced Dean Isaacs murdered Laura. She was breaking up with him and he couldn't stand that. He admitted going back to the house. He'd gotten her to steal the pills from Zblewski. He probably had possession of them. If not, he sure knew where they were. He could have crushed them and put them in her soft drink without her ever knowing. And that plastic bag? He'd used that on a cat not long before. Ask Ed Radey about that.

"You can't just let Isaacs go. Yes, he served twenty-five years for a murder he didn't commit. But nothing for the murder he *did* commit. Because his perfect alibi for the murder he was convicted of was that he was committing the one that wasn't investigated as a murder."

Every person in the room agreed with my statement. I could feel it. Including Sheriff Conrad.

That didn't stop him from saying, "Your conviction is worth nothing." I had to wonder if there was any wishful thinking in his directing the words *your conviction* at me. "Evidence—that would be worth something. Have you got any of that?"

"No," I admitted.

"No," he repeated. "And the one man who might have shed light on it, might have given us testimony—"

"He didn't have information about—"

He rolled over my argument. "—is dead. So we'll never know."

The floor suddenly became fascinating to a lot of people.

"If—" Everyone turned toward Kitty at the soft word. "—Dean Isaacs had been convicted of Laura's murder back then instead of Yolanda's, he'd be out on parole anyway. The same laws that released him now would have applied."

I didn't know if it was realism or forgiveness. Either way it was remarkable.

I couldn't have reacted with such grace. I *wasn't* reacting with such grace. What I wanted was to forget that he'd served twenty-five years for a crime he didn't commit and toss him back in prison for the one he did commit.

"Toss him back in prison," I repeated aloud, pivoting toward Shelton. "We can do that. Not for Laura's murder, but for violating parole, for fraud."

He met my gaze for a moment with his usual impenetrable stare, then said distinctly, "For impersonating a law enforcement officer."

"*What?*" Russ Conrad demanded.

I grinned. "It's a long story, but it's one with an ending you'll like, Sheriff. Lots of witnesses. All of them very much alive."

WE MADE IT back to Mike's with a good half hour to spare before midnight.

Aunt Gee, Mrs. Parens, and Shadow were all there.

Aunt Gee had taken Mike's call about us being tied up with the police and run with it. Not only bringing the additional revelers, but making herself at home in Mike's kitchen.

We devoured the appetizers, chips and dips, and nuts set out on the kitchen island. Shaking off our hunger just in time to pour champagne and count down with the TV.

"Happy New Year!" we all shouted.

There was an instant of motionless, then I turned to hug Mrs. P, bending to kiss her on the cheek. We did hugs and cheek kisses all around.

Did I think about other kinds of kisses with Tom and Mike, Mike and Tom?

I will not start the New Year with a lie. Oh, hell, yes, I did.

And yet, this was right. For now.

That's what I was thinking about some minutes later, when Diana came up beside me as I looked out a window not blinded by the interior lights.

"Thinking about where you were a year ago?" she asked.

"What? Why?"

"You had that faraway look. Like you might be remembering the life you used to have."

A year ago, I had been wrapping up my final network stint, working New Year's Eve while the hot properties got the night off. By that point, I'd been so not-hot, that they'd made me come back to work that final day after two weeks of vacation, spent with my family in Illinois.

"I know this job doesn't compare to what you were doing and what you have to work with here doesn't compare, either," Diana said.

She was right. The studio, editing bays, control room, bullpen, and other physical facilities of a year ago had every imaginable advantage over KWMT-TV. So did the software and support and—I stopped before I depressed myself.

"Not even in the same solar system. But you work with the same leftovers from decades gone by and so does everybody else at KWMT."

"We're used to it. Besides, this hasn't been the easiest year for you in other ways, but…"

She stalled there.

"But what?"

"But I hope you're not too unhappy here."

I reached out and hugged her. Wasn't sure who was more surprised, her or me.

"You want to know what I was thinking? Not where I was a year ago. I was thinking about how far I've come in the past year."

"They're worried about you going back there," Mrs. Parens said.

At her voice, I looked around and saw they were all watching and listening.

"Why?"

"Because everything here seems temporary with you," Diana said. "You bought the vehicle you said would fit better into another life. You keep saying you're not going to stay permanently in the bunkhouse, but you also haven't looked for anywhere else to live. It's like you're poised to pack up everything into your all-wheel-drive and go. And when I say *everything*, it's not all that much, considering you didn't bring much to start and after the fire, you had nothing except Shadow. So I guess that's the one thing you'd take with you when you left. Shadow."

He tipped his head at us, hearing his name.

"But I'm not talking about leaving," I said to him.

"The signs are there."

I looked back to Diana. "What signs?"

"Like you going to Illinois for Christmas."

"I've always done that. It's family. It's home——"

She pounced. "Exactly. You said it right there. It's home to you."

I had to laugh.

"What?" she demanded.

"You know what my family got on me about the whole time I was there? Referring to Wyoming as home. I got to the point where I was saying I was leaving home to go home. Crazy, huh?"

No one answered, which was a good thing, because then words poured out of me.

"It's been on my mind for a while and after the holiday, I'm going to call a real estate agent and start looking for a place here. My own place. Where I'll have my own things. Everything that's been in storage and maybe some new things. I'll find the perfect place—I wonder if Linda Caswell would sell. Preferably for a song... What? Why are you all laughing?"

"You're not getting the Caswell place. Better set your sights considerably lower than that," Aunt Gee said.

It hit me that that's what the world I'd come from thought I'd done by being here in Wyoming—setting my career sights, my life sights, considerably lower.

The thing was I'd discovered that I kept seeing a lot of new and enjoyable things with my sights at this level.

"I can do that," I said. "I can definitely do that. Here's to the New Year and a new house for me and——"

"New adventures for all of us," Mike said.

We raised our glasses and toasted each other again.

Epilogue

THE KWMT NEWSROOM is as repopulated as it ever gets, including Jennifer in her rightful spot as czarina of the computers.

Diana's kids are back in school. She and the sheriff are officially dating, even in front of her kids. Unofficially, they're doing a lot more, but so discreetly nobody could prove it.

Shadow, showing how far he's come since the spring, has been moping about the lack of company. He's so desperate, he's coming to me voluntarily for petting. I hardly ever cry anymore when he does that.

Dean Isaacs is in prison again, his parole forfeited for bad behavior as proven by the techies who tracked his scam. The victim who sent him money—twice—was the woman who'd been principal of Cottonwood County High School during his brief time there.

The Cottonwood County Sheriff's Department and county attorney continue to look at the possibility of charging him in Laura Roy's death.

It doesn't look good.

But having him back in prison helps. So said an email to Diana, Mike, Tom, and me from Javier Cruz on behalf of his family.

The sheriff and the county attorney briefly discussed Isaacs' account of Nora Roy being the real murderer of Yolanda Cruz. Javier told them the family would prefer that not be pursued. He said he spoke for the family, but I suspect he'd steered that discussion, in order to spare Kitty at least that.

Isaacs has tried to raise interest in his account of what happened from prison. He's repeated the claim that he had proof without producing any. So far he's been right about nobody listening to cons. At least nobody has listened to him.

One interesting point. He went red, then white, then red again when he was told that Sally Tipton had burned everything he'd left at her house. In addition to genealogy papers, that included a small recording device … and whatever was recorded on it.

Sally is happy and fluffy again. Her secret, whatever it is, remains a secret. Perhaps until another Dean Isaacs comes along to threaten it.

Belknap skipped town on New Year's Day, leaving Jasmine Uffelman to pay his bill at the Haber House Hotel, including a case of champagne ordered to celebrate the "discovery" of the fake document supporting his theory of the Battle of Cottonwood County. There's a warrant out for him. Word is that Graham Young is helping Jasmine find a position at a small school in Arkansas where she can start fresh.

Mrs. Parens remains irate that Belknap has not yet been punished for invoking the name of her ancestor in his scheme. The guy better never come back to Cottonwood County.

Graham and Kitty Young are preparing to sell the Roy ranch—it's not in my price range and even if it were… No.

The co-op program involving Cottonwood County Community College is continuing, but starting next school year, it will involve multiple universities. Graham has been named chair of the program, but not of the Bison University department, which is being reorganized.

Mike took a few days off and went to see his parents. He swears it was a coincidence that the wind chill in Cottonwood County was twenty degrees below zero the day he left. Then he had the gall to say, "The good thing is when it's that cold it doesn't snow."

Of course it snowed.

Tom is preparing his ranch and road construction company for the better weather everyone keeps promising is coming.

Tamantha has already done one demonstration for the elementary school of her drone skills. The response, said Needham Bender in the *Independence,* was shock and awe.

As for me, I'm arranging a trip to the East Coast for a hearing Mel instigated over the real estate proceeds. He says I'll likely see Wes. What I'm looking forward to is checking on my items in storage and arranging for them to be sent west.

Not long ago, on a blue sky and clear roads day, I went to see CeeCee Wynn. I held her grandson, ate her brownies, and told her unofficially that she'd been right. There had been a crime and she had helped solve it for her friend, Laura.

~ THE END ~

If you enjoyed Back Story, I hope you'll consider leaving a review, to let your fellow readers know about your experience.

For news about upcoming books, subscribe to Patricia McLinn's free newsletter.
www.PatriciaMclinn.com/newsletter

Caught Dead in Wyoming series

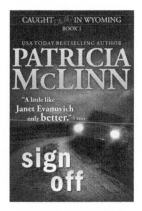

SIGN OFF

With her career derailed by her ex, top-flight reporter Elizabeth "E.M." Danniher lands in tiny Sherman. But the case of a missing deputy and a determined little girl drag her out of her fog.

LEFT HANGING

From a rodeo queen's tiara to the manure ground into the arena dirt, TV reporter Elizabeth Danniher receives a murderous introduction to the world of rodeo.

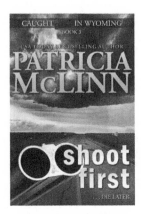

SHOOT FIRST

Death hits close to home for Elizabeth Danniher—or, rather, close to Hovel, as she's dubbed her decrepit rental house in small-town Sherman.

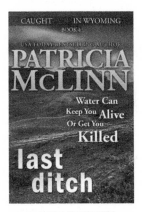

LAST DITCH

A man in a wheelchair goes missing in rough Big Horn Basin country. KWMT's Elizabeth Danniher and Mike Paycik join the search, but soon they're on a search of a different kind.

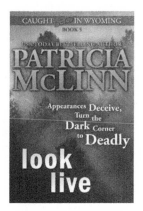

LOOK LIVE

Elizabeth Danniher and her supporting sleuths take on another mystery, with help—and hindrance—from intriguing out-of-towners

Get LOOK LIVE now!

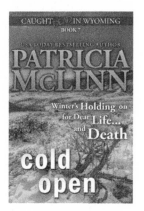

COLD OPEN

Elizabeth Danniher is ready for spring and looking for a place of her own. Until she discovers homicide at her front door.

Get COLD OPEN now!

What people are saying about the
CAUGHT DEAD IN WYOMING series

"While the mystery itself is twisty-turny and thoroughly engaging, it's the smart and witty writing that I loved the best."
—*Diane Chamberlain, bestselling author*

"I loved this book. Colorful characters, intriguing, intelligent mystery, plus the state of Wyoming leaping off every page. A terrific start to this series. I'll be standing in line for the next one."
—*Emilie Richards, USA Today bestselling author*

"She writes a little like Janet Evanovich only better."

"E.M.'s internal monologues are sharp, snappy and often hilarious."

"McLinn has created in E.M. a female protagonist who is flawed but likable, never silly or cartoonish, and definitely not made of cardboard."

Romantic Suspense by Patricia McLinn

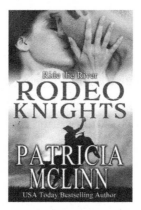

RIDE THE RIVER

In Ride the River: Rodeo Knights, a new western romance with suspense, Regina Moran is tracking bank robberies on the Wyoming rodeo circuit when she discovers her ex is a prime suspect. One of the towns she visits is Sherman, so look for some cameos by some of your favorite Caught Dead in Wyoming characters.

Get RIDE THE RIVER now!

If you particularly enjoy connected books—as I do!—try these:

Wyoming Wildflowers series

A Place Called Home series

The Bardville, Wyoming series

The Wedding Series

Seasons in a Small Town series

Marry Me series

Explore a complete list of all Patricia's books

Or get a printable booklist

patriciamclinn.com/patricias-books

About the author

USA Today bestselling author Patricia McLinn's novels — cited by reviewers for warmth, wit and vivid characterization — have won numerous regional and national awards and been on national bestseller lists.

In addition to her romance and women's fiction books, Patricia is the author of the Caught Dead in Wyoming mystery series, which adds a touch of humor and romance to figuring out whodunit.

Patricia received BA and MSJ degrees from Northwestern University. She was a sports writer (Rockford, Ill.), assistant sports editor (Charlotte, N.C.) and — for 20-plus years — an editor at The Washington Post. She has spoken about writing from Melbourne, Australia to Washington, D.C., including being a guest-speaker at the Smithsonian Institution.

She is now living in Northern Kentucky, and writing full-time. Patricia loves to hear from readers through her website, Facebook and Twitter.

Visit with Patricia:

Website: patriciamclinn.com

Facebook: facebook.com/PatriciaMcLinn

Twitter: @PatriciaMcLinn

Pinterest: pinterest.com/patriciamclinn

ISBN: 978-1-944126-27-8